PROTECTED

A Deadly Secrets Novel

May 18

PROTECTED

A Deadly Secrets Novel

ELISABETH NAUGHTON

 Montlake
Romance

Published by Montlake Romance, Seattle

www.apub.com

Amazon, the Amazon logo, and Montlake Romance are trademarks of Amazon.com, Inc., or its affiliates.

ISBN-13: 9781503900783
ISBN-10: 1503900789

Cover design by Michael Rehder

Printed in the United States of America

For Rachel,
Who's always there to rescue me when I'm lost in
every book.
Never leave me, girlfriend, because I don't know how
I'd do any of this without you.

CHAPTER ONE

Congratulations. The papers were signed by the judge last night. You're a free woman.

Kelsey McClane breathed a sigh of relief as she read the text from her attorney. Eight months of hell dealing with her ex were finally over. She felt as if a giant weight had been lifted from her shoulders. The only thing that could make this day any sweeter was if she'd never married the jerk to begin with.

Rolling her eyes because her track record in her personal life was shit and she knew it, she set her cell phone on the counter as she checked her reflection one last time. The lights on both sides of the mirror highlighted her blonde hair and showed every imperfection in her features. She knew the cameras would pick up each annoying freckle across the bridge of her nose, but it was too late to do anything about that now. In a matter of minutes she was scheduled to be on air with Portland's hottest morning show, and not even the good news from her attorney could settle her frazzled nerves.

She fluffed out her shoulder-length hair one last time, thinking how stupid it was to get worked up over a local TV show. She'd recently had her big moment, sharing her designs with the world during New York's famed Fashion Week, and even then she hadn't been this nervous. Of course, back East no one knew her. Here, every person she'd grown up with would be judging whether she was a success or a total flop.

Please don't let me be a total flop.

She breathed deeply and silently repeated the words that had gotten her through way worse than this.

Keep it together. Stay strong. You can get through this.

"Ms. McClane?" a woman called from the doorway. "Five minutes."

Glancing over her shoulder toward the dark-haired woman wearing a headset and holding a clipboard, Kelsey forced a smile she hoped covered her nerves. The woman was some kind of assistant to the producer, but Kelsey couldn't remember her name. Meeting the cast and crew of *Good Morning Portland* this morning had been a complete blur. "Okay, thanks. I'll be right out."

Instead of turning around and bustling out as Kelsey expected, the woman narrowed her eyes and tipped her head. "Has anyone ever told you that you look like that actress? The blonde who played in all those romantic comedies. What was her name?"

Annoyance pulsed inside Kelsey, but she was careful not to let it show. "Vivienne Armstrong?"

"Yeah. That's the one."

"Yes. I've heard that once or twice." In fact, she'd been asked the same question more times in her life than she cared to admit. And right now it wasn't helping settle her nerves any. "They say everyone has a twin. Mine happened to be famous." And a drug addict. *Lucky me.*

"Too bad she's dead. You could have done look-alike work for her."

As if Kelsey had the time. Or interest.

"Oh well. Four minutes now. Don't be late." The assistant ducked out of the room and disappeared.

Frowning, Kelsey turned back to the mirror. Maybe it was time she colored her hair. She wanted people to start recognizing her for her designs, not because fate had decided she should be some dead actress's doppelganger.

Enough wasting time.

Drawing a deep breath, she smoothed her blouse and repeated her inner pep talk. *Keep it together. Stay strong. You will get through this.* Then she grabbed her cell, stuffed it in the front pocket of her slacks, and headed for the door.

Just as she stepped into the doorway, a shadow filled her line of sight. She gasped but wasn't able to stop her momentum. Seconds later she smacked face-first into a hard male body and ricocheted back.

"Shit." Hunter O'Donnell's long fingers and wide palms closed around her upper arms and jerked her forward, preventing her from hitting the ground on her butt. "Sorry. Dammit, I didn't see you."

Kelsey stumbled on her three-inch heels and reflexively lifted her hands to steady herself. Her fingertips landed against solid muscle, and the familiar scents of citrus and leather filled her senses, leaving her light-headed and weak in the knees in a way that made her feel fifteen again.

"Are you okay?" He ducked his head when she didn't immediately look up at him. "Kelsey?"

As soon as she had her footing, Kelsey dropped her hands and stepped back, hating and liking the way his hands felt all at the same time. Stupid thoughts like that had gotten her into a bad marriage, and she had no intention of repeating past mistakes. Besides, even if she was interested, Hunter O'Donnell was her brother Alec's best friend and off-limits.

"Yes, I'm fine." Gently, she shrugged out of his grip, avoiding eye contact so she wouldn't draw attention to how awkward she felt around him. "They're ready for me out on set."

"Yeah, I know." Hunt stepped back so she could pass. "Everything looks good out there so you're free to go."

A whisper of disbelief rushed down Kelsey's spine, and she looked up into his deep-brown eyes. She'd known Hunt more than half her life, and normally she'd look at him as an ally, but today, regardless of how good he smelled, he felt more like her enemy. She didn't need him telling her what she could and couldn't do. Julian had done that for three damn years during their marriage, and she'd vowed never to let any man boss her around again. If it weren't for her overprotective brothers, she wouldn't even be dealing with Hunt today. But they were so worried Julian was going to do something to retaliate because of the divorce that they'd hired Hunt to follow her around like a guard dog.

Clenching her teeth so she wouldn't say something she'd regret, Kelsey moved out of the greenroom and stepped past him into the hall, heading for the set. She knew her brothers meant well, and she knew Hunt—a former Army Ranger who now ran a PI and security firm here in Portland—was good at what he did, but it still grated on her last nerve that he was here hovering at all. Julian was a bully, nothing more. He'd bullied her into dating him. He'd bullied her into marriage. And for the last year, he'd been trying to bully her into calling off the divorce. She'd been stupid to get involved with the man from the start, but she wasn't afraid of him. Bullies only had power when you cowered from them, and she was done cowering from Julian Benedict. In a couple of days, when he realized it was finally over, he'd leave her alone. She was sure of it.

Thoughts of Hunt and Julian faded as she stepped into the studio and spotted the hosts on set. A red light to her right blinked, signaling the cameras were live. Her nerves kicked in full force as she watched the hosts banter back and forth during the opening segment, knowing she was almost up. Glancing around the room at the people gathered on the fringes to watch, she spotted the three models already dressed in designs from her latest line and decided to head that way.

They didn't really need her. They looked gorgeous and totally show-cased her work. But she needed something to keep her nerves at bay, and fussing with their collars and hems was the only thing she could think to do at the moment.

"Looks good," she said to the closest model, running her hand down the sleeve of the girl's jacket. All three were taller than she was, at least five years younger, and way more attractive, but Kelsey barely noticed. She was too fixated on making sure her clothing hung correctly and that the models hadn't missed any buttons or loose threads.

The hosts continued to chat behind her on set. When the female production assistant tapped her elbow, Kelsey knew it was go-time. Those nerves went haywire in her belly, like Mexican jumping beans amped up on speed, and not for the first time she wondered how she'd let herself get talked into doing local television. New York Fashion Week had nothing on this insanity. Why did she care what her old peers in high school thought of her, anyway?

Because you've always cared what people think. Because you've never been good enough. Never smart enough, never talented or exciting enough for anyone to love the real you.

All her old neuroses came screaming back. With one simple thought, she wasn't twenty-seven and an up-and-coming fashion designer on the cusp of real success. She was ten years old again, wondering why the hell Michael and Hannah McClane wanted to adopt *her*: a mousy little wallflower who'd flitted from foster home to foster home, never fitting in or connecting with a single person in her life.

Lifting her shaky hand from the model's jacket, she told herself she wasn't that kid anymore. She was strong. She was independent. She was so much more than she'd ever been before *because* of the McClanes and everything they'd given her.

Turning toward the set, she spotted Hunt standing not more than three feet away from her in the shadows, looking all dark and sexy and ruggedly imposing. But instead of being annoyed by his presence as she'd been before, a calm she didn't expect settled over her, allowing her to take a deep breath that filled her lungs and gave her strength.

He'd never treated her as if she were less. He'd never acted like she was lucky to be in his presence, as Julian had since the day she'd met her ex. From the time she was a teenager, she couldn't remember Hunter O'Donnell being anything besides a solid, quiet presence in her life, coming and going from the McClane home whenever he was with Alec. He hadn't teased her as her brothers constantly did. Hadn't talked down to her. Hadn't done anything but just be nice to her, which was exactly what she'd needed during those crazy teen years.

So, okay. Maybe she was frustrated with the reason he was here now, but she couldn't say she didn't appreciate his presence. Because it did relax her in a familiar, comforting kind of way she could definitely use right now.

Before she realized what she was doing, she smiled at Hunt. It surprised him. She could tell by the way his brows lifted in response. All morning she'd been salty and brusque with him when he'd only been doing a favor for her brothers. For her family. For *her*.

"Speaking of celebrities," Rachel Brown said on set, snagging Kelsey's attention. Reluctantly, Kelsey turned toward the host, who was currently flipping her auburn hair as she glanced at her cohost, Adam Lancaster, then back to the camera. "We've got an up-and-coming local celebrity with us today. Fashion designer Kelsey McClane recently returned from New York's Fashion Week and is here to share all the ins and outs of the big event. So stay tuned after the break to hear about her whirlwind experience and to see some of her work, which is being compared to that of Vera Wang, Stella McCartney, and Donatella Versace."

"Oooh, I love Vera Wang!" Adam Lancaster exclaimed.

Someone on the edge of the set signaled the small audience in bleachers behind the cameras, and a chorus of claps and cheers filled the room. Seconds later, a voice yelled, "Clear!" indicating they'd gone to commercial break, and then things happened so fast all Kelsey could do was go with the flow.

The production assistant grasped her elbow and pulled her to the far side of the set. Voices echoed through the room as people darted right and left, fixing props and touching up the hosts' makeup and hair. Across the stage, Kelsey spotted her three models, waiting in the wings for their signal to parade out.

Her nerves kicked back up as the assistant rattled off directions in her ear, so she searched the set for Hunt's familiar face, hoping it would calm her again. The space where he'd been standing before was empty, and for a moment, panic crept in. But then she spotted him behind the camera, heading her way around the outside of the chaos, sticking close as he'd said he would.

The tightness in her belly relaxed once more, and she breathed deeply, knowing it was both stupid and juvenile to react to him like this but not wanting to think about that too much. When this was all over, she'd go back to keeping her distance, but for now she supposed having him around wasn't such a hardship. He was easy to look at, after all, and when she thought about how nice his touch had felt against her arms just a few minutes ago . . .

Her belly warmed at the memory, and her gaze followed his movements as he stopped just past the third camera. One corner of her lips curled because, yeah, he really was gorgeous. All gathered strength and cut muscles. She guessed his physique was a result of his time in the military, but a lot of guys let themselves go when they got out. Not Hunt. He was still in tip-top form. Definitely in better shape than Julian had ever been. In better shape than 99 percent of the male population, for that matter.

Behind her, the producer started counting down from ten, signaling their return from commercial break, but she barely noticed. She was too busy admiring Hunt's strong profile, his deep-brown eyes, and that tiny scar on the left side of his jaw that made her wonder how he'd gotten it . . . and when.

Her gaze skipped back to his eyes, and in a rush of heat that flamed her face, she realized he was watching her checking him out. Knew, because one corner of his lips lifted in a quirky half smile that told her loud and clear she was busted.

She quickly looked down at her feet, cursing herself for being so damn obvious. But she could still see the way his smile widened to encompass his whole face, and dammit, all she wanted to do was look back at him because the force of that smile was absolutely hypnotic.

A vibration radiated into her hip, distracting her—thankfully—from making an even bigger fool of herself. Geez, what was wrong with her? Blushing? Her cheeks absolutely burned. She never blushed. Tugging her phone out with a hurried motion, she tapped the button to turn it on.

Then froze when she read the words on her screen.

You might think you have everything, but soon you're going to get exactly what you deserve. I know the real you, and this isn't it. You're nothing but a disappointment. A gigantic failure. Your own mother didn't want you. No one wants you. The world will be a better place when you're dead. And in a matter of minutes, starlet, the world will be able to thank me because I'm about to make that happen.

Her stomach rolled. She looked up and around the set, over the hosts' laughing faces and the sea of onlookers bordering the room. Her vision blurred at the edges, and her head grew light as she looked from face to face, searching for the person who'd sent the text. Faintly, she recognized her name being called from a great distance, heard muffled claps indicating she was being introduced, but her feet wouldn't move. All she could do was replay those last few words in her mind again and again as she continued to search.

When you're dead . . .

I'm about to make that happen.

Panic wrapped icy fingers of dread around her chest, constricting her airway. She couldn't see Julian in the crowd. He wasn't here. She swallowed hard and tried to breathe. Tried to think logically.

It was just a threat, right? He wouldn't be so stupid as to try to follow through on that threat. He was a coward, not a killer.

Turning quickly, she searched for Hunt in the sea of faces. The text was nothing more than Julian being upset about the divorce. Just Julian being a bully, trying to scare her like always . . . *right?*

She spotted Hunt, ten feet away, moving around equipment, still trying to get close to her. The smile faded from his lips when their eyes met, and his deep-brown gaze dropped to the phone in her hand then lifted back to her face. He quickly looked past her and over the people around them, but the way his shoulders stiffened and his body tensed told her he already knew something was wrong. She took a step toward him.

The production assistant stepped in her path, plucked the phone out of her hand, and shoved her toward the hosts. "Go!" she hissed. "You're on!"

"Kels!"

Hunt's hissed voice echoed at Kelsey's back, and the heat of his hand brushed her forearm for a split second. But the push from that assistant sent her stumbling forward, out of his reach, and when the camera swung her way with its flashing red light, she knew it was already too late.

Somehow, she managed to catch herself before she hit the ground and straightened her spine so she didn't look like a complete idiot on live TV. She had to get through this interview without freaking out. When it was over, she'd show Hunt the text and let him decide what she should do about it. That's why he was here, after all. Drawing a breath, she put one foot in front of the other and forced a smile she didn't feel.

Her heels clicked along the hardwood floor. Her pulse raced. Her skin was hot and sticky. But she told herself she was safe—Julian couldn't get to her in this studio. Everything would be okay. If she looked at this logically, she could see his text was actually a *good* thing. Now she had proof of his threats, and she could get a restraining order against him. Even though she was sure Julian would never act on those threats, at least now she could keep him from messing with her mind once and for all.

She reached Rachel and Adam on set. Shook their hands. Even managed to make a joke about how clumsy she was. Sinking into her chair, she crossed her legs, remembered to keep her spine straight, and began answering questions about Fashion Week. And from the corner of her eye she spotted Hunt on the fringe of the set and relaxed even more because . . .

Because he was here.

He was good at his job. His company was wildly successful and had several big-name clients thanks to the booming film industry in the Portland area. Nothing bad would happen to her because Hunter O'Donnell wouldn't let Julian anywhere near her.

"Should we bring out the models?" Rachel asked.

"Sure." Pushing to her feet along with Rachel, Kelsey stepped down from the raised set and moved to an open area of the stage, set up like a runway. The first model was already moving toward her. Just as she was about to open her mouth and talk about the model's outfit, a shiver rushed down her spine, and a feeling that something was wrong hit her square in the chest, stealing the air from her lungs.

She whipped around and searched for Hunt in the faces on the edge of the stage. But she couldn't see anything more than bright lights. Perspiration dotted her spine as she squinted to see better, but she still couldn't find him. Where was he?

"Kelsey?" Rachel asked. "Uh, the model's over here."

In a daze, Kelsey turned to look at the hosts, both eyeing her as if she'd lost her mind. But the feeling wouldn't go away. She swallowed hard and glanced past them, looking to the far side of the set for any sign of Julian.

He wasn't there. He couldn't be there. But the feeling was growing stronger. Making her think something awful was about to happen.

Adam cleared his throat. "So our first model is Claire, right?"

When a hand grasped her at the elbow, Kelsey blinked and looked up to see Adam standing right beside her, holding her arm and smiling down at her. But his eyes were filled with a pull-yourself-together look she didn't miss. And in a rush she realized . . .

This was exactly what Julian wanted. To scare her. To make her look like a fool on live TV. To humiliate her.

He was playing the bully again, like always, and she was falling right into his trap.

Straightening her spine, Kelsey blinked and forced a smile for the camera. "Right. This is Claire. What I love most about Claire's ensemble is the versatility. She's wearing a deep-blue—"

The sound registered first—a low rumble that cut off Kelsey's words and increased in strength until it was a roar in the studio. Eyes wide, Kelsey looked around the room. But before she could even ask what the sound was, the lights went out, and a shock wave jolted the building, nearly knocking her off her feet.

And as screams rose up around her in the darkness, one thing became clear: the text she'd read only moments before hadn't just been a warning. It had been a promise. And too late she realized she should have listened to her instincts.

CHAPTER TWO

The second he felt the shock wave jerk the building, Hunt lurched forward with only one thought in mind. "Kelsey!"

"It's an earthquake!" someone shouted.

"Take cover under a desk!" another voice hollered.

"Get to a doorway!"

The shrieks and screams filling the soundstage were drowned out by debris crashing down in the darkness. People streaked past Hunt, trying to get to the exits before the walls collapsed.

Something hard hit him on the back of his head, on his shoulder, and across his left arm, but he ground his teeth against the pain and pushed on.

"Kelsey!" he yelled again, hoping she could hear him, fighting back the panic that wanted to grab hold because he couldn't see her. "Get to the back of the couch. Lie on your side on the ground next to it! Cover your head!"

More screams reached his ears in the darkness, followed by one faint shriek he recognized. One off to his right, telling him . . . she was there. That she'd moved toward the couch in the middle of the set. That somehow she'd heard him in the chaos.

"Kelsey?" He shifted direction and rushed that way, but his foot collided with something solid, and before he could stop himself, he lost his balance and flew forward.

His body hit the ground with a grunt. The air whooshed out of his lungs. He sucked in a breath but took in dust that made him cough. Flattening his palms, he pushed up and tried to listen. The cracking and rumbling had subsided, and the building didn't seem to be shaking anymore. He couldn't see shit in the dark, but there was still air around him, which meant the ceiling hadn't completely collapsed. At least, not yet.

He struggled to his feet, groaning at the pain in his left shoulder. "Kels? Talk to me? Where are you?"

Silence, then a faint voice off to his right called, "I'm here. I'll come to you."

"No, don't. There's too much debris. Are you against the couch?"

"Yes," she answered in a frightened voice. "Was that an earthquake?"

"I don't know. Stay where you are. You're safest next to something sturdy. If the walls buckle they'll hit the couch, which will create a triangular area that'll protect you. Stay as close to the back of the couch as you can. And keep your head covered."

"If the walls buckle?" she squeaked.

Shit, he was scaring her. "It probably won't happen. Just stay there, okay?"

"O-okay."

A groan echoed somewhere to Hunt's left. At his back, someone screamed, "Help me!"

Six years as an Army Ranger had taken him into some of the world's deadliest situations. He'd freed children from bombed-out buildings in Iraq, rescued hostages in Africa, and helped take an entire airfield in Afghanistan from Taliban forces in the dead of night. His instinct was not to leave those in need behind, but he knew if he turned around, if he tried to offer help, he could lose Kelsey in the darkness. There was so much debris in his way—beams, chunks of cement, destroyed camera equipment—he could be lost in seconds. Not to mention if the ceiling did collapse, he'd never reach her in time. She was his focus, not only because he'd been hired to keep her safe but because the McClanes were like family. He'd never forgive himself if something bad happened to her on his watch.

He tuned out the sounds around him and zeroed in on her voice. "Keep talking to me, Kels." More dust filled his lungs, and he coughed. "So I can find you."

"I'm here. Here," she repeated. "Over here." Another deafening crack echoed from above, growing steadily louder. "Oh, God. What the hell is that?"

Instinct made Hunt look up even though he knew he couldn't see anything in the dark. The rumble grew louder. His chest constricted when he realized the building definitely wasn't done settling and that all holy hell was about to rain down around them.

"Cover your head!" He hurled himself toward the last place he'd heard her voice. His right shoulder slammed into something hard, and his body smacked against the floor. Pain spiraled though his arm and torso, but the roar above kick-started his reflexes. Pulling his legs in, he rolled into a fetal position as quickly as he could, covered his head with his arms, and shifted back into whatever object he'd hit.

Please let it be a couch or a table or something strong enough to create a pocket of air.

He barely had time to wish let alone pray. The building crashed down around him in a deafening boom. As cement and bits of metal pummeled his body, he screamed Kelsey's name one last time.

And hoped that wherever she was, she was safe.

————

It was dark. So dark Kelsey couldn't even see an inch in front of her face. And cold. The kind of cold that seeps into the bone and makes a person think they'll never be warm again.

"Hunter?" she whispered, shaking in the darkness. "Someone? Anyone?"

For the hundredth time, no one answered. Nothing moved around her. No sound met her ears but her own labored breaths as she struggled to hold back a sob.

She had no idea how much time had gone by, but it felt like an eternity. Once the debris had settled, she'd found herself wedged into a two-foot wide, four-foot long space against the back of the couch. Some kind of ceiling beam had crashed down on top of her during the building's collapse, but it had hit the back of the couch, forming an angled, protective barrier above her. She wasn't sure how Hunt had known she would be safe beside a piece of furniture rather than under a table or desk as she'd always been taught, but she was thankful he'd called out to her in the chaos. Even more thankful she'd listened.

"Hunt?" she called again, coughing over the word from the dust in the air. She was desperate to hear his voice. To know where he was. To find out if he was okay or if he was trapped under something and needed help.

Not that she could help anyone in her current situation but . . . she needed to know.

"Hunter O'Donnell!" she screamed.

Still no response.

Fear pushed in, condensing in her chest until she couldn't breathe. Gasping caused her to shift in her confined space, which only sent dust into the air that made her cough harder. She fought through the hacking spell and mentally told herself to calm down. Panicking wasn't going to help. But as her coughing subsided and silence filled the space around her, a new sense of dread took hold. One that told her she had no one to blame for this situation but herself.

If she'd stayed in New York for the rest of Fashion Week, or even if she'd traveled to Orlando with her parents and siblings for the big family trip to Disney World they'd all planned, she wouldn't be here.

She'd be somewhere else, smiling. Maybe even laughing in the sunshine. But instead, because she'd been so caught up in her blossoming career, because she hadn't been able to say no to free promo, she'd agreed to this interview and flown home early. And now, all thanks to her laser-focused drive—something Julian had once told her would be her downfall—she might never be found. Everything she'd worked so hard for the last few years was on the verge of being snuffed out. She could very well die down here in the dark alone, and she would never have a chance to say goodbye to the people she loved.

"Hunter?" she called again.

Still nothing.

Keep it together. Stay strong. You will get through this.

She repeated the words in her head, over and over, until they ran like a loop in her mind. But each second the silence stretched in the dark, the harder it was to believe them.

———

A muffled sound dragged Hunt from the silence. Followed by a groan somewhere close. Forcing his eyes open, he blinked several times into utter blackness that caused his lungs to constrict with a quick shot of panic.

His breath caught. The groaning stopped. Which told him . . . the sound had come from him.

Slowly, his senses righted, and he tried to figure out where he was and what had happened. Memories flashed in his mind—the morning-show set, watching from the sidelines, a loud boom, complete darkness, and searching for Kelsey in a sea of screams and crashes and complete pandemonium.

That panic came back full force, lodging beneath his breastbone. Pulling his hands in front of him, he tried to push his body up so he could go find her. "Kels—"

Dust immediately filled his mouth, and he coughed. He rolled to his stomach as best he could and tried to pull his legs beneath him, but they wouldn't move.

As his hacking and wheezing died down, he pushed up on his hands and tried to glance down his body, but it was so dark he couldn't see even an inch in front of his face. Something was definitely blocking his movement. Rolling to his side, he felt another solid object wedged at his back, and when he lifted his hands out in front of him he registered beams and slabs of concrete on all sides.

Panic wrapped around his chest and squeezed like a boa constrictor, but he forced his mind to stay calm, knowing he was safe for the moment with a pocket of air around him. If he gave in to the fear and freaked out, he could use up all his oxygen. He'd been in enough tight spaces to know losing control wouldn't accomplish anything but making him crazy. Focusing on his leg, he braced his hands against the concrete at his front and pushed, trying to pull his lower half from whatever held him in place, hoping he didn't dislodge something that would put him in a worse situation.

Nothing budged.

Sweat slicked his skin, and the effort made him draw deep breaths that caused him to cough all over again. Knowing he needed to conserve energy, he gave up the fight and concentrated on sucking in air through his nose so he wouldn't take in too much dust. As his lungs slowly relaxed, he took stock of his body, searching for any major injuries. He was sore in places, and the back of his head hurt like a motherfucker, but one touch of his hand confirmed he hadn't cracked his skull open. His legs, on the other hand, were definitely stuck. They didn't hurt, but he couldn't be sure that was good news. Either something had his pant legs pinned, holding him in place, or he'd snapped his vertebrae when the ceiling had come down and was now paralyzed.

"Better fucking be the pant legs," he muttered. He had not survived three tours with the Rangers in the world's deadliest hot spots only to lose his legs now.

Dust filled his mouth once more, making him cough harder. And shit, he needed to get control of that, or he was going to black out.

"Hunter? Oh my God, Hunt, is that you?"

He swallowed the coughing fit the second he heard Kelsey's voice. Lifting his head, he struggled through his lungs' attempt to expel the dust and strained to listen, hoping he hadn't hallucinated the sound.

"Hunter?" Kelsey's voice lifted an octave in obvious panic. "Hunter, answer me!"

Relief spread through his whole body. She sounded close. Really close. As if he could reach and touch her. "I'm here," he managed, willing his lungs to relax. "I'm right . . . here."

"Oh, thank God." Her voice was muffled but strong, and he took that as a good sign. "I've been calling and calling for you. I was sure you were dead."

"Not dead." Definitely not dead, and for that he'd never been more thankful. He cleared his throat to keep from coughing once more. "Are you hurt?"

"I don't think so. My left hip is sore. I got hit by something when the walls came down. Whatever it was, it landed against the back of the couch and didn't crush me. It's cold and metal. I think it actually kept other things from hitting me."

He breathed easier, relieved she'd listened and reached the couch before the building had collapsed.

"What about you?" she asked. "Are you hurt?"

"I don't know. My legs are stuck."

"Oh shit." Her voice rose again. "Are they broken?"

"I don't know. They don't hurt."

"Well, that's good."

He hoped like hell that was good. But considering she sounded as if she were fighting the edge of hysteria, he decided not to tell her the other option.

"How did you know we'd be safe against the couch instead of under a desk or table?"

"Experience." His muscles slowly relaxed. Hearing her voice, knowing she was safe, eased his greatest fear at the moment. "When I was a Ranger, every person we pulled alive from any kind of rubble was found next to something solid instead of under it. I have a friend from the military who now heads an international rescue team organization. They respond to natural disasters all over the world. They've seen the same thing in numerous disasters. When buildings collapse, the people who took cover under something solid usually wind up dead because objects will collapse under heavy weight." He paused to cough again, then added, "But those who get trapped next to a solid object survive because the object won't completely compact. It creates a pocket of air near the ground and a protected space just big enough for a human to survive in."

"Oh my God," she said in a low voice. "I was just about to dart under the newscaster's desk before I heard you yell for me to find the couch."

His chest pinched, but he told himself she was safe. She was okay. That she'd listened. "It's a good thing you didn't."

Silence settled between them.

Unsure what she was thinking, he shifted, trying to find a more comfortable position, but it was virtually impossible with his legs immobilized. He finally gave up, knowing conserving energy was more important. Remembering his phone, he patted his hip pocket and silently rejoiced when he found his cell. He tugged it out and hit the button to turn it on, but no light filled the space.

"Shit." One touch told him the screen was shattered and the casing was cracked.

"What was that?" Kelsey asked.

"Nothing," he said quickly, not wanting to upset her. "Just trying to find a comfortable position."

"You won't find one."

He didn't like how bleak her voice sounded. "Have you heard anyone else?"

"No. It's been quiet for a long time. I called and called for help but no has answered. I . . ." Her voice wavered. "I think we might be the only two left alive."

He could tell she was right back on the edge of panic. He needed to focus on keeping her calm so she didn't give in to fear. "Don't waste your energy yelling. All it will do is increase your heart rate and make you breathe harder. There's a lot of dust in the air." And toxic fumes, but he kept that to himself too. He coughed once more. "You don't want to take too much of that in. Besides, we need to conserve energy for when we're found."

"But what if . . ." Her voice grew so quiet he had to strain to hear the rest of her words. "What if no one ever finds us?"

Something in his chest squeezed tight. Something he only felt when he was around her. He'd always had a soft spot for Kelsey McClane, though he wasn't sure why. Maybe it was because she was the outcast in her family, always making choices no one approved of. Maybe it was the way she dove into her work, sometimes at the expense of her own personal life. And maybe it was the tough-girl persona she showed the world but which he sensed was a façade. Whatever the reason, he'd known there was something special about Kelsey the first moment he'd met her, even all those years ago when she'd been nothing but an awkward teenager trying to hold her own with rambunctious brothers who didn't have a clue what to do with a little sister. Which was why hearing her so frightened now tore at something deep inside him.

"They're coming, Kels," he said softly. "Don't worry. A million people saw this building collapse on live TV. It's just going to take the rescue workers a while to get to us. There's probably other damage in the area from the gas main eruption, and streets might be blocked. The best thing we can do is sit tight and wait. But I promise, someone is definitely coming for us."

"You think it was a ruptured gas line?"

"That'd be my guess. When I came in this morning, I noticed they're building on the lot next door. I saw a backhoe and construction workers messing with the gas lines. There's no fire here, which means it had to have been next door. A gas main explosion can level an entire block."

When she didn't respond, his brow wrinkled. "It definitely wasn't an earthquake, if that's what you're thinking. There was an explosion first. I'm not sure if it was in the basement of the building or outside, but I recognized that sound."

"I know. It's just . . ."

"Just what?"

"Just . . . before we heard the explosion, I got a text."

He couldn't see the connection between any text she might have received and the explosion, and he was just about to say so when a memory flashed behind his eyes. One of her standing in the wings of the morning show, seconds before she was about to go on, staring down at her phone. Followed by the full-on panic in her soft brown eyes when she'd lifted her gaze to his.

"A text from who?" he asked. "About what?"

"From Julian. Telling me that in a matter of minutes I was going to be dead."

For a heartbeat, Hunt wasn't sure he'd heard her right, but then her words sank in, and every muscle in his body contracted in understanding. "Do you have the phone? Can you turn it on? Read me exactly what it says."

"I don't have it."

"What do you mean you don't have it? It was in your hand. I saw you looking at it before you went on."

"I don't have it," she said louder. "The production assistant ripped it from my hand just before she pushed me onstage. And don't you think I would have tried to use my phone already to call for help if I had it right now?"

He was getting worked up. *She* was growing agitated because he was on the verge of freaking out. Drawing a deep breath through his nose, he reminded himself to stay calm. But, holy shit. If what she said she'd read was true . . .

"Tell me exactly what the text said. Everything you can remember."

She audibly exhaled, and the sound told him she was fighting hysteria again, but he had to know. "It came through just after the hosts introduced me. It said that I think I have everything but that soon I was going to get exactly what I deserve. It said I was nothing but a disappointment. That he knew the real me, and this—I guess he meant the designer, public part of my life—wasn't it. It said no one wanted me. That"—she hesitated—"that my own mother hadn't wanted me." She paused again. "Then it said the world would be a better place when I was dead, and that in a matter of minutes the world could thank him for making that happen."

Disbelief turned to a red-hot rage that curled Hunt's hands into fists. "And it was from Benedict? You saw his name on your screen?"

"No. I mean, I didn't see his name. I blocked his number several months ago, but I know it was from him."

"How do you know for sure?"

"Because he's been harassing me since I filed for divorce. I haven't been able to prove it because he keeps doing it from different numbers. My attorney thinks they're burner phones. You know, those throwaway cell phones you can buy preloaded with a certain number of minutes? We've never been able to track the calls back to Julian, which is what

I needed to get a restraining order, but I know it was him. He's been sending me threatening texts for months."

Hunt wanted to jump on blaming Benedict—he'd never liked the asshole, not just because Benedict acted like he was the shit, but also because the dick had treated Kelsey like a second-class citizen all through their marriage. Only experience told him to consider all the possibilities. "Alec told me some of what's been going on with Benedict. Tell me about the other messages he's sent you. Were any others like this?"

"They were pretty similar. He liked to point out how useless I was. That my business was going to fail. That my designs sucked. That no one wanted me or my clothing line. That I'd come crawling back to him like a dog before long, and that when I did, he'd have to think long and hard about how he was going to make me pay for humiliating him."

Hunt's jaw clenched down hard. The urge to slam his fist through Benedict's face was stronger than ever. So strong the muscles in his arm ached from contracting.

"I just ignored them, you know?" she went on. "I thought if I did, the texts would eventually stop. They slowed down a little, but my brothers were still worried, which is why they asked you to keep an eye on me while they were gone."

Hunt knew that. Her brother Alec had told him Benedict was being an ass about the divorce and that they were worried he might do something to retaliate. But Hunt had never expected something like this. To orchestrate the take-down of an entire building, all to get back at her . . .

His mind raced. Julian Benedict was an investment guy. He worked for some big financial company in the city. No one would suspect him of knowing anything about bombs or how to rupture a gas line. But Hunt remembered something Kelsey had told him when he'd first come home from the military and discovered she was dating Benedict. That the guy had double-majored in college—in finance and chemistry. That he'd hoped to work in pharmaceuticals but had found a job in investments that had paid too much to turn down.

Chemists knew about bombs and gas lines. And hell, these days if you didn't already know that kind of stuff, you could find it on the fucking Internet.

A sniffling sound met Hunt's ears. And realizing Kelsey was crying hit him hard, like a punch right to the stomach. Enough to calm the storm brewing inside him.

"If he's the one who did this, Kels, the Feds will find out. They'll get him, don't worry."

"I know." She sniffled again. "I just . . . I can't stop thinking about the other people who were in the building with us. The ones we haven't heard from since everything happened."

Hunt's memory flashed back to someone calling for help in the darkness, between the first shake and the second that had brought the ceiling down. Even though he knew he'd made the right choice, guilt twisted in his gut. "This wasn't your fault. You didn't do anything wrong. Do you hear me? You didn't cause any of this to happen."

"I could have prevented it, though." She sniffled again. "If I hadn't been so hell-bent on coming back here for this stupid interview, those people would all still be alive. I-if I'd stayed on the East Coast with the rest of my family, you wouldn't be here. You wouldn't have felt obligated to babysit me, and you definitely wouldn't be trapped in the dark with your legs pinned or"—her words faltered—"or broken."

His chest squeezed tight again. "Kels, listen to me. First of all, we don't know where anyone else is. Just because we can't hear them doesn't mean they're dead. People were running toward the exits when the walls started to go. They could be buried too far away for us to hear them. They could already have been rescued for all we know. Don't assume the worst right now, okay? I need you to think positive. Second of all, I'm fine. I've been through way worse than this, trust me. I could tell you stories from my time in the military that would make this look like a party. But more than that, I want you to know that I'm here with you because I wanted to be here. Not because I felt obligated. Not because your brothers forced me to babysit. Because you matter. I'd do whatever I could to keep you safe."

She sniffled again. And the silence that followed was more deafening than the roar of the building coming down.

"You would?" she finally said.

He relaxed a little because in those two simple words, her voice had sounded stronger. If he was going to get her through this, he had to keep her focused on something other than her fears.

"Of course I would."

"Why?"

"Why? Because you're family. I've known you almost as long as I've known Alec."

"So you'd do whatever you could to keep me safe because you see me as Alec's annoying younger sister and you feel what . . . responsible for me?"

Relief made the corner of his mouth turn up. This was the Kelsey who could drive him wild. The smart, snarky, teasing woman he'd watched spar with her brothers more times than he could count. "Trust me, I don't see you as an annoying younger sister at all."

"You don't?"

"No. Believe me when I say you are only an annoying younger sister to your older brothers. To every other guy who meets you, you're an incredibly attractive woman with an amazing talent."

She was silent so long, he wasn't sure she was still there. "Kelsey? Did you hear me?"

"I heard you," she said softly. "I just . . . I never thought you noticed when I was around."

His stomach tightened all over again. Man, Benedict had really done a number on her. The urge to find the son of a bitch and pound him into the ground whipped through Hunt once more, but he focused on keeping Kelsey calm and distracted. Told himself that was all that mattered right now.

"Of course I noticed. I always noticed. I mean . . ." *Shit.* He had to phrase this right. "When I first met you, you were only like thirteen, and I didn't notice you were attractive then. I mean, you were cute but . . . young. Innocent." Holy hell, this was totally coming out wrong. "I mean, I didn't look at you like a guy would then. That would have been creepy because I was like nineteen. And I'm definitely not into, you know, *that.*"

"I get it," she said with a smile in her voice. "Keep going. You're finally getting to the good part."

"The good part?" *Shit,* he was sweating. He lifted a hand and swiped his forehead, dragging dust and tiny bits of rock across his skin in the process. How the hell had he gotten himself on this topic?

"Yes, the part where you tell me what you thought of me when we met."

"I thought you were sweet. I liked you. Like a friend," he added quickly so she wouldn't get the wrong idea.

"And what about later?"

"Later?" *Fuck,* did his voice just crack? He shifted uncomfortably, knowing he was screwed if he didn't steer the conversation in a different direction fast.

"Yes, later. You didn't see me for a long time. After you graduated from college you joined the military. The few times you visited my family when you were on leave, I was away at college. You didn't see me again until I was like twenty-two. What did you think of me then?"

Perspiration dotted his spine, and he swallowed hard because he remembered exactly what he'd thought then. He'd thought she was the hottest woman he'd ever seen. Taller than he remembered, curvy in all the places she'd been straight before, with thick, blonde hair down to the middle of her back, tempting pink lips, and insanely long eyelashes framing her deep-brown eyes. The only part of her that had looked the same was the spray of freckles across her nose. Everything else had been all woman. And after he'd spent some time with her, he'd realized she wasn't *just* another hot chick. She'd been smart and witty, mature in ways other twenty-two-year-old women he'd encountered were not, and as sweet as sugar.

All of it had thrown him for a loop. Somehow, in the six years he'd been away, she'd transformed from that awkward, shy teenager with braces he remembered into his ideal version of the perfect woman. And he'd been seconds away from asking her out.

Then Julian Benedict had blown into the McClane house as if he lived there, dropped down beside Kelsey on the couch, wrapped a possessive arm around her shoulders, and made it more than clear that she was off-limits. Which Hunt would have been able to accept if he hadn't seen her stiffen under that arm. In a heartbeat, she'd shifted from a clever, sexy, confident woman who'd made him want things he'd never wanted before to one who was nervous, self-conscious, and afraid to do or say the wrong thing in front of Benedict.

His jaw tightened once more because he should have realized Benedict was a threat back then. He'd been too disappointed in the fact Kelsey was already taken to waste much thought on Benedict, though. And now, because he hadn't done a damn thing to stop the son of a bitch when he'd had the chance, Kelsey's life was in danger, and innocent people could be dead.

The only way he could make up for it was to ensure the fucker never hurt another person again.

CHAPTER THREE

"Hunt?" Unease wedged its way between Kelsey's ribs as she waited in the silence for him to say something. Anything.

Possibilities whipped through her mind. What if he'd passed out? What if the rubble pinning his legs had shifted and crushed him? She didn't think that could have happened—she hadn't heard any debris moving—but what if he'd been cut when the ceiling had come down and hadn't realized it? What if he'd blacked out from blood loss?

Worst-case scenarios filled her mind as she scooted closer to the cold cement separating them and fought against the panic threatening to drag her under. "Hunter?"

"Yeah. Sorry. I, uh, lost my train of thought. I must have hit my head harder than I realized. What were you asking?"

Relief filled her chest like a balloon inflating. Closing her eyes, she laid her cheek against the cement beneath her and tried to slow her pulse. He was okay. A hysterical laugh filled her chest when she realized where her mind had gone, and she only just held it back.

She breathed deep. In and out, focusing on the whoosh and pull of air in her lungs to calm her fears. She probably shouldn't be asking these questions, knew she was likely setting herself up for a letdown but didn't care. She could very well die in this rubble. If this was going to be one of her last conversations, she wasn't holding anything back. Besides, Hunt had started it, and part of her was glad he had.

Because she knew exactly what she'd thought when he'd walked into her parents' house that sunny July day just after she'd graduated from college. She thought she'd fallen into a dream.

Her lips curled as she lay still with her cheek against the cold cement. Warmth spread through her chest at the memory. She'd been the only one home that afternoon. Her parents had still been at work, her older brothers hadn't been living at the house then, and the youngest McClane—Thomas—hadn't been adopted yet. Alec had called earlier in the day to tell her he was swinging by after work to meet Hunt at the house and to let Hunt in if he got there first. She hadn't paid much mind to Alec's heads-up because Hunter O'Donnell had always just been that gangly, quiet roommate of her brother's.

"Yeah, whatever. He's coming by. Got it. I'll give him a magazine or turn on the TV for him until you get here. Just don't expect me to entertain him or anything. I have plans."

Then the doorbell had rung, and she'd pulled the heavy wood slab open to find that Hunter O'Donnell wasn't at all what she'd remembered. Instead of gangly, he'd been tan and ruggedly muscular after six years in the military. A little bit dangerous with that thick mahogany hair, the dusting of dark stubble on his jaw, and a collection of new scars on his hands and cheek and arms that made her wonder what he'd been up to. He'd also been a whole lot enticing, especially with those dark-brown, almost black eyes that had seemed older and wiser and brimming with mystery. But it was when he'd come in, sat in the living room with her, and talked to her as he waited for Alec that she really felt like she'd dropped into a dream. Not because of what he'd said but because he *listened.* Really listened. The way guys do when they're interested.

That had been a good day. A really great day. Her smile widened as she remembered the way he'd laughed with her, the chemistry that had sizzled between them in that room. Somehow the conversation had drifted to the latest movies—what she'd seen and when—and for a moment she'd thought he might ask her out. Then Julian had shown up for their date—a date she'd completely forgotten about as she'd been chatting with Hunt—and everything had changed.

Her smile faded in the dark, and that warmth inside her cooled. Hunt hadn't asked her out that day. In fact, his demeanor had totally changed as soon as he'd met Julian. And after that, every time she'd seen him in passing he'd been nothing more than the strong, silent, stand-offish friend of her brother's—just as he'd been when she was in high school. They'd never again talked like they had that afternoon—nothing more than polite chitchat at family events. But part of her had always wondered . . . what if? What if Julian hadn't shown up that day? What if they'd had more time together? What had he really been thinking about her before he'd realized she was already seeing someone?

Courage swirled in her chest. If this was her last chance to find out, she wasn't going to let anything stand in her way. She'd let too many good things pass her by over the years. "I was asking what you thought of me after you saw me again."

Silence, then he said, "I thought . . ."

She braced herself for the rest. To hear him say he'd thought she was immature or flighty or just plain stupid for dating someone like Julian Benedict.

"I thought you were amazing. Not at all what I remembered. And I was pretty damn mesmerized by you."

Mesmerized? She blinked into the darkness. "You were?"

He chuckled. "Yeah. I, uh, had a little bit of a crush on you then, I'm afraid."

A smile pulled at her lips as she lifted her head and looked toward the sound of his voice, wishing she could see him. "You did?"

Okay, now she sounded like she was fifteen. *Dial it down a notch, Kels.*

"Yeah." He laughed again, only this time it sounded a tiny bit nervous, and knowing he was nervous made her stomach flop like a fish out of water. "I can't believe I'm admitting this, but I was about to ask you out that day. Which, in retrospect, probably wouldn't have gone over well with your brothers or your folks, but I didn't care at the time. Only then your, uh, boyfriend showed up, and I realized you were already seeing someone, and . . . well, the rest is kind of history."

No, it wasn't history. It wasn't history at all because she was no longer *with* Julian.

Her heart pounded hard. She told herself not to get her hopes up, but part of her just couldn't stop from hoping.

For the last eight months since she'd left Julian, she'd sworn off men. She didn't need a guy to be happy, didn't need a relationship to be successful, didn't want a man messing up her life—a life that was finally back on track after a disastrous relationship that never should have happened. And only a couple of hours ago, if Hunt had admitted he'd been interested in her all that time ago, she probably would have been flattered but still walked away.

Now everything was different, though. Now she was facing her own mortality. Now she was in the middle of a life-threatening disaster she might not survive. And all this time alone in the dark, staring into an abyss of her greatest fears, had led her to one truth.

There was only one thing in life that truly mattered, and it wasn't her career or money or her status, because in the end, all those things were worthless. It was the people who touched her that mattered most. The ones who made her feel alive. The ones she knew she didn't want to live without.

Her parents were at the top of that list, the two people who'd taken a chance on her when she'd been an orphaned kid, who'd given her a home and a family and a future. And her brothers, of course, who—even at their most obnoxious—were her biggest fans and strongest supporters. But, lying here in the dark, she'd realized that her list also included Hunt. He'd been part of her life almost as long as her brothers. A silent, steady, resilient part she'd taken for granted because she'd just assumed he'd always be there.

Nerves rattled around in her belly, and she licked her lips, thought about staying quiet, then told herself if she did, she'd always regret not asking. "Why didn't you ever tell me that?"

For a heartbeat, he didn't answer, then quietly, he said, "Because it wouldn't have made a difference."

"It might have."

"I doubt it. You were already with Benedict. If you hadn't been in love with him, you wouldn't have stayed with him, right? Definitely wouldn't have married him."

Her chest deflated. Yes, she had been with Julian, but their relationship had been new then. She'd been unsure whether he was the guy for her. She knew now, in retrospect, that Julian most definitely had not been good for her, but back then she'd naively thought that was the way things were supposed to work: fall for someone in college, graduate, get married, have kids.

Clearly not. Look how great that plan turned out.

Sickness rolled through her belly. Thankfully, she'd wised up shortly after she and Julian were married. Once she'd seen his violent mood swings, she hadn't wanted to discuss the topic of kids. Not until he chilled out. But that had been her biggest mistake, hadn't it? Thinking she could change him. People didn't really change. She'd wasted three years figuring that out.

"I don't know." Hunt sighed. "Maybe things are only supposed to happen at a certain time. In the long run, it's good we didn't go there because relationships never work out. I never planned to tell you any of this—never wanted things to be weird between us, you know? I hope they won't be weird now. I value you as a friend, Kelsey."

As a friend.

The three worst words in the English language. Her disappointment was swift and all-consuming, but in the end . . . did she really have anyone to blame for that disappointment but herself?

She shoved aside the feeling and tried like hell to keep her voice steady when she said, "No. They're not weird. I'm glad you told me."

And she was. Because in the last fifteen minutes, when they'd been talking, she hadn't thought about how tightly she was confined or how dark it was around her or what had happened to the others caught in the rubble. His little "confession" had completely distracted her from their current situation. Which could very well have been his intention all along.

Panic threatened to overwhelm her again, but she repeated her little pep talk—*Keep it together. Stay strong. Help is coming*—and laid her cheek back on the cement. Only as the cold seeped into her skin, that feeling hit her again. The one she'd felt just before the lights had gone out. The one that sent a shiver down her back and made her feel as if impending doom was just waiting for the right moment to strike.

———

Hunt tried to shift to his side to take some weight off his arms, but his pinned legs made it impossible to move.

He had no idea how much time had passed, but it felt like ages. A shiver racked his spine, and he rubbed his hands across the parts of his arms he could reach, hoping to ease the chill.

"Kels? Are you still awake?"

Silence met his ears, amping up his stress level. She'd gone quiet after their chat about the past. He'd mentally kicked himself for confessing any of that, then decided it wasn't a big deal. Aside from that one afternoon, she hadn't shown any romantic interest in him over the years. And according to Alec, since her divorce, she'd announced she was done with men in general. The fact he'd admitted he'd *kinda* had a crush on her a bazillion years ago shouldn't be an issue. Yet she still wasn't talking . . .

"Come on, Kels. You're starting to make me worry here. Say something so I know you're still there. Otherwise I'm gonna think you got your ass rescued while I'm still stuck here in the dark."

Silence met his ears again, then softly he heard her say, "It's still dark here too."

His chest warmed with relief. But something in her tone worried him. *Something like . . . being terrified she might never get out of this freakin' rubble?*

"You need to stay awake," he said, not wanting to think like that. They had to stay positive. Someone was coming for them. He was sure of it. "Tell me about Fashion Week. When Alec called me from New York, he said your designs were a huge hit."

More than a hit. Alec had told him she'd been inundated with orders since the show. So many that her small company, operating out of a warehouse in North Portland, couldn't keep up. The interview this morning was only part of the reason she'd flown back early. The other reason was because her employees had been working overtime since the show and were desperate for production help. Which meant Kelsey'd had to come back here and miss out on a relaxing trip to Disney World with the rest of the McClane clan.

He nearly snorted because he couldn't imagine anything relaxing about being surrounded by ten million kids at Disney World. He did, however, get a sick sort of pleasure imagining Alec's five-year-old daughter, Emma, forcing her dad to take her on It's a Small World for the hundredth time.

"There's not much to tell. It was just a lot of models and clothes and cameras."

"There had to be parties, right? I bet there were some great parties. How many celebrities did you see?"

"I don't know."

"I'm sure you saw some European royalty too, right? I heard they always go to those shows." He could give a rip about celebrities and stuffy parties and "royal" anything, but he was desperate to distract her.

She sighed. "I don't know. A few, I guess."

"Like who? Give me some names."

"God, you're irritating, you know that?"

He grinned because "irritating" was good. "Irritating" kept her mind occupied. "I know. Start talking."

She sighed again. "Um . . . Alaina Pierce."

His smile faded as he racked his brain. He'd heard that name but couldn't remember whether she was a singer, actor, or just some rich billionaire's kid. He was pretty sure she wasn't European royalty, but he couldn't be a hundred percent certain.

"Alaina Pierce, the award-winning actress," she said before he could come up with the answer on his own, drawing the last word out in a way that made him think she was on to him.

"Alaina Pierce, the actress. Right. I knew that."

She snorted, telling him loud and clear she *knew* he was full of shit.

He cleared his throat. "Isn't she married to one of those famous sextuplet guys who own that big hotel here in wine country?"

"Evan Archer. Yes, they own the Alex Hotel."

"Have you ever been to the hotel?"

"No. Alaina invited me to come down sometime and check out their new spa, but . . ."

"You should go."

"I don't know. I don't have a lot of time for the spa. Besides which, we may never get out of this nightmare, so what's the point in even thinking about it?"

Damn. She'd steered the conversation right back where he didn't want it to go.

"We're going to get out of here, Kelsey. You have to think positive."

"I'm trying to, I just . . ."

"Just what?"

"Nothing. Never mind."

He didn't like the way she was shutting down. He wanted to comfort her but couldn't reach out to her. The best he could do was remind her she wasn't alone. "Did Alec ever tell you about my mom?"

"No," she said hesitantly. "I don't think so."

He knew she had to be wondering about his abrupt change in topic, but he kept going. "She was a nurse. She died when I was twelve."

"Oh . . . I had no idea. I'm so sorry. Alec never said anything."

No, he probably wouldn't have. Hunt had asked him never to talk about it.

An ache filled his chest, one that was always there but which he kept locked down tight. One he was only letting himself feel right now in the hopes it helped Kelsey here in the dark. "It happened a long time ago, and I've dealt with it. Anyway, she was one of those people who was always the first to come running if someone was hurt. At events if someone fell down, at church if one of the elderly collapsed, even at my sporting events when kids twisted their ankles, which used to embarrass the hell out of me."

"Sounds like a great woman."

She was. His mom had been the best, but he wasn't going to let himself think about her because it would just open up old wounds he'd let close long ago.

"We were coming home from one of my baseball tournaments. It was the middle of the summer, hotter than hell. Right about dusk, this huge thunderstorm rolled through. Slashing rain, hail—it was insane. We were on the freeway, and my dad was driving. I was snoozing in the back seat because I'd played three games that day and was exhausted. I remember feeling the car slow down and hearing my parents talking quietly about an accident ahead. It must have just happened because cops weren't even on the scene yet. When my mom popped the door and said she was going to see if anyone needed help, my dad tried to stop her. She told him not to worry. They argued for a few seconds. He said he should be the one to go help, but she wouldn't let him. She had the medical training, he didn't. She asked him to stay in the car with me to keep me distracted in case I woke up, then she left."

A thousand emotions he didn't want to feel rolled in, but he forced them away, not wanting to acknowledge any because this wasn't about him. It was about Kelsey. "I remember coming fully awake then, sitting up and seeing the mangled metal out the front windshield. There were like six cars in the wreck. The hail had caused the visibility to drop, and the driver of the first car had slammed on his brakes, which set off a chain reaction. I remember a layer of white dusting the ground and the twisted vehicles, but everything was distorted because of the rain and the windshield wipers going back and forth at the highest setting. I couldn't be sure what I was seeing, so I asked my dad what was going on, and he kind of mumbled that there was an accident, but he was only half paying attention to me. He was focused on my mom, rushing up to the scene, talking to the other people who'd seen the accident and gotten out to help, then moving to the crumpled vehicles to check on passengers."

The images hit him hard and fast, filling his vision with the same things he'd seen that day: watching his mom rush up to the busted-out window of a white SUV upside down on the pavement. Seeing her speak to whoever was inside. Registering the flames even before he heard the explosion.

"What happened then?"

Her soft voice pulled him back, and he blinked hard to rid the pictures from his mind. "Then the SUV she was checking exploded. It happened so fast she didn't have time to move back or even react. The crash had ruptured the fuel line."

"Oh my God. I am *so* sorry."

He blinked back tears that still stung his eyes, even twenty years later, and cleared his throat. There was no sense even responding to her comment. He'd heard the same over the years too many times to count, and while he knew people meant well, it never really did help. Not in any way that mattered. "My dad lost it then. He bolted right out of the car, only there was nothing he could do. Nothing anyone could do. The coroner said she was dead within seconds. That, at least, is a comfort, I guess."

"Oh, Hunt."

He kept going as if she hadn't even spoken, thankful she couldn't see him and that he could get all this out where she could hear him but not touch him. He didn't like people trying to comfort him when they heard his sob story. Probably why he never talked about it anymore.

"It is what it is," he said. "I didn't bring it up to be a downer or to imply something like that is going to happen here—it isn't. If this place were at risk of going up, it would have happened already. I mentioned it only because my dad gave up that day. He stopped living. He burned his arm, trying to get to my mom. He had to have a couple skin grafts over the years to fix it, and I know his arm still causes him pain, but he won't talk about it. Won't even acknowledge he was ever hurt. The only thing he's ever been able to focus on is his grief. He gave up on life, because according to him, life gave up on him."

"I think that's understandable," Kelsey said softly. "He lost his wife."

Hunt huffed, any pain he'd felt before replaced by a familiar resentment he'd never been quite as good at keeping locked down. "Yeah, he lost his wife, but he still had me. I lost her too, only he never thought about that. Instead of being the dad I needed, he turned into this shell of a person I don't even recognize some days. I had to become the adult that day. I spent most of my teen years taking care of him. Making sure he was okay. I'm still doing it, even now when he's in his sixties. I do it because I love him and because he's my father, but it's not a way to live. It's not a way to be."

He took a breath, hoping she heard what he was trying to say. "Yeah, life sucks. It sucks in a thousand different ways for a billion different people, but you don't just give up. Bad things happen, and you can't predict them. All you can do is keep living. Because the reality is, it can always get worse. Always. He could have lost me that day, but he didn't. My dad never wanted to see that, but it's true. There's always something to be thankful for in every tragedy if you just look hard enough."

Silence met his ears. He had no idea what she was thinking, and as the silence stretched, he wondered if he'd just crossed a line he shouldn't have gotten near. Yes, he considered her family in a weird sort of way, and yes, at one point he'd even had a crush on her that he'd kept to himself, but at the end of the day, they'd never been more than friendly acquaintances. And he had no idea if she'd take what he'd just said as encouragement or as a reprimand.

"You're right," she said softly. "We can't stop bad things from happening. Worrying about when they'll happen doesn't help either."

He wasn't quite sure what she meant by that. But before he could ask, she said, "And I can easily see why Emma tells everyone she meets that she's going to marry you someday, Hunter O'Donnell."

A laugh he didn't expect pushed up his throat. "Why's that?"

"Because you're a very special man."

"Not that special. I'm a pain in the ass most days. Ask Alec."

"I don't have to. I already know the truth. So does anyone who really gets to know you, I'm sure. Thank you for being here with me. There's no one else I'd rather be stuck in the dark with than you."

A strange feeling twisted in his belly. One he wasn't used to. "There's no one I'd rather be with right now either, Kelsey."

Silence stretched between them. One that made his heart beat even faster because he'd meant those words. Every one. And he wasn't entirely sure what to do with that knowledge.

She finally sighed. "Let's talk about something normal. What are you doing for vacation this ye—"

A rumble sounded.

"Did you hear that?" she gasped.

"Yeah." Senses alert, he looked up even though he couldn't see anything and strained to listen. "It could just be more debris settling abo—"

The rumble turned to a roar, which kicked his adrenaline sky high.

"Kelsey!" Every muscle in his body contracted. "Cover your head!"

The rest of his words were drowned out by a deafening crash.

And the lingering sound of Kelsey's scream.

CHAPTER FOUR

Hunt coughed against the dust filling his lungs as the roar faded.

The debris around him had shifted. He wasn't sure what had happened, but his little air pocket was now smaller than before. Cement and rock pushed against him from every side, but at least it hadn't completely collapsed on top of him.

"Kels"—he coughed again—"Kelsey, answer me."

Silence met his ears, sending his pulse right back into overdrive.

He blinked and tried to rub the grime from his eyes. There was so much dirt and debris he was sure he'd never be clean again. "Kelsey? Talk to me. Tell me you're okay."

Every second that passed with no sound from her caused his chest to cinch tighter until it felt three sizes too small for his lungs. "Kelsey, dammit. Answer me."

Still no response.

He pressed his palm against the cement near his head that separated his space from hers and used every ounce of strength he had to try to shove it aside, but it wouldn't budge. Muscles burning, he finally dropped his arm and breathed deep, filling his lungs with the foul dust that only made him want to cough again.

There were plenty of times he'd felt powerless in his life—when his mom had been killed, when his dad had refused to get help for his depression, during his time in the military when he'd arrived too late to save a civilian or even a fellow soldier from a roadside bomb. But this—being stuck here in this rubble, able to hear everything that happened around him but unable to move a single muscle to help—was the absolute worst.

He closed his eyes. "Come on, Kelsey, say something, baby. I need to know you're still there. Say anything. Kels?"

An eerie silence echoed around him. One he didn't like. One that made his mind spin with images of Kelsey being crushed in the debris only inches away from him.

No. She wasn't dead. She couldn't be dead. Defiance and anger welled inside him. He shoved hard against the cement inches in front of his face again, determined to get to her. "I know you're there, Kelsey. Say something, dammit."

His muscles burned. Perspiration slicked his skin. He grunted as his lungs seized, not just from exertion but also from a misery he wasn't going to survive.

Another rumble sounded, but he didn't stop pushing against the stones. Debris moved around him. Dust filled the small space, causing him to cough all over again. But faintly, over the sound of his hacking, over the blood roaring in his ears, he thought heard a voice.

He slowed his struggle, sucked in a breath, and stilled. "Kelsey?"

"There!" the muffled voice called. "I knew I heard someone there. Hurry."

Rocks and concrete shifted above him, and more dust rose in the air, forcing him to cough even harder. And then a blinding light broke through the darkness.

Hunt slammed his eyes shut. More rocks shifted. The voice grew louder, followed by another. And another. Blinking rapidly, he held up a hand to block the growing light as he tried like hell not to suck in too much dust. One by one, chunks of concrete were moved out of the way. Fresh air rushed all around him. And then hands were on his arms, pulling him free.

The cement near his legs shifted. The pressure holding him down released, allowing him to move the lower half of his body for the first time in hours. Fingers closed around his wrists. Pins and needles stabbed into his legs and feet as he was hauled up, and his weight almost went out from under him, but two rescue workers were there, tugging his arms over their shoulders so they could help him stand.

He blinked against the bright lights as he tried to see clearly. His eyes weren't working right yet. All he could make out were shapes and shadows and a flurry of activity as he was helped over the broken cement and mangled steel. Sound registered. Voices shouting orders, the hum of machinery being used to sift through the debris, sirens, even the whir of helicopter blades above. But the one sound he couldn't hear was Kelsey's voice. The one thing he couldn't see was her.

"No." He shifted his weight to his feet, ignoring the pain in his legs as he pushed back against the two men helping him. "I can't. She's still stuck down there. I have to go back."

"You're in no condition to help," the man on his left said.

"I can't leave her." Hunt pulled his arms from their shoulders and let his legs take the full brunt of his weight.

And nearly gasped because *holy hell*, his legs hurt like a mother-fucker. But one step was all it took to realize there was no perma-nent damage. He was scraped, bruised, and probably bleeding in a few places, but he could walk.

He turned back toward the rubble and faltered when his eyes focused and he saw the damage for the first time. "Holy shit."

The bottom two floors of the building were completely blown out on one side, and it wasn't the side closest to where city workers had been tampering with that gas line. Piles of concrete and twisted metal covered the ground, along with papers, shattered glass, demolished furniture, and crumpled tiles.

He'd seen enough blown-out buildings overseas to know what a bomb could do. And his heart beat hard and fast, knowing this hadn't been an accidental gas-line rupture as he'd hoped.

"Here!" a first responder standing in the rubble yelled, not far from where Hunt had been pulled free. "We found another one!"

Hunt's heart shot into his throat, and even though his legs felt as if they might go out from under him at any second, he hobbled back toward the destruction, trying to see around paramedics and firemen and rescue workers, searching for any sign of Kelsey.

Someone stepped in his way. He spotted a hand being lifted from the rubble. His pulse went stratospheric as he tried to move around people blocking his path. Another arm appeared from the debris, white with dust.

Someone stepped in his path, blocking his view again. Hands landed on his upper arms. "Sir, you can't help here. You need to get checked out by the EMTs. We can handle this."

"I need to see if it's her." He struggled against the first responder's hold, ducking his head so he could see around the man.

Please let it be her, please let it be her, please, please, please . . .

A dusty arm rose from the destruction, then a slim body, coated in dust. He couldn't tell if it was a man or woman. Couldn't tell if they were alive or not moving. Couldn't see where the rescue workers were taking them.

More bodies stepped in his way, pushing him back. Frustrated because his muscles weren't working right, because he couldn't get past this firefighter he could normally drop with barely any effort, he yelled, "Kelsey!"

"Hunter?"

Kelsey's voice was weak, but it was real. And it gave him the strength he'd been missing. He broke free of the firefighter holding him back and spotted two rescue workers heading toward him, helping her over the rubble.

She was covered in fine white dust, her face and arms and every inch of her body filthy and scraped and bruised, and she was squinting and blinking to see through the bright light. But she was whole. She was breathing. She was alive.

"Kels . . ." His relief was all-consuming. He met her at the edge of the rubble, captured her around the waist, and pulled her from the rescue workers until her body was flush against his. And then he lowered his mouth and kissed her.

Her hands landed on his shoulders. She sucked in a surprised breath. But before he could make himself stop, she groaned, tangled her fingers in his shirt, and opened to him, kissing him back with the same desperation he was kissing her.

His brain short-circuited. The only thing that mattered was her. Safe. Alive. In his arms, right here and now. He fisted her ripped blouse, drawing her even tighter against him, and kissed her deeper. Needing to taste every part of her if for no other reason than to prove to himself she was real.

Someone nearby chuckled.

A voice muttered, "I think these two are okay."

Farther away, someone else hollered, "I found another one!" Then footsteps sounded on concrete before fading until he didn't hear anything but his roaring pulse echoing in his ears.

Breathless, he finally drew back from her mouth, just a fraction of an inch. But he didn't loosen his hold, wasn't ready to release even an ounce of her heat that felt so damn good plastered against him.

"I thought . . ." Words lodged in his throat, and a rush of emotions he wasn't ready for wrapped like tentacles around his chest. "When that last rumble sounded, and you didn't answer me, I thought I'd lost you."

She trembled and pressed her forehead against his. "I . . . I couldn't hear you. I called and called. I was so scared something had happened to you."

He lifted his hands to her face, drawing back just far enough so he could see her eyes. His fingers grazed a scrape on her cheek. He brushed a lock of hair back from her temples, so dusty it looked white instead of blonde. A nasty bruise was forming along her jawline, but he was relieved to see her eyes were clear. Clear and as brown as the blessed earth beneath his feet. Clear and so damn fathomless, staring up at him with truth and compassion swimming in their depths, his heart turned over beneath his ribs.

"I thought I was never going to see you again," she whispered.

He knew people were watching. He knew he needed to let her go so the EMTs could make sure she was all right. He knew the way he'd kissed her moments ago had been rooted in relief and was nothing but a life-affirming reaction. He also knew he had no right or reason to kiss her again. Not when that life-affirming moment had passed. But he wanted to kiss her again. His gaze dropped to her lips, and a hunger so sharp it was all he could focus on took control of his body.

He lowered his mouth to hers once more. Only this time he didn't kiss her with relief or to reassure himself she was alive. He kissed her the way he'd wanted to kiss her for five damn years. With every bit of passion he hadn't realized he'd stored up inside for her.

She opened the minute their lips met. Groaned into his mouth. Dug her fingertips into his shoulders as she held on and lifted herself in his arms so she could press her body even closer to his. And then she kissed him back as if she never wanted to stop.

A little voice in the back of his head told him this was wrong. But it felt too damn good to stop. His hand slid from her cheek into her hair. The other wrapped around her lower spine, moving her against him. Vaguely, he heard footsteps and voices coming closer, but they didn't deter him. Didn't stop him either. Cupping the back of her head, he angled her mouth so he could kiss her even deeper. And when she answered with a tiny gasp and stroked his tongue harder, all he could do was wonder why the hell it had taken him so long to kiss her in the first place.

"You son of a fucking bitch!" a man yelled.

Kelsey lurched back from Hunt's mouth and stumbled out of his arms. Blinking, Hunt reached for her, his mind hazy, his senses in a fog as to why she'd pulled away. Then he registered her shriek. Heard a thud as she hit the ground at his feet. But he didn't have time to brace himself before a fist slammed into his jaw.

———

Kelsey's eyes flew wide as she looked up to see Julian drawing his arm back to hit Hunt again.

"She's my wife, asshole. Keep your fucking hands off her!"

"Julian! No!" She scrambled to her feet and grappled for Julian's arm, but he was already throwing it forward, straight toward Hunt's face.

She stumbled in the dirt. Looked up to see Hunt's eyes widen. But instead of the sickening sound of Julian's fist hitting bone, all she heard was the whoosh of air as Hunt ducked beneath the swing.

She scrambled back even farther, her heart in her throat. Julian whipped around and arced out with his fist again, but he was too slow. Hunt's fist plowed into Julian's gut before Julian even got his arm all the way around.

Julian grunted and doubled over. "Fucking asshole. I'll kill you."

Hunt lifted both hands in front of his face like a prizefighter. "Try it and you'll regret it."

Julian looked up at Hunt, but he didn't make another move to go after him. Instead, he threw a vicious look Kelsey's way. And the second her eyes met his, fear shot straight into her throat because she knew that look. The one that told her he was past any kind of sanity and engulfed in a rage that this time wouldn't be mollified.

Her legs shook as she stepped back and lifted her hands in front of her. "Julian, don't."

"You." Baring his teeth in a growl, he lurched toward her. "You unfaithful, no-good whore."

Kelsey shrieked and stumbled. Lifting her hands in front of her face, she ducked and closed her eyes, her body tense in anticipation of his fist. But the blow never came. A grunt echoed, followed by a thud. And when she pried her eyes open, she found Julian splayed on the ground at her feet.

"You're done threatening people." Hunt grasped the back of Julian's jacket and jerked him to his feet. "And you're done using her as a punching bag."

Julian scrambled to find his footing, tried to pull free of Hunt's hold on his shirtfront, and lifted his fists. But before he could even utter a protest or pull his arm back, Hunt's fist smashed straight into his nose.

Bones cracked. Blood spurted. And when Hunt let go of Julian's shirt, the man crumpled to the ground like the broken cement all around them.

Kelsey gasped, unable to look away from the man who'd made her life a living hell for the past three years, writhing on the ground as he clutched his bloody nose. She should be happy. She should be ecstatic someone had just done to him what he'd threatened to do to her too many times to count, but she wasn't. She was suddenly shaking and didn't know why.

Footsteps sounded close. Hunt's footsteps. She sensed others were rushing toward them, probably to intervene, and she knew she was safe. But instinct pushed her back another step.

"Kelsey," Hunt said firmly. "Stop."

The harsh command stilled her feet, but it didn't slow her racing pulse or her rapid-fire breaths lifting her chest as if she'd just run a marathon.

"Are you hurt?" Hunt moved in front of her, gripped her at the jaw with warm fingers, and tipped her face up toward his. "Look at me. Did he hurt you?"

She blinked and shook her head, unable to meet his gaze. She knew Hunt was only trying to help her, but she couldn't look at him right now. She wasn't afraid of him. She knew he wouldn't hurt her, and she knew he'd never blame her for what had just happened. She wasn't even upset that Julian was currently moaning on the ground feet away from them—he deserved that and more after everything he'd done, especially if he'd had anything to do with the building collapse here today. But she still couldn't make herself look at Hunt right now, because she was afraid if she saw even a fraction of the rage she'd seen seconds ago in Julian's eyes, it would forever tarnish her impression of Hunt and what he stood for.

Her eyes slammed shut. A tremor she couldn't stop racked her body. Wrapping her arms around herself, she repeated her mantra: *Keep it together. Stay strong. You can get through this.* Only it didn't help. The shakes intensified, making her painfully aware she was teetering on the edge of a hysteria she might not be able to hold back.

"Shit," she muttered, stepping back again. *"Shit."* She'd just survived a collapsed building, for crying out loud. Why was she losing it now?

"Just breathe, Kels." Strong arms closed around her like steel bands. And then all she felt was heat. Against her cheek, around her waist, sliding down her spine. The scents of citrus and leather hit her, scents that were familiar and comforting. But it was the rhythmic thump in her ear grabbed her attention. The steady beat that slowed her pulse. That gave her something solid to focus on. That drew her back from the edge of madness.

"You're okay," Hunt said softly as he held her. "Everything's okay." Slowly, she became aware of sounds around her. Of Julian scream- ing that he'd been assaulted. That Hunt needed to be thrown in jail. That he needed a doctor before he bled out. Then she heard another voice, closer but muffled and clipped, sounding official, asking all kinds of questions about her and Julian and what had just happened.

"No, she's fine," Hunt said above her in a calm voice, talking to someone she couldn't see. "Who let him in here?"

"Officers at the barricade said he went nuts when he saw his wife. He pushed past them before they could stop him."

"They're not married anymore. They've been separated for eight months, and their divorce went through this morning. He's been harass- ing her for the last year. Just before the bomb went off, he sent her a text, threatening to kill her."

"You're sure of that?"

"I saw her face when she read it. That was seconds before the bomb blew. The timing can't be a coincidence."

"Does she have the phone?"

"No, she lost it in the explosion."

"Miss?" the man asked gently. "My name's Officer Callahan. Are you feeling up to answering a few questions? I guarantee Mr. Benedict won't be able to hear or touch you."

All Kelsey wanted to do was go on letting Hunt hold her, but that time was up. Steeling herself for what she'd see on his face, she untangled her arms from her waist and pressed her hands against Hunt's stomach. For a second his arms tightened, and she was sure he wasn't going to let her go. Then he released her. But he didn't step back as she expected, and even though she knew it made her weak, especially after she'd very nearly had a nervous breakdown right in front of him, she was glad. Even more relieved when he reached for her hand, wrapped his strong, solid fingers around hers, and squeezed.

"Brett's an old friend, Kels. He knows better than to throw bullshit at me."

Officer Callahan chuckled. And for whatever reason, the sound eased more of the tension inside her.

She chanced a look up at Hunt's face. A smile tugged at the corner of his mouth, and his eyes were calm, not the least bit enraged as Julian's had been. The last of the panic she'd felt before unwound inside her.

"I-I'm sorry. I'm not usually such a wreck." Brushing the filthy hair back from her face, Kelsey looked to Officer Callahan. He was shorter than Hunt by several inches, with a receding hairline and a nose that looked as if it had been broken more than once. But his hazel eyes were kind, and the way he smiled and hooked his thumbs in his belt in a nonthreatening way relaxed her even more.

"No judgment from me," he answered. "You've been through hell today."

She had been. But she still didn't like the way she'd very nearly crumbled a few minutes ago. Or that she'd almost done it in front of Hunt.

Glancing past Callahan, Kelsey spotted several officers surrounding Julian at the back of an ambulance. She couldn't hear what they were saying, but their aggressive stances needed no explanation.

"Hunt was just telling me about the text you received." Callahan pulled a small pad of paper and a pencil from his breast pocket, drawing her attention his way. "Can you describe the cell phone for me?"

"It's an iPhone. Silver. In a clear case with pink flowers."

"When was the last time you remember having it?"

A scream echoed from the direction of the ambulances. Kelsey's gaze shot in that direction to where Julian was now bent over the back of the ambulance with his cheek pressed against the floor of the vehicle while two officers wrestled his hands behind his back and snapped cuffs over his wrists.

"Um . . . I . . . the production assistant took it from me just before I was supposed to go on air."

"Sir?" A female EMT with brown hair tied in a neat ponytail reached for Hunt's arm with gloved hands. "Your leg is bleeding. We need to take a look at that."

Kelsey's gaze dropped, and for the first time she noticed Hunt's left pant leg was shredded from hip to ankle and that his thigh was red and oozing beneath the torn fabric. "Oh my God." Sickness swirled in her stomach. "You're hurt."

"It's nothing." Hunt brushed the EMT's hand away, tightening his hold on Kelsey's hand when she tried to release him. "I'm fine."

He wasn't fine. She stared at the wound, remembering how he'd said his legs had been pinned in the rubble. Her gaze lifted to his face, but she could tell with one look he wasn't feeling any pain. His focused eyes were locked on her as if *she* were the one who was injured. As if making sure she was okay was all that mattered.

Emotions slammed into her from every side. Emotions that stole her breath and drew her right back to that moment in the destruction when he'd told her she mattered. That he cared. That there was no one else he'd rather be with. Followed by the overwhelming way he'd kissed her when she'd been pulled from the rubble. Not once, but twice.

He'd meant those words. Meant every single one. Her lips tingled as the memory of those kisses flooded her mind. And in the aftermath, her skin warmed and her heart sped up until the only thing she wanted was for him to kiss her again.

"She's fine, O'Donnell." Officer Callahan glared at Hunt. "Go get your leg patched up before it falls off."

Hunt shot a frown Callahan's way, then looked back at Kelsey. "I can stay."

Words lodged in her throat. She couldn't seem to make her tongue work. And this inability to speak had nothing to do with fear or a breakdown or anything to do with Julian. It had to do with the man in front of her. With the way he'd protected her. With the way he was *still* protecting her. And all the ways she wanted to thank him for being exactly what she needed.

The best she could do was shake her head.

His brow wrinkled, as if he were unsure, and knowing he wouldn't leave her when he was worried, she said, "I'm fine, Hunter. Go."

"Are you sure?"

She nodded. "Very. I'm fine."

His features relaxed. Releasing her hand, he pointed toward the line of ambulances. "I'll be right over there if you need me."

"Holy hell," Callahan breathed. "Get out of here already, O'Donnell."

Hunt glared Callahan's way once more, then looked down at the EMT. "Okay, lead the way.

The EMT placed a gloved hand around his arm, helping him as he hobbled toward the ambulance. And as Kelsey watched, she hated that she'd been so wrapped up in herself and what had happened with Julian that she hadn't noticed he was injured. At the same time, though, something inside her warmed with the knowledge that he'd been so wrapped up in her he hadn't even noticed himself.

"Stubborn jackass," Callahan muttered at her side. "You must have the magic touch."

Kelsey blinked and looked toward the officer. "I do?"

"You must. He never listens to me. Never listens to anyone, as a matter of fact."

As Callahan jotted something in his notebook, Kelsey watched as Hunt carefully climbed up on the open tailgate of an ambulance and extended his leg for the EMT to inspect. He was strength and resilience and family, she realized. Not in a way that made her feel confined, as her brothers and parents often did, but one that made her feel safe, protected, cherished. And for reasons she didn't quite understand, she suddenly wanted to have the magic touch for him. Wanted to *be* the magic for him that he'd just been for her. Couldn't keep from wondering what that would be like.

"We should probably get you checked out too," Callahan said, flipping his notebook closed.

Kelsey blinked, still unable to look away from Hunt. "I'm fine. I'm not hurt."

"Humor me, will ya? I'm sure you are fine, but I'll feel better when I know for sure. Plus, I want you to tell me about Benedict before the FBI gets wind of you. Hunt said you've had problems with the man in the past. If he had something to do with this bombing, trust me, Portland PD wants a piece of him before the Feds get involved. And if you're at the center of all this, I want to know every damn thing about you and Benedict before the Feds come looking for you."

CHAPTER FIVE

Hunt had a sinking feeling he'd seriously fucked up. But for the moment, there wasn't a thing he could do to fix it.

The doctor tied off the last of the stitches in his thigh in the emergency bay at the ER where Hunt had been taken even though he'd argued he didn't need a hospital. A little of the tension in Hunt's chest eased, knowing this part of his day was almost done. He was itching to get out of here. Itching to get back to Kelsey. And his eagerness had absolutely nothing to do with that never-should-have-happened kiss, and everything to do with the fact he didn't have a clue where Benedict was at the moment.

Damn. What the hell had he been thinking, kissing Kelsey like that? She was his best friend's sister. There was a bro-code there he knew better than to cross. He needed to get out of this hospital and find Kelsey, not just because she was technically his client at the moment, but because he needed to talk to her about that kiss. Apologize. Explain . . .

Explain what? Just how long he'd been fantasizing about kissing her? Or how badly he wanted to kiss her again?

"Fuck me," he muttered, gripping the sides of the table. Just what the hell *was* he going to say to her?

The dark-skinned nurse at his side chuckled as the doctor stepped back, and she moved in to bandage his leg. "You're cute and all, but a little dirty for my taste. 'Sides which, I'm married."

Hunt's face warmed, and he glanced up when he realized he'd said that out loud. "Sorry. I was thinking about . . . something else."

"Uh-huh." She placed a square bandage over his stitches. "Did you call her yet to let her know you're all right?"

"She knows." But her question made him suddenly remember her family. And his dad. And what the hell they were all thinking at the moment.

The twentysomething doctor stripped off his gloves. "These stitches need to stay dry for at least forty-eight hours. Ellen's putting a waterproof bandage over the dressing. You can shower when you get home, but briefly. Try not to get the bandage too wet." He tossed his gloves in a trashcan and moved to the counter to sign Hunt's paperwork. "Take the plastic covering off tonight. Check the dressing. If it's wet you'll need to get the gauze off and rebandage it."

Hunt nodded. "I was in the army. I know how to take care of a dressing."

"Good." The doctor clicked his pen and tucked it in the chest pocket of his scrubs. "The stitches will need to stay in seven to fourteen days. Follow up with your primary care physician to have them removed, or call him if you notice any signs of infection."

He swept out of the room before Hunt could even respond. Since the ER was packed with people from the disaster and Hunt could tell the kid was stressed, he cut the guy some slack. Glancing past the nurse still wrapping his thigh, Hunt looked up toward the clock and realized it was already after seven in the evening.

Shit. Seven p.m. The blast had happened at just after nine fifteen that morning. He and Kelsey had been stuck in that rubble for almost eight hours, then there'd been that whole scene with Benedict at the site, followed by coming here . . . Both of their families were probably freaking the hell out.

He reached to his back for his phone only to find his pocket empty. He'd lost his cell somewhere in the blast, but his thoughts had been so scattered, he'd completely forgotten until just now. He really needed to call his dad. He needed to call the McClanes. But more than anything, he needed to find Kelsey and make sure she was okay.

The nurse tugged off her gloves and dropped them on the tray at her side, then stepped back so he could stand. "I'm going to grab your discharge papers from the printer. There's a pair of scrubs on the counter there. They aren't pretty, but they'll get you home in something more than your undies. Go ahead and get dressed, and I'll be right back."

"Thanks." Hunt climbed off the gurney, wincing at the ache in his legs. A little pain was better than being paralyzed, though, and today he'd take it over the alternative.

By the time the nurse came back, he was dressed in the teal scrubs. She went over the discharge instructions with him again and made him promise to call if he had any problems. Just as she was finishing, footsteps sounded in the hallway. "He won't call. Too bullheaded."

Hunt's heart lurched into his throat when he spotted Callahan alone in the doorway. "Where is she?"

"Relax." Callahan flashed a wide smile at the nurse, then stepped aside to let her pass. "She's fine. In the waiting room with one of my officers. FBI wanted to keep her for questioning, but I told 'em a bullshit story about her being too exhausted to go through it all again. Though I'm sure they'll call her tomorrow just for shits and giggles." He glanced over his shoulder toward the nurse who'd just left. "You didn't catch her name by any chance, did ya?"

"Ellen. And she's married."

"Bummer. She's hot."

Hunt breathed a little easier, knowing Kelsey was close, but not much. He'd feel better when he saw her with his own two eyes. He tugged on his filthy shirt, cringing at the twinge in his back. The doctor had insisted on looking at a scrape on his shoulder, but it, thankfully, hadn't needed stitches. "Where's Benedict?"

"Being booked right now for assaulting an officer." Callahan followed Hunt out into the busy ER hallway. "Guy was whining about needing a hospital, but the EMTs patched him up. Nice work on his nose, by the way. Not broken, but you definitely did a number on his profile."

Hunt wasn't exactly proud of that. Violence didn't always solve things, and he definitely didn't like that he'd dropped the guy right in front of Kelsey. Especially with the way she'd reacted to it.

"Have the Feds questioned him?" Hunt asked, moving around a trio of doctors standing in the middle of the hallway.

"Not yet. But I'm sure they will. They also want to talk to you."

Hunt expected that. His night was far from over. He glanced at his friend as they approached the double doors that led to the lobby. "And what did Kelsey tell you about Benedict?"

Callahan exhaled. "Enough to give me a not-so-pretty picture of their not-so-happy marriage. Guy's clearly got anger issues. He never hit her, if that's what you're wondering, at least not that she's admitting. But he did enough behind closed doors to scare her. Guys like him use threats and bullying to get what they want."

Hunt stopped and turned toward his friend, unease churning in his gut. "That's exactly what Kelsey said. Even if he did send that text, he doesn't fit the profile of someone who'd set off a bomb in the middle of a city."

"Yeah. That was my thought too."

Hunt stared at his friend. "So what happens to him now?"

"At this point we have no evidence he was involved, but the investigation is only just beginning. We'll keep him for questioning as long as we can, but, Hunt . . . Kelsey never filed a restraining order, so we can't even hold him for violating that. Benedict's attorney will likely argue

Benedict was distraught over the bombing, and that's why he reacted aggressively. If he does that, it'll be hard for us to make the assault charges stick, and my guess is the DA will decline to prosecute in that situation. If we can't find anything linking Benedict to the bombing, he'll probably be out on the street tomorrow."

Hunt didn't like the sound of that. Regardless of whether Benedict was or wasn't involved in that bombing, he was still a threat to Kelsey. Today he'd become violent, even if she wouldn't admit he had before. "Can she file a restraining order now? Considering the way he went after us today?"

"Yes. And I had her file a temporary restraining order before I brought her over here. Judge Halliwell already signed it, and she's got a copy. She'll have to appear in court in fifteen or twenty days to make it permanent. The key will be whether she goes through with it then, when she has to face him in front of a judge."

Hunt would make sure she went through with it.

His chest pinched. He didn't like thinking about Kelsey being hurt—now or in the past. Didn't like thinking how his growing need to protect her was crossing over from professional into way-too-damn personal. Reaching a hand out, he hit the button on the wall at his side to open the wide double doors. Just as he did, Callahan's phone went off. His friend lifted the cell to his ear and answered as he and Hunt stepped into the lobby.

Hunt's gaze swept the two dozen or so people waiting to be seen by a doctor. Around him the hustle and bustle of a busy emergency room echoed in his ears. A baby cried. People chatted in low voices. At the counter to his left someone was arguing with the receptionist. But he couldn't find Kelsey.

Panic reformed beneath his ribs. He looked over each face again, sure he had to have missed her. Just when he was ready to rip the phone out of Callahan's hand and ask where the hell she was, a woman with powder-white hair and familiar brown eyes emerged from what he realized was a small hallway that led to a couple of restrooms. And behind her, an officer dressed in the familiar PPD blue colors.

The air whooshed out of his lungs, and relief filled the space behind. He stepped toward her, but Callahan's hand on his arm stopped him.

"Yeah, hold on," Callahan said into his phone. "He's right here." He held the phone out to Hunt. "It's McClane. For you."

"Which one?" Hunt closed his hand around the phone. "And how'd they know we were together?"

"Alec. And he guessed. What happened in Portland this morning is all over the national news. When he couldn't get ahold of you, he called the station. Someone there gave him my number. Talk to him."

Hunt pressed the phone to his ear. "Hey. Things have been crazy here. Sorry I didn't call. I lost my phone."

"Is Kelsey okay? We've been going out of our minds here."

"She's fine." Hunt focused on Kelsey, walking toward him, looking way better than any woman should look after everything she'd been through today. "We're both fine. She's right here with me, safe and in one piece." And, damn, he wanted to hold her again. Ached to wrap his arms around her right here in the middle of this waiting room just to prove to himself she was warm and solid and real.

"The news said it was a bomb. What the heck is going on there, Hunt?"

Hunt had roomed with Alec in college and knew his friend didn't always handle stress well. At this point, there was no sense bringing up theories and hunches that would just cause Alec more anxiety. "No one's sure yet. Callahan says the Feds are on it, though."

In the background, Hunt could hear Kelsey's other brothers rattling off rapid-fire questions for Alec to ask. The most insistent was Rusty, desperate to know where Benedict was. Hunt tensed, not wanting to get into Benedict's location at the moment. Doing so would only force him to explain what had set Benedict off, and he wasn't ready to go there with any of the McClanes, especially Rusty. Of all Kelsey's brothers,

Rusty was the most protective of her. Considering everything Kelsey had been through with Benedict, Hunt didn't doubt Rusty would be the first to get right in his face and demand to know what the hell had happened and why Hunt hadn't stopped it before it had gone down. And, oh yeah, if Rusty happened to catch any footage of Hunt kissing Kelsey, that wouldn't go over well either.

"Who is it?" Kelsey mouthed, stopping at Hunt's side while Alec ranted in his ear about everything he'd seen on the news, avoiding his brothers' questions.

Hunt tipped the phone away from his mouth. "Alec."

A frown tugged at Kelsey's lips as she held out her hand. "Here, let me talk to him before he bursts a blood vessel."

Hunt relaxed, more than happy to hand the phone off to her.

Kelsey listened for several seconds, then said, "Calm down, Alec. Yes, I'm fine. No, I'm not lying. Well, if you'd chill out for ten seconds and let me talk, I'd tell you."

Hunt watched her, awed by the way she took charge and put her brother right in his place. She'd always been able to do that with her brothers. As the only girl in the McClane family, she'd learned early on to stand up for herself. He just wasn't sure why she hadn't done that with Benedict. The memory of the way she'd cowered away from the confrontation with Benedict at the blast site replayed in his mind, making him wonder where her fighting spirit had been then. And if she'd had it at anytime during her marriage.

"Yes," she said into the phone with a roll of her eyes. "Yes, of course I want to talk to them." Her voice softened. "Hey, Dad. No, I'm fine. We're at the hospital. Hunt had a cut on his leg he needed stitched. Yeah, he's okay too."

Hunt couldn't hear what Kelsey's father was saying on the other end of the line, but he did see the way Kelsey's eyes grew damp, and he heard the sudden waver in her voice that told him the people that mattered most in her life were on the other end of that phone.

A quick shot of guilt hit him in the chest as he watched her reassure her father, mother, then Rusty, Thomas, and finally Ethan that she was safe. He should have called her family sooner. Should have called them the moment she'd been freed from the rubble instead of spending all that time kissing her. The McClanes weren't just friends to him, they were family. They'd trusted him to watch over Kelsey, and he didn't want to do anything to let them down. And that meant he needed to cool it with any romantic thoughts where Kelsey was concerned and get back to what they'd asked him to do. Which was to make sure nothing happened to their girl.

"Yes, okay," Kelsey said once more, any previous sign of being choked up long gone. She glanced Hunt's way. "He's right here." Pulling the phone away from her mouth, she whispered, "It's Alec again. He wants to talk to you before he hangs up."

Hunt's fingertips grazed hers as he took the phone, and warmth shot up his arm at the casual touch. And even though he told himself Alec couldn't see and had no idea about their kiss, he tensed just the same. "Yeah," he said into the phone. "I'm here."

Callahan pointed toward two men in suits and mouthed for Hunt to join him in the hall when he was done. Hunt nodded, but his stomach dropped when he spotted the two Feds. He'd been hoping to get home and take a shower before they got ahold of him, but it looked like that was a pipe dream now.

"Listen, man," Alec said in his ear. "None of us can get flights back into Portland for several days. Even Seattle's a mess. Flights are packed solid. I don't want her staying alone after all this."

Hunt wasn't about to let Kelsey stay anywhere alone. Especially not after that scene with Benedict. "Don't worry about it. I'll stay with her until you get back."

At his side, Kelsey's eyes widened in an *oh really?* way that made her whole face light up and her lips curl in a gentle smile.

Her—*dammit*—soft, plump, seriously tempting lips that he was already thinking about kissing again.

"Good," Alec said. "And make sure you take her to your place, not hers. This is just the kind of situation Benedict will try to take advantage of. He'll act all concerned for her safety when we all know in reality he's pissed she had the nerve to go through with the divorce."

"I'll take care of her. Don't worry." And he would. Without any more kissing. Definitely without more kissing.

He said goodbye without giving himself away, hit "End" on the phone, and lowered it to his side. But his anxiety didn't lessen any because the woman he wasn't supposed to be thinking about kissing was currently standing in front of him, looking sweet and vulnerable and staring up at him as if he were her hero. Which, damn, he suddenly wanted to be. Not just today but every day.

"Thank you," she said softly. "I know he's a pain in the ass right now. He's just worried."

"I'm used to him. I think Rusty's more stressed. If he knew how to fly a plane, I'm pretty sure he'd steal one just so he could get back and see for himself you're in one piece."

One corner of her lips curled in a sad smile. "I know. He's overprotective of me. It has very little to do with me and mostly to do with what happened to his biological sister."

Hunt knew all about Rusty's sister's death. Alec had told him about it years ago when Hunt had asked how Rusty had gotten all those scars. "Maybe a little. But his overprotectiveness is ninety-nine percent about you. He loves you. They all do."

"I know they do."

The sad way she glanced down at her ruined flats made him ache to wrap his arms around her. Clearing his throat, he turned away so he wouldn't give in to the urge and moved toward the ER's doors. "Callahan said you already talked to the Feds."

"Yeah, I did." She fell into step beside him. "They want to speak with you, though."

Hunt moved out into the hallway. Callahan and the other officer were standing in a circle with the two Feds halfway down the corridor, waiting for him. His back tightened reflexively. He really hated dealing with law enforcement of any kind, Callahan being the exception only because they'd become more like friends over the years rather than adversaries. But in his line of work, being questioned by cops—especially Feds—wasn't something he looked forward to. Most tended to look down on private security contractors as bugs worthy only of being squashed beneath their feet. And after the day he'd had, he really wasn't in the mood for a face-off with some uppity agent who'd probably never drawn his gun and likely knew nothing about real-life tragedy.

"Better get this over with then." He drew a deep breath and stepped toward the group.

The discharge papers he held rolled up in his left hand slipped from his grip. Before he could look down to see where he'd dropped them, warmth encircled his palm, followed by a zing of electricity that felt way too damn good.

Kelsey's small fingers wrapped around his much bigger ones and squeezed. And then her lips grazed his cheek, causing his footsteps to falter and his whole body to light up like a Roman candle.

"For luck," she whispered when his eyes met hers. She squeezed his hand again and winked. "And for speed. Make it fast, O'Donnell, because I'm more than ready to go home with you."

CHAPTER SIX

Kelsey eyed Hunt warily in the entryway of the rundown brick building he'd brought her to in the Goose Hollow neighborhood. He'd been acting strange since his meeting with those federal agents. Not worried, exactly, but standoffish, quiet, almost a little cold.

She wasn't sure what to make of that. She waited while Hunt slid a key into the panel outside the elevator and pushed a button. Had his meeting with the Feds not gone well? Had her brother said something on the phone that had upset him? Or did his demeanor have something to do with the fact she'd kissed him outside the ER?

The elevator doors whooshed open, and Hunt held out a hand for her to enter the small car first. Stepping in, she turned to watch him, hoping for any sign he was stressed over something other than that kiss.

The elevator jolted as if it were a hundred years old, then hummed as it began to move. She didn't want to think he could be upset over that; after all, *he* was the one who'd kissed her earlier in the day. Kissed her so thoroughly she could still feel that kiss smoldering in her toes. But the truth was . . . she couldn't be entirely sure. Before today, she hadn't spent a whole lot of time with Hunt one-on-one. And even though they'd both been through a pretty traumatic experience and they'd each pretty much bared their souls to each other in that rubble, the reality was . . . she didn't know him that well. Definitely didn't know his moods or how to read him.

Her mind skipped back to stumbling out of that rubble and seeing him. She'd been so relieved he was all right that she'd all but thrown herself at him. And when he'd grabbed her and looked down, she'd instantly lifted her mouth to his. But what if he hadn't been trying to kiss her then? What if he hadn't even planned to hug her? He was a protective guy—heck, he protected people for a living. What if he hadn't been reaching for her at that moment for no other reason than to steady her because he'd seen her wobbling toward him?

A hiss sounded, but she barely noticed. Had she totally misread him? Was she the one who'd forced that kiss? If that were the case, then yeah, her kissing his cheek at the hospital would totally make a guy like him standoffish.

"Kels? You okay?"

Startled by Hunt's voice, she swallowed and fought back the nausea. "Yes. Why?"

"Because we're here, and you haven't moved."

Blinking, she realized he was holding the elevator door open for her. Feeling like an idiot, she stepped forward on shaky legs. Then faltered when she noticed the twinkling Portland skyline in the wall of dark windows across the vast room and realized the elevator opened right into his apartment—his huge, loft-style apartment—not a hallway like she'd expected.

"Oh my." Wide eyed, she took in her surroundings. The old building in the southwest hills had nearly a complete view of downtown Portland. The walls were brick, with old steel beams that looked as rugged as Hunt littered throughout the space. An enormous kitchen decked out in more stainless steel opened to her left. To her right an entire home gym was set up, complete with free weights, bench press, chin-up bar, speed bag, and a treadmill. Ahead, the main portion of the room housed the living space—a gigantic flat-screen TV over a modern fireplace; an enormous U-shaped sectional and a few leather chairs; a variety of dark wood tables; a tall ficus tree that was clearly well cared for; and two vast paintings on the walls—one of a gorgeous beach house set on a cliff overlooking an ocean, the other of what she thought might be the Tuscan countryside.

The apartment was modern, masculine, and not at all what she'd expected. And even though the outside looked rundown and shabby, the inside was top-of-the-line everything.

"This is amazing." She stepped farther into the room, still unable to believe he lived here. On the top floor. "And big. You live here all alone?"

"Yeah. This is the only apartment in the building. I guess you could say I like my privacy." He stepped past her, moved through the massive living space, and headed for a door off to the right, not far from the wall of windows. "This is the guest room." He pushed the door open and reached inside to flip on a light. "I'm sure you're dying to take a shower. There are fresh towels in the guest bath. I'll get a clean pair of sweats and a T-shirt and leave them on the bed for you to change into. If you need something else, just holler."

He headed for another door on the far side of the room that seemed to match the one he'd left open for her.

"Wait." She looked after him. "The only apartment? You mean, no one else lives anywhere in this building?"

"Nope. Just me."

"How?"

"Because I own the building. Take a shower, and we'll talk later if you still want to."

He disappeared into the master bedroom, and she moved into the guest room, more confused than she'd been before. She knew he owned his own company, but Alec had never said anything about his owning an entire building.

The guest room was just as nice as the main room, with a plush queen bed, two end tables, a dresser, a club chair in the corner, and another vast view of the twinkling city. Moving into the guest bath, she flipped on the shower and peeled out of her filthy clothes, hoping she wasn't leaving too much grime behind on his spotless floor. As she stepped under the warm spray, she closed her eyes and tipped her head back so the water could wash away her worries. But it didn't. It only made her think about Hunt again. About this place. About the fact she knew virtually nothing about the man who'd saved her life today. And that meant it was absolutely possible she'd completely misread his intentions when she'd stumbled out of that rubble and forced that kiss that had rocked her world.

By the time she finished her shower, her skin was pink and wrinkly, but her brain was still completely scrambled. Wrapping herself in a plush taupe towel, she moved into the cushy bedroom with its dark wood furnishings and looked down at the sweats and T-shirt Hunt had left for her on the bed.

The sweats were nothing fancy, just the traditional heather-gray men's variety she knew would be too big. But the T-shirt brought a smile to her face. Printed in white letters across the front of the blue shirt, it said, "Make Portland Weirder."

She fingered the soft cotton, knowing Julian would have died before he'd own a T-shirt like this. And he definitely wouldn't have suggested she wear something so silly. But instinctively she knew Hunt had picked this of all his shirts for her because it would make her smile.

She glanced toward the closed bedroom door, her belly warming at the simple act of kindness. Did she know him? She thought back over everything they'd shared today. She wanted to know him. She didn't want to jump to conclusions. Knew she was second-guessing herself. Knew she was awful at relationships and completely out of practice with what was normal and healthy and rational when it came to the way men acted. And she could think of only one way to find out the truth.

Dropping her towel on the bed, she pulled the T-shirt over her head and tugged the sweats up her legs. As she'd expected, both were too big, but she was able to roll the waistband down on the sweats several times to make them stay up. One look in the mirror told her today was not the day to worry about her looks. Her cheek was scraped, and a nice purple bruise was forming across her jaw. She didn't remember getting hit in either spot, but things had happened so fast in the dark, she'd barely been paying attention.

Every limb was stiff, and she was sore in places she didn't know a person could be sore. She knew she'd likely find other bruises all over her body, but she didn't want to waste time looking. After finger-combing her hair, she headed for the door, intent on facing Hunt and figuring out just what was going on between them once and for all.

The enormous TV was tuned to a national station as she entered the living room, the volume on low, but she didn't need to hear the anchor's words to know what he was reporting. Images of the destruction in Portland flashed across the screen, followed by numerous filthy and bloodied bodies being pulled from the rubble.

Her stomach pitched all over again, but she was unable to look away from the carnage. Slowly, she lowered herself to the edge of the ottoman across from the TV as she stared at the screen. Memories of being trapped in that pitch-black rubble bombarded her from every side and sent a shiver down her spine. But seeing it from the outside . . . A surreal feeling floated around her, knowing she'd been underneath all that broken concrete and twisted metal.

"No, same number." Hunt's voice echoed from his open bedroom door, but Kelsey didn't turn to look. "I already switched everything online to the new phone. Yeah, convenience of having a closet full of phones for just this kind of situation." He hesitated, then said, "Yeah, I'll talk to her when she finishes showering."

He'd moved into the living room and was staring at her. She could see him from the corner of her eye with a phone to his ear, but she still couldn't turn to look at him. Didn't even catch whatever else he said into his phone when he lowered his voice because all she could suddenly hear was the newscaster's words echoing in her ears.

"So far two are confirmed dead, but officials expect that number to rise as the night goes on."

Her stomach twisted tighter, and she swallowed the bile rising in her throat.

Hunt leaned down to pick up the remote from the coffee table in front of her. "You shouldn't be watching thi—"

"No, don't." She lifted her hand to block him from pointing it at the screen. "Leave it on. Please."

He frowned. But she still didn't look at him.

"Authorities as of yet have no confirmed suspects in custody, and no known terrorist groups have taken responsibility for what most officials think was a bomb."

"You don't need to listen to the spin on this," Hunt muttered, still holding the remote. But he didn't make any move to flip the TV off. And seconds later the ottoman cushion dipped as he sat beside her and looked toward the horror unfolding on the screen.

They watched in silence for at least twenty minutes, and only when the station went to a commercial did Hunt finally flip the television off.

Even with the screen black, Kelsey could still see the destruction. Could still hear the sirens. Could still feel the bitter cold deep in her bones in that darkness. *Two confirmed dead . . .* She blinked rapidly, trying like hell not to envision the blood that had been all over Hunt's pants when she'd realized he was injured. It could have been him. It could have been them. She'd spent all this time worrying about kisses that meant nothing when people were hurt. Suffering. When they were dead.

"Hey." Hunt's arm slid around her shoulder, tugging her against the warmth of his chest. "You have to focus on the positive, Kels, not all the bad shit they're reporting. Every hour, rescue workers are pulling people alive from that rubble. They'll find everyone. They'll catch whoever did this, I promise. Terrorists want you to be scared. That's the definition of terrorism. Don't give them what they want. Don't let them win."

She knew that but . . . Knowing and believing were two very different things.

She closed her eyes and leaned against him, just for a moment. Let him be the strength she needed as he lightly ran his hand up and down her arm. Told herself to be tough but . . . really liked the way this felt. "I'm sorry. I'm not usually such a mess."

"I know you're not. And you have nothing to apologize for."

"I don't like being an emotional mess."

"I know that too," he said with a smile in his voice. "But cut yourself some slack, okay? You had a really shitty day."

She wasn't sure how he knew just what to say to make her feel better, but that one comment eased the tension inside her. "So you think this was a terrorist attack?"

His fingers stilled against her biceps. "It could have been. That's the logical assumption. That was Callahan on the phone, calling to give me an update. They found evidence that points to a bomb, not a ruptured gas main. Similar to bombs terrorists have set in Europe recently."

She didn't want to move away from him, but she wanted to see his eyes when they had this conversation, so she pushed back. "So they don't think Julian did this?"

Hunt dropped his arm from her shoulder. But he didn't make any move to scoot away, and she liked that too. "They don't have any evidence yet that ties him to it. The Feds have been questioning him for hours, and he hasn't cracked. That doesn't mean he won't, but Callahan said they're leaning away from the theory he was involved."

Kelsey wanted to be relieved by that fact but wasn't. Her gaze slid from Hunt's eyes to the black T-shirt stretched seductively across his chest, then down to the worn jeans on his thighs. She didn't want to believe Julian could be involved in something so heinous, but she couldn't shake the feeling what had happened today had somehow been linked to her. The same way she hadn't been able to shake that feeling of impending doom she'd experienced right before the building had come down.

"How long can they keep him in custody? Until they know for sure if it was him?"

"No. Without probable cause they can only hold him for about twenty-four hours."

Which meant by tomorrow this time, if not sooner, he'd be out on the streets. She turned back toward the black screen and told herself he wouldn't do anything stupid when he was released. But she hadn't really expected him to do anything today, and look what had happened when he'd seen her with Hunt.

"Hey." Hunt's hand grazed her back, gently tracing the length of her spine. "The cops will figure this out. I have total faith in Callahan. He's one of the good guys."

Kelsey didn't doubt that. She couldn't see Hunt being friends with someone who wasn't.

"Even if they can't hold Benedict, they'll keep a close eye on him until they know for sure he wasn't involved. And I promise he won't get anywhere near you. You're safe here with me, Kels."

She knew she was. She was lucky. But what about the other people who'd been caught in that blast?

"I know what I saw on my phone," she said, trying to convince herself she wasn't crazy. "It wasn't a coincidence that the threat came through right before the building went down."

"I believe you. And they'll find your phone. Don't worry. Callahan's got everyone looking for it."

She wasn't sure what good that would do. It had probably been crushed in the collapse.

As quickly as the thought hit, her mind shot to that production assistant who'd ripped the phone from her hand, and her stomach pitched all over again. She had no idea if that woman was alive or dead. Hadn't even caught her name so she could listen for it on the news.

"In the meantime, I've got some burner phones here. I'll get you set up with one so you don't feel disconnected from the outside world."

"Burner phones?"

He smirked. "Techno-toys. Perk of the job."

A buzzing sounded from the direction of the main elevator before she could ask more, and Hunt dropped his arm from her back and pushed to his feet. "That's the food I ordered. I don't know about you, but I'm starving."

Kelsey didn't feel like eating. Didn't think she'd ever feel like eating after this day. But she didn't say so. She slowly pushed to her feet as Hunt hit a button on what looked like an intercom by the front door, told whoever was downstairs he'd be right there, then grabbed his keys from the kitchen counter and glanced her way.

"I gotta run down and grab it. Why don't you find something to drink? There's water, juice, and beer in the fridge. Or you can choose a bottle of wine from the sideboard. I'll be right back."

He flashed her a weak smile just as he stepped onto the metal car, and she returned it. But the second the elevator doors closed, her face fell, and alone she glanced around the massive apartment, wondering what the hell was really going on.

If Julian hadn't set that bomb, then who had? And why had they threatened her just before it had gone off? She was a nobody. She moved toward the sideboard in the dining area and pulled open the bottom cupboard doors. Okay, she could admit she wasn't a total nobody, not after her fashion debut in New York, but barely a somebody on the scale of famous somebodies. Why would a random terrorist threaten her just before destroying that building if she wasn't somehow personally involved?

Frustrated at the questions swirling in her head, irritated her emotions kept swinging from one extreme to the other, she stared down at the impressive wine collection in front of her, surprised yet again by what she was seeing. In all the times Hunt had visited his parents' house or they'd both attended a get-together at Alec's place, she hadn't once seen him with a glass of wine in his hand. Beer, yes. But wine? Never.

Since she'd never been good at picking wine, she looked at the labels and spotted one that looked familiar. Setting the bottle on the table, she moved into the kitchen, found two wineglasses in the cupboard, and was just bringing them back when the elevator doors opened and Hunt stepped into the room carrying two white plastic bags.

Her stomach instantly warmed, a reaction she told herself had nothing to do with that crazy kiss earlier that meant nothing and everything to do with simple fact he carried food.

"I wasn't sure what you felt like eating, so I figured comfort food was the safest bet." He set the bags on the table, moved around the counter into the kitchen, and grabbed plates and forks.

The sweet and spicy scents of Italian food filled the air. Suddenly ravenous, she pulled at the bag closest to her and flipped the box open and stilled at what she saw.

Hunt's footsteps sounded close, and he slid a plate near her hand. "I hope I got that right. Spaghetti Bolognese is what you always order, right? There's lasagna in the other box if you'd rather have that instead."

He'd remembered. Tears sprang to her eyes again, irrational tears that came out of nowhere. Tears that had nothing to do with what had happened today and everything to do with the fact he'd not only paid attention to what she liked the few times he'd eaten out with her family, he'd remembered.

She blinked rapidly, trying not to let her reaction show. "Yeah. That's . . . that's right."

"Good." He reached for the wine she'd set on the table and moved into the kitchen with the bottle. "Sit down and start eating while I get this open."

She slid into a chair, spooned a helping of her favorite dish onto her plate, and lifted a bite toward her mouth. And as she did she tried not to think about how sweet the man currently taking care of her was. How considerate. How unlike Julian and every other guy she'd dated. And how stupid she was for overreacting, overthinking, and just plain overinternalizing everything.

She smiled as he set a glass of wine in front of her and told herself she didn't care what she knew about him or didn't, what was normal for him when he was protecting a client or not. She needed this. She needed him tonight. She wasn't going to worry about looking needy or weak. She was going to let him be her strength for as long as it lasted. And she was going to be thankful that tonight of all nights, she wasn't alone.

———

He never should have refilled her wineglass. Definitely shouldn't have suggested they watch a movie together on the couch after dinner. And absolutely should not have sat close enough for her to lean against him.

Hunt had no idea if Kelsey was awake or asleep against him. All he knew was that her heat was like a furnace pressing against his side, and even though he'd known it was a terrible idea to slide his arm around her to make them both more comfortable, he hadn't been able to stop. Now he didn't want to let go.

The credits rolled down the screen. He'd barely caught any of the movie and couldn't describe the plot even if his life depended on it. The minute Kelsey had leaned against him, his gray matter had short-circuited, and every bit of his focus had zeroed in on her. On how soft her skin was and how hot her body was, on how feminine and sweet and perfect she felt tucked under his arm.

Holy hell, he needed to let go of her. Needed her to go into the guest room and lock the door so he wouldn't be tempted to give in to every primal urge now circling in his brain. She was his best friend's little sister. Totally off-limits. He was assigned to protect her. Not screw her into next week.

Fabulous. Thanks to his little internal pep talk, now all he was going to fantasize about was the sounds she made when she came. *Way to go, dumbass.*

A heavy sigh echoed from beneath his arm, and then she stretched and gently pushed against his chest to peer up at him with a sleepy, sexy-as-hell expression he itched to kiss right off her angelic face. "Is it over?"

"Yeah." Slowly, so she wouldn't notice, he tugged the throw pillow across his lap so she didn't accidentally see what all her sultry heat had done to him. What it was still doing to him. "Just finished."

She yawned and rubbed her eyes. "I didn't see how it ended."

He hadn't even seen how it began.

He cleared his throat, averting his eyes from her features because she looked delightfully rumpled and all he wanted to do was rumple her up even more. "Why don't you go on in to bed? I'll turn everything off out here."

"Are you sure?"

No, he absolutely wasn't sure. He could think of a thousand other things he wanted her to do, but none of them were safe.

"Yeah," he forced himself to say. "Go on."

She stared at him a moment. Blinked in that sleepy way that told him she was only half seeing him, then smiled weakly and leaned forward. "Thanks."

Her soft lips brushed his cheek, just as they had outside the ER earlier, and the simple action sent blood screaming right back into his groin.

Her lips were gone way too fast. Before he could even think about pulling her back, she was on her feet and shuffling toward the guest room.

Where she belongs, idiot.

"'Night, Hunter."

God, he even liked the way she said his name.

"'Night, Kelsey," he managed.

He waited until he heard her door close. Waited even longer for her to stop moving around in her room. And only when he was confident she was in bed and out for the night did he lean forward and swipe a hand down his overheated face. "You are so fucked, O'Donnell."

He was. And not in any way he wanted to be.

Shaking that thought off, he pushed to his feet and moved through the apartment, flipping off the TV and lights, cringing at the pain in his leg. Just as he was stepping into his own room, intent on passing out so he wouldn't be tempted to do any of the dozen things he knew would get him in trouble, his home phone rang. He grabbed it from his nightstand, hoping it was Callahan with an update, then frowned when he recognized the number.

Shit. He wasn't in the mood to answer, but he knew if he didn't, she'd only call back. And a twinge of guilt cut through him when he realized he hadn't even thought of texting her about what had happened today.

Closing his bedroom door, he hit "Answer" and moved toward his bed. "Hey, Genevieve."

"Oh my God, Hunter! Are you okay? I just found out what happened in Portland. Were you there?"

"Yeah." He sank down to the end of his bed, wishing like hell he could have just hit "Decline" on his phone even more. "I was there. I was with a client who was about to appear on that morning show when the building collapsed. I'm fine, though."

"Why the hell didn't you call me after you were found, you asshole? I had to hear about the bombing from my coworker during my layover this morning! And then I had to see it on the news tonight!"

Two things hit Hunt at once: First, Genevieve had heard the news but hadn't called to check on him until now—more than twelve hours after the fact. And since he'd talked to her last week, she'd known he had a client scheduled to appear on that show. But secondly—and more importantly—she'd said she'd seen "it" on the news. He wasn't sure what "it" was, but if "it" had made her suddenly call when she hadn't been interested before, he had a strong hunch "it" wasn't just footage of the bombing aftermath. "It" was either him getting into a fist fight with Julian Benedict or him kissing the hell out of Kelsey McClane.

Fuck. He raked a hand through his hair, suddenly wondering who else had seen that damn footage and why the hell he hadn't stopped to realize there had probably been cameras rolling the minute he'd grabbed Kelsey and kissed her.

"Who was she?" Genevieve asked with a bite to her voice.

Bingo. There it was. He rubbed his suddenly aching temple, wondering why the hell her brothers hadn't grilled him in the same way when they'd spoken earlier.

"Hunter?"

Dammit, he should have put an end to this no-strings fling he'd had going with Genevieve long ago. The only reason he hadn't was because he just hadn't wanted to deal with the drama.

He definitely didn't want to deal with the drama tonight, especially over the phone, but he also didn't want to wait a week to do what he should have done months ago.

He dropped his hand to the edge of the bed. "Just a woman who was pulled from the destruction."

"So just some random woman you were consoling?"

He wasn't about to get into his relationship with Kelsey with her or anyone else. "We're not exclusive, Genevieve. You date lots of guys when you're not with me. I'm sure you even kiss them too."

"You were *kissing*? The camera didn't show that part."

Holy hell. He bit into his tongue. He was only making things worse now.

"Well," she said when he didn't respond. "I guess you're only human. I can forgive you for that, considering the situation. But I think it's time we discussed being exclusive."

No way. This conversation was way past due, and he didn't care whether doing it over the phone made him an asshole. Waiting would only make him an even bigger one. "No, we don't need to discuss that. The long-distance thing is too much work."

She had the audacity to sound shocked when she said, "What are you talking about?"

He worked for patience even though he was close to the end of whatever patience he had left. "You know exactly what I'm talking about. If this thing meant anything to either of us, you would have been down from Seattle as soon as you heard about the accident, and I would have tried to contact you as soon as I was rescued. Neither of us did that, which means it's not that important. And that's not a bad thing. It just means . . . it's run its course."

"But . . . I would have come down right away, only I was so busy with work. You know I can't text when I'm on a flight. I could come now, though. I'm off tomorrow. You shouldn't be alone tonight. I could be there in a few hours."

Yeah, no. Not happening. The last thing he wanted was her here in his apartment. And that had zero to do with what had happened today and everything to do with the fact he just wasn't interested anymore.

"We had some fun times together, Gen. Let's just leave it at that and move on. We both know it's time."

She was silent so long he wasn't sure she'd heard him. Then she said, "You're wrong. And you're just reacting like this because of what happened to you today."

He wasn't. But he breathed easier knowing she wasn't crying or getting hysterical or lashing out in anger over the phone. Which was another sign this conversation was way overdue.

"I'm really sorry." Man, he sucked at endings. Always had. No wonder he was still single.

The best way to be. Safer that way.

"You'll change your mind," Genevieve said. "I know you will."

He wouldn't. But he didn't say so. "Thanks for checking on me. I appreciate it. The day's catching up with me, and I need to crash before I fall asleep on the phone. 'Night, Gen."

She didn't respond, and after several seconds of silence, he gave up waiting and just hit "End."

Tossing his phone on the side chair in his room, he blew out a long breath. Not the conversation he'd wanted to have tonight of all nights, but he couldn't deny that part of him felt lighter just getting it over with.

He stripped off his T-shirt and tossed it on top of the phone on the chair, then flopped onto his back on his bed without even pulling off his jeans. Was he a total slime because he'd kissed Kelsey earlier in the day when he'd kinda sorta still had something going with another woman? Was he a prick because he'd been thinking nonstop about kissing Kelsey since then? Maybe. Probably, he realized. But both were nonissues since he was never kissing her like that again. The only thing he was going to do was focus on keeping her safe, doing his damn job, and not fucking things up worse with her or her family.

That and figuring out what Benedict was really up to.

CHAPTER SEVEN

Kelsey couldn't sleep. She'd been tossing and turning for the last two hours, but every time she closed her eyes, she was right back in that pitch-black darkness, surrounded by all that debris, unable to get out.

Throwing back the covers, she breathed deep and stared up at the ceiling in Hunt's guest room as she fought the panic trying to squeeze the air out of her lungs. She'd left the bathroom light on and the door separating the two rooms open to remind herself she wasn't in that nightmare any longer, but even that wasn't helping. It was too quiet in this building. The walls were obviously some high-tech variety that blocked out city noise. If she could just hear something other than her rapid pulse and erratic breaths, maybe she could get some damn sleep. Maybe she wouldn't feel like she was about to hyperventilate.

Unable to stand the silence a moment longer, she pushed out of bed and crossed the floor. The living room was dark and quiet, but there was enough city light coming in through the wide windows to illuminate the room. Enough to see that Hunt had left his bedroom door open wide. Enough for her to spot the end of his bed and his bare feet on top of the comforter.

Her heartbeat quickened. She bit her lip, knowing she needed to go back to her room. But she couldn't seem to look away from his feet.

Normally, she liked being alone. After the ugliness of her marriage, she'd valued her independence and solitude. But tonight that solitude was driving her mad, and she was afraid if she spent one more minute by herself, she might just scream.

Before she could change her mind, she crossed the living room and stepped into his room.

He hadn't closed his curtains. Light from the street spilled into the room from windows on both sides of his wide bed, illuminating his room. It was bigger than hers, all dark woods, sleek lines, and gray fabrics, but her focus was on him. On his strong body reclined on top of the comforter, his legs covered by the low-riding, faded Levis he'd had on earlier, one hand resting on his muscular chest, his other hand on the mattress at his side while he slept.

Her gaze drifted to his face. To the dusting of dark stubble covering his square jaw. The skin around his eyes was smooth, showing none of the stress of their earlier day, his mouth barely open as he breathed. She knew she was invading his space. Knew if he woke and saw her, she'd look like a creepy stalker. But she didn't want to leave because the simple sound of his steady breath eased the tightness in her chest. Made her muscles unlock one by one. Reaffirmed that she wasn't really alone after all.

Warmth prickled her skin. A warmth that told her she was absolutely alive and aching as she stood still in the darkness. She wanted to slide onto that bed next to him. Wanted to feel his arm wrap around her and hold her close just as he'd held her when they'd watched that movie on the couch. Wanted to let his strength and body heat melt the last bits of ice inside her.

That ache was so strong, so insistent, she knew if she didn't get out of his room right this second, she was going to forget all the reasons she wasn't supposed to be here.

"Pathetic," she whispered to herself, turning away and moving back toward his open door as quietly as she could. She wasn't alone in this apartment as her stupid brain was trying to make her believe. She wasn't back in that rubble. She was a strong, independent woman who didn't want or need a man to take care of her, so why was she acting like such a basket case tonight?

"Kels?"

The sleepy sound of his voice stopped her feet.

Fabric rustled at her back. "What's wrong? Are you okay?"

Shit. Her eyes slid closed, and she cursed herself for being so completely pitiful. People had died today. She should be thanking her lucky stars she was alive. Instead, she was a gigantic mess she just bet he regretted having in his house.

"I-I'm fine." She turned just enough so he could see her profile in the dim light, but not enough so she had to meet his eyes. "Nothing's wrong. I thought I heard something." She cringed because that sounded completely ridiculous and quickly swiveled back toward the door. "Sorry. I didn't mean to wake you."

"Having trouble sleeping?" he asked before she could even take a step. "Because I am."

Her pulse picked up speed. She told herself to go back to her own room. Right now. Knew better than to glance back at him. But couldn't seem to stop herself.

He'd pushed himself up on the bed so he was leaning back on his hands, looking relaxed, but his gaze was locked on her. His sleepy, sexy, way-too-tender gaze that made her pulse skip a beat.

"Y-you were sound asleep a second ago."

"Not sleeping. Just dozing. Pretty sure I haven't slept yet tonight. You haven't either by the looks of you."

Nerves rolled through her belly. "No, I, uh . . . it's too quiet."

"I know. That's usually not a problem for me, but tonight it is. Come here."

For a moment, she was sure she'd heard him wrong. Then he held out a hand to her, and she realized she hadn't.

A little voice in the back of her head screamed it was way past time to get back in her own room, but she didn't move. Couldn't, because the draw toward him was too strong.

He sat upright. "You were able to sleep on the couch next to me earlier. Maybe all you need is just someone else in the room so your brain knows you're not alone and it can finally slow down." He raked a hand through his hair. "God knows, after the day we both had, I'm pretty sure I could use that too."

He was trying to make her feel better. She was pretty sure he had no problem being alone tonight or any night. But the tender offer touched her, and before she could stop herself, she was moving toward the bed, then stretching out on the soft mattress beside him.

She was careful not to get too close, to stay on her side. But as soon as she lay down she instantly regretted the fact she'd taken off those baggy sweatpants he'd given her. The fact she was wearing nothing but his oversize T-shirt hit her like a bullet to the brain.

She tugged the hem as low across her thighs as she could. And was relieved when he grabbed the throw from the end of the bed and spread it over her.

"Thanks," she whispered, pulling it up to her chest.

"If you're cold you can climb under the covers." He lay back down on his side and tucked an arm behind his head on the pillow. But he didn't try to share her blanket, which, considering how weird she was acting, was probably good.

"No. This is fine. You're not cold?"

"No. Hot-blooded."

Yes, he was. And way too damn sexy for his own good.

Not wanting to think about that too much, she closed her eyes and tipped her face toward the ceiling, listening to the ebb and flow of his breaths, hoping it would lull her into sleep.

Long minutes passed. His steady breaths didn't do a thing to relax her. All they did was make her skin tingle with the urge to touch him.

Do not give in to that urge.

Silence stretched between them. She forced herself to lie still. Counted sheep. Listened to the whir of the ceiling fan turning slowly above. Tried everything she could think of, but nothing worked. Hoping maybe a change in position would help, she carefully rolled away from him.

The bed dipped. Something warm slid across her hipbone. Then heat pressed against her spine, her buttocks, all the way down the backs of her thighs, causing her whole body to tense.

"Close your eyes, Kels," Hunt whispered into her hair.

Oh dear God . . . that felt good. Too damn good for words.

He smoothed her hair up and over the pillow so it wouldn't tickle his face, then wrapped his arm around her belly and tugged her tighter to his chest. "You're safe right here with me. Close your eyes and relax. I won't ever let anything bad happen to you."

His body heat penetrated her skin and eased the tension in her muscles. And for the first time in hours—maybe even days and months—all the stress and worry and fear uncoiled inside her.

Screw the consequences and whether or not this made her weak. She liked this. Tonight, she needed it. And for the moment, she planned to savor every moment.

She savored him because she knew tomorrow everything would be different.

—————

Hunt never did fall completely asleep. He was hyperaware of every sound Kelsey made and every twitch of her body.

He'd moved back to his side of the bed not long after she'd fallen asleep, knowing touching her like that was a really bad idea. He shouldn't have invited her to sleep in his bed. Should have sent her back to her room the minute he'd seen her. But he hadn't been able to. Not just because that quiver in her voice had hit him like a punch to the gut, but because the lost look he'd seen in her eyes had completely upended his resolve to keep his distance.

She was a contradiction of behaviors and reactions. Independent one minute, vulnerable the next, feisty when she dealt with her brothers, then nervous and unsure as soon as the lights were out. He knew a lot of that was because of the trauma she'd experienced today, but as he lay beside her in the dark and thought back over every interaction he'd had with her over the years, he realized the odd shift in her moods had been going on a lot longer than just today. She'd been unpredictable for a while now. And her reactions had only become more unpredictable the longer she'd been married to Benedict.

He glanced sideways at her, still asleep on her side, her blonde hair splayed over the pillow, her slim body looking small and defenseless in his big bed. Callahan had said Benedict hadn't hit her, at least not that she'd admitted. But Hunt knew there were a lot of ways a man could abuse a woman that didn't involve his fists.

A slow rage burned through him. If he found out Benedict had anything to do with that bomb, he wasn't sure he could stop himself from inflicting serious bodily harm. And if the man made any kind of move to go after Kelsey again . . .

"No," Kelsey mumbled. "No, can't."

Hunt pushed up on his arm to make sure she was all right. She didn't move. Didn't make any indication she was awake. As her breaths evened out, he carefully lay back down and stared up at the ceiling, knowing she was just dreaming.

Okay, enough thinking. He closed his eyes and tried to focus on nothing. If he fell asleep right now he could get two hours in before dawn.

"No." Kelsey jerked, the movement shaking the bed. Rolling to her back, she kicked the throw blanket off her legs. "No. Let me go. Let me out. I don't want to be alone."

Hunt's eyes shot open. Hers were still tightly closed, but the way she thrashed brought him fully awake. And the haunted sound of her voice made him desperate to comfort her from whatever nightmare was tormenting her.

He scooted across the bed toward to her, careful not to startle her. He'd lived through enough of his dad's nightmares to know the worst thing he could do was shock her awake. Bracing his elbow on his pillow, he grazed his fingertips against her arm and kept his voice gentle when he said, "You're okay, Kels. You're safe. You're right here with me in my apartment, remember?"

Her arms and legs slowed their flailing, and she tipped her head his way. But she didn't open her eyes. Didn't speak. Just breathed in and out until the tension unwound from her muscles.

"That's better." He continued to trail his fingertips over her arm, her shoulder, up her neck, and through her hair. "See? Nothing to worry about. Just you and me here together."

Man, her hair was soft. Like satin. He slid his fingers through the long locks again and again, knowing he should stop now that she was drifting back to sleep but not able to let go of her just yet. Her warm breath tickled his lips, torturing him in a new and anguishing way, but he still didn't move away from her. He looked from her lips to her throat, to the tiny birthmark on her collarbone, visible where the neck of his too-big T-shirt fell open over her silky-smooth shoulder.

"Hunt?"

Her quiet voice caught him off guard. He looked up to find her sweet brown eyes open and focused on him. Only these eyes weren't filled with fear or shock or confusion as he expected. They brimmed with heat. A heat that pushed him right to the edge of control.

Everything inside him stilled. He knew he needed to move away. Knew he was dangerously close to taking something she wouldn't be offering on any normal day. But still couldn't make his muscles work.

Her gaze slid from his eyes to his lips. And then she pressed her hand to his chest, and, *holy God*, the silky touch of her fingertips against his bare skin was like absolute heaven.

He closed his eyes. Breathed in and out as her fingertips slid over his skin. Tried like hell not to react in case she was still half asleep. And completely lost the fight when her lips brushed his collarbone.

Desire overtook logic. He sifted his fingers into her hair and lifted her face toward his. And then he kissed her the way he'd been dreaming of kissing her. The way he knew he shouldn't be kissing her. The way that lit up his body and made him want to kiss every inch of her until they were both sweaty and sated and limp.

She opened at the first touch, drawing his tongue into the soft, wet intoxicating heat of her mouth. Fire licked like flames across his skin as her hand captured his shoulder, as her tongue stroked his with frantic movements, as she groaned and pulled him toward her.

He pushed her to her back as he explored her tongue, lips, and teeth, kissing her deeper with each pass, desperate for more. She shifted her fingers up into his hair and nipped at his bottom lip, then groaned and sucked his tongue back into her mouth, just as frantic and hot and needy as him. And as she pulled him on top of her, and he felt the swell of her supple breasts and her nipples hardening against his chest, every ounce of blood in his body shot straight into his groin, making him ache for more, for as much as she'd give him.

He trailed his fingers down her throat and over her shoulder as he kissed her, then lower to her ribs, loving the way her nails dug into his flesh and the sexy sounds she made. Desperate to feel more of her, he shifted his palm to her front and closed his hand around her breast and the soft cotton of his T-shirt. She sucked in a breath but didn't push him away. And then she was kissing him harder and arching her back, offering more, making him high with the need to touch her bare skin, to take her nipple into his mouth, to make her moan in pure ecstasy.

She groaned long and deep as he squeezed the supple mound. Did it again when he moved to her other breast and slid his fingertip over her nipple, circling the tip until it formed a taut bud. God, she was responsive. Bracing one arm on the pillow near her head, he slid the other down her ribs and over her hip to the hem of her T-shirt resting against her silky-soft thigh.

A buzzing sounded in his head. A buzzing that told him he was dangerously close to forgetting every one of the reasons this was wrong. It didn't feel wrong. It felt right as hell. She felt fucking right. And she wasn't making any move to stop him.

Her fingertips grazed his ribs, sending a shiver over his skin. She nipped at his bottom lip, then sucked it between her teeth before groaning and sliding her tongue back between his lips. Blood pounded in his groin as he tugged the T-shirt up her leg and kissed the corner of her mouth, her jaw, as he tilted her head back with the hand near her head so he could trail a line of kisses down her throat.

"Hunter."

God, he loved the way she said his name. He nipped at her throat, then drew the delicate skin between his lips and sucked. Her fingertips curled against his sides, then dropped to the waistband of his jeans. He tugged the shirt higher, grazing his knuckles across the sensitive area where her leg met her torso as he found another delectable spot to lick and suck and kiss, groaning himself when she trembled and flexed her hips, telling him just how much she liked his touch.

Another buzz sounded in his head. Followed by, "Hunter, answer me."

Kelsey's hands stilled an inch from finding out just how turned on he really was. And confused about why she sounded irritated rather than turned on like he knew she was, he lifted his head a fraction of an inch and said, "Answer what, baby?"

"Huh? I didn't say anything."

"You told me to answer you."

"No, I didn't. You're hearing things." Lifting her head, she pressed her lips against his throat, then nipped and licked and sucked just as he'd done to her. "Kiss me already, Hunter."

He groaned and turned his head, capturing her lips and kissing her the way she wanted. The way he wanted. The way that made him abso-fucking-lutely on fire.

She groaned into his mouth and slid her hand down the front of his jeans, right over his straining erection.

Sparks shot off behind his eyes. But before she could find the snap on his jeans, that damn buzzing sounded again. And this time it didn't stop.

Kelsey jerked back from his mouth and looked toward the open bedroom door. "What is that noise?"

The sound finally registered, bringing Hunt's head up. "My downstairs intercom. Shit. Someone's here."

He didn't want to let go of her, but he forced himself to push off all her succulent heat.

"It's like four in the morning." She tugged the T-shirt down her legs and reached for the throw hanging halfway off the bed. "Who would be visiting you now?"

"I don't know." He climbed off the bed and ran a hand through his hair. It could be Callahan. Or the Feds. Or even her family.

Shit. He seriously hoped it wasn't her family.

"Stay here. I'll see who it is and get rid of them."

Just the thought her brothers could have found a red-eye and were home nearly killed his arousal, at least enough so he could walk. But he'd only given the building's access code to a handful of people, Alec being one of them, and he couldn't think of anyone else who could get into the lobby. He was confident Alec couldn't get up to his apartment to surprise them—he needed a key for that—but once inside the lobby Alec could buzz the hell out of Hunt to get his attention, which his visitor was clearly doing.

Son of a bitch.

Tugging the bedroom door closed behind him, he swiped a hand down his face, trying not to look like a guilty fucking friend as he crossed his dark living room and headed toward the security panel near the door. The buzzer sounded again, this time in several short, rhythmic bursts, telling him whoever was pressing the damn thing was irritated beyond belief that he hadn't yet responded. His gaze zeroed in on the screen—from farther back he could only make out a shape moving around downstairs in the lobby. Then the person turned and faced the camera just as her voice echoed through his living room.

"Dammit, Hunt. I drove all the way down here from Seattle. Let me in already."

Oh fuck. Genevieve.

His adrenaline surged as he sprinted to turn the volume down before Kelsey heard her. Way too late he remembered he'd given Gen the lobby access code months ago when she'd come by on one of her layovers. He hadn't been stupid enough to give her access to his apartment, but he hadn't wanted her standing out in the rain until he got home.

"Hunt—"

He hit the button to respond, killing her voice in the room. "Hold on. Stop hitting the damn button. I'll be right down."

Her irritated expression flashed on the screen, but he reached up to turn the screen off, not really caring about her reaction. All he wanted was to get rid of her before Kelsey spotted her.

"Who's that?"

He jerked around at the sound of Kelsey's voice behind him. "No one. Just someone who's lost."

"At four in the morning?"

"Yeah." He grabbed his keys from the counter and hit the elevator button. "I'll be right back."

He didn't wait for her answer. Didn't draw a full breath until the elevator doors closed behind him. His entire focus was on the shitstorm currently swirling around him.

A shitstorm he had no one to blame for but himself.

CHAPTER EIGHT

A knot wedged its way into the center of Kelsey's chest the second the elevator doors closed. She wasn't sure what was going on; she only knew Hunt wasn't being truthful. The person downstairs wasn't a stranger. She'd used his first name.

Unease swirled inside Kelsey as she moved across the living room and stopped at the security panel he'd turned dark before leaving. She didn't know a thing about his fancy system, but she was pretty sure he hadn't killed the entire mechanism. Running her fingers along the side of the console, she found a button and pushed it. An image lit up the screen, and she blinked against the bright light until she finally focused on a woman with long dark hair and a clearly perturbed expression, who stood with her arms crossed, facing the closed elevator doors.

Seconds that felt like an eternity ticked by as she watched, wondering who the woman was. Then the elevator doors opened, Hunt stepped out of the car still as shirtless and sexy as he'd been in his bedroom only moments before, and the brunette threw herself into his arms.

Kelsey's pulse turned to a whir in her ears. On the screen, Hunt eased out of the woman's arms, but he didn't jerk back from her touch, and he didn't push her away, which told Kelsey loud and clear that this was way more than a "someone." This was a coworker or friend or—she swallowed hard, hoping she was wrong—even a lover.

The woman dropped her arms with what looked to be a huff, held one hand out toward the elevator. Since there was no sound, Kelsey couldn't hear them, but the tension in her shoulders and the way Hunt lifted his hands in front of him told her they were having some kind of argument. Desperate to know what was going on, why he'd lied to her, and who this woman was, Kelsey frantically pushed buttons on the screen, searching for the volume.

"I told you not to come down." Hunt's voice crackled through the speaker. "This is not a good time. We talked about it on the phone earlier."

"Because we talked about it is exactly the reason I'm here," the woman answered. "Excuse me for being concerned when my boyfriend is nearly killed in a bombing."

Kelsey sucked in a sharp breath and dropped her hand from the panel as if it had burned her.

Hunt rested his hands on his hips. "Gen, we talked about that too."

"No, you talked." The brunette moved close and lifted her hands to Hunt's bare chest—a bare chest that only minutes ago Kelsey had been touching. "I only listened."

He frowned down at her. "Clearly not very well."

She smiled up at him, the look in her eyes speaking volumes about what was going on between them. "I think we definitely need to talk some more. Or not talk. Either works for me."

Bile shot up Kelsey's throat. As the woman slid her arms around Hunt and pressed her body flush against his, she hit the button to kill the sound, not wanting to hear any more. Her fingers shook as she fumbled with the buttons on the side of the screen until she finally turned that off too, and the panel went dark.

Resting her forehead against the wall, she drew a deep breath and called herself ten kinds of stupid. Dear God, she'd all but thrown herself at Hunt—when he had a girlfriend—and he hadn't done a thing to stop her. But what did she expect? He was a man, and men were assholes. She was a complete fool for thinking he was different. He might not push women around, like her ex, but he clearly had no problem fucking around on them.

Disgusted with herself, with what she'd almost let happen, she whipped away from the door and rushed for the guest room. She quickly stripped out of his T-shirt and changed back into her ripped pants and filthy blouse. Her flats were scuffed and nearly trashed, but they'd do. Right now she didn't care how she looked; she wanted out of this nightmare as fast as possible.

She didn't bother with a note. Knew Hunt would figure out why she'd left when he came back. In the living room, she faltered because the elevator opened right into his apartment. She hadn't seen a set of stairs when Hunt had brought her up here, but she knew there had to be one in case of a fire. Heart pounding, she checked every room, then finally located it behind a door off the kitchen.

The stairwell was only dimly lit, but she didn't let that stop her. Skipping, she hit the ground level, then hesitated with her hands on the steel bar of the door, listening for any voices beyond.

If this door opened into the lobby, she did not want to accidentally walk in on Hunt and his girlfriend reuniting. Nausea swirled in her stomach as she pressed her ear to the solid steel and strained to listen. No sound came through. Nothing but an eerie silence that sent perspiration dotting her spine.

Deciding it was probably safe, she pushed the door open, then breathed easier when she realized she was in a parking garage beneath the building. In front of her were three vehicles: a deep-blue Ram pickup truck, a sleek white BMW SUV, and a black Audi sedan. She bypassed the trucks, reached for the driver door of the sedan, and silently rejoiced when it pulled open. Rejoiced even more when she realized the keys were sitting in the tray of the console.

It was four in the morning. She'd never find a cab at this hour, and she was clear across the city from her place. But more than that, she was pretty sure this garage was locked up tight, and if she tried to leave on foot, she likely wouldn't find a way out before Hunt realized she was gone. He might be a jerk who got off stringing women along, but he was still technically supposed to be watching out for her, and she didn't doubt he'd try to make her stay regardless of what was going on between him and his girlfriend. She also had a strong hunch that somewhere in this car was a remote to open the garage doors.

She slid into the seat and slammed the door before she could change her mind. The engine hummed with a touch of a button. She cringed at the sound, even though common sense told her he couldn't hear the car a floor up in the lobby where he was still probably making out with his girlfriend, then shoved the car into "Drive" and maneuvered around the concrete columns until she spotted the ramp leading up to street level.

As she expected, the garage doors were closed. Since she hadn't seen a remote, she took a chance he'd programmed the car. She lifted her hand to the three buttons above the rearview mirror and pushed the closest one. The first opened the sunroof. The second tilted the mirror down. But the third caused the heavy metal garage door to slide to the left, bringing the dark and empty street into view.

Kelsey stepped on the gas, not even bothering to look back. She didn't care that technically she was stealing his car. Didn't care that he was going to be pissed when he found out she was gone. Didn't even care that she looked weak and pathetic by running away. He'd get his car back—she had no desire to keep it. He'd even get his money because she was fairly certain now he hadn't agreed to babysit her for free. But she would never regain her dignity after the way she'd let down her guard with him, and that, more than anything, burned like lava right through her.

Men were all the same, and she was done being a fool. The sooner she accepted the fact she was the only person she could count on, the better off she'd be.

———

Hunt glanced down at his wrist as Genevieve rattled on—trying to convince him to take her upstairs—only to remember he'd taken his broken watch off in the ER and left it in the pocket of his ripped jeans he'd tossed in the garbage.

He didn't care about the watch. Didn't care what Genevieve was saying either. The only thing he cared about was getting back upstairs to Kelsey before she got the wrong idea.

Or the right idea, asshat.

"Gen, stop."

Genevieve's mouth fell open when he interrupted her, and he knew what he was about to say wasn't going to go over well, but he didn't give a rip about that either.

He placed his hands on her shoulders, hoping his touch might soften the blow, but really, if she hadn't gotten it from his phone call, there was no way to let her down softly. "I appreciate that you came down to check on me. I'm fine, as you can see. But I'm tired, it's been a long day, and I need you to leave now."

Shock drained the color from her face. "But I drove three hours to get here. In the middle of the night."

He fought the frown because he was well aware she'd driven down to Portland in the middle of the night to see him—something she'd never done before, and had never even once shown any interest in doing. The only time he saw her in Portland was when she was on a layover and it was convenient for her.

He let go of her. "I didn't invite you, Gen. I have oth—"

A low alarm bell sounded through the lobby, causing his adrenaline to spike. His gaze shot past Gen to the glass doors. Seeing nothing but darkness, he glanced quickly to the security panel on the far wall where several lights were blinking, indicating a breach.

"Hunter. Let's talk about this upstairs. It's late, and I'm cold."

Hunt barely heard her. He was across the floor in three strides, punching numbers into the panel and pulling up the cameras. The camera in his apartment showed no movement. He checked the elevator. Back stairwell. Fire escape. Garage. Didn't see anything out of the ord—

"Motherfucker." He flipped back to the garage camera and stared wide-eyed at the empty parking place where his Audi usually sat.

He hit the button on the elevator. It opened immediately. Rushing inside, he typed in his code. The doors closed. Vaguely, he was aware Genevieve had slipped into the elevator with him, but all he could think about was Kelsey. Where she was. Who she was with. And what the hell had been happening upstairs when he'd been down here dealing with Gen.

As soon as the doors opened, he rushed into his apartment and scanned the darkness. Nothing moved. Flipping on the light, he swept through the living area, checked his bedroom and the guest room, found nothing out of the ordinary. Nothing but his T-shirt on the floor in the guest bath and Kelsey's filthy clothing long gone.

"Son of a bitch." He scrubbed a hand through his hair as he bent and picked up the shirt, knowing exactly what had happened. She was a smart girl. She'd clearly heard Genevieve's voice on the intercom. She hadn't bought his shit that Gen was just a lost stranger.

His mind spun with thoughts of where she could have gone. Even though Benedict was in custody, he didn't like the thought of her in the city alone. Especially when they still weren't a hundred percent certain Benedict was the one who'd sent that text. And when she was clearly upset at what she'd overheard.

"Why are you in here?" Gen said from the doorway at his back. "And why is the bed in here messed up. Do you have company?"

He didn't have time to deal with Gen now. He needed to find Kelsey and make sure she was safe, then explain things to her before she got the wrong idea.

He swept past Gen and headed for his room to grab a shirt and a pair of shoes. But the whole time that little voice in the back of his head whispered, *How are you going to fix this? You know Kelsey didn't get the wrong idea. She got the right idea, jackass.*

Dropping the T-shirt Kelsey had worn on his bed, he moved into his closet where he tore a Henley from the hanger and shoved his feet into a pair of boots, then headed for the living room.

"Hunter," Gen exclaimed in a nervous voice, rushing after him toward the elevator doors. "Will you stop for two seconds and tell me what the heck is going on?"

He whirled on her, at the end of his patience. "What's going on is I'm done. This is over, Gen. Get out of my apartment and don't come back."

Disbelief shot her eyes wide, but he didn't back down. He hit the button for the elevator. The doors immediately sprang open. Holding his arm in front of one side, he waited while Gen snapped her mouth closed, lifted her chin, and silently moved into the car.

"You'll regret this," she said, not looking at him.

No, he wouldn't. The only thing he regretted was the fact that his stupidity had now put Kelsey at risk.

Dawn was just peeking over Mount Hood as Kelsey pulled Hunt's Audi to a stop in front of her building and killed the ignition.

The road was quiet, the sidewalk empty. The Central Eastside neighborhood where her business was located was trendy and hip with new restaurants and storefronts opening all the time. But it didn't feel like home. To her, this side of the river would always be the Warehouse district, and she couldn't wait until life slowed down a little and she could find a place of her own. For now, though, it was enough, and she'd been thankful she had the option of living in the loft above her design company after she'd left Julian.

She grabbed the keys, climbed out, and slammed the door. She was pretty sure Hunt's fancy car wouldn't get broken into here, but nothing was guaranteed in life—as she'd painfully learned over the last few hours. Feeling like an idiot for kissing Hunt yesterday, for staying at his place, for—she cringed and rubbed at the pounding between her eyes—climbing into bed with him, she hit the lock on the fob and headed for the side door of the old building.

She pulled her keys from the pocket of her ruined slacks, thankful she hadn't tucked them into her purse at the station. Even more thankful they hadn't fallen out of her pocket when she'd been buried in all that rubble. She could call a cab or Uber but didn't want to wait, and without her wallet or car, and with every member of her immediate family in Florida, she didn't have a lot of options. Which was something else she could be thankful for, she realized. That her brothers weren't around to see what a gigantic mess she'd made of her life—yet again.

Shoving her key in the rusted lock, she called herself ten kinds of stupid and twisted. A scraping sound echoed, then the lock gave. With one hand on the tarnished door handle, she shimmied the key in the lock and slammed her hip against the steel door just as she always had to do to get into the old building.

The door gave with a pop. She yanked her key free and stepped into what was her storefront, consisting of several different mannequins dressed in her latest designs. A few racks held various sizes and styles. Since she didn't sell to the general public, the storefront was primarily used to meet buyers, but she'd spent a pretty penny to make the space look professional and cutting-edge with expensive lighting, crisp paint, high ceilings, and upper-end furnishings. She'd even added a small runway off to the right surrounded by white leather couches where buyers could view models parading out in her trendy fashions.

The hinges creaked as the door swung closed behind her. Not wanting to think about the work, she didn't bother with the lights, just turned to flip the deadbolt on the old door. She needed sleep. Needed to crash for the next twenty-four or maybe forty-eight hours. Needed to somehow find a way to forget the last day had even happened.

Her fingers grazed the lock, but before she could flip it, the heavy door shot back toward her face. She gasped and stumbled. A shadow filled the doorway.

"You fucking bitch."

The voice was male, irate, the body moving toward her big. But those were the only things she registered. Hands grasped her at the upper arms and shoved hard, sending her sailing backward.

She hit the tile floor with a grunt, jarring every bone in her body. Head spinning, she groaned and tried to push herself up, tried to roll to her side, tried to figure out what was going on. She still couldn't see whoever was standing over her, but the flight response kicked in hard, sending her adrenaline surging and her fear sky high.

Strong fingers gripped her at the shirtfront and yanked before she could crawl even a foot away, jerking her to her feet. Gasping, she clawed at the hands, found her footing, and shoved as hard as she could against the man's hold, but he had a death grip on her clothing.

"Do you have any idea where I've been, you dumb cunt?"

Julian. Kelsey's eyes flew wide, and fear stole what little breath she had left. That was Julian's voice. She still couldn't see him clearly—her vision was watery—but she didn't need to see his face to know he was in the grip of a bitter rage. One her instincts told her she wasn't going to survive this time if she didn't break free fast.

"Do you have any fucking clue what I've been through tonight because of you?" He pulled her in close enough for the whiskey on his breath to make her eyes water, then shoved hard, sending her flying through the air once more.

She crashed into a mannequin with her shoulder and hip, bounced off, and hit another. As the hard plastic bodies crashed to the ground, she crumpled with them, groaning at the pain suddenly erupting across her elbow, ribs, shoulder, hip, and knee.

The coppery taste of blood filled her mouth. Stars fired off behind her closed eyelids. She struggled to find her balance, knew she needed to get up, to run before he killed her. A scraping sound echoed close, drowning out her groans. She kicked a mannequin's arm out of the way, rolled her to stomach. Pushed up on her shaky hands to—

Julian wrapped his fingers through the back of her hair and yanked hard. Kelsey screamed as pain shot through her scalp like a thousand knives stabbing into her brain.

"No, I doubt you do." Julian jerked her to her feet. "Judging from the fancy car you drove up in, I know exactly what you were doing while I was getting my ass kicked in jail."

He wrenched her back against his body. Kelsey gasped and swung out, trying to knock his hold loose, but his grip was too strong, and since he was behind her, she couldn't see him. With one hand still wrapped in her hair, he used the other to clasp her chin and squeezed so hard she saw spots.

"Tell me," he hissed in her ear. "Was he as good as you always thought?" He squeezed tighter, and she slowed her thrashing and cried out, afraid he was going to shatter her jawbone. "If I'd have known you were such a slut, I'd have taken advantage of that a long fucking time ago. Guess there's still time for that now, isn't there, *wife*?"

He jerked her back against his body, and in a heartbeat of horror, she realized he wasn't just enraged, he was aroused.

Terror clawed up Kelsey's chest. This was different from every other time he'd gotten mad at her and shoved her across the room or slammed her into a piece of furniture or pinned her to the ground until she stopped arguing. Those times—when he'd lost his temper and become aggressive—he'd been so disgusted by the sight of her he hadn't even wanted sex for days, sometimes weeks afterward. This time, he was turned on by hurting her. Which meant this time, she didn't have a clue what he was capable of. Or what he had planned.

"You want to be a whore? Do you?" he snarled. "I can fucking make that happen."

Bile shot up her throat, churning with the panic and revulsion spinning inside her. There would be no reasoning with him this time. Her only hope was to break free and run.

She dug her fingernails into his hand at her jaw. Skin ripped. He screamed in pain. He loosened his hold on her chin, and she jammed her elbow back into his gut and stomped on the inside of his foot. And the second he let go of her and doubled forward, she ran.

She ran and knew with absolute clarity that the feeling of impending doom she'd experienced yesterday had nothing to do with Hunt or that collapsed building. It had to do with Julian and her stupidity for believing she'd ever be free of him.

———

Hunt wove around a semitruck and swerved into the right-hand lane to take the exit ramp toward the Central Eastside district.

The GPS on his Audi told him Kelsey hadn't driven out to her folks' house in Lake Oswego. She'd run to her warehouse where she was currently living.

That was both good and bad news as far as Hunt was concerned. Since Kelsey had only flown in from New York the night before her interview with *Good Morning Portland*, and because her family had all still been back East, Hunt had picked her up at the airport and brought her home. He'd never been to her warehouse before that, and one look had made it glaringly obvious it was sorely lacking in security, which he'd pointed out to her. That hadn't gone over well—she'd already been irritated her brothers had insisted he look out for her until they got back—and she'd claimed to be too tired to listen. He'd ended up sitting outside in his vehicle, keeping an eye on her place overnight just to be safe, but on the drive to the TV studio the next morning he'd gotten her to agree to let him overhaul her entire system. He'd even convinced her to stay at her parents' place until it was done. Which she'd clearly ignored when she'd run back here.

Yeah, the fact she was here and not down in Lake Oswego meant he could get to her faster if something went wrong. But it also meant Benedict or whoever was harassing her could also get to her quicker. And that thought didn't just cause his pulse to beat faster, it left him with a knot the size of a boulder right in the middle of his throat.

He tore off the freeway and laid his foot on the gas, not caring about his speed. Luckily, at this hour, there was barely anyone on the streets. Even though his head told him that Kelsey was fine, that nothing bad could have happened to her in the thirty or so minutes she'd been out of his sight, his gut screamed he hadn't thought that damn TV station would come crumbling down around them either.

"Come on, come on, come on," he muttered, slamming on his brakes and laying on his horn because a cab was blocking his path, waiting for a homeless man to cross the street.

His new cell phone rang, the one he'd programmed with his previous number when Kelsey had been taking a shower last night. He hit "Answer" and held it to his ear without looking at the name. "Kels?"

"No, it's Callahan. Aren't you with Kelsey, O'Donnell?"

Shit. He didn't want to get into his fuck-up with Callahan. Hunt hit the gas as soon as the cab moved out of the way. "It's a long story."

"Jeez, you could screw up a wet dream, you know that?"

Sadly, he did.

"Listen." Callahan's voice grew serious. "We found Kelsey's cell phone in the rubble."

"And?"

"And the text she mentioned was there. Definitely sent up all kinds of red flags, considering what happened just after it was sent. But it doesn't look like the text came from Benedict."

Hunt whipped his SUV around a corner and spotted his Audi parked on the right ahead. A little of his anxiety eased as he scanned the street. There were no people milling about, no signs of trouble, just a few parked cars here and there. Nothing out of the ordinary. "How do you know?"

"Because we traced it back to an address in southern California. And Benedict doesn't have any ties to southern California that we can find."

Southern California . . .

Hunt parked behind his Audi and killed the ignition. "Maybe he had it registered to a different address to throw the Feds off. He had to know the number would be traced."

"It's possible. We'll keep digging. In the meantime, you might want to find your girl."

Hunt's stomach flipped as he shut off the ignition. Kelsey wasn't his girl. He didn't even want a girl. "Why?"

"Because we let Benedict go about two hours ago. His attorney did exactly what I thought he'd do. The DA caved"

"Fuck me." Hunt grabbed the Sig from his glove box, jerked out of the vehicle, and let the door slam behind him. "You could have called me before you let the asshole go, you know."

"I was going to. At a decent hour. Figured you'd both be asleep this early after yesterday. Never occurred to me you wouldn't be with her since that's your freakin' job at the moment."

Hunt should still be with her. He *would* still be with her if he hadn't fucked things up royally. He mentally kicked himself the hundredth time and checked the magazine on his 9mm.

"I already found her." He reached back to tuck the pistol into the back waistband of his jeans as he crossed the sidewalk. "She's at her warehouse on—"

A crash sounded from inside Kelsey's warehouse, followed by a shrill scream.

Kelsey's scream.

Hunt's heart lurched into his throat. He drew his firearm and stepped back from the door. "Did you hear that?" He gave Callahan Kelsey's warehouse address, and added, "Get your ass over here *now*."

"Shit." Shuffling sounded in his ear. "We're on our way."

Hunt stuffed his phone in his back pocket and gripped the gun in both hands. Another crash echoed from inside, followed by a grunt that sent his adrenaline soaring.

Gripping the gun in one hand, he twisted the door handle and found it unlocked. Kelsey's scream filled his ears. Chest tight, he shoved his shoulder into the old steel door. The hinges groaned, and the door cracked against the wall as he swept into the room and scanned the scene.

The showroom was in shambles—tables overturned, clothing strewn across the floor, mannequins in pieces. But it was Benedict looming over Kelsey on the ground, one hand on the back of her head as he held her pinned face-first to the floor, that made Hunt see nothing but red.

He'd known the asshole could be dangerous. He'd seen Benedict's temper firsthand at the bomb site when Benedict had shown up and yanked Kelsey away from him. He'd even heard Kelsey's brothers' theories that Benedict was abusing her. But he hadn't envisioned this. And the image of her on the ground, struggling and screaming, unleashed a fury of rage inside him he didn't expect. One that brought everything else to a standstill and made him focus on only one thing—inflicting as much pain as possible.

He crossed the floor in three strides, grasped Benedict by the back of the shirt, and wrenched him off her. Benedict stumbled and turned wide, shocked eyes Hunt's way. The man opened his mouth, but before he could even utter a sound, Hunt slammed the butt of his gun into the side of Benedict's face.

Blood spurted from Benedict's mouth. He grunted and staggered back. Stuffing the gun into his back waistband, Hunt grasped Benedict by the shirtfront with both hands and plowed his fist into the asshole's bandaged nose.

"Hunter!" Kelsey screamed.

A crack echoed through the room. Benedict collapsed onto the ground and clutched his nose, screaming in pain. Shuffling sounded at Hunt's back, but he didn't turn to look at Kelsey. Couldn't because all he could see was the image of her on the floor, pinned beneath the fucker in front of him. That, and a blinding red rage that fueled his need for vengeance.

He straddled Benedict and pulled his arm back. "You like beating up on women? Let's see how you like being on the receiving end, dickhead."

CHAPTER NINE

Kelsey stumbled to her feet, bruised and sore but wide-eyed and unable to look away from what was happening in front of her.

Blood spurted from Julian's mouth, and his head jerked from one side to the other as Hunt slammed his fist into Julian's bruised and swollen face again and again.

Her heart shot into her throat. Yes, she hated Julian for what he'd just done to her. Yes, she wanted him to suffer. But not like this. And not at the hands of someone who was supposed to be one of the good guys but who at the moment looked to be more of a threat than her ex-husband.

Hunt drew his fist back once more, and Kelsey stumbled forward, wrapping her hand around his wrist and yanking hard so he couldn't land another blow. "Hunter, stop!"

The sound of her voice gave him pause. Or maybe it was her fierce hold on his arm. Whatever the cause, he swiveled toward her, and for a split second there was no recognition in his familiar brown irises. A new sort of panic ripped through her chest. But before instinct sent her staggering back from him, his eyes widened, and he lurched to his feet.

He grasped her face with his bloody hand. "Are you all right?"

She flinched out of his reach, not wanting to be touched by him right now. She'd known he was in the military. She'd assumed he was more than capable of providing protection to his clients. But in all the times she's been around him, she'd never thought him violent. What she'd just witnessed made her think otherwise. Made her wonder if he was more like Julian than she'd realized. And the fact he could shift gears so quickly brought her right back to the fact she knew very little about the man she'd foolishly thrown herself at last night.

"I'm fine." She stepped to the side and rubbed at her aching arms as she fought the nausea swirling in her stomach. "But you're not. Look at him. Y-you could have killed him."

He glanced once at Julian, who was moaning on the ground and making no move to get up. But in his expression Kelsey didn't see regret for what he'd done. She saw nothing but disgust. And that sent her back from him another step.

Hunt's gaze lifted to her, but this time when their eyes met, something hardened in his gaze. Something she hadn't known had been soft until just now. "You're defending him? After what he just did to you?"

Her stomach swirled faster. She wasn't defending Julian, but she didn't completely trust Hunt right now either. And even though common sense told her he wasn't the threat, her flight response was pushing her to get away from both men before something worse happened.

"I-I'm calling the police." She wobbled through the doorway that led to the stairs and her loft above.

"Shit," Hunt muttered at her back. "Kelsey, wait. The cops are already on their way."

She wasn't sure how that was possible, but she didn't wait around to discover the answer. Gripping the banister, she pulled herself up the stairs as quickly as she could, wanting only to put as much space between her and what had happened downstairs as possible, focusing on taking deep breaths to keep the panic at bay.

Every inch of her body hurt, but it was her heart that hurt the most. That and her pride. Because once again, reality had proved her judgment was shit. Julian wasn't the man she'd thought, and neither was Hunt. And that meant she didn't have a clue whom she could trust.

Herself included.

———

As the cops finished taking his statement, Hunt glanced over the handful of rubberneckers on the street and searched for Kelsey.

She was no longer with the paramedics. He'd been relieved to learn she hadn't needed medical treatment beyond an ice pack and a few bandages. Somehow, in the midst of Benedict's rage, she'd managed to keep him from doing any serious harm. Hunt was awed by that fact. Awed by everything she'd been through in the last few days and survived. And more than a little worried about the way she'd jerked back from his touch and raced for the stairs.

He hadn't missed the look of horror on her face. As the paramedic finished wrapping his split knuckle, his mind flashed to the way Kelsey had stumbled back from him at the blast site when he'd dropped Benedict to the ground. He'd bet his left arm this wasn't the first time Benedict had hurt her. She reacted to violence the way a beaten dog would. And that didn't just fire him up and make him want to slam his fist into Benedict's jaw all over again, it sent off a swirling sickness in his gut because he had a sinking feeling she now thought he was the same kind of shit as her ex-husband.

"We're taking off," Callahan said, moving up on his right. "Got everything we need from Kelsey. Benedict won't be bugging her for a nice long while. You good here?"

"Thanks," Hunt mumbled to the paramedic. Then to Callahan, "Yeah. Fine."

But the news Benedict would be preoccupied for a while didn't ease his stress any. His stomach pitched with the need to talk to Kelsey and set things right—on multiple fronts. Problem was, he had no fucking clue where to start.

He turned to look toward Kelsey's door where the last two officers were filing out. "Any news on that number trace from California?"

"Not yet. I'll let you know when I hear." Callahan moved around his car and reached for the door handle. "She's still rattled by what happened but moving quickly toward pissed. Watch your back when you go in there. I got the distinct impression she wasn't happy with you."

Hunt's stomach swirled stronger as he rubbed his thumb over the bandage on his hand. "Thanks for the warning."

Callahan grinned and slid into his vehicle.

Hunt watched the cars pull away. He should be relieved Kelsey was okay. That he'd gotten here in time. But all he could think about was the sound of her screams when Benedict had been holding her down. And all he could see when he closed his eyes was the terror in her features when she'd stopped him from beating the shit out of Benedict and stared up at him as if *he* were the real monster.

"Fuck." Scrubbing a hand through his hair, he stepped up onto the sidewalk and moved toward Kelsey's door. He had no experience with battered women. Didn't have a whole lot of experience with women's reactions, period. He'd purposely steered clear of relationships and emotional entanglements most of his life, never wanting to get close to any one person for too long. Life was safer that way. And he knew life would be a whole lot safer now if he just backed off and stood guard outside her door like the security professional he was. But he couldn't do that. Because the thought Kelsey had lumped him in with her ex, that she could even fathom he'd do anything to hurt her, made him nauseous and gave him the itch to fix every single thing he'd fucked up.

He moved into the warehouse and flipped the lock on the door at his back. Her studio was still in shambles, and blood spots stained the concrete. Forcing back the bile, he headed for the doorway that led to her loft, reminding himself Benedict couldn't get to her now. As he hit the stairs, he thought back to what Callahan had shared earlier about the text they'd traced.

It was still possible Benedict had orchestrated the bombing. He could have had someone in California send that text so it couldn't be traced back to him. God knew, he'd just proved he was violent and unpredictable. But Hunt wasn't convinced Benedict had the patience to orchestrate and follow through with that kind of plan. And if he wanted her dead so badly, why not use a gun or a knife, or hell, even a car? There was no rational reason Benedict would turn to a bomb.

Which meant someone else wanted that building to come down. Someone who may or may not be linked to Kelsey. Someone neither he nor her family had considered.

The shower was running when he reached her loft. Images of her bare skin, wet and pink from the steam, flashed in his mind, but he quickly shut down the thoughts. He'd already screwed things up enough by crossing from professional to personal. He needed to focus on getting things back on track. He needed to apologize for what happened at his apartment and reassure her he was focused on nothing but her safety, then go back to being what he'd been to her before the last two days had ever happened—nothing more than her brother's friend.

For some reason, the thought of being an acquaintance again—not even her friend—shot his mood right into the basement. But he knew it was the safest plan. The smartest plan. And at the end of the day, he had a sinking feeling it was probably the only plan she'd go for.

Not wanting her to see him when she came out of the bathroom, he went back downstairs and spent the next twenty minutes putting her storefront back together and cleaning up the mess he'd helped create. He didn't have a clue how she'd folded some of the sweaters on the big square shelves—there was only one on each wide shelf that he could see, which seemed like a huge waste of space—but he did the best he could. When the place looked pretty good and enough time had passed for her to have gotten dressed, he turned toward the stairs again, intent on going up and talking to her, but something sparkly in the smoke detector above caught his attention.

His brow wrinkled as he moved closer and stared up at the round plastic device. Whatever had caught the light was now gone, but a shimmer like that made him think of glass. And he couldn't think of a single reason for there to be glass in the smoke alarm of her shop.

A tingle ran over his nape. Telling himself he was being overprotective, he moved into the production facility behind the storefront and searched for a ladder. He'd probably just seen the light reflecting off the battery casing. After locating a fifteen-foot ladder, he hauled it back into the storefront and set it up beneath the smoke alarm, then climbed up and dislodged the cover.

"Holy shit." Disbelief churned inside him as he stared at the mini surveillance camera on the end of a flexible wire casing. He followed the casing back and discovered the camera was plugged into the outlet along with the smoke alarm.

He jerked the camera out of the outlet and climbed down the ladder, that tingle turning to full-on warning vibrations. In the production facility, he found another camera hidden in one of the light fixtures. And upstairs in the living area of Kelsey's loft apartment, which she'd managed to make homey and even cozy since moving in only a few months back, he discovered another hiding in a speaker beside her flat-screen TV.

"Son of a bitch." He stared down at the three cameras in the palm of his hand. Something in his gut told him Kelsey hadn't placed these herself to keep an eye on her employees.

His gaze lifted and swept over the small loft. She'd set up a living area adjacent to the small galley kitchen. Her design desk and a couple of tables were pushed up against a far wall. Natural light shone in from skylights above, and through an open doorway he could just see into a back room that looked like a bedroom.

He didn't want to scare the crap out of her, so he cleared his throat and closed his hand around the cameras, deciding he'd save them for later. Before he showed her what he'd just found, he needed to get their relationship back on solid ground so she could trust him again. And that meant eating crow, proving he wasn't the shit she thought he was.

Seconds passed in silence—seconds that only increased his pulse because he knew she knew he was out here—then she appeared in the doorway wearing slim jeans and a baggy OSU sweatshirt, her damp hair twisted into a messy bun on the top of her head, her adorable feet completely bare on the old wood floor.

Just the sight of her freshly showered with morning light shining down from above hit him like a swift punch to the gut. Her skin was devoid of makeup, but bruises had already formed along her jaw where Benedict had held her down. Internally, Hunt cringed, only he didn't let the reaction show because he knew it wouldn't help his cause. He also didn't want her to think she looked bad, because to him she never could. She, on the other hand, didn't have the slightest trouble letting her honest reaction to him show. The scowl that settled across her pretty face told him loud and clear he was the last person she wanted to see.

"Yes?" she asked, as if she couldn't wait to get rid of him.

"Cops left."

"Good." She moved out of the bedroom, swept past him, and headed into the small kitchen. "You can follow them out. I don't need you hovering over me anymore."

The citrusy scent of grapefruit hung in the air as she moved, and he instantly wondered if it was her shampoo or lotion or just the natural scent of her silky soft skin. Even though the professional side of his brain screamed *that's not any of your concern!*

Pushing the thought aside, he turned to look after her and stuffed his hands in the front pockets of his worn jeans, hoping he looked non-threatening. "I'm not leaving. We need to talk about earlier."

She pushed to her bare toes and pulled coffee filters out of the cupboard above her head, the movement accentuating her ass in those form-fitting jeans. "Trust me, we don't."

He blinked and focused on the back of her head so his mind wouldn't wander. "I wouldn't hurt you. I'm not like Benedict."

"I am *not* talking about this." She dropped back to her heels and reached for the carafe from the coffeemaker.

"Not all guys get off hurting women. I know what you saw me do downstairs freaked you out, but I would never use my hands to hurt you or another woman like he did. I was trying to protec—"

She slammed her palm against the counter. "I said stop talking about it. I do *not* want to talk about this with you. Ever."

The quiver to her voice, the way her shoulders shook, the fact she wouldn't turn to face him all swirled together and hit Hunt like a swift punch to the gut.

She was ashamed. Because Benedict had attacked her? Because she hadn't gotten away on her own? Or because Hunt had witnessed it? He wasn't sure. But the nausea swirling in his stomach told him it could very well be from all three.

"Kels." He softened his voice and cautiously stepped toward her. "What happened wasn't your fault."

"I know it wasn't my fault," she snapped, jerking toward the sink to flip on the water and fill the carafe. "And you can spare me the psycho-babble bullshit. I don't need you trying to make me feel better. If you want to make someone feel better, go find your girlfriend."

Something else hit Hunt hard. The reality that she wasn't just ashamed of what had happened downstairs, but that she was still smarting from what had pushed her out of his apartment in the first place.

"Gen is not my girlfriend. I don't have a girlfriend. I don't have girlfriends, period. What you saw was—"

"I'm not talking about this either." She flipped the water off and moved back to the coffee maker. "So drop the subject right now, or I'll call the cops back and have them drop it for you."

Hunt's mouth slid closed, and he watched her tense shoulders and jerky movements as she finished making the coffee, feeling like an even bigger shit than he already did. He'd hurt her. More than he'd thought he had the power to hurt her. And every second he stood here trying to fix his mistakes, he was only making things worse.

"Look," he said softly, wishing she'd just turn and look at him. Once. "I know you want me to take a hike right now, but your family's not back yet, and they asked me to look after you."

"No, my family hired you because of Julian. Who, thanks to you, is in the hospital now. So you can stop with the fake concern. We both know I don't need a babysitter anymore."

Frustration welled inside him. "It's not fake, Kels."

"Uh-huh." She reached for a cup from the cupboard. "Coulda fooled me."

He clenched his jaw, fighting for patience. Part of him wanted to grab her and shake some sense into her. Another part wanted to kiss her until she realized he was serious. Since neither would help his cause, he said, "I'm not going to apologize for hitting Benedict. I'd do it again in a heartbeat if he came after you."

"Good thing we don't have to worry about that." She moved to the fridge and grabbed a carton of half-and-half.

"No, we don't. But that doesn't mean you're not still in danger."

She poured a generous dollop of creamer in her cup. "My ex-husband will be in jail for at least the next few weeks. Callahan already confirmed that. And my brothers will be back before a judge even sets his bail, so I'd say I'm safe."

"Benedict isn't the one I'm worried about."

Her hand stilled against the carton, and her shoulders tensed all over again, but she still wouldn't turn to look at him. "What does that mean?"

"It means I'm not convinced Benedict's the one who sent you that threatening text message. And neither are the cops."

She finally glanced his way, and he didn't miss the fear in her pretty brown eyes. The same kind of fear he'd seen when she'd grabbed his arm downstairs. "What do you mean?"

He didn't like scaring her, but he didn't want to hold anything back from her either. He relayed what Callahan had told him about the text being traced to California. "I'm also not sure Benedict could come up with or execute the kind of planning it would take to set off a bomb. After seeing the short temper he displayed today, I don't think he has the patience."

"Wait a minute. You think someone else targeted me?"

"Maybe not. Maybe that text wasn't related to the bombing at all. On the other hand, you're a public figure now."

She reached for the carafe of freshly brewed coffee and poured the steaming liquid into her mug. "I'm a nobody."

"You're not a nobody. Not after your big debut in New York. I ran a search while you were getting your scrapes bandaged. That actress friend of yours has worn several of your designs on the red carpet. And in interviews, she's shared your name. You're on peoples' radars even if you don't think you are."

Rolling her eyes, Kelsey lifted her cup from the counter and moved past him into the living room. "I don't have time for this. I have a business to run."

"You're going to have to make time." He held out his hand as she passed. "I found these all over in here."

She slowed her steps and stared down at the thin tubular objects in his hands. "What are those?"

"Surveillance cameras." When her wide-eyed gaze shot up to his, he added, "And judging from your reaction, you didn't know they were there."

Shock and a good dose of *holy shit* ran across her features, telling him, yep, she'd had zero clue they'd been there. "How . . . ?" She swallowed hard, looking down at the cameras, then back up at his face. "Where? How did they get here?"

"Two I found downstairs, one up here. I'm guessing there's more. And as for how they got here? You don't have a security system. It'd be easy for someone to jimmy that lock downstairs, slip in and plant them, then slip right out again without you ever knowing."

A sick look passed over her features. "Someone's been watching me? How long?"

"I don't know."

"If they're cameras, they have to be relaying images somewhere. How do they work? Were they hooked to some kind of computer?"

"No. These send a wireless signal." He glanced around her loft. "My guess is whoever planted them also hooked up a remote server of some kind. We just need to find it."

"Like a router?"

"Technically, yeah, they could hook these to a wireless router. But only if the network is unsecured."

When she didn't respond, a warning tingle ran down his spine. He tipped his head. "You don't even have a secure router, do you?"

"No, I do."

He breathed easier.

"But my password's on the side of the box."

Of course it was. He forced himself to take a calming breath and made a mental note to hit each of her brothers upside the head for not talking to her about basic security measures. "Show me."

She moved across the room. "Over here. In the cabinet under the TV."

Just as she'd said, he found her secure password on the side of her router, hidden in plain sight for anyone who looked. He was absolutely sure whoever had set the cameras in her warehouse was using her own router to send the images.

He tugged the phone from his back pocket and dialed his office. Taren Davies answered on the first ring. "Hey, boss. Didn't expect to hear from you so early, especially after yesterday. What's up?"

Hunt had talked to Davies last night after he'd called his dad, so the guy knew all about the bombing and that Hunt was still with a client. "I need you to get Monica on the line and set up a complete security overhaul on a warehouse in East Portland."

"Sure thing. But I think Mon said we were scheduling out at least three weeks on new jobs."

"This one gets bumped to the front of the line. I want it done ASAP."

"That'll piss some clients off."

"I don't give a shit. I also have a router here I want you to check out. See if you can trace any connected devices and figure out where they're relaying images."

"That's not going to be easy to do. Especially if it's a basic router."

"It is."

"If the person using the device is at all tech savvy and set up a hidden IP address, you're SOL."

Hunt knew that. "Just see what you can find."

"Will do. You coming into the office today, or you still with the McClane client?"

Hunt glanced toward Kelsey, who was watching him with wariness and a sea of nerves as she sipped her coffee. "Not coming in. I'll call you in a bit with an update and the address for the warehouse."

"Gotcha."

Hunt hit "End" and slipped the phone in his pocket. After unhooking Kelsey's router, he pulled the device from the cabinet and pushed to his feet. "You can't stay here."

She gripped the mug in both hands, no longer looking angry, just way-the-fuck freaked out. "There's still a chance Julian is the one who set these cameras. And he's in jail now."

"Yeah. There is. But until we know for sure, it's not safe here."

She looked down at her bare feet, and in the silence, Hunt knew scaring and bullying her would never get her to see reason. So he opted for the only choice he had. He opted for honesty.

"Look, I know you're mad at me, Kelsey. You have every right to be mad at me for last night. I crossed a line I never should have gone near. But this isn't about me. This is about you and your safety. You shouldn't be alone right now. Not until the cops figure out what's going on and if it has anything to do with you. I promised your family I'd keep you safe, and I promise you that's all I'm interested in doing. But if you don't trust me enough to do that, then at least let me call someone who can."

"What do you mean?"

He didn't like leaving her safety in the hands of anyone else, but at this point it was better than the alternative. "I've got several guys working for me who are completely capable of keeping you safe. And if you can't trust someone from my company, then I know a few guys in town at other firms who are just as good. I can call one of them to take you back to your parents' place or wherever else you want to go."

"You'd do that?"

"Absolutely."

"My family hired you, though. Wouldn't you lose out on your fee if you handed me over to some other firm?"

"You think I give a shit about the money? I didn't agree to watch over you because I thought I could make a quick buck. I did it to make sure nothing bad happened to you."

When she didn't answer, only blinked and stared at him, he told himself he was letting his emotions get the best of him. But, man, it really grated on him that she thought he was only here for the money. "Sorry. I didn't mean it like that. I meant—"

"Where?"

"Where what?"

"You said I should go somewhere safe, but you didn't say where." She stared at something on his shirt, not meeting his eyes. "I really don't want to go back to your apartment."

Was she saying . . . ?

"You wouldn't have to," he said before the thought could even circle in his head.

"If this—person—turns out not to be Julian, and they really are targeting me for some reason, I don't want to do anything to lead them to the rest of my family."

"You wouldn't. I can take you to my place on the coast."

Her gaze lifted to his. "You have a house at the beach?"

"Technically it's on a cliff overlooking a beach. It's highly private and has the same security setup as my apartment. No one will find you there. And you can stay as long as you want."

"I don't want to stay very long."

He tried not to be disappointed by that comment. "Then you can stay as long as it takes the authorities to confirm it was Benedict who sent that text and planted these cameras or figure out who did."

She chewed on the inside of her lip. Seemed to be debating her options. And in the silence, he told himself the only thing that mattered was her safety. He didn't care who made that happen, only that she listened to reason.

"Fine." She dropped her arms and turned away. "I'll pack a bag and meet you out here in ten minutes."

His chest tightened. "Does that mean—"

"I'll go with you to your beach house," she said from the doorway of her bedroom. "For now. Just don't make me regret it."

When she was gone, he drew what felt like his first full breath since she'd walked into his bedroom last night. He'd absolutely make sure she wouldn't regret it. He, on the other hand, was pretty sure he might.

Because having her in his house—close but not close enough to touch—was going to be nothing but pure torture for him.

CHAPTER TEN

This was the dumbest thing she'd ever agreed to.

Kelsey glanced toward the bedside clock in the guest room of Hunt's beach house, then looked back up at the dark ceiling and sighed. Two forty-three a.m. She'd yet to do more than doze since she'd said good night and closed herself in this room at not even nine thirty, and the way her brain wouldn't stop spinning, she had a pretty strong hunch she wouldn't be getting any sleep tonight no matter what time the clock read.

"Dumb, dumb, really dumb idea," she muttered, rubbing a hand across her forehead.

She hadn't seen Hunt since he'd given her a tour of the house, shown her the safe room and how to work the security system, then led her to this room. She should have taken him up on his offer to have another security firm protect her. Especially after the fiasco at his place and what he'd seen Julian do to her at the warehouse.

Her cheeks burned with mortification at the way she'd thrown herself at him at his apartment. But it didn't even compare with the rolling sickness in her belly every time she imagined what he must think of her after that scene with Julian. She already knew she was weak for ever having been with Julian. Hunt probably thought she was the most pathetic woman in the world for letting a guy treat her like that.

"Enough." She dropped her arm and closed her eyes. "Sleep, Kelsey."

Somehow she drifted to sleep, but her dreams were filled with disjointed images of cameras and text messages and exploding buildings that made no sense. And in all of them, she was trapped in the darkness, unable to break free, and powerless to stop something horrible from happening.

The scent of freshly brewed coffee pulled her eyes open. Blinking, she focused on dawn's early light spilling across the floor and queen-size bed. Her first instinct was to pull the covers over her head and go back to sleep, but the little voice in the back of her head told her that was the coward's way out, and she was done being a coward. Regardless of what had happened between her and Hunt, or of what he thought of her, she needed to get back in control of her life. Because no one could do that but her.

Her muscles were sore, and every joint felt stiff as she dug through her suitcase and pulled out an oversize gray sweatshirt with her design logo in gold on the front and paired it with black leggings from her recent line. The ballet collar fell open over one shoulder, and the hem dropped to her thighs. After twisting her hair up into a knot, she wandered into the bathroom to brush her teeth and found a bottle of ibuprofen on the counter.

Something in the center of her chest pinched. He'd left her drugs. Common sense told her to be creeped out he'd been in her room without her knowledge, but she wanted the pain relief more than she wanted to be upset. And he was just being nice. She didn't need to read anything into that.

After brushing her teeth and swallowing the meds, she checked her reflection. One glance in the bathroom mirror told her she needed concealer and a thin layer of powder to cover the dark circles under her eyes and the slight bruising on her jaw, but she resisted the urge to make herself look nice.

Barriers firmly in place, she tucked the new cell she'd picked up yesterday before leaving Portland into the hidden back pocket of her leggings, pulled her bedroom door open, and moved out into the living area.

Hunt's house wasn't that old—maybe five years—with soaring ceilings, thick trim moldings, wide windows in every room that overlooked the ocean and beach far below, and top-of-the-line everything. From a design perspective, the place was pretty incredible. But the view this morning was what stopped her cold. Miles of pristine blue water filled the windows, instantly calming her the longer she looked out across the ocean.

The coffee pot gurgled from the kitchen, and she finally pulled her gaze away from the windows and moved into the industrial kitchen with its white cabinets, granite counters, and fancy appliances. Hunt was nowhere to be found, but she didn't mind. The view in the kitchen was the same as the living room, and she couldn't keep from staring out at it again as she found a mug in the cupboard and poured herself a cup of coffee.

She took her mug to the table in the breakfast nook, tucked one leg under her, and sat on the padded white chair. Her gaze drifted from the water to the beach below, where a man in tennis shoes, running shorts, and a long-sleeved T-shirt was playing with a golden retriever on the sand.

Maybe she should think about getting a dog. Julian had never wanted one, but she didn't have to worry about him anymore. And staying at the loft, she didn't have a landlord to tell her no. Plus, dogs were good for security, right?

Thinking about security made her mind flip right back to those cameras Hunt had found. And thinking about those cameras made her remember the scene yesterday at her warehouse and what she'd let Julian do to her.

Mood slinking south, she looked away from the view and finished her coffee. She knew she should probably grab something to eat—she couldn't remember when she'd eaten last—but she had no appetite now. Carrying her cup to the sink, she looked back down at the beach once more, but the man and dog were gone.

The kitchen door opened, and she glanced over her shoulder. Hunt stepped into the room wearing athletic shorts, a long-sleeved dark-gray T-shirt, and running shoes. And even though she told herself not to, she tensed at the sight of him and wished she'd stayed in her room.

"Hey." He closed the door, looking sweaty and windblown and too damn sexy for any one man to look. "I hope I didn't wake you when I left for a run."

Her first instinct was to flee to her room, but she was done being a pathetic female. The sooner she started standing up to men—Hunt included—the better off she'd be.

"You went for a run?" She rinsed out her cup, trying to look bored. "I didn't even notice."

"Yeah. With Princess."

"Another girlfriend?" *Shit.* She bit her lip. Had she said that out loud?

He chuckled. "No. Neighbor's dog."

Dammit. Her face heated. She had said it. She fumbled for something to say, a way to brush it off as a joke.

"She's my running partner anytime I'm here," he added before she could come up with a pithy retort. "Though she just had puppies so she hasn't been as available lately."

He stopped only inches from her, and this close the sweet scent of his sweaty skin surrounded her, distracting her from everything but the way his body heat knocked the temperature in the room up a good ten degrees.

He lifted his hands and smiled.

"What?" She blinked, completely confused.

"Need to wash these."

Good God. Now she looked like a complete idiot. She quickly let go of the counter at her back, realizing she'd been so completely distracted by him she'd been holding on to the thing with a death grip, and stepped out of the way. "Sorry."

"No problem." He flipped on the faucet and went to work washing his hands. "The house is yours while you're here."

She wasn't sure what to say to that, but as she moved to the end of the island and leaned a hip against the surface, she also realized that had been him out there on the beach playing with that dog.

"Why don't you have a dog?" she asked before she could stop herself. "I'd think a security guy would be all over having a guard dog around."

He shrugged and dried his hands on a towel. "Depends on the breed. My systems work just fine without dogs."

She watched as he moved to the fridge and pulled one side open. "You clearly like dogs, though."

He shrugged and cracked the lid on a bottle of water. "I'm gone a lot. Wouldn't really be fair to leave a dog alone that much." Downing a large sip of water, he grabbed a gallon of milk and set it on the island, then shoved the fridge door closed. "Plus dogs don't live all that long."

An odd comment. Especially coming from someone who clearly liked dogs. "Also depends on the breed," she said, using his own words as she watched him move to the pantry, pull out a box of Lucky Charms, and turn to wave it her way. "No, thanks."

He shrugged like it was her loss, then found a bowl and spoon and carried everything to the table.

Crossing her arms over her chest, she turned to look after him. "Small dogs can live up to eighteen years."

He grunted as he poured cereal into his bowl. "Do I look like a small-dog kind of guy?"

No, he looked like a sexy-as-hell-athlete kind of guy, especially sitting there all sweaty and tempting, eating something she couldn't even think about touching because it would go straight to her hips.

She wasn't about to say that, though, so instead she said, "Even sporting dogs like Princess live ten to thirteen years. That's not exactly short."

He swallowed around a mouthful of cereal but didn't look up at her. "Not exactly long. What's the point in getting attached to something that's going to be gone in ten years?"

She grew silent as he ate, his comment circling in her mind. It was a pretty sad take on life. With that attitude, why get married? Fifty percent of marriages failed these days. Better yet, why get involved with anyone at all? Most relationships didn't work either. She and Julian were a perfect example of that.

Out of nowhere, Hunt's words from yesterday hit her.

"Gen is not my girlfriend. I don't have a girlfriend. I don't have girlfriends, period."

An uneasy feeling settled in her chest as he finished eating. She wasn't about to discuss the fiasco at his apartment, but thinking back to what she'd heard on that intercom, she realized he hadn't referred to the woman in his lobby as his girlfriend. She'd called herself that. He'd actually seemed ticked she was there. At the time, Kelsey had assumed it was because she'd been upstairs in his bed. But what if he'd been telling her the truth? What if he didn't do relationships at all?

Her memory skipped back to their time together in that rubble, when they'd talked about their mutual attraction all those years ago. He'd made a comment about relationships then too. When he'd justified why it was good they'd never dated. He'd said, *"Relationships never work out."* And she couldn't deny that in all the years he'd been coming to McClane family events, he'd never brought a date. Not one.

He was a good-looking guy. Successful. Nice. What would make a guy like Hunter O'Donnell gun-shy when it came to relationships?

His spoon clattered against his bowl, the sound making her blink. Seconds later, his chair scraped the tile floor as he pushed back from the table and stood.

"I need to shower and call Callahan. See if he's got any info on your texts." He stepped around her and set his dishes in the sink. "Since Lucky Charms aren't your thing, help yourself to any breakfast fixings you can find. I had the housekeeper stock the fridge before we came out, so there should be plenty of stuff."

"Thanks," she absently answered, still thinking about his comments.

"Oh, one more thing." He paused on the edge of the kitchen and glanced back. "I know you have work to do, so feel free to spread out wherever you want. My office is downstairs, so I'll stay out of your way. Odds are good the next few days will pass without you even knowing I'm here."

For some reason, that comment unsettled her more than the rest. She didn't answer. Didn't know how to answer. Just watched in silence as he left the room.

When he was gone, the air felt as if it was leaking out of her, like a balloon stuck with a pin and slowly deflating. The hours of stress and no sleep were catching up with her. Sinking into a chair at the table, she stared out at the view that minutes before had relaxed her but now left her feeling empty.

She couldn't deny that she and Hunt were not all that different. They were both workaholics, both wary of getting close to others, both loners at their cores. The difference was that she knew why she was alone. Because of choices she'd made—some bad, some good, all leading her to the place she was in right now. He, on the other hand, didn't seem to have a clue.

She thought back through his comment about dogs not living very long. And then the story he'd told her about his mom's death fluttered through her mind.

Her gaze darted to the empty doorway. Was that why he didn't do relationships? Because he was afraid of losing someone he cared about? He'd said he'd watched his father fall into a deep depression after his mom's death. That would screw anyone up. She knew all about fear and how it could hold a person back. Hell, she'd watched her brother Rusty live half a life for years because of fear. He did many of the same things Hunt did—kept his distance from people, didn't really date, was often cold and closed off emotionally.

Except . . . Hunt hadn't been closed off like that when they'd been trapped together. He'd been honest and straightforward and not the least bit afraid to admit how he'd felt about her that day years ago. And when he'd kissed her after they'd been freed . . .

The memory of that kiss heated her blood and made her toes curl against the kitchen tiles. A man who could kiss like that was not destined to spend his life alone.

Perspiration dotted her forehead. A little voice in the back of her head urged her to get up, to go find him, to talk to him about . . .

About what? That whole girlfriend/nongirlfriend thing? His fear of relationships? Or did she want to talk to him about that kiss and what had almost happened in his bed?

Her hands grew damp, and she swiped them down the thighs of her leggings. The answer to all three questions was yes, but she was smart enough to know she wasn't in any kind of rational frame of mind to have even one of those conversations. She was still processing the bombing, that someone may or may not be stalking her, and, oh yeah, the way Julian had attacked her yesterday. Hunt's fear of relationships and what had *almost* happened between them should be the last thing on her mind. So why was it the only thing she could think about?

The cell in her pocket buzzed. She pulled it out and glanced at the screen, expecting it to be Hunt telling her something else about the house he'd forgotten earlier. He was one of only a couple of people who had her new number. But it wasn't. And one glance at the words on the screen caused everything inside her to go cold.

Feeling safe because you found a way out of that rubble? You're not safe. I know where you are. I can get to you whenever I want. You took everything from me, and in return I'm going to take everything from you. Including that new boyfriend you've got. So enjoy that view, starlet, because it might be the last one you ever see. I'm coming for you. I'm coming for you very soon.

———

Hunt was trying his best not to lose his shit.

He'd held it together with Callahan when he'd called PPD earlier to find out if his friend had any news—which he didn't. But the cap he usually kept on his temper as he talked to his employee now about Kelsey's latest text was about to blow, and he really didn't want to let it loose with Kelsey leaning against the desk in his office, watching him like a hawk as he made this call.

He swiveled his chair away from her and glanced out the windows toward the ocean view beyond, working like hell not to crush the cell phone in his hand, working even harder to keep his voice even when he said, "What's taking so long on this, Davies? It's a simple search."

"Not as simple as you think," Taren Davies tossed back. "Whoever sent that text knew it would be traced. He went to a lot of trouble to route the number around so it'd be hard to pinpoint."

Which was why the police hadn't been able to trace it yet.

Hunt's stomach tightened as he glanced at the words on her screen. The fact the fucker had used the word starlet in both texts told him it was the same guy. And his gut was almost 100 percent sure now that her ex, Benedict, wasn't that fucker because as of ten minutes ago when Hunt had checked in with Callahan, Benedict was still in PPD custody.

Kelsey shifted against the edge of his desk where she was leaning. He glanced up, relieved she'd brought him the phone as soon as the text had come through, ready to pound whoever had sent it to her into the earth at the same time.

He forced a smile for her benefit and tipped the phone away from his mouth. "This will probably take a while. Why don't you go relax, and I'll come find you when I have some news."

"I'm not leaving."

Three words. Short and sweet. And filled with so much anxiety he knew she meant them.

Hunt's adrenaline kicked up another notch as their eyes held. She had the same terrified look in her eye she'd had just before the building had collapsed around them. The same horrific one he'd seen when Benedict had snatched her away from him at the blast site and gone after her. The same one he'd focused on when she'd grabbed his arm and stopped him from pounding on Benedict at her warehouse.

That look—knowing she was scared shitless all over again—set off that protective instinct inside him he'd felt at the bomb site. One that left him completely rattled in a way he didn't like.

He glanced back down at her phone in his hand again. "Well?" he prodded into the receiver pressed to his ear.

"Patience you must have, my young padawan."

Keys clicking sounded over the line, and Hunt's jaw clenched as he imagined Taren Davies parked at his workstation, running a dozen different searches on a dozen different screens. "You're a fucking nerd, Davies."

Taren chuckled. "Yeah, but I'm the best damn nerd you've got on your payroll." Keys clicked again, then Taren said, "There it is."

"You got it?"

"Just came up."

"Put him on speaker," Kelsey said.

Hunt didn't want to, but one look at her fierce expression told him she wouldn't be deterred. "Hold on, Davies, I'm putting you on speaker." He pulled the phone away from his face, hit the speaker button, and set it down on his desk. "Taren, say hello to Kelsey McClane."

"Hey, Ms. McClane. Sorry this is how we get to meet. The boss man there rarely unchains me from the basement."

"Hi, Taren." She uncrossed her arms and braced her hands against the surface of Hunt's desk as she glanced at the phone by her side. "That's okay, I'm going to keep your boss chained up here in this basement until he figures out who's harassing me."

Heat exploded in Hunt's belly. A heat he knew he should not be feeling and which he couldn't keep from shooting straight into his groin. *Holy shit*, she had no idea what she'd just said. Or what kind of dirty thoughts were suddenly spinning in his mind.

From Davies's silence, Hunt knew his employee had heard Kelsey's words and taken it as a sexual innuendo as well. Good thing he was keeping his trap shut.

Davies cleared his throat. "Okay, well. Moving on. O'Donnell, you still there?"

Kelsey's brow lowered as if she'd missed something, and she glanced toward Hunt.

Shifting uncomfortably, not wanting her to know where his mind was running, Hunt said, "Yeah. I'm here. What did you find?"

"CBG Industries. The address is on the outskirts of LA."

Hunt glanced up at Kelsey. "You said Benedict doesn't have any family or friends in southern California, right?"

She shook her head. "No. He's from the Midwest."

"Callahan said they can't find any business associates or clients there for him either. Did he ever mention anyone in southern California to you?"

"No."

"What about CBG Industries? Ever heard of it, or do you ever remember Benedict mentioning it?"

"No. It's not familiar at all."

"Do you know anyone in LA?"

"A few acquaintances. No one special."

Glancing down at the phone, he said, "Davies, I want you to get me everything you can on this CBG Industries. I want to know what they do and when they do it."

"Hold on," Davies announced. "The trace is running again. Okay, I've got a home address is Palm Desert, California. Looks like the owner of that number worked for CBG Industries until about eight months ago."

Bingo.

"What's the name?" Hunt asked.

"Graham Foster."

Hunt jotted the name and address on a piece of paper as Davies read it off. When he was done, he looked back up at Kelsey. "Does that name ring a bell?"

Her brow was drawn and wrinkled, her eyes confused but just as focused and intense as they'd been since she'd stepped into his office and shown him that text. "No. I've never heard it before."

Hunt glanced at the receiver on his desk. "Davies? I want you to run a background on this guy for me. I want to know everything about him, where he works now, what he does for fun, who he knows, what he ate for breakfast. And I want it all within the hour."

Davies sighed. "That it? Yeah, no problem."

Pushing to his feet, Hunt glanced at his watch, "Call me on my cell with whatever you can find. If I don't answer it means I'm out of range. Leave me a message."

"Will do. You going down there?"

"Yeah." He reached for the phone. "I want to surprise this guy before he realizes we're even on to him."

Davies clucked his tongue. "Okay, don't do anything stupid."

"I won't. Have Monica book me on a flight in three hours. Then call Branaugh and have him meet me at the office. I need him to come back here with Kelsey."

"Done," Davies said.

Plan in place, Hunt clicked "End" on the cordless phone, set it back in its cradle, and moved for the door.

"You're going to California?" Kelsey asked at his back.

"Yeah." He jogged up the stairs to the main level of the house and headed for the master bedroom while Kelsey followed. "I'm sorry to drag you back to Portland, but it'll be safer for you to go with me to my place then come back here again with Branaugh. I don't want you here alone, just in case. Branaugh's a good guy. He's worked for me for three years. There's no one you'd be safer with than me."

She stopped in the doorway to his bedroom and crossed her arms over her chest while he tugged a duffel from the closet and started throwing clothes inside. "I'm not coming back here with someone else."

"Don't be stupid, Kelsey. You're safer here than in Portland."

"I'm not being stupid. I'm being smart. I don't know this Branaugh guy, and I certainly didn't agree to let him watch over me. I agreed to let you do that. So if you're going to California, then so am I."

He stopped what he was doing and glanced over the bed toward her. "That's a bad idea."

"Why? Because it's not your idea? News flash, O'Donnell. I make my own decisions."

He stared at her. Blinked. Knew he needed to tell her *no way in hell* but couldn't force the words past his lips. He didn't want her anywhere near the guy. But more than that, *he* didn't want to be anywhere near her right now because his reactions to her were out of control and bordering on obsessive.

What was it about her that was making him so crazy? When he'd walked in on her in his kitchen earlier, looking sleepy and sexy and delightfully rumpled, all he'd wanted to do was kiss her. When she'd brought him her phone minutes ago and he'd seen the terror in her eyes from that text message, he'd wanted blood from whoever had sent it. And watching the strength and defiance grow in her features right now as she challenged him head-on made him absolutely ache to grab her and claim her and never let go.

"I really don't think that's a good idea, Kels—"

"I'm going with you, Hunter. Don't even try to tell me otherwise." She dropped her arms and turned for her room. "I'll be ready in ten minutes."

The air whooshed out of his lungs as soon as she was gone, and he braced his hands on the mattress, wondering what the hell he'd just agreed to. Or hadn't agreed to. Or, *fuck*, been too damn stupid to stop.

"Way to go, dumbass," he muttered, straightening and tossing clothes in his bag with more force than necessary. "You better start thinking with your head instead of your dick so you don't fuck this up again."

And he would. Because he did not form attachments. He was not *going* to form an attachment to Kelsey McClane, dammit. He was going to focus on his job, make sure nothing happened to her, and solve this damn case. In that order.

He had to, because it was the only way he was going to get the hell away from her before it was too late.

CHAPTER ELEVEN

Hunt's plan was already backfiring. Ten minutes in the air, and Hunt knew agreeing to let Kelsey accompany him on this quick trip to California had "bad news" written all over it.

She hadn't done anything wrong, she hadn't said anything wrong. He just didn't like how close she was in the cramped cabin of the small plane. And he definitely didn't like that citrusy scent he kept picking up every time she moved. The one that left him light-headed and completely distracted him from the reason he was on this damn plane in the first place.

Since the flight had been last-minute, they'd been stuck with whatever seats they could get—two in the back of coach. He'd spent most of the two-hour flight reading e-mails and writing replies on his phone, doing anything he could to keep his hands and mind occupied so it wouldn't wander to the woman flipping through a magazine at his side. But he knew he'd failed miserably when he had to retype an e-mail to Alec for the fifth time, explaining where the hell he was taking his friend's little sister.

"What if your family gets home while you're gone?" Hunt asked, sending the last e-mail to his outbox as they started their descent into Palm Springs.

"Then they get home before me."

"That's not what I meant," he said with a frown. "What are you going to tell them if they get back before us?"

"The same thing I always do when it comes to them," she answered absently, flipping a page in her magazine without looking his way. "Whatever the hell I want."

She'd been full of sass ever since he'd tried to talk to her in her loft after the nightmare with Benedict. He was sure some of that snarky attitude was spurred on by anger she was still feeling toward him because of Gen. But another part of him wondered if this was all a mask. If pulling out the tough-girl Kelsey image he often saw her use with her brothers was her way of proving to him she was strong and resilient and didn't need anyone all because he'd witnessed her at one of her most vulnerable moments.

His frustration with her waned as he looked at her sitting next to him in her designer white slacks and trendy blue blouse, her blonde hair falling straight and sleek around her face as she continued to flip through her magazine. He already knew she was strong and resilient. Anyone who'd lived through what she had, not just in her childhood but with Benedict, couldn't have come out sane on the other side if they weren't resilient as hell. Why did she feel like she had to prove that to people? Why couldn't she just relax and be herself?

She'd been herself with him in the rubble, he realized, thinking back to their conversations in the dark. She hadn't hidden her fear then, hadn't pretended to be hard as steel as she was doing now. Even when she'd come to him later that night in his bedroom, when he'd opened his eyes to see her standing in the doorway, and he'd realized she hadn't wanted to be alone, she'd been herself. Nervous, yeah, but soft around the edges and without all the barriers she had up now, willing to let him see a glimpse of the sweet and special woman she was inside.

He liked that woman. Liked her a lot. And every time he thought about that woman, he couldn't help but remember the way she'd felt pressed against him—warm and curvy and perfect—and just how hot it had been when she'd pressed her lips to his and kissed him.

She glanced sideways at him, her brow dropping. "What?"

"What do you mean, what?"

"You have a weird look on your face. Are you feeling all right, Hunter? You're not about to get sick, are you? Should I call for a barf bag? I might have agreed to this little trip, but I did not agree to play nursemaid."

He frowned again because her snark was back stronger than ever. Looking toward the seatback in front of him, he gripped his phone and told himself that was a good thing. It would keep him from doing something stupid while they were on this trip. It would definitely keep him from kissing her again.

Except, now all he could think about was how he could coax the real her out from beneath all that armor. And if he succeeded in doing that, then all guarantees meant nothing, because there was no way he could resist the real Kelsey McClane if she decided to show herself.

———

As they unloaded from the plane, made their way through the airport to grab their bags, and rented a car, Kelsey didn't miss the fact Hunt did just about anything to keep from looking at her.

She wasn't sure what to make of that. Was he upset by the joke she'd made on the plane? Angry she'd tagged along on this trip? Frustrated she wouldn't sit back at his beach house and wait as he'd told her to do? She didn't think any of those things could be causing his mood, but she couldn't be sure. Hunter O'Donnell was still a mystery to her. One she told herself not to try to figure out, but which her brain couldn't seem to ignore.

Questions spun through her mind as he climbed into the driver's seat beside her, typed in the address on the GPS, and clicked his seatbelt. "I'm going to drop you at the hotel first so you ca—"

"No dropping me anywhere," she said, realizing he was trying to brush her aside already. Just like her brothers. Just like Julian. "We came down here to surprise Foster. We're going out to his place first. We'll check into the hotel later."

Hunt frowned as he slid on his sunglasses but was careful not to meet her gaze as he glanced over his shoulder and backed out of the space. "I really don't think that's a good ide—"

"I don't care if you think it's a good idea or not. I'm the client. I get what I want."

He glanced sideways at her. She couldn't see his eyes behind his sleek Ray-Bans, but the clench to his jaw told her loud and clear he wasn't happy. Too bad. She wasn't particularly happy at the moment either.

"I'm not your enemy, Kelsey. I'm here to help you." Glancing back toward the windshield, he maneuvered the vehicle out of the parking structure. "Sometimes it's okay to let people help you, you know. It's even okay to ask for help."

His comment made her spine stiffen. She knew that. Why was he telling her that? She didn't need a lecture from him.

She crossed her arms over her chest as they left the parking structure, refusing to answer that comment. Late-afternoon sunshine shone through the windows. Desert mountains rose around the Coachella Valley, and palm trees lined the streets. Kelsey loved the green of Oregon, but she could see how appealing the warmth of the desert could be. It was beautiful with its vibrant colors and jagged peaks. Beautiful and calming in a way she hadn't expected.

Her gaze strayed to Hunt beside her as they left the city, and a twinge of guilt passed through her for the way she'd been treating him. Was that what was eating at him? Her bitchy attitude? She had been pretty hard on him lately. But he'd hurt her with that whole girlfriend thing. She had every right to be upset about that. Any woman would be.

Except he'd said the woman wasn't his girlfriend. And you even admitted to yourself he might have been telling the truth.

She shifted uncomfortably in her seat and looked out the passenger window at the tumbleweed blowing by. She didn't like being a bitch. It didn't make her feel good. But she liked being taken advantage of even less. There was only one way to find out the truth.

She focused on a mountaintop far in the distance. "So your girlfriend the other morning—"

"She's not my girlfriend."

"So you said. But she called herself your girlfriend when you were in the lobby with her, and you didn't correct her."

From the corner of her vision, she saw the way he tensed. But he didn't turn to look at her, and she made more than sure she didn't look at him either. Was afraid if she did she wouldn't be able to get through his conversation.

"Gen is not my girlfriend," he said calmly.

"Then what is she?"

"Nothing. Nothing more than a fling. She's a flight attendant. We met on a trip and hooked up a few times. That's it."

"That's it?" Kelsey didn't buy that. She'd seen the woman. She'd been busty and built and had "sure thing" written all over her.

"Yes, that's it. I'm not dating her. Last time I saw her was three months ago. We weren't serious."

"Not serious? And she just conveniently shows up at your apartment at four in the morning?"

"I told her not to come down. I broke things off with her. Neither of us has ever been serious about the other. She dated lots of guys besides me."

"When?"

"When what?"

"When did you break things off with her?"

He shifted in his seat and gripped the wheel tighter. But he still didn't look at her, and the tick in his jaw answered her question long before he did. "When she called to check on me."

"After the bombing," she guessed. "When I was at your apartment."

When he didn't respond, another wave of stupidity washed over her. She focused on a fence post, calling herself a complete moron for even entertaining the idea—again—that he was different. "I see."

The vehicle slowed, and Hunt pulled to the side of the road. Shoving the car into "Park," he turned to look at her. And even though she could tell from his expression that he was ticked, she still didn't look at him. Couldn't, because it just made her feel more stupid.

"Look," he said in a way that told her he was working to stay calm, "I didn't plan what happened between you and me. And I didn't officially break things off with Gen earlier that night in the hopes something would happen between us. If you remember, you're the one who came to my room. Not the other way around."

Her face heated with both embarrassment and mortification. She tightened her arms across her chest. "I remember. And you don't have to bring that up now. Can we just go, please?"

"No, we can't." He tugged off his sunglasses and pinned her with very focused, very serious brown eyes. "I know you're mad at me, but I didn't set out to hurt you. Yes, Gen called me earlier in the evening and said she wanted to come down. I told her no, not because of you, but because I wasn't interested. And I broke things off with her over the phone because I realized I'd let things drag on way too long, even if it was nothing more than a casual fling. She didn't listen, obviously, but that doesn't change the facts. She was not who I wanted to be with that night. You were. And not because I was trying to score or get lucky or take advantage of you, but because I really like spending time with you. When you're not ready to bite my head off, you're sweet and compassionate and real. Qualities I don't see a whole lot of in my job. And when you actually drop your guard and let me see the real you for five damn minutes, you make me absolutely cr—"

The abrupt end to his rant brought her head around. Her stomach tightened as she stared at him in his white button-down rolled up to his elbows, loose khaki pants, and casual boots, wondering why he'd stopped. Wondering even more what he'd been about to say. "It makes you what?" she asked before she could stop herself.

"Nothing." He shoved his sunglasses on and quickly shifted into "Drive," pulling back onto the highway with a sputter of gravel. "Forget I even said anything."

Silence filled the car. A silence she should have been thankful for. Only she wasn't. Because in the silence, everything he'd just said was suddenly swirling in her brain, mixing with what she'd seen in his eyes just before he'd looked away.

Honesty. She'd seen absolute honesty in those deep-brown irises. He liked her. He really liked her. Maybe not the bitchy her, but the real her. The one she didn't let many people get close to. But on the heels of that honesty, she'd also seen fear. A great big giant dose of it that had caused him to pull way back before he'd said something he might later regret.

Her pulse picked up speed. Her skin grew hot. Knowing he was scared—of her—set off a weird tremor deep inside her. One she didn't understand or particularly like. One that made her rethink everything she'd said to him over the last day—the last few days that had brought them to this point.

"I don't know what we'll run into out here," Hunt said, his voice once more even as he turned the vehicle onto a gravel road. "So if I say stay in the car, I mean stay in the car."

He was back in security mode. Their earlier conversation was over, which should relieve her, only it didn't. All she could think about now was what he'd said, what he'd been about to say, and why a strong, take-charge guy like him could ever be scared of a weak, nobody woman like her. "I will."

He glanced sideways at her, his jaw tight, and even though she couldn't see his eyes she knew they were filled with skepticism.

"This is your area of expertise." Releasing her arms, she folded her hands in her lap. "I'll just sit in the car and wait until you tell me otherwise."

He frowned and focused on the road once more, but he didn't respond. And in the silence, she knew he was waiting for a pithy retort, but she didn't have one. She didn't want to have one. What she wanted was more of the easygoing, relaxed relationship they'd had during the bombing, when he'd made her feel safe even though she'd been in the most dangerous moment of her life.

"What did Davies find in the background check on this guy?" she asked, working for casual and real. He was right. She didn't let people see the real her very often. She didn't want to hide from him anymore. "I'm assuming you already read through that on your phone? I don't think you'd be heading out here without knowing what you're walking into."

He didn't immediately answer, and she glanced his way, afraid he was still angry. His jaw was definitely still tight, his shoulders tense, but his voice sounded calm, even a little surprised when he said, "CBG Industries is a multitiered conglomerate that runs a number of different businesses. Foster worked for the company in a low-level management position for twenty-two years before retiring here."

"In what business?"

"Oil and gas. He managed a distribution center that coordinated trucking deliveries to fuel stations."

He slowed the vehicle and made a right-hand turn onto another gravel road. "Callahan also got back to me. The FBI confirmed the bomb was parked in a truck outside the TV station's building. It wasn't big, which is why it didn't do as much damage as it could have. But it was a smaller version of the kind McVeigh used in Oklahoma City, made up of fertilizer, chemicals and—"

"Diesel fuel," she finished on a tight breath.

He glanced her way. "You know about bombs?"

"I read the news. I also went to college and remember studying the Oklahoma City bombing. Did you tell Callahan what you learned about Foster?"

"Yeah. I texted him when we landed. Which means the FBI will be here in a matter of minutes if they aren't already. I want a look at the guy before they get ahold of him."

She wasn't sure how she felt about that. This guy could be—probably was—dangerous. Staying back at the hotel might not have been a bad idea.

Hunt slowed the vehicle as they approached a short gravel driveway. The house was set back a good twenty yards from the road, more like a dilapidated old cabin than a home. There were no trees surrounding the aged structure in the middle of the desert, no yard either. Nothing but scrub brush and waist-high, yellow weeds. In the driveway sat a beat-up pickup truck that looked as if it hadn't run in years.

He parked the car on the side of the road, glancing all around them for signs of life. They were in the middle of nowhere—no other homes within sight, no buildings or trees or even bushes big enough for anyone to hide behind.

"Doesn't look like anyone's home," he muttered.

It didn't to her either. Maybe Davies had given them the wrong address.

He popped the driver door. "Climb over here. If anyone drives up while I'm gone, or you hear anything strange, get the hell out of here."

And leave him? He didn't know her too well if he thought she'd bail like that.

As he climbed out of the vehicle, she slid over the console and dropped into the driver's seat. He checked the magazine of the 9mm he'd tucked into a holster at his lower back before they'd climbed in the rental car and snapped it closed.

Nerves shot all through her belly as she gripped the steering wheel. "How long will you be gone?"

"Hopefully only a few minutes." He wouldn't meet her eyes. He kept checking their surroundings, looking for any kind of threat. "Stay here. Keep the doors locked. I'll call you on your cell if it's safe."

She swallowed hard, not because she was afraid, but because she didn't like this tension between them. Tension she'd created by jumping to conclusions and being so distrusting.

"Hunt." She wrapped her fingers around his hand before he could take a full step away, pulling him to a stop.

He glanced down at her through mirrored sunglasses that completely hid his eyes from view, preventing her from knowing what he was thinking, but the flex to his jaw screamed of discomfort. "What?"

Her stomach tightened. She was not good at apologizing. Or leaning on people. Or letting people in. "I'm sorry. For jumping to conclusions. I should have asked instead of assumed. That's not always easy for me. Very few people surprise me."

His jaw released, and his fingers curled around hers where she held him, warm and rough and strong. "Maybe that's because you don't give people the chance to surprise you. Not everyone's an asshole like your ex."

His words stung, but they were spoken softly and without any bite, and she couldn't deny he was right. "I know that. Believing it, though, is not always easy."

"You can believe it about me. I would never intentionally hurt you, physically or emotionally."

Her heart beat hard and fast as she blinked up at him. "I know that too," she whispered, fighting a wave of emotion that seemed to come out nowhere. "I-I'll try to be better about showing it."

"Okay."

He didn't pull away. Didn't release her hand. Didn't make any other move toward her. And she was thankful for that, because her emotions were all over the map, and she wasn't sure what she would do if he touched her right now—push him away or hold on tight and never let go.

"Are you going to be okay out here?" he asked.

She nodded.

"Are you sure?"

"Yes." The sun was sinking in the sky behind him, making it hard to see his face. Knowing he was worried and wouldn't leave until she reassured him she wasn't about to fall apart, she forced a smile and squinted up at him. "I'll be fine."

"Okay." Gently, he released her. "I'll be right back."

"Be careful."

He flashed a warm smile. "Always."

He closed her door and walked around the back of the car. Alone, she drew a ragged breath that did little to ease the tightness in her chest and followed him in the rearview mirror until he disappeared behind the car and headed for the house.

She should feel better that she'd set things right with him. She should be relieved that she knew the truth about that woman who'd interrupted them the other night and that he wasn't upset with her anymore. But she wasn't. Lifting a hand, she rubbed against the tight spot in her chest, hoping it would help the pressure, but it didn't. It almost felt like . . .

Her head jerked around as she realized what she was feeling. The same damn thing she'd felt just before that bomb had gone off and again before the rubble had shifted and she'd lost contact with Hunt. A sense that something horrible was about to happen.

Hunt was already at the front of the house, quietly moving up the three rickety porch steps. If she jumped out now and yelled to stop him, she could alert anyone inside that he was there. She watched with bated breath as he peered through the dirty window. His gun was still holstered, his body language didn't hint at any kind of danger, yet her heart continued to pound fast and erratic, and that pressure inside was only growing stronger.

He knocked on the door. Long minutes stretched with no answer. He knocked again. When still no one answered, he glanced back at her in the car and pointed to the side, telling her he was going around back.

"Shit." She swallowed hard. Rubbed her damp palms against her slacks. Wanted to scream at him to stay where he was. But he was already on the move. Seconds later she couldn't see him anymore.

The temperature inside the vehicle rose with every passing second. She wasn't sure how much time passed, but it felt like hours. Perspiration formed along her forehead and down her spine. Unable to handle the rising heat in the car anymore, she glanced forward and back, and not seeing any other cars anywhere close, she popped the driver door open and pushed to her feet.

A light wind blew her hair back from her face and rustled the scrub brush. Somewhere in the distance, a hawk called, but there was no other sound. Nothing besides an eerie silence that only amped her already sky-high adrenaline.

"C'mon, c'mon, c'mon," she muttered, looking over the roof of the vehicle toward the quiet house. What was taking so long?

Movement caught her attention through the front room window of the house.

She sucked in a surprised breath only to let it out again when she realized the movement was Hunt, one hand on his hip, the other on the phone pressed to his ear as he looked down at his feet.

The air whooshed out of her lungs. He was safe. Nothing bad had happened. The fact he didn't have his gun drawn and was talking on his phone told her there was no threat inside the house. Which meant she was out here stressing for no reason.

Feeling like an idiot, she closed the door and headed toward the house. Since she hadn't seen him move to the front door, she assumed it was still locked, so she went around back, the way he'd gone.

Chipped cement steps let up to an open kitchen door. Cautiously, she moved inside, and called, "Hunt?"

The smell hit her first. A moldy, stale smell that made her nose wrinkle. One quick glance around the filthy kitchen told her the smell was probably coming from the dirty dishes stacked in the stained sink or the table to her right littered with old pizza boxes and empty milk cartons.

The room was empty. Looking ahead, she spotted a small hall that cut the house in two. She headed that direction. "Hunt?"

A shuffling sound echoed from the front room, and seconds later Hunt stepped into the hall with the phone pressed to his ear. "Shit. Hold on." He pulled the phone away from his mouth. "Kelsey, stop. Don't go any farther."

She made it one more step before his words registered, drawing her to a stop. A fluttering movement to her left caught her attention. Hunt headed like lightning straight toward her, but she turned to get a better look before he could reach her. She was standing in front of an open office door. Dozens of black-and-white newsprint pictures were scattered across the shaggy carpet, rustling in the breeze coming through the open window. And in every one, she saw her face.

"Dammit." Hunt reached her side and tried to gently tug her away. "You don't need to see that."

"No, don't." She pushed against his hold, her eyes growing wider as she scanned the photos. They weren't just pictures of her. They were all pictures taken over the last few weeks. Some at her fashion shows in New York. Others at parties with industry professionals. Still others of her hailing a cab on the street in Times Square.

But those weren't what made her suck in a sharp breath. The photos of her on the desk with the words BITCH, CUNT, and DEAD, scrawled in red lettering across her face were the ones that chilled her to the bone.

Those and the one in the center of the desk. The one of her smiling as she stood on stage with her models in New York. The one someone had stabbed right through her heart with the blade of a vicious hunting knife.

CHAPTER TWELVE

Kelsey paced in the drive of the rundown house, the fingers of one hand pressed against her lips, the other hand wrapped around her waist as the sun sank low on the horizon and she fought to keep from freaking out.

Hunt had already called the police by the time she'd gone inside looking for him, and a sea of county and FBI vehicles now lined the driveway and narrow road beyond. She hadn't stayed inside long before exiting to get fresh air, but what she'd seen in that small time frame had been enough.

There was no question those texts were meant for her. Her stomach rolled all over again, and she breathed deep, fighting back the nausea. She just didn't understand why. Or who, really. She didn't know anyone here. She didn't know anyone named Foster.

Gravel crunched somewhere close, and she breathed even deeper, fighting not to lose her lunch in front of some poor, unsuspecting police officer.

"Hey," Hunt said softly at her back. "You okay?"

The sound of his voice calmed her in a way she didn't want to over-analyze right now. She was simply thankful he was here.

She turned toward him and brushed the hair back from her face. "Not really."

"Come here." He moved into her, and when he wrapped his arms around her shoulders and closed her into the heat of his body, she didn't stop him because she absolutely needed this right now.

She closed her eyes and slid her arms around his waist, breathing in the familiar scent of him as she pressed her cheek to his chest. God, this felt good. Safe. Right. She didn't want to question why. She just wanted more.

She tightened her arms around his waist, and he took the cue, holding her closer. Against her ear, he whispered that everything was going to be okay, that she was safe, that no one could get to her, but words of reassurance weren't what she needed. What she needed was him. A solid, calming presence in her life, just as he'd always been.

Feeling steadier, she finally released him. For a second she didn't think he was going to let her go, which she absolutely loved, but then he released her. Telling herself to keep it together, to stay tough, she brushed the hair back from her face and looked up at him. But it took every bit of strength she had not to close herself off from him like she normally would.

"What's happening in there?" she asked, fighting for normal when it was the last thing she felt.

He raked a hand through his hair and glanced back toward the house where a couple of law enforcement personnel stood on the decaying front porch, deep in conversation. "The deed for the property's in the name of Graham Foster. They're gathering fingerprints. There's no sign of the guy. Place looks like it's been empty for a couple of days."

She wasn't sure how she felt about that. A couple of days was plenty of time to get up to Oregon and set that bomb. But the fact Foster wasn't here and that the texts had come from here unnerved her. "Can they locate him?"

"They will. They put out an APB on him. He's in his sixties. He shouldn't be hard to find."

She chewed on her lip. "Do they think he has any link to Julian?"

"They'll be looking into that. That's why I came out here. The Feds want to talk to you again. See if you know something you might not be aware you know."

That comment hit her as just plain funny, especially considering everything else. "You're supposed to protect me. Not let the Feds scramble my brain."

He chuckled, and the sound was so light, especially when he smiled in that way that made him look sexier than any man should, it eased the last of the pressure inside her chest. "I'll stay with you to make sure there's no brain scrambling. How's that?"

Right now, that sounded perfect. "Thanks. I appreciate that."

"Do you want to call your folks? Let them know what we found here?"

"Absolutely not." When one side of his lips tipped up, she realized how that must have sounded. "I don't want to worry them yet. There's nothing they can do about it, and if we tell them about this, it'll just cause unnecessary stress."

"I get it."

She eyed him warily. "I'm safe here, right? Foster isn't here."

"You're completely safe. No one's getting near you but me."

Her belly warmed. She knew he didn't mean that the way she wanted, but she liked it just the same.

Sighing, not wanting to think about that too much, she looked toward the house. "I guess I should go get this over with."

He reached for her hand, stopping her from stepping away. "I told them to come out here."

She glanced down at his warm fingers wrapped around her cold ones, awed by the way he seemed to know exactly what she needed. Surprised even more by the fact her first reaction wasn't to pull away. She could lean on him and still hold it together. In fact, holding it together when he was by her side made the whole thing a hell of a lot easier to do.

"When we're done here, what do you think about checking in to the hotel, getting cleaned up, then finding a place to grab dinner?" he asked. "They probably won't have any info for us on Foster until at least tomorrow."

To her, what he was describing sounded heavenly. And a lot like a date, which she knew could be dangerous, especially right now when she didn't want to let go of his hand. "I think that sounds nice. And just what I need."

His smile widened, and his grip tightened on her hand in a way that didn't just supercharge her blood, it infused her with even more strength. "Me too. I'll keep you safe, Kels. I promise."

She smiled back, knowing he'd do everything he could to keep his word. But knowing and believing were two very different things, and after what she'd seen today, there were no guarantees.

Because she knew now they weren't just dealing with a jilted ex-husband. The person who'd cut out all those pictures and stabbed that knife through her heart was unhinged in ways that made him completely unpredictable.

———

Hunt braced his elbows on his knees as he sat on the plush, rolled-back, tufted side chair in the living area of the hotel suite and flipped channels on the TV with the remote.

There was nothing on the local news about Foster or what the cops had found at that property in the desert, and no indication the FBI was doing anything out of the ordinary in the area. Finally settling on a basketball game, he turned the volume to low so it wouldn't disturb Kelsey in the bedroom, set the remote on the coffee table in front of him, and checked his phone for the umpteenth time.

Still nothing from the cops. And nothing from Callahan in Portland. He'd called Davies earlier and told him to look into Benedict's and Foster's backgrounds as well, hoping for some kind of link between the two men, but so far Davies had come up empty on both. Logic said they had to be connected in some way, but that tingle along the back of Hunt's neck anytime he thought about the two men told him he was reaching.

He swiped a hand across his nape, then grabbed the water bottle he'd opened and left on the coffee table. The suite his office manager, Monica, had booked them into was all modern lines, plush furnishings, and warm desert colors—a mix of creams and browns and oranges that matched the colors outside as the sun set over the jagged mountains. It had two bedrooms—the biggest of which he'd given to Kelsey—and balconies that overlooked the pool area. She was currently in her room, getting ready for dinner. Had been locked in there for the last hour. And even though he knew she was safe and that nothing bad could happen to her here right under his nose, he was itching for that damn door to open so he could see for himself she was all right.

Because he wasn't completely sure she was as fine as she said. She'd seemed okay on the drive to the hotel. She was acting normal—better than normal, in fact. She was acting like the Kelsey he'd spent all those hours talking to in the rubble, not the snarky, closed-off Kelsey he'd taken to his beach house. But he knew what she'd seen at Foster's house had freaked her out. He'd seen it in her eyes before she'd gone outside. And he'd felt it when he'd hugged her and she'd clung to him as if she never wanted to let go.

The master bedroom door opened just when he was seconds away from knocking to make sure she was still alive, and Kelsey stepped out into the living room with a one-sided smile and his iPad cradled in her hands.

He breathed deeply, knowing she was safe, but frowned because she wasn't dressed and ready for dinner as he'd expected. She was wrapped in a plush white bathrobe, with her wet hair covered by one of those weird towel things he didn't know how girls made stay on their heads.

"Sorry I'm running late," she said as she moved past him toward the bar and pulled the fridge open. "I'll be ready in twenty minutes."

"It's fine." He tracked her across the room, watching her carefully as she popped the top on a water bottle, tipped her head back, and took a long sip. Her features weren't drawn or tight. Her eyes weren't puffy from crying. She didn't look upset in any way. And she absolutely shouldn't look sexy in that bathrobe and head towel, but, *holy hell*, she did. Free of makeup, she was gorgeous. And he was a complete louse for thinking about shit like that after what she'd just been through.

Water bottle in hand, she moved to stand next to him and stared at the television above the fireplace. "Who's playing?"

She also smelled divine. Her grapefruit scent made him completely mad. "Playing what?"

"The basketball game?" She pointed toward the screen with an adorable smile. "The one you're watching?"

"Oh." He glanced toward the TV even though all he wanted to do was go on looking at her. "Warriors and Celtics."

"Hmm." She watched for a few seconds as she sipped her water, then said, "I'll be ready in a few minutes. Thanks for letting me use your iPad." She set the tablet on the coffee table and turned back for her room. "I took a bath and got distracted reading."

"Sure. No problem." He watched her go, part of him wishing she'd stay. Another part really wishing she'd plop down next to him and keep watching the game in that sexy robe. "What were you reading?"

She paused at the threshold of her room and gripped the doorframe to glance back. "A book."

When he frowned, the cutest smile spread across her fresh face, one he liked seeing way more than the worry he'd seen earlier.

"A biography," she clarified. "On Vivienne Armstrong."

"The dead actress? Why?"

"Because I saw a copy of it on Foster's desk. One of the officers was paging through it before I walked out of the house. There were long sections inside highlighted in yellow."

Hunt wasn't one to follow the Hollywood gossip scene, but Vivienne Armstrong had been a rising star until her death from a drug overdose sometime in the last year. "Why would Foster be highlighting a dead actress's autobiography?"

"I don't know. Thought maybe if I looked I could find a connection between them, but I didn't see anything. It's filled with all kinds of juicy Hollywood gossip, but nothing about Foster. You can keep looking if you want. I only read the first three chapters before I realized it was a waste of time." She pushed away from the doorjamb. "I'll be ready in a few minutes."

She left her bedroom door open but disappeared around the corner into her bathroom. Relaxing back into his seat, he reached for his iPad and glanced through the book she'd been reading while he waited.

Kelsey was right. The book was filled with long sections about movies the actress had worked on, actors she'd dated, and the actresses who hated her for being Hollywood's latest "it" girl. Nothing of interest—at least, not to Hunt. He was just about to close the reading app when he spotted a chapter entitled "My Biggest Regret."

He skimmed the first paragraph, then went back and reread it word for word when he realized what the chapter was about. A child. A child the actress had given up for her own good.

The hair on his nape tingled as the story unfolded before him. Vivienne Armstrong claimed she'd come from an abusive home, that when she'd been no more than sixteen, she'd gotten pregnant and her parents had thrown her out of their house. She'd moved in with her boyfriend, a mechanic who was a few years older and living on his own. But when she lost the baby, their relationship deteriorated, and she eventually moved out. She was at the end of her rope, had no one to lean on, and fell back on the one thing she'd always been good at: theater.

She moved to LA with the dream of making it big in the movie business. She auditioned for parts and waitressed to make the rent. Slowly, she started earning roles—first in commercials, then as extras in sitcoms and TV dramas. And she fell in love with a man she shouldn't have—someone not in the film industry who didn't understand her dream.

Hunt flipped pages faster, reading with more interest, sensing without even asking that these were the pages that had been highlighted in the book at Foster's house. A child had resulted from that union—a little girl—and Vivienne had been overjoyed. But the relationship fizzled soon after because of what the actress called the girl's "special needs," and Vivienne soon found herself single, still struggling to make it in Hollywood, but now raising a daughter on her own and working three jobs to pay for child care, rent, and her acting classes.

Hunt wasn't sure how much of the story he was reading was true. A large portion was probably dramatized to sell books. But Vivienne Armstrong painted herself as the struggling, devoted single mother. According to the actress, her infant daughter had attachment issues. Vivienne couldn't leave her to work. She couldn't quit her jobs, or they'd starve. Social services convinced her the child needed specialists and medical intervention Vivienne couldn't afford. She took on yet another job but was fired when she repeatedly had to leave to deal with the girl's emotional outbursts with the sitter. And at the end of her rope, unable to take care of her daughter, and now struggling to take care of herself as well, Vivienne began to believe what the social workers repeatedly suggested, that perhaps the best care for her daughter could be found somewhere else. With a new family who could give her the stability and support she needed.

The next few paragraphs were vague but got the point across. Vivienne turned the girl over to a friend in her old hometown, one who promised to give her the attention she needed and raise her in a loving environment. Vivienne went back to Hollywood, but she was so heartbroken at yet another failure, she vowed to make a million dollars so she could hire all the people she'd need to help her bring her daughter home. Only when she finally reached her goal, when she did make it big in Hollywood and finally went back to retrieve her daughter, the girl was gone. The woman who'd taken her in had become ill and given her up for adoption. The last paragraph in the chapter claimed by the time

Vivienne learned the news, the caregiver was dead and her daughter had been lost in the system. And she'd spent years trying to find her only to come up empty.

Hunt stared at the page, the tingle at his nape shifting to a full-on vibration as he remembered a conversation he'd had with Kelsey's brother Alec years before.

"I'm all set."

From the corner of his eye, he was aware of Kelsey stepping into the room. She was doing something with her hair, running her fingers through it or fluffing it out, he wasn't sure which because he couldn't turn to look.

"Hunt? Are you all right?"

"Alec told me once that you changed your first name when the McClanes adopted you."

"I did," she said hesitantly. "A lot of adopted kids do. Why are you bringing that up?"

He looked up at her, standing feet from him, wearing a slim black dress with cap sleeves and a wrap bodice that accentuated her cleavage and the curves at her hips. Standing in the early light of evening with her blonde hair hanging in gentle waves past her shoulders, she looked angelic and gorgeous. Ready for a night out away from the nightmare of the last few days. Which she deserved. But she wasn't going to get it. And he felt like a complete ass for being the one who was about to destroy it.

He pushed to his feet and handed her the iPad. "Because I think it just became important."

Wary, she took the iPad and glanced from his face down to the screen. The second her wide eyes shot back up to his face, he knew he didn't even need to hear her say her birth name.

"I need to make a call." He stepped past her, gently brushing his hand over her shoulder in the process. "And you need to sit down and read that."

She didn't answer, just slowly sank onto the chair he'd vacated as she furiously scrolled back to the start of the chapter and began reading.

He watched her for a second to make sure she was okay. She would be, he knew. Not because she was made of steel or tough under pressure, but because she was a survivor. She might have trouble trusting others. She might keep her emotions closed off and tightly guarded. But he knew now why she did those things. Because she'd learned at an early age it was safer than being rejected. If she was that child he'd read about in Armstrong's book, if she'd had those attachment issues even from birth, it explained a whole lot more than he'd ever imagined. Even her relationship with Benedict made a sick sort of sense when he thought about it. For someone like her, who was scared to death to get close to anyone, he was a safe choice because she'd known from the start he'd never push her to let him in.

His heart beat hard and fast as he watched her, sitting in the chair reading. They were the same, really. Both alone, both wary of relationships, both scared of taking a chance on someone else. Only her reasons were so much stronger than his. After everything he now knew about her, after everything she'd survived, his just seemed . . . cowardly.

Especially when she was the one person he was starting to think might be worth risking everything for.

———

Kelsey swirled her wine and watched the red liquid stick to the sides of the glass as she sat at a table on the sparsely populated balcony of the bistro where she and Hunt had grabbed dinner in downtown Palm Springs. She knew she needed to snap out of the melancholy mood she'd slipped into after reading that chapter in Vivienne Armstrong's autobiography. But she just couldn't.

Was it possible? Could she really be the late actress's long-lost daughter?

Logic said no, but Kali-Shae was not a common name. And the backstory . . . the dates . . . they matched up.

Footsteps sounded close, then the chair across from her scraped the floor, and she glanced up to see Hunt sitting across from her. "That was the detective."

"Well?" She sat up straighter, her pulse ticking up at those four simple words. Hunt had left a message for the detective in charge of the investigation before they'd left the hotel, and the man had called back in the middle of their meal.

"You were right. That was the chapter that was highlighted."

Her stomach rolled, and she looked down at the food she'd ordered but barely touched.

"He also said they got a positive ID on fingerprints in the house. They're Foster's. The last time he was seen was four days ago at a gas station outside LA."

"Plenty of time for him to fly from LA to Portland to set that bomb."

"Yeah." A worried look passed over his features.

"What else?"

His jaw clenched, then he said, "The cops found an outbuilding on his property with some interesting contents. Several barrels of diesel fuel, a couple pallets of fertilizer bags, and wiring that could be used to build a bomb."

Her shoulders tensed.

"The cops also told me Foster has a reputation in this area for being a bit of a recluse who likes to complain about the evils of Corporate America, the media, and the US government."

"So he's a conspiracy theorist."

"Sounds like it."

All the scenarios she'd tried not to let invade her brain came crashing in. "So what are we hypothesizing here? That Armstrong was my mother? That this guy Foster was my father? That he set that bomb in

Portland because he knew I'd be there and he . . . what? Wanted to get back at Armstrong in some way for leaving him?"

"Let's not get ahead of ourselves." Hunt placed his hand over hers against her wineglass.

The heat of his touch was gentle and warm, and it calmed her just enough so she didn't freak out. "We both know that's the logical assumption."

"Maybe. But it doesn't make sense. Why go after you? You didn't know her. We don't even know if you're related to her. And if you really were the target, why set a bomb? There are a dozen easier ways to hurt someone that will draw way less attention."

"Unless he didn't want anyone to know I was the target. If I'd died in that bombing, it would have just looked like a random accident."

"Then why send the text message?"

"To scare me. To make me crazy." Exactly as she was right now. "And you just explained he's a nutjob. If he hates the media and Corporate America so much, setting off that bomb at a major television studio would hit two targets at one time."

"Maybe," he said, squeezing her hand. "But it's just as likely Foster is nothing more than a crazed fan. Until we know how you're connected to both Armstrong and Foster, it's not worth stressing over."

She wasn't sure about that. She couldn't shake the things she'd seen in that house and the fact her name—her birth name—was in that book.

Hunt released her hand, and even though she knew she couldn't lean on him as she wanted, part of her wished he'd hold her hand just a little while longer, the way he'd held her against him outside Foster's house. "The detective gave me the name of Armstrong's attorneys. I think we should try to set up a meeting. They should be able to either confirm or deny everything I know you're worrying about right now."

She nodded as he cut back into his steak, cold now because he'd had to leave to take that call. Her own meal was cold, but she didn't care.

She couldn't eat it. Lifting her wine, she swallowed what was left in her glass and signaled the waiter, knowing it wasn't smart to keep drinking but needing it at the same time to keep her sane.

Hunt eyed her warily as she thanked the waiter for refilling her glass and then took a large sip. Her brothers eyed her like that when they thought she was being reckless. She hated that look from them almost as much as she hated it from Hunt now. The only plus was that Hunt was smart enough to keep his opinion to himself.

He tried to change the topic and talked to her about the city and what they should do after dinner—get dessert, walk through the shops, or hit a few galleries. She nodded where appropriate but barely heard what he was saying. All she could focus on was that chapter she'd read in Armstrong's book.

"Even if Foster was nothing more than a crazed fan," she said when he paused long enough to finish his meal, "it doesn't change anything."

He swallowed his last bite, lowered his silverware to his plate, then used the napkin to wipe his mouth. Pushing his plate to the side, he said, "Okay, tell me why not."

"Because his being a crazed fan actually explains my situation. He transferred the grudge he had against her to me."

"Kels," he said softly, leaning his forearms against the table, "you don't know that she's your mother."

"Yes, I do." She looked back at her wine. "And you do too, even if you're not ready to admit it."

"The name and timing are similar, I'll give you that."

"It's more than that. The developmental delays she wrote about? The attachment issues? I had those, but they weren't from any sort of special-needs birth defect like she made it sound. They were a direct result of fetal alcohol syndrome. My mother drank when she was pregnant with me. I was a fussy baby and a difficult child who was developmentally and socially delayed for a long time. I went through three foster homes because I was so hard to manage, and the only reason I'm not an alcoholic myself as an adult is because the McClanes adopted me."

"And you think that proves she's your mother?"

She knew she sounded irrational, but she didn't care. "It goes one step further in proving it. Vivienne Armstrong died of a drug overdose. I've seen pictures of her online, and in every one she always had a drink in her hand. And don't tell me you don't see the similarities. People have told me for years that I look like her. You heard that production assistant at the studio say so just before that damn bomb went off."

He reached for her hand, but she snatched up her wine before he could touch her, not wanting his calming presence or strength right now. She wanted to wallow and rant and rage because life was being so goddamn unfair to her. Again.

"Don't do that."

She paused with the glass to her lips and swallowed the large sip in her mouth, looking across the stem at his eyes, realizing what she was doing.

Realizing exactly how similar she was to the actress.

Nausea swirled in her stomach as she lowered the glass to the table with a shaky hand, wishing she could get up and run out of this restaurant, wishing she could run away from her pathetic issues in the process.

"Don't do that either." He captured her fingers before she could pull her hand away, only this time his grip was fierce and insistent, and the edge in his voice matched the chill she'd seen moments before in his eyes. "Don't sit there looking like I'm scolding you because I'm not. I don't care if you have a drink or ten. I'm not your brothers, and I'm not your ex. When I said don't, I meant don't shut me out."

Wary, she lifted her gaze to his, but she didn't see lies in his deep-brown eyes, she saw truth. The same truth she always saw when she looked at him because Hunter O'Donnell was not the kind of man who lied.

"Did you ever look for your birth mother, Kels?"

She shook her head and stared down at his hand holding hers. "Why not?"

"Because I was never interested in finding her."

"Is that what's bothering you tonight? That you might now know when you never wanted to know before?"

She shook her head, fighting the irrational urge to cry.

"Then tell me what is," he said softer. "It's more than the possibility this actress could be your mother because God knows that's the least of our problems at the moment. Something else is bothering you. Something you're not telling me. I've watched you handle way worse than this." He shifted their hands until their fingers intertwined, and his thumb stroked a soft path of heat across her palm. "Tell me what that is, Kels. Tell me so I can help you."

Tears burned the backs of her eyes, tears that were both useless and familiar. Closing them quickly so he couldn't see, she breathed through her nose, hating that he was right, that this was getting to her in a way nothing had before. Hating even more that he was seeing it. She'd vowed to be tough in front of him ever since he'd seen her at her weakest with Julian.

"You can't help me," she managed.

"Let me be the judge of that."

She exhaled a breath that was half-huff, half-laugh because the comment was just so . . . male.

When he didn't let go of her hand, she sighed and opened her eyes to stare down at their joined hands. She knew she couldn't get out of this conversation now, and part of her didn't want to. She liked how he held her hand. Liked the way they fit together. Liked even more the way it felt to open up to him. Even just a little.

"You're right," she said. "It's not her. It's not even knowing she could be the reason I had so much trouble when I was younger. It's knowing the truth at all. All my life I've had this fantasy about my mother. It's stupid, really. All kids have it. The fantasy that you really weren't given up. That either your birth mom was forced to let you go or you were kidnapped or she thought you were dead. Alec and I used to talk about it, actually. Used to imagine what had happened to both of us. Except in his case, that actually came true, and in mine . . ."

"Except in yours," Hunt said softly, continuing to stroke her palm with his thumb, "what we found today proves that your fantasy can't be true."

She blinked back the useless tears. "Yeah. Stupid, isn't it?"

"No. It's real. There's more to the story than what's in that book. If she's your mother, I'm sure there's a lot more."

"Does it matter? The bottom line is she didn't want me."

"She wrote about wanting to find you after she hit it big."

"That's the point, Hunt. She wrote about it. But she didn't do it. That book was published five years ago. Oregon adoption laws were eased in 2014. If she really wanted to find me, she could have. The truth is she didn't want to find me. That was all BS for her book."

"You don't know that."

She tugged back from his hand and reached for her wine. "I do know that. She didn't want to find me, which means she didn't really care. And that's what's eating at me. Not that she could be some big actress. Not that she drank and left me with the repercussions that made my life hell when I was a kid. But that at the end of the day, she just didn't give a shit about me."

All her old inadequacies came racing back as she drained the last of the wine in her glass. *No one wants you. Your mother didn't even want you.* That was what the first text message had said, and it was true. No one but the McClanes had ever really wanted her. She'd thought that was enough in her life, but the older she got the more she realized it wasn't. It was why she dated men she wasn't initially interested in, why she chose the wrong kinds of men—like Julian. Why she'd gotten married when she hadn't even loved the jerk. Because somewhere inside her troubled mind she thought if she could make someone who didn't want her want her, then she'd finally be good enough. Only it hadn't happened with Julian, and she had a sickening feeling it wasn't ever going to happen with anyone else either.

She pushed back from the table, feeling worse than she had before, wishing this day—this whole fucking week—would just disappear. "Can we just go back to the hotel? I'm really tired."

"Yeah." He eased back in his chair and signaled the waiter.

The waiter scurried off to grab their bill, and in the silence, as she gripped her purse at her side, Kelsey stared at the tablecloth and wished she had more wine. Or that she'd just kept her mouth shut tonight.

"There's just one thing," Hunt said, breaking the silence.

She couldn't muster up the strength to look at him.

"Maybe you're right." He leaned his forearms on the table again. "Maybe she didn't come looking for you when she could have. But that doesn't mean she lied. It just means she was scared. The same way you've been scared to look for her. Those laws made it easier for adoptees to find their birth parents in 2014 as well."

The waiter set the bill next to his hand, and Hunt spoke quietly with the man as he reached back for his wallet, but Kelsey didn't listen to their conversation. She was too busy digesting what he'd said.

He was right, but not in the way he thought. She hadn't looked for her birth mother because she was scared. She purposely hadn't searched for her because she knew the truth might prove she really never would be enough.

And knowing that didn't just have the power to break her in a way nothing else ever had. It could destroy the shaky foundation on which she'd built her entire life.

CHAPTER THIRTEEN

Kelsey was silent on the walk back to the hotel.

Hunt knew she was dealing with a lot, so he didn't push her to talk. But he wanted her to. He'd liked the way she'd turned to him outside Foster's house and held on to him. He'd liked the way she'd opened up to him at dinner, even if it had caused her to shut down now. He wanted her to trust him again, to let him be what she needed, he just wasn't sure how to make that happen.

As they entered the suite, he closed the door at his back, tossed the keycard on the entry table, and watched her drop her purse on the couch. She moved to the fridge to grab a water bottle. Since they'd left the balcony door cracked, jazz music from the outdoor bar's band filtered into the room along with a cool breeze that rustled the gauzy curtains.

She tipped the water bottle back and took a long sip, the sexy line of her throat and the hourglass shape of her silhouette accentuated by the lights shining in through the windows. And not for the first time, he wondered how the hell Benedict could have ever laid a hand on her in anger.

She pushed the fridge door closed with her hip and turned for her room. "It's been a long day. I think I'm just going to go bed."

He knew he should let her go. He knew that was the safe choice. But tonight he didn't want to play things safe.

He stepped in her path, blocking her door. She drew up short and frowned. "What are you doing?"

"Something I probably shouldn't."

She sighed, but when he reached for her hand, she didn't pull away, and it was all the encouragement he needed. "I know you think I'm freaking out, but I'm not. I'm just tired. Really, I'm fine."

"I know you're fine. You always are. But that's not why I stopped you."

When she rolled her eyes, he lifted his hands to her cheeks, forcing her to look up at him. "You don't always have to face everything alone. It's okay to lean on someone else. It's okay to be vulnerable now and then."

Her whole body stilled, and as she stared up at him, her eyes grew damp. So damp something in his chest turned over. "I don't like being vulnerable. Especially in front of you."

"You shouldn't be. You have nothing to fear from me."

Her pretty brown eyes slid closed, and she made that sound again that was a huff and a laugh all rolled into one and so damn cute he ached to kiss her. "Easier said than done."

"Why?"

"Because you're . . . you. Because I saw the kind of women you like to hang out with. And because I've read all the fashion magazines. Women are supposed to be mysterious and intriguing in front of the men they're interested in, not weak an—"

Her lips snapped closed when she realized what she'd just said, and a blush stained her cheeks. A blush that heated Hunt's blood way more than her words ever could because it was a reaction she couldn't fake.

He brushed his thumb over her silky smooth cheek, awed by her strength and spirit all over again. "For the record, if that was the kind of woman I wanted to hang out with, I'd be with her. And call me crazy, but I'm pretty sure the authors of those articles in your fashion magazines are nothing more than twenty-year-old computer nerds who don't know a thing about what guys really want."

Her shoulders relaxed, and a reluctant smile toyed with the edge of her lips, urging him on. "And you are the least weak woman I've ever met. I don't know many people—male or female—who could survive what you have in your life. Not just survive but triumph over. And to me, you are mysterious as hell. I never know what you're thinking or what you're going to say next. You've more than kept me on my toes these last few days."

She snorted, but she still didn't open her eyes, and her lips quivered when she said, "That's because I'm borderline mental."

"No, you're not. You're smart, you're funny, you're beautiful and sexy. And when you open up to me like you did tonight, when you make yourself vulnerable, it's not a turnoff, Kels. It's a massive turn-*on*. Because it means you trust me enough to let me in."

Slowly, she opened her eyes and blinked up at him. And when her gaze met his, it was filled with so much tenderness, his heart felt like it flipped over beneath his ribs. A reaction that didn't just surprise him, it completely rocked his world.

"I do trust you," she whispered. "You're probably the only person besides my brothers I truly trus—"

He lowered his lips to hers. Couldn't stop himself. And when she opened and drew him into the soft, wet heat of her mouth, all the reasons he wasn't supposed to be kissing her faded from his mind.

She groaned. Wrapped her arms around his shoulders and lifted to her toes. Then pressed her body flush against his as she tipped her head and stroked his tongue with long, languid strokes. And the contact shot a shock wave of electricity through every cell in his body. One that lit him up and made him ache for more. For her hands on his bare skin, for her body laid out beneath his, for everything he'd almost had that night she'd come to him in his room.

That want was so strong, so insistent, so not what he'd planned when he'd stepped in her path tonight, it drew him back from her lips and everything he was seconds away from taking.

She breathed heavy against his chest as she dropped to her heels. But she didn't move back, didn't make any attempt to release him, just dug her fingertips into his sides and held on. And damn, she felt good. Too good. So fucking good she was about to shatter what little self-control he had left.

He swallowed hard. "I, uh, I like vulnerable. A lot. But I don't want to take advantage of it."

Her lips curled, and she shifted one hand from his ribs to his chest and laid her palm right over his heart. "You're not."

Holy hell. He closed his eyes and breathed deep, fighting for restraint. "I'm about to. Which is why you should probably go in your room and lock your door."

She tipped her head back and smiled up at him, still not making any move away. And the sexy look smoldering in her eyes was so damn hot, it lit him up like a firework. "It doesn't feel like you want me to go in my room alone."

No, he knew it didn't. His growing erection was already pressing into her belly.

"It feels like you want to go in there with me," she added.

Dear God, he did want that. He wanted it so much he was about to forget every single reason he'd stayed away from her all these years. But he was deathly afraid of screwing this up again. "I don't want you to feel pressured or regret trusting me."

She glanced down at his chest where her hand rested over his heart, and his pulse raced as he watched a nervous look creep into her eyes. "You were right when you said I don't let people in. I don't. But I'm trying to fix that. And I want to start with you. You're not pressuring me. And the only thing I may regret about this night is not taking a chance. But if you don't want that, then I—"

His resistance snapped. Just shattered under the crushing weight of his desire. He captured her words with his lips and kissed her. Mouthed, "I want you," against her lips again and again. And when she kissed him back just as frantically, he knew neither of them could stop what was about to happen.

He turned her toward her bedroom, continued to nip and lick and taste every part of her mouth as he stepped forward, forcing her back. Her fingers tightened against his sides, then released, and as they moved into her bedroom, her hands shifted to his chest and began working the buttons of his shirt free with swift movements.

God, she tasted good. She felt even better. He slid his hands to her shoulders, then down her sides and around her back, searching for a zipper or hook or something to free so he could get her out of this dress. "Kelsey."

"Yes." She drew back from his lips just long enough to unhook the last button of his shirt and tug the tails free of his pants. Then her lips were on his again, kissing him crazy as she swept her warm hands up his bare chest and pushed the shirt from his shoulders.

Just the simple skim of her fingertips over his skin was better than anything he'd imagined. He kissed her hard, then drew back a breath. "Don't stop touching me."

Her smile was so damn sexy, he smiled too. Lifting to her toes, she pressed her tempting lips to the corner of his mouth until he ached to taste her again, then dropped to her heels and leaned forward to trace the tip of her tongue around his left nipple. "I won't."

Sweet Jesus, if she kept that up, his brain was going to completely short-circuit. Sifting his fingers into her hair, he lifted her face back to his and dove into her mouth, kissing her deeply. She groaned, slid her hands down his stomach, and found the button on his waistband.

He forced her back a step until her legs hit the mattress. Kissed her deeper. Never wanted to stop kissing her. But he also wanted more. He wanted everything. His hands slid down her sides, over her hips, and grasped the fabric of her dress at her thighs. Drawing back from her swollen lips, he tugged straight up. "Lift your arms."

She flicked the button free on his pants and lifted her arms over her head. And in one swift move he stripped her of her dress and tossed it on the floor, then stared down at her gorgeous body wrapped in nothing but a sheer lace bra, low-riding lace panties that hugged her slim hips, and a pair of perfect fuck-me black heels.

Whatever blood was left in his head shot straight into his groin. Licking his lips, he palmed her right breast and rubbed the pad of his thumb across the smooth lace covering her taut nipple. "Is this from your collection?"

She dropped her head back when he moved his thumb across the straining tip again. Reached for his hips and whispered, "Yes."

"I like it." He brought his other hand up, palmed her left breast, and toyed with her neglected nipple. "I like it a lot." Tugging one cup aside, he lowered his mouth and breathed hot over her quivering skin. "But I like this more."

He traced his tongue around her nipple, loving the way she trembled and dug her fingernails into his sides. Then he drew her into his mouth and sucked. And the groan that erupted from her throat made him as hard as stone.

Wrapping his arms around her, he flicked the clasp on the back of her bra and tugged it from her body. She slid her fingers into his hair as he tormented one nipple with his tongue, then the other. With one arm supporting her around the waist, he lowered her to the mattress, then trailed his lips back up her throat to claim her mouth again in a hard, hot, incredibly wet kiss.

Breathless, he braced one hand on the mattress near her head and drew back to look down at her, just enough so he could see her eyes and make sure she was still with him.

She blinked several times. Her eyes shimmered. But in her gaze he saw nothing but lust. "Why did you stop?"

"Because I want to see you." He glanced down her body so he could take all of her in. The swell of her breasts made his mouth water, but the scrap of lace between her legs made him completely ravenous. Pushing back on hands, he slid down her body and lowered his knees to the floor. "Spread your legs. I want to see all of you."

She blushed but did as he said, making room for him between her thighs. And as he tugged on the sides of her panties, she pushed up on her elbows and bit her lip, watching him as he pulled the lace from her legs and took a long, slow perusal of every inch of her body.

"My God. You are absolutely stunning. Everything I envisioned and more."

She swallowed hard, watching him as he pressed a kiss to the inside of her knee and slowly worked his mouth higher. "How long have you been envisioning?"

He smiled. Kissed another spot. This one higher on her inner thigh. "Way too long."

Her muscles tensed, and her breath caught. "Recently?"

He moved his lips to her other thigh and nipped at her tender skin. "Absolutely."

"W-when?"

He was careful to keep his touch light and teasing, even though all he wanted to do was dive in and claim her. She licked her lips and rocked her hips forward, searching for contact, but he held back, not giving her what she craved. He wanted her trembling first. Wanted her so hot she was practically begging. "On the plane." He pressed his lips to the sensitive skin between her leg and hip. "In the car." When she groaned again, he moved closer to her mound. "All through dinner." He breathed hot over the sensitive flesh between her legs, growing light-headed from the scent of her arousal. "Only every damn time I've seen you over the last ten years."

"Oh God." Her eyes slid closed, and her head fell back. She rocked up against him again and slid her fingers into his hair, drawing his mouth right where she desperately wanted it. "Stop teasing me already, Hunt. I want you."

He growled and licked up her center, tasting her excitement and desire. Her arms went out from under her, and she fell back on the bed. He circled her clit while she planted her feet on the mattress and lifted to meet every stroke. And when he felt her getting close, he slid a finger deep inside her, licked faster, and drove her hard into an orgasm that tore a scream from her mouth.

She was still quivering when he pressed his lips to her thigh, her hip, when he worked his way up her body and finally found her mouth. She opened immediately and shoved his pants down his hips as he swept his tongue along hers. Her fingers fumbled with his trousers, helping him shuck them off. Rolling to his side, he tore his lips from hers just long enough to grab his wallet and kick his pants and boxers the rest of the way off.

Her hand wrapped around his erection. He jerked at the contact, then moaned as she stroked him and lifted her mouth back to his. Her small hand was like velvet wrapped around his shaft, so good he was afraid he might come if she kept that up. He pulled back from her mouth once more and glanced at the wallet in his hand, searching for a condom. "Hold on. Just a second."

She moved to her knees, stroked him again. He sucked in a breath at the wicked sensation. His fingers closed around the condom, and he yanked it out of his wallet. Then absolutely lost his fucking mind when he felt her lips close around his shaft.

"Oh fuck." He fell back in the pillows before he could stop himself. His eyes rolled back in his head. She sucked him deep, let him slip almost all the way out of her mouth, swirled her tongue around the head, then drew him deep all over again.

Blood pounded in his groin as she worked him over with her mouth. Her small hand stroked the base of his cock while her lips and tongue focused on the head. He felt his orgasm screaming toward him. Knew he could come in a matter of seconds. But he didn't want this to be over so soon. And when he came, he wanted to feel her come all around him at the same time.

His hands shook, but he managed to push himself up, to grasp her by the arms and draw her back. She gasped as he slid from her mouth and looked up him with lust-glazed eyes. Pulling her close for a quick kiss, he said, "I need to be inside you. Climb over me."

"Yes." She straddled his legs as he made quick work of the condom. "Hurry." As soon as he got it on, she wrapped her arms around his neck and kissed him hard.

She tasted like heaven. Felt like pure bliss. Grasping her at the hips, he pulled her toward him while she licked into his mouth. The tips of her breasts grazed his chest. Her slick core brushed the head of his cock. Electricity raced down his spine as he lined her up and tugged her down so he pressed inside her just a fraction of an inch.

He drew back from her mouth just enough so he could see her face. "Kelsey, look at me."

She eased back, lips swollen, eyes glazed, body trembling. But it was the trust he saw in her gaze that absolutely undid him.

"Take me." His fingers flexed against her hips. "I'm yours if you want me."

"I want you. I want all of you." She closed her lips over his and sucked his tongue into her mouth just as she lowered and drew his length deep in her body. And the taste of her was so wicked, the feel of her so hot and slick and tight, all he could do was groan against her lips and thrust hard to meet her.

Her hips pressed flush against his. She gasped and lifted, tightening as she rocked her hips, making him twitch and tremble with every stroke.

He wrapped one arm around her waist, holding her tighter. Drove deeper inside her. Grunted every time he bottomed out and her wet core squeezed all around him. He could feel her growing wetter, tighter. Knew she was close. Pulling his mouth from hers, he kissed the corner of her lips and whispered, "God, you feel good." He palmed her breast and gently pinched her nipple. "Ride me, Kelsey. Use me. I want to feel you come all around me."

She moaned and tore her mouth from his, breathing hard as she moved over him, faster with every thrust. "Oh yes, there." Her fingernails dug into his shoulders. Her hot breath brushed his lips. "Right there. Don't stop."

He couldn't. He was seconds away from detonating. "Do it." Holding her tight against him, he plunged deep again and again, his eyes locked on hers as he watched her spiral blindly toward her release. "Come for me, baby. And take me with you when you go."

Her climax slammed into her, stealing her breath with a gasp that echoed in his ears. And the second it did, the instant he felt her body quiver and quake all around him, he let go of the tension in his body and grunted through a shattering release that didn't just consume him, it flipped his entire world upside down until only two things were clear.

One, this wasn't wrong. In the middle of complete chaos, they'd found each other, and it was the most pure and honest thing he'd ever known.

And two, that scared the shit out of him because he finally had something he never wanted to let go. Something someone else seemed dead set on destroying.

CHAPTER FOURTEEN

The man definitely had some wicked talents.

A smile tugged at Kelsey's lips as she rolled toward the closed bathroom door and listened to the water running on the other side. She liked that Hunt was in there, using her shower. Liked that he'd stayed in her room all night. Liked even more what he'd done to her in this bed.

Her cheeks heated as she remembered how assertive she'd been last night. She'd never been like that with a man before, but then she'd never been with a man like Hunt either. It was easy to drop her guard and just be herself with him, especially when she'd seen how turned on he'd become when she'd taken charge and shown him what she liked.

The shower flipped off. Nerves rattled around in her belly as she tugged the sheet up to her breasts and shook back her hair, hoping it looked sexy and alluring on the pillow instead of the major bedhead it probably was. Since Hunt had slipped out of bed before she was awake, she didn't know what he was thinking now that morning had hit. She desperately didn't want him to regret any of last night, but she knew there was a chance that was possible. Especially since they'd clearly cut the sexual tension between them and the wine from last night's dinner had worn off.

Oh man. I really hope that wasn't because of the wine . . .

The bathroom door quietly opened, and Hunt stepped into the bedroom with a white towel hooked low at his hips and another in his hand as he rubbed his hair.

"Hey," she said, pushing herself higher in the pillows while trying not to look at that low-riding towel that accentuated the dark line of hair on his belly and did crazy things to her blood.

"Hey. You're up. I hope I didn't wake you."

"You didn't." She fixed a smile on her face, hoping she looked calm and casual. That's how she needed to play this regardless of what he was thinking this morning.

"Good. I contacted Armstrong's attorneys last night. They left me a voice mail this morning and said they could see us at two. I was going to let you sleep a little longer, then thought we could get breakfast and drive into LA."

Real life. She didn't want to think about real life just yet, but there was no avoiding it. "Yeah, that sounds fine."

"Good." He tossed the hand towel onto a small chair in the corner and eyed her carefully.

An awkward silence filled the room, one she didn't like. She glanced down at her hands, trying to think of something mature to say.

He moved toward the bed, and those nerves went haywire in her belly. She still didn't know what he was thinking, but instead of grabbing his clothes from the floor or telling her he needed to go get dressed as she half expected him to do, he placed a knee on the mattress, angled diagonally toward her, then stretched out on his stomach and reached for her hand. "I had a good time last night."

The relief suddenly swirling inside her was sweeter than any summer wine. "So did I."

Pushing up on his elbows, he closed both hands around hers and played with her fingers, looking sexy and adorable and just the slightest bit nervous. And, *oh boy*, she *really* liked that he was nervous. "Not what I expected, of course."

Her heart skipped a beat. Had she been *too* aggressive? She was completely clueless when it came to what guys liked. "I, um, hope I didn't force you to do anything you didn't want to do."

He laughed and glanced up at her, and his smile made him so devastatingly handsome, she caught her breath. "That's not what I meant. No, I definitely liked *that*. Loved it, actually, and absolutely want more."

Oh, thank God.

He glanced down at their joined hands again. "I meant this. You and me. I think it's safe to say I've stayed away from you on purpose because . . ."

When he didn't seem to want to go on, she mustered her courage and said what he was thinking. "Because it complicates things."

"Yeah." He looked up at her. "It does, big-time."

That little burst of happiness deflated like a balloon losing air. She loved what he'd said, loved the way he was touching her, but she hated what he was about to say next.

"Your brother. My best friend. Your other brothers. Your parents."

Yep. There it was. He was already listing off all the reasons this couldn't happen again. She'd been silly to think last night was a good idea.

"But here's the thing." He brushed his thumb over her knuckles. "I don't really give a shit what your parents or brothers or even Alec think about this."

She blinked, sure she had to have heard him wrong. "What did you say?"

One corner of his lips tipped up in the sexiest smirk. "I said, I don't care what they think. And I don't want you to either. I know this complicates things with your family in a million different ways, and it's probably gonna tick Alec off royally, but neither of us planned it. And this morning when I was in the shower, I was just thinking, you know, who cares if we planned it or not? This isn't about them or anyone else. It's about you and me. And now that it's happened, I wanna do it again."

"You do?"

"Yeah." He tightened his hold on her hand. "I do. What about you?"

Every nerve ending in her body tingled with excitement. "I do too." Smiling, she pushed up from the pillow and leaned toward his lips. "I definitely do."

He met her kiss, opened, and drew her into his mouth as he shifted to his side, wrapped an arm around her, and pulled her flush against him. Deepening the kiss, she pushed him to his back and straddled his hips, part of her unable to believe that last night—that this morning—had actually happened.

Drawing back from her mouth, he laid his head on the pillow and looked up at her. "There is one thing I'm a little worried about, though."

"What?" Her gaze drifted from his lips to his scruffy jaw, then down the line of his throat to his sexy chest. God, the man was built. And right now he was laid out before her like an offering.

He brushed the hair back from her face, drawing her eyes back to his. "Your divorce was just finalized."

She blinked down at him, unsure where this was going. "And?"

"And . . . I told you last night I've had a thing for you for ten years. I don't want to ruin it before it even starts because my timing suc—"

She kissed him. Dove right in and kissed him hard. And when he drew in a surprised breath, she swept her tongue into his mouth and tasted him, wanting him even more than she had last night.

His hands fisted in her hair, holding her close so he could take charge of the kiss. And beneath his towel, his erection lengthened and pressed against her low belly, telling her he wanted her the same way she wanted him.

When she was breathless, when she knew he was too, she drew back just enough so he could see her eyes. "You have nothing to worry about."

"No?"

She loved the hopeful sound of his voice. "Not at all. Julian and I have been separated for eight months, but I was over him years ago. The truth is, I never should have married him."

His gaze dropped to her hair falling across his chest. "That's good."

She sensed there was something more. Eyeing him carefully, she said, "What else?"

"Why do you think there's something else?"

"Because I've spent ten years watching you too. You're not the only one with creepy stalker tendencies."

He laughed, and the sound was so light it released a little of the pressure building in her chest. "I will remember that."

"So tell me."

His smile faded, and his expression grew serious. "I'm . . . not great with relationships. I avoid them, to be honest. Women have told me in the past that I'm bullheaded, emotionally closed off, and noncommittal, all of which is true. And a big part of the reason I've stayed away from you. I just . . ." He glanced back down at her hair and toyed with a wayward strand. "I don't want to avoid you anymore. I don't think I can. But I definitely don't want to screw this up either."

His words touched her in a way nothing else ever could. Not just because he'd said them, but because he meant them. Her ex certainly hadn't ever cared about their relationship like this.

"Hunter." She stretched out on top of him so they were eye level. "Look at me."

His gaze drifted to hers, and in his dark irises she saw heat and nerves and hunger. All the same damn things she felt. And that one look supercharged her blood and told her no matter what, this—them—was absolutely not a mistake she would ever regret.

Sliding down his body, she pressed her lips to his chest, then moved lower, skimming hot, wet kisses the length of his abs to the top of his towel. "Unless you plan on stopping me right now, there's not a whole lot you can screw up at the moment."

Relief filled his eyes, but it quickly heated and darkened, intensifying all that hunger she'd seen earlier in his gaze. "I think I like the sound of that."

She knew he would. Reaching for the knot at his hip, she planned to make sure he liked it a whole lot more than he had last night.

———

All those nerves Hunt had fought through the night had completely dissolved when Kelsey had climbed over him this morning and rocked his world. And it wasn't because of the sex—though that had been soul-shatteringly amazing. It was because they were finally on the same page. Both ready to see where this thing growing between them went.

He glanced sideways at her as they stepped into the elevator at the trendy Beverly Hills law offices and Kelsey pushed the button for the top floor. Unlike him, she *was* nervous today. He could tell by the way she repeatedly fiddled with the hem of her blouse and smoothed her hand down the hip of her slacks. But he was confident these nerves had nothing to do with him, and he was also sure—especially after last night—that he was the only person who could calm her.

As soon as the doors slid closed, he reached for her hand at her hip and pulled her toward him.

Surprise drew her brows together as she glanced down where he held her then up at his face. "What are you—?"

He closed his mouth over hers and pushed her up against the back wall of the elevator. She sucked in one surprised breath and tensed, but the second he dipped into her mouth and stroked her tongue, she sank into him with a groan and slid her arms around his waist.

God, he loved the way she tasted. Adored the way she melted under his touch. And couldn't stop himself from feeling more than a little victorious when the tension and stress released from her muscles, all because of him.

When she was breathless—when he was nearly ready to hit the "Stop" button and completely distract both of them—he drew back and gazed down at her. She blinked her sweet brown eyes up at him before pursing her lips and reaching to wipe the lipstick from his mouth. "Point taken, Mr. O'Donnell."

He grinned, loving that she knew exactly what he'd been doing. "It's just a meeting." He pressed his lips to the tip of her nose, then stepped back so she could smooth out her shirt again. "Nothing bad is going to happen."

She smirked his way, then focused on the silver doors. "Famous last words."

"Kels—"

"I'm fine." She shook back her hair. "Really, I am. But I'm glad you're here with me." Drawing a deep breath, she added, "Promise not to get too far away, just in case."

Something in his chest turned over as he watched her, shoulders back, spine straight, eyes focused and intense. Something he wasn't prepared for.

He knew she saw herself as weak, but she wasn't. Not just because of all she'd been through in her life and survived, as he'd told her last night, but because she hadn't let any of it jade her. She'd been rejected numerous times. She'd failed more than she'd succeeded. And right now, some unknown person wanted to hurt her, and they still didn't know who that was or if that person was even a threat anymore. But she hadn't been hardened by any of it. She hadn't closed herself off emotionally, as he had for years. And she wasn't letting the past dictate her future, as he still did every damn day. She was taking chances, moving forward, living life by her rules and no one else's . . . the way he should be.

"Kelsey." His fingertips skimmed hers.

She glanced up at him with the prettiest brown eyes he'd ever seen. "Yeah?"

Words lodged in his throat. Words he wasn't ready to say but couldn't keep from forming in his mind.

He wasn't just attracted to her. He was falling in love with her. Had probably been halfway in love with her for a really long time, only he'd been too stupid to see it. And he didn't know what the hell to do with that information because his lungs suddenly weren't working and it felt as if a thousand daggers were piercing his chest from every side.

The elevator dinged, and the doors slid open. Kelsey's head swiveled toward the lobby of the law offices, and she squared her shoulders as she released his hand. "Go-time. Come on. Let's get this over with."

His head felt as if it were floating in a fog as he watched her step off the elevator and cross the immaculate lobby toward the high, sleek counter on the far side. A receptionist, seated in front of a waterfall held back by a wall of glass etched with the words Lange, Hanson & Associates, looked up and smiled.

Hunt's heart raced as he stepped off the elevator and Kelsey quietly spoke to the receptionist. He couldn't hear what they were saying. All he could hear was the rapid pounding of his pulse and that little voice in the back of his head that was screaming he was playing with fire. Liking her and loving her were two very different things. Liking her was safe. Loving her made him vulnerable. It also made her a weakness he could never completely keep safe.

He swallowed hard as he stilled in the middle of the lobby and shoved his hands into the pockets of his jeans. Yeah, security was his business, and yes, he was confident he could protect her from whoever was harassing her, but he hadn't been able to stop what had happened to his mom. His dad hadn't been able to stop it. No one could. No matter what he did, he couldn't protect Kelsey from everyday dangers, and there were a shit-ton of them in today's world. Which meant, at some point, he was going to lose her, regardless of what he did and how much he loved her. And he already knew that would gut him. Knew because just the thought of it was already burning a hole right in the center of his chest. He just didn't know if he'd be able to survive it a year, five years, or even twenty years down the line if let himself fall all the way in love with her the way he wanted.

"Yes," Kelsey said to the receptionist. "Two o'clock."

Footsteps sounded close, and Hunt blinked, focusing on Kelsey's silky blonde hair and her gorgeous face drawing near.

"It'll just be a few minutes," Kelsey said to him. "He's in a meeting right now." A frown pulled at her lips as she shot a glance over her shoulder, then looked back at his face. "The secretary eyed me like I had a giant wart on the end of my nose. I don't have something on my face, do I?"

Emotions closed his throat. Unable to speak, unconcerned with who could see, he wrapped both arms around her shoulders, pulled her up against him, and lowered his mouth to hers.

She tensed, then relaxed as she always did when he kissed her, and he drank it in. Drank her in. Kissed her with everything he had in him, never wanting to let her go, scared to death at the same time because he suddenly didn't trust himself. He wanted this. He wanted her. But he was suddenly terrified if he didn't let her go soon, if he pushed this relationship further and something bad happened to spook him, it might cause him pull back completely. And that wouldn't just hurt her, it would amplify all the rejection he already knew she struggled with and shake the foundation on which she stood.

When he finally drew back from her mouth, she blinked up at him with soft, sweet, trusting eyes that only made that lump in his throat grow even bigger. God, he didn't want to hurt her. He'd hate himself forever if he hurt her.

"What was that for?" she whispered.

He didn't have an answer. Couldn't make his lips form one. All he wanted to do was kiss her again and hold on tight until he was forced to let go.

"Hunt?" Kelsey's brows drew together. "Are you all right?" Drawing her hand from his waist, she pressed her palm against his forehead. "You look pale. Are you sick?"

He closed his eyes, soaking in the heat of her hand against his head. *No, I'm not sick.* He breathed deep, fighting to slow his pulse. *I'm head over heels in love with you, and I don't have a fucking clue what to do now.*

"Ms. McClane?"

A male voice rang out to his left. At his front, Kelsey dropped her hand from his forehead and said, "Yes?"

"My God."

Footsteps echoed across the floor, then stopped. And as a heartbeat and another passed in silence, Hunt forced his eyes open and blinked, searching for the person who'd pulled Kelsey's attention away from him.

A sixtysomething man with thinning gray hair and a pudgy build stared at Kelsey with wide eyes. "I can't believe it. The similarity is completely uncanny."

Kelsey shot Hunt a nervous look, one that snapped his attention away from his turbulent emotions and back to the reason they were here. Straightening, he cleared his throat, hoping it would snap the suit out of whatever trance he seemed to have fallen into.

The man gave his head a quick shake and held out his hand. "I'm sorry. I've completely forgotten my manners. I'm Charles Lange. It's good to meet you."

"Thanks. I'm Kelsey McClane. This is Hunter O'Donnell. I think he spoke with your assistant on the phone earlier."

"Yes, of course." Charles Lange shook Hunt's hand, then held his arm out, indicating the open office door. "Please, this way." As Kelsey and Hunt moved in that direction, Lange said to his secretary, "Hold all calls for the next two hours. We're not to be disturbed unless it's you-know-who. And send David in right away."

"Yes, sir, Mr. Lange."

Hunt followed Kelsey into the office, but he didn't miss the nervous look she shot his way, and all those emotions tightened in his chest with the urge to close his hand around hers and reassure her everything would be okay.

He resisted, though. Not because he wasn't desperate to touch her, but because he didn't totally trust himself at the moment. His emotions were dangerously close to the surface, and he wasn't sure what might set him off. As much as he ached to hold on to any part of her he could reach, he didn't want to trip back into that fog and do something stupid that would embarrass her in front of these lawyers, like grab her and kiss her and never let go.

So he settled for placing a hand at the small of her back as she moved through the doorway in front of him. Then wished like hell they were alone so he could strip off her slim-fitting slacks, toss her up on that desk, and devour her with his mouth until the taste of her consumed his mind and shoved aside all that shit still swirling in his head.

Lange closed the office door at his back and motioned toward a sitting area to the left where two couches were separated by a low coffee table. "Please, have a seat. Can I get you anything to drink?"

Hunt shook his head and lowered himself to the couch that faced a wall of windows and the view of LA's high-rises in the distance. Sitting next to him, Kelsey said, "No, thanks. We're fine."

With a sigh, Lange sat across from them, unbuttoning his suit jacket in the process. Perching one Armani shoe on his opposite knee, he leaned back in his seat and smiled with a shake of his head. "It really is amazing. When my secretary, Melanie, told me you wanted to meet today, I thought this was another dead end. I looked you up online, Ms. McClane. Your picture doesn't do you justice."

Kelsey's back tightened. It was a subtle move, but now that Hunt's brain was working again, he caught it. "Thank you," she said, clearly not knowing how to take that comment.

"Terrible incident up in Portland. The news reports said you were caught in that blast. How are you feeling?"

Kelsey shot Hunt a nervous look before refocusing on Lange. "Fine. A little sore, but it could have been much worse. I consider myself lucky."

"As you should."

"We both were."

This time, when Kelsey looked at Hunt, Lange noticed. He shifted his gaze to Hunt. "You were there as well?"

"Yeah. Long story." And one he didn't particularly want to get into right now.

Questions lurked in Lange's eyes, but Hunt sidestepped them by saying, "We appreciate you seeing us today. We're actually here because we're investigating whether there was any link between your client, Vivienne Armstrong, and a man named Graham Fost—"

A door on the far side of the office opened, and a tall man in his late fifties with jet-black hair graying at the temples stepped into the room with a file folder in his hand. "I'm sorry to keep you all waiting. I—"

He stopped in his tracks when Kelsey glanced his direction. "My God."

Lange chuckled and shot to his feet. "I'm not the only one bowled over by the resemblance. Ms. McClane, Mr. O'Donnell, this is my associate, David Hanson."

Kelsey and Hunt both pushed to their feet and shook the man's hand as he drew close. When he only continued to stare the way Lange had, Kelsey looked back at Hunt and rolled her eyes. And that one simple action eased some of the tension inside Hunt. At least enough so he could reach for her hand and not feel like he was about to lose his shit.

Hanson sat next to Lange on the couch across from them and flipped the file folder open on the table. "My apologies. I saw your picture online earlier; it's just way more obvious in person."

Lange propped his foot on his knee again, leaning back with a grin as wide as the cat that swallowed the canary. "Incredible, isn't it? We almost don't need to know her background to call the lab."

"The lab?" Kelsey blinked.

"Routine, my dear." Lange waved his hand. "We've had a number of women claiming to be Vivienne's long-lost daughter ever since her memoir was published. After her death, you can only imagine how many opportunists came out of the woodwork, seeking fame and fortune."

"I'm not seeking fame and fortune, trust me. I'm just here to get some information."

"Which makes you all the more intriguing to us," Hanson said. "You're already quite successful with your design business."

Kelsey glanced Hunt's way. They'd done their research.

Lange dropped his foot to the floor. "Why don't you start at the beginning and tell us how you wound up here today?"

Starting at the beginning seemed logical, so Hunt explained how their investigation into Kelsey's cell phone messages had brought them to California, looking for Graham Foster.

For their parts, Lange and Hanson didn't say much, just listened intently as he and Kelsey relayed the story. At one point, Lange pushed to his feet and brought a pen and pad of legal paper back to his seat where he jotted notes as they spoke, but aside from nodding, neither interrupted, and neither asked any questions. Not until Hunt said, "And that brought us here."

"Forgive me if this is an insensitive question considering the circumstances." Hanson removed his glasses and rubbed at the bridge of his nose before sliding them back on. "Have you seen a photograph of Mr. Foster, Ms. McClane?"

"Yes. The police showed me one when they were questioning me."

"And did you recognize him?"

"Not at all. I've never met him."

"The cops put out an APB on him," Hunt said, "but as of this morning they still have no lead on his whereabouts."

Lange made another note. "We'll call over and see what we can find out." He looked up at Kelsey. "The online bio you published for your business says you were adopted."

"I was."

"Tell us about that. How old were you? And do you have any memory of your birth mother?"

Kelsey glanced once at Hunt. Knowing she was nervous, he squeezed her hand, but he knew she didn't really need it. She was solid steel whether she believed it or not.

"There's not much to tell, I'm afraid. I don't remember my birth mother at all. I wasn't even two when I was placed in foster care. From what my parents told me—the McClanes," she clarified when the attorney began jotting notes again, "that was somewhere in southern Oregon. Klamath Falls, I believe. I was relocated several times. By the time I was eight I'd already been with three different families, and I was living in Ashland. But I was about to be moved to a new family."

"And why was that?" Hanson asked.

"Because I was termed difficult. I don't think anyone really knew the reason at the time. I was small for my age, but I was also socially behind other kids my age. I had trouble expressing myself. When I'd get mad, I'd have emotional outbursts and trouble controlling my reactions. I also didn't always understand cause and effect, which made it hard for me to assimilate into my foster families."

"But you were eventually adopted," Lange said. "By the McClanes. How did that come about?"

Kelsey shifted next to Hunt, clearly uncomfortable but not about to back down. "The year I was eight was the year Oregon had that really wet spring. You might remember it from the news. Rivers in the southern part of the state were all above flood stage because of the unrelenting rain, and there was so much damage that the governor finally declared the area a state of emergency. Hannah McClane, my mother, is an ER doctor in Portland. She volunteered to help during the disaster relief. The house I was living in at the time was within the evacuation zone, and my foster family was relocated to a shelter. Hannah was at the shelter, providing medical aid, while we were there. I didn't realize it at the time, but my caseworker was there one day, arguing with my foster mother because they didn't want to keep me anymore, and Hannah overheard them. She came over, sat next to me, and talked to me for a while, then she went and spoke with both of them. It all kind of happened really fast. The next thing I knew, I was going home with Hannah and Michael McClane."

"A little unorthodox," Lange said.

"Very." Kelsey smirked. "But the McClanes are like that. I have three older brothers, all adopted when they were twelve or thirteen years old, and a younger brother, also adopted, who's still in high school. We've each come from some rough and troubled backgrounds, but the McClanes gave us a chance for a permanent home and a real family, and I don't know, somehow it worked. Shouldn't have." She smiled. "But it did."

"Sounds like a movie script." Hanson shot Lange a mischievous look, then glanced back at Kelsey.

"Maybe." Her expression grew serious once more. "But it wasn't all unicorns and rainbows by any means. It was a lot of work. I was lucky. My parents are also both medical doctors. It's because of them I'm where I am now. I've never been officially diagnosed because no one examined me after I was born, but both of my parents suspect my delays are linked to mild fetal alcohol syndrome, or, since I didn't have the facial abnormalities FAS kids have, ARND—Alcohol-Related Neurodevelopmental Disorder. Whatever you want to call it, my struggles were related to my birth mother's prenatal drinking. And had the McClanes not adopted me, put me in therapy, and gotten me the help I needed, I'd probably be living on the streets and struggling to hold down a job today."

A somber look passed over Lange's face. "I'm going to guess for that reason, you never tried to look for your birth mother."

"Your guess would be right. I don't expect either of you to believe this, but I'm not here for publicity or fame or money. I don't care about any of those things. I'm only here because I'm trying to figure out who Graham Foster is and how he's connected to me. That's it."

Silence settled over the room. The two attorneys glanced at each other and conversed in that nonspeaking way attorneys do. Long seconds later, Lange finally sighed and tossed his notepad on the table in front of him. "Graham Foster was Vivienne's high school sweetheart. He was a few years older than her. They dated on and off for about three years when she was a teenager in Klamath Falls and lived together for roughly six months after she graduated from high school."

Kelsey's face paled. "Are you sure it was Foster? His name wasn't in her memoir."

"No, it wasn't," Hanson said. "And I'm sure. She kept his name out of the book intentionally. The split wasn't amicable. Foster wasn't happy when she left for Hollywood. Told her she'd never make it as an actress. I think part of her hated him for that. At the same time, it motivated her to prove him wrong. Sadly, he never forgave her for that."

"Foster had a pattern of harassing her," Lange continued. "He moved to the LA area just after she hit it big in film and tried to force a reconciliation. Vivienne wasn't interested at that point. Foster didn't listen, and over the years Vivienne filed multiple restraining orders against him in the hopes he would leave her alone. According to him, they were meant to be together. He was never violent, but he was mentally unstable, and twice he was admitted for psychiatric evaluation. The last five or so years of Vivienne's life, Foster was mostly quiet. A letter now and then, but he didn't try to see her."

Kelsey reached for Hunt's hand on the sofa between them and squeezed tight. "She wrote in the book that the child she'd been trying to locate for so long was from a different relationship. Was that true? Or a lie?"

"No, it was true," Lange answered.

Kelsey released her tight grip on Hunt's hand.

"Vivienne's daughter was born about three years after she moved to LA." Lange went on. "Vivienne had a brief relationship with a man who moved into her apartment complex for a short time when he separated from his wife. It didn't last long, and as far as we know, he was out of Vivienne's life rather quickly. But Graham Foster was most definitely not her daughter's father."

Kelsey exhaled and glanced at Hunt with half grin. And though he wanted to share her relief, he couldn't. Not quite yet.

Focusing on the attorneys, he said, "What about Armstrong's death? I remember seeing tabloid articles claiming it wasn't really an overdose."

Both attorneys stiffened. It was the first time Hunt had seen them flinch all day. Even when they'd seen Kelsey for the first time, they hadn't seemed uncomfortable, but they definitely were now.

Hanson adjusted his glasses, then looked across the table. "What we speak of in this room goes no further, agreed?"

Hunt and Kelsey exchanged glances, then nodded toward the attorneys.

Hanson drew in a breath. "I believe—"

"We believe," Lange interrupted, shooting a look at his colleague.

"We believe," Hanson corrected with a nod, "that Vivienne was murdered. We haven't been able to prove that yet, but we've hired a private investigator to look into the matter. For the last six months, since Vivienne's death, he's been gathering information."

"It's no secret that Vivienne struggled with alcohol." Lange leaned forward to rest his elbows on his knees. "Her addiction was well documented in the media. She liked her wine, and she liked to flaunt the image of herself enjoying her wine. Vivienne was 'old-school Hollywood.' We often joked she should have been working in the thirties and forties instead of today. But she was never a fan of hard alcohol, and she never did recreational drugs."

Hanson shifted in his seat. "When she was found dead by her housekeeper, we were immediately suspicious. The official autopsy report said they found a cocktail of painkillers and sleeping pills in her system. But none of those fit with what we knew of Vivienne. After all the years we'd worked together, not just on her film deals but on her personal deals, neither of us could reconcile what we knew of Vivienne with the media's story of an accidental overdose. Just didn't fit."

Hunt glanced between the two men. "You have a theory about who killed her, obviously. Otherwise you wouldn't be hiring a PI to dig."

The men exchanged glances again, then Lange said, "We do. Our money has always been on Foster. The fact he grew quiet the last few years concerned us. It was out of character for him."

Hanson sighed and leaned back in his chair. "Only a few people know this. Vivienne kept it tightly under wraps. But she married Foster in a civil ceremony right after she graduated from high school. She was only seventeen at the time and lied about her age. We weren't even aware of the marriage until after her death when Foster petitioned the courts for fifty percent of her estate. California's a community property state, and they were never legally separated or divorced. It's caused all kinds of red tape, as you can imagine. Her assets are technically in limbo until the courts rule on the legality of that marriage."

A tingle rushed down Hunt's spine. That gave Foster motive.

"Foster is unstable," Hanson said, glancing Kelsey's way. "He has been for a long time. We're confident the courts are not going to rule in his favor, but we want you to be aware of everything going in. I know it's not much help, but if what you told us is true, that Vivienne's memoir was found in his place not far from pictures of you, then I would suspect he already believes you're Vivienne's daughter, and he's not happy you're alive."

Kelsey stiffened, and this time Hunt didn't even hesitate to reach for her hand. He closed his fingers possessively around hers and held on tight when he said, "He won't get to her. Do either of you have any idea where he might go?"

"No." Hanson blew out a breath. "The only person who might know—and it would be a stretch—is his son."

"He has a son?" Kelsey asked.

Hanson nodded. "He's a few years older than you. From a previous relationship. He works for a tech company in San Francisco. He and his father had a tense relationship most of his life, but whenever we had problems with Foster harassing Vivienne, he was always willing to help us get him reined in. For all his faults, Vivienne never wanted Foster arrested. She just wanted him to leave her alone."

Hunt glanced toward Kelsey. "I think we need to talk to him."

She nodded in agreement.

Hunt looked back at the attorneys. "What about the man Vivienne wrote about in her memoir? Her child's father? Do either of you know where he is?"

Lange shook his head. "She never told us who he was."

"Is there anyone who might know his name?"

Kelsey shot a look his way, and he didn't miss the *what the heck are you doing?* warning in her eyes.

Hanson brushed his thumb over his lips, considering. "The only person who might know is her best friend. Catarina Brunelli."

"The actress?" Hunt asked.

Hanson nodded. "Vivienne and Cat broke into the industry at the same time. They had a lifelong friendship."

"I thought I read somewhere they couldn't stand each other," Kelsey interrupted.

Hanson dropped his hand. "Oh, they had their ups and downs, but any quarrels they had over the years were usually about roles. They were often up for the same parts, which, sadly, become harder to come by for women as they age in this industry." He looked toward Hunt. "I can have my secretary give her a call if you'd like, see if she'll meet with you both this afternoon? I'm sure she'd be more than happy to talk to you."

"Yeah, I think we'd like that." When he caught Kelsey's confused look again from the corner of his eye, he quietly said, "She might be able to give us information they can't."

She didn't seem thrilled by that idea, but she didn't argue.

Lange jotted a name and number on a piece of paper, ripped it off, and handed it across the table to Hunt. "This is Trey Foster's number." Looking at Kelsey again, he said, "The good news is you're safe now."

That was the good news. Hunt tucked the paper in his pocket. But for how long? That second text Kelsey had received proved Foster wasn't ready to give up his need for revenge just yet. And until he knew more he wouldn't be able to relax.

"Mr. Lange?" The intercom on Lange's desk rang out with his secretary's voice. "I'm sorry to bother you, but the lab is here."

"Wonderful." Lange rose and crossed to his desk where he pushed a button and said, "Send them in." He looked Kelsey's way as she stood. "After we read your bio, we called the lab to come over and take a DNA sample. It's highly routine, I assure you. Just a swab of your cheek and possibly a blood sample."

A nervous look passed over her face. "Are you saying—?"

"That it's highly likely? Yes. Everything you've told us today coincides with what we know about Vivienne's daughter, right down to dates and locations."

Hunt moved up beside her and placed a hand at the small of her back, just in case. She eased a half step closer to him.

"Vivienne's estate is quite large." Hanson moved up on Lange's left as the double doors opened and two lab techs entered the room carrying trays of medical instruments. "We've been looking for you since she died."

"But I . . ." Kelsey swallowed hard. "We don't know yet that I'm her daughter."

"Not yet." Lange grinned. "But we will soon. Lab results take about two to three days. If they come back the way we expect, your entire life is going to change. For the better."

"Oh, I really don't care about finding out if I'm—"

"It's really all routine," Hanson said, pushing her gently toward the lab techs at the table. "I promise."

The waver to Kelsey's voice pushed Hunt into protective mode. "Do we really have to do this today? She's already been through a lot recently, and—"

"The sooner we know the truth, the better it'll be for everyone," Lange cut in, positioning himself between Hunt and Kelsey so Hunt couldn't get in the way of the test. "There are legality issues that need to be resolved for the estate. Trust me." He patted Hunt's arm in a way that did nothing to ease Hunt's stress. "It'll be better all around once we have the results."

Hunt wasn't so sure. And the wary look Kelsey shot him tightened his chest, but not for the reasons she thought. Not because he was afraid her world was going to change for good or bad, but because he knew in that moment he'd do whatever it took to protect her from being hurt. From a long-dead mother, from her unhinged ex, from a crazed stalker even, if that's what this turned out to be.

He'd even do whatever it took to protect her from himself.

CHAPTER FIFTEEN

Kelsey stared at a gigantic framed painting of a Tuscan vineyard that engulfed one entire wall in Catarina Brunelli's living room as she and Hunt waited for the actress to join them. Kelsey wasn't entirely sure how she'd ended up in the palatial Beverly Hills mansion, but she was eager for Hunt to ask whatever questions he wanted answered so they could get the heck out of here.

A low whistle echoed from the other side of the room, where Hunt stood with his hands in his pockets, examining yet another elaborate painting that had to cost a fortune. "Looks like she's quite a collector."

The maid had let them in, then left them alone in this room with its white furniture with gold accents. They'd been waiting for at least fifteen minutes, and Kelsey's patience was starting to dwindle. Sighing, she turned his way, feeling more uncomfortable by the minute.

He glanced her way, concern darkening his eyes, then moved across the room toward her. "Hey. You okay?"

"Not really. Why are we here again?"

He drew his hands from his pockets and reached for her arms, rubbing her tense muscles. "A hunch."

When she tipped her head and frowned, he smiled. "She knew Vivienne personally. In a way her attorneys didn't. She might be able to give us more insight into Vivienne's relationship with Foster."

"Except Vivienne didn't know Catarina when she was with Foster."

"All the more reason to find out what she said about Foster over the years." His expression darkened further. "And find out who the other guy was."

Her back stiffened. There it was. The whole reason he'd brought them here. "I don't care who he is."

"Are you sure?"

"Yes, I'm sure." She shrugged out of his grip, not wanting to be touched right now. "He's not involved in any of this, and I have zero interest in finding him."

"Kels—"

She moved her hand when he reached for her, knowing she was probably being irrational about this but unwilling to budge. "No matter what those test results say, Vivienne Armstrong is not my family. This married man she had an affair with twenty-eight years ago is not my family. My family is flying home from Florida as we speak. They're the only family I know, and the only family I want to know. And I don't think I should have to explain that to you."

"Okay." His expression softened, and this time when he reached for her hand, she didn't pull away because she could see in his eyes that he got it. "You're right. I'm sorry. I didn't think about it from that perspective. I only thought about—"

"Finding answers. Yeah, I get that."

His shoulders dropped. "I'm only trying to help. But if you want to leave, say the word. We'll split right now and head back to Palm Desert."

She shook her head and frowned, knowing leaving now would just make her look like a coward. "We're already here. We might as well stay."

He reached for her other hand. "Are you sure?"

She nodded. "But no matter who this guy is, we're not visiting him next."

"Fair enough." He tipped his head, looking way too damn sexy for his own good. "You're amazing, you know that?"

She rolled her eyes. "Why? Because I just had a little temper tantrum?"

He wrapped an arm around her shoulder and pressed his lips to her temple. "No, because you're smart enough to know when you've had enough. I should have been paying more attention to how you were handling it all instead of focusing on what I wanted to know."

She closed her eyes and breathed in his familiar scents of citrus and leather, wishing like hell that comment didn't make her sound weak. But it did. And she wasn't sure what to think of that or what to do.

The click of heels on hardwood floors sounded from the archway at Kelsey's back, followed by a curt female voice, saying, "And I want the finalized guest list on my desk this evening. There's not a lot of time left to whip this gala into shape."

Kelsey turned toward the archway where a maid and a very petite fiftysomething woman in a flowing peach chiffon blouse, white ankle-length trousers, and three-inch heels entered the room. To the maid, she said, "That's all for now, Stella."

Kelsey straightened as Catarina Brunelli moved toward them. "I'm sorry to keep you waiting." She brushed a lock of her famous curly red hair back where the rest of her hair was twisted in neat chignon and smiled with perfectly painted lips. Her makeup was flawless, her outfit impeccable, her long nails manicured and painted a soft shade of pink. "I don't normally entertain visitors this late in the day, but Charles said you have some questions about—"

Her words cut off as she drew close and focused on Kelsey's face. "Well, I'll be."

She blinked and stared, much as Vivienne Armstrong's lawyers had. And the reaction wasn't exactly welcome to Kelsey. Her stomach tightened with that strange feeling of impending doom again. She cleared her throat and held out her hand. "Thank you for seeing us on such short notice, Ms. Brunelli. I'm Kelsey McClane, and this is my friend Hunter O'Donnell. We'd like to ask you a few questions about Vivienne Armstrong if you don't mind. We promise not to take up too much of your time."

Catarina Brunelli haphazardly shook each of their hands, but her eyes never left Kelsey's face. Several seconds later she finally blinked and shook her head again, muttering, "Of course. Please. Come and sit."

She motioned toward a pair of white couches that looked as if they'd never been sat on before. Kelsey moved toward the closest while Hunt followed.

"It really is remarkable," Catarina said, shaking her head as she sat across from them and continued to look at Kelsey. "Charles said you looked like her, but I didn't expect . . ." She pursed her lips. "It's the eyes. They're exactly like Vivienne's. And the nose. Your chin and jaw-line are different, but the eyes are what're so strikingly similar."

Kelsey shot Hunt a nervous look, then refocused on why they were here. "As you know, we just came from the attorneys' office."

"And?" Catarina sat up a little straighter. "Were they able to send you for testing?" When Kelsey hesitated, Catarina said, "Don't worry, dear. I'm well aware of what's been happening with Vivienne's estate. Vivienne and I were the best of friends. We shared everything. Charles and David have been frantically looking for Vivienne's missing child for the last six months, and I've helped out where I can. I'm the executor for her will, you know. So tell me, did they send you for testing?"

"Yes. Sort of. I mean, the lab came to the attorneys' office."

"Good." She leaned back against the leather cushion. "That means they verified your story and believe you have a very strong claim. It's way past time Vivienne's estate was settled." She folded her hands neatly on her lap. "Now, what can I do for you?"

The comment hit Kelsey as odd. Not relief that her friend's long-lost daughter might be sitting in front of her, just relief that Vivienne's estate could soon be settled.

Hunt leaned forward to rest his elbows on his knees. "We were mostly hoping you could give us some personal insight into Vivienne's relationships. Did she ever mention a man named Graham Foster?"

Catarina frowned. "Many times. That man was a menace. He should have been put in jail a long, long time ago. I was always telling Vivienne to stop being so softhearted and have him locked up. But she would never listen. She was a fool when it came to men. Always was. Every man she was ever involved with either used her or ruined her." She focused on Kelsey. "Word of advice, dear. Don't be like your mother. Men are not to be trusted. Get a dog instead. Way better companions."

Kelsey's cheeks heated, and she fought back a smile as she looked at Hunt, who was trying not to roll his eyes, then at Catarina. Okay, maybe she wasn't insensitive, just blunt as hell. "Thanks. I'll remember that. But we don't know for sure yet that she's my mother."

"Charles would not have sent you over here if he didn't strongly suspect."

That thought made Kelsey's stomach roll all over again.

"Ms. Brunelli," Hunt said, "we've heard speculation that Vivienne's death was not an accident. Do you have any reason to believe that yourself?"

Catarina sighed. "Are you asking if I think she was murdered? My answer is yes. Charles and I have spoken at length about this. I was the first person he and David confided in when they were considering hiring a private investigator to look into her death. I absolutely believe her overdose was not an accident. Vivienne had too much to live for. Oh, I know some people think she was getting too old to keep working, but she had plenty of offers still rolling in, and she was quite happy living off her millions. Did you know she had a young lover in Italy? A twentysomething art student she met when she was vacationing at her villa there a few months before her death." She sighed again. "You tell me what fiftysomething woman would foolishly overdose when she's got a young stud like that warming her bed?"

Kelsey smirked. Apparently, according to Catarina Brunelli, men were to be enjoyed, just not trusted. She glanced at Hunt and made a mental note. He caught the mischievous look in her eye and sent her his own quizzical expression in return.

"Besides which," Catarina went on, oblivious to their silent communication, "I never knew Vivienne to be careless about painkillers and alcohol. Yes, she loved her wine, but she never mixed the two. And I firmly believe Graham Foster had something to do with her death. He had an unhealthy obsession with Vivienne. Why, he filed a petition for half her estate before her body was even cold."

Hunt looked back at the actress. "Yeah, we were made aware of that. Doesn't sound like he has a strong case, though."

She huffed. "I sure hope not. I would hate to see that man get a single penny of her money."

Catarina turned her eyes toward Kelsey and leaned forward. "I don't know what people have told you about Vivienne, dear, but most of the rumors you've read in the tabloids just aren't true. Hollywood is a nasty place, and the paparazzi are vile creatures. Vivienne was a free spirit who lived her life without rules and without caring what most people thought of her. For that, I always admired her. The only things you should believe are her own words. She wrote in her biography how much she regretted giving you up. That was all true. She desperately wanted to find you."

"Then why didn't she?" A lump formed in Kelsey's throat, followed by a good dose of resentment she didn't like feeling. "Forgive me, but I really don't think she looked all that hard. Her biography was published five years ago. If she was so intent on finding me, she could have hired a private investigator to track me down. I found her within a day of looking."

Catarina's face fell. "You're right. Of course you're right." Sighing, she leaned back against the seat cushions once more. "She probably could have found you if she'd looked. I don't know why she didn't, except that I think she was scared. The fantasy was easier to live with than the reality that she might be rejected. Regardless of how free-spirited Vivienne was, deep down, she was always afraid she wouldn't be enough for you. It's easier to play the role of a mother than to be a mother, you know? Or so I'm told. I don't have any children of my own."

That was the first thing anyone had said about Vivienne Armstrong that Kelsey could relate to. A little of the animosity inside her eased.

"Regardless," Catarina said, "I'm glad you're here now. And I'm glad you found Charles and David so we can all find out if you really are Vivienne's daughter. It will be nice to have this whole nasty mess behind us."

She pushed to her feet. "I'm sorry to end our discussion, but I have a dinner party I need to get ready for." When Kelsey and Hunt both stood, she said, "If you have any other questions about Vivienne, feel free to contact me through Vivienne's attorneys."

Kelsey shook her hand, feeling marginally better than she had when they'd first entered the house. "Thanks. I appreciate that."

She and Hunt moved toward the steps that led to the entryway.

"Oh, one more thing," Hunt said, turning to look back. "You wouldn't happen to know who the father of Vivienne's child was, would you?"

Catarina Brunelli flinched. It was the first time she'd look rattled. She glanced warily toward Kelsey. "Yes, I do."

Kelsey and Hunt both waited for an answer.

"But I'm sorry, I can't tell you. You have to understand, he's a very wealthy man with a family of his own. Vivienne never wanted news of their brief affair to destroy his reputation. I promised Vivienne I would never reveal his identity."

"Not even to her daughter?" Hunt asked.

She considered a moment. "When the test results come back and we have confirmation she is Vivienne's daughter, then you can ask me that question again. Until then, I'm bound by an oath."

Kelsey could respect that. She nodded and looked toward Hunt with raised brows. "That's doable."

He didn't seem so convinced, but he thanked Catarina Brunelli one last time and followed Kelsey toward the massive double front doors.

Outside, the sun was heading toward the ocean. Hunt slipped on his sunglasses as he placed a hand at the base of Kelsey's spine and guided her down the steep steps toward their car parked out on the street in the ritzy neighborhood. "Well? What did you think?"

"I think she's a loyal friend who's not afraid to say what's on her mind."

"I agree." He pulled the car door open for her. "What did you think of what she had to say about Foster?"

"It wasn't anything we didn't already know." Kelsey smirked as she slid into the passenger seat. "Except the part about dogs being more loyal than men."

He frowned and moved to close her door. "Very funny."

Her mood was a whole lot lighter than it had been before. And as he slid behind the wheel, she wanted him to know that. She reached for his hand and brought it to her lips for a kiss.

He glanced sideways at her. "What was that for?"

"Just for being you. Thanks for bringing me here."

Something in his eyes softened. "You're welcome. Not as bad as you thought, huh?"

She chuckled and released his hand so he could start the ignition. "No. It wasn't."

And as they pulled out onto the street, she knew why. Because Vivienne Armstrong was a real person to her now, not just some Hollywood starlet who'd abandoned her daughter for fame and glory.

Catarina Brunelli had brought Vivienne to life for Kelsey by simply revealing Vivienne's fear about finding her daughter. And in that one moment, Kelsey found her reason to let go of twenty-seven years' worth of resentment.

———

Hunt glanced up at Kelsey as he crossed the trendy Palm Desert coffee shop with their drinks and headed toward the table he'd already scoped out for her in the back of the restaurant, relieved she seemed more relaxed this evening than she'd been this morning. He had to admit, he'd been worried before their meeting with Armstrong's attorneys. She'd looked ready to bolt at a moment's notice.

Out the wide windows, the sun sank low over the mountains, fading into the dim light of dusk, and as the last rays of sunshine drifted over her face, she smiled and reached for one of the drinks in his hands. "Thanks."

"I hope I got that right." He moved around the table and pulled out a chair at her side, back against the wall so he could scan the restaurant for any kind of threat. Too bad all he really wanted to do was look at her.

Man, she was beautiful. He knew he needed to be focused on this investigation and what was going on around them, but he'd rather spend all day focused on her. To him, she didn't look like some famous movie star. She would always be the girl he'd been crushing on most of his adult life.

"Even if you didn't, any kind of caffeine will work." She took a sip from the iced latte and sighed. "Yep, you got it right."

He sipped his own iced coffee, relieved she wasn't upset with him. Maybe he shouldn't have pushed her to meet with Brunelli, but he was glad now that he had. There was a calmness about her that hadn't been there before, and he knew it was a direct result of something the actress had said. "You were pretty quiet on the drive back here."

"Processing."

He nodded and took another sip of his drink. "It's been a busy day."

"It has."

"You okay meeting Foster's son now?"

"Yes. I'm anxious to find out what we need to so we can go home."

He knew she was anxious to get home. Anxious to see her family. He was too, in a way. But another part of him liked the privacy they had down here. Once they returned to Oregon, real life would be upon them too soon.

He glanced around the coffee shop. Nothing seemed out of order. "So, I'm not sure if you heard the attorneys talking to me when you were giving your DNA sample, but Vivienne Armstrong was pretty loaded."

"I figured. Catarina mentioned a villa in Italy. Just how loaded are we talking, though?"

"Very. She's worth over two hundred and fifty million. She's got property in Beverly Hills, on Cliffside Drive in Malibu overlooking the Pacific, a spread on Columbus Circle with a view of Central Park, and the modest villa in Naples on the edge of the Mediterranean. That's a lot of reasons for Foster to want to kill her. Especially if she didn't have any intention of sharing any of it with him."

"Assuming he did kill her, do you think that's why? Because of her money? You heard her attorneys. They don't think the courts will rule in his favor. Their marriage wasn't legal because she was underage."

"It could be. If there's no heir, he might think he has a chance. He had to know her attorneys are searching for her daughter."

"Which gives him a reason to come after me. Yeah, I get the logic. I just don't understand why he would set off a bomb. There are easier ways to get rid of me. Planting a bomb is sociopathic."

Hunt reached for her hand, closing his fingers around her cold ones. "Fits with what we know of his recluse reputation. Who knows why he chose a bomb? Maybe he wanted to send a message while making your

206

death look like an accident? Bottom line is he made a mistake." He squeezed her hand. "A guy like that can't hide forever."

She nodded, then looked up at him with narrowed eyes. "So tell me, Mr. O'Donnell, is that your latest theory? That Foster set that bomb? Twenty-four hours ago you were convinced Julian was the big bad guy."

He frowned. "Benedict *is* a bad guy. I've not ruled him out completely. But Occam's Razor says—"

"That the simplest explanation is usually the right one. Yeah, I've heard the philosopher's problem-solving theory." She tipped her head and smiled as she flipped her hand over and twined her fingers with his. "It just seems like such an optimistic theory for you."

Heat rushed through his belly. "Don't do that."

"Don't do what?"

"Don't look at me in that coy way."

Her smile widened. "Why not?"

He leaned toward her and in a low voice said, "Because it makes me want to have my way with you right here."

She leaned forward and met his lips across the table. "I absolutely would not mind that."

She was toying with him, and, *holy hell*, he liked it. Wrapping one hand around her nape, he tugged her in for a hot, wet, scorching kiss he felt everywhere.

Someone cleared their throat.

Kelsey drew back from Hunt's lips way before he was ready to let her go. Above them, a male voice said, "Sorry to interrupt."

Shit. There he went being completely distracted by her when he shouldn't be. Hunt immediately released her and pushed to his feet. A thirtysomething man dressed in jeans and a wrinkled polo stood beside their table.

The man ran his fingers through his dark hair. "I'm not sure I have the right couple. Are you Hunter O'Donnell?"

Hunt glanced past the man and scanned the coffee shop again. No threats, no signs of trouble or anything even watching them. He looked back at the man. "Trey Foster?"

"Yeah."

"Thanks for meeting us. This is Kelsey McClane."

"Nice to meet you both." Trey Foster pulled out the third chair and sat.

He looked wrecked. It was Hunt's first impression as he sat back. His clothes were wrinkled, his hair disheveled, and there was one, maybe two days' worth of stubble on his chin that told him he hadn't shaved recently.

"Can I get you something to drink?" Hunt asked.

"No. Thanks. I've had enough coffee for an entire week. I swear the stuff at the station was straight caffeine."

"You were with the police?" Kelsey asked.

"Yeah. Trying to help out as much as I can. I'm still having trouble believing my dad was involved in that bombing up in Portland."

Hunt wasn't sure what to say in response to that. "Are you close?"

He shook his head. "Not particularly. My dad can be . . . difficult. 'My way or the highway,' you know? We rarely see each other these days. He's always been opinionated, but the older he gets, the harder it is to talk to him about anything, really. Everyone's out to get him, especially the government."

That coincided with what they'd been told by the police. "When was the last time you saw your father?" Hunt asked.

Trey Foster blew out a breath. "Gosh, probably Thanksgiving. I spent a couple hours with him that day, but that was it." He looked up. "The cops told me you were both caught in that building in Portland."

"We were." Hunt glanced at Kelsey, remembering the screams and chaos before the building had come down around them and everything had gone dark and silent. And how relieved he'd been when he'd seen her dust-covered face emerge from that rubble. "A lot of people were. Some weren't as lucky as us."

Trey nodded and looked down at the table. "I heard the death toll's still rising."

"Stands at four, from what I heard this morning," Hunt answered, watching the man closely. "With many more still in the hospital."

Trey shook his head. "So awful." With a nervous look, he glanced at Hunt and then at Kelsey. "Did you know any of the victims?"

Odd question. "Not me personally," Hunt answered with narrowed eyes.

"Me either," Kelsey said. "Though one of the hosts and a production assistant I worked with that morning are both still in the hospital recovering."

Foster looked back down at the table. "Hopefully they're both going to be okay."

"Yeah," Kelsey said quietly. "I hope so as well."

Hunt wasn't sure how to read the man. He sounded overwhelmed, but Hunt couldn't tell if he was fishing for information or just plain curious.

"Damn." Trey Foster sighed. "I'm really sorry it happened. And I'm really sorry those people were hurt, especially the ones who were killed. I've tried to convince myself for a long time that he wasn't violent. A kid just doesn't want to think that about his father, you know? But . . ." He stared at a spot on the table and shook his head in a way that left him looking dazed. His voice wobbled when he added, "I should have seen this coming."

"Why do you say that?" Kelsey asked softly.

He cleared his throat. "Because he's bipolar." Running a hand through his hair, he shifted in his seat, and added in a stronger voice, "Whenever he goes off medication, he's prone to manic episodes and unpredictable behavior. I've been dealing with this kind of shit for years, though not to the extreme of the last few days."

He glanced up at them. "I know you both talked to Vivienne Armstrong's attorneys today. About six months ago, right after she died, he stopped taking his meds. He was completely distraught after her death. I tried to get him to start taking them again, but he refused. I tried to get him to see his psychiatrist, but he refused that too. In the past, whenever he went through one of these episodes, he'd try to contact Vivienne, and it usually resulted in his harassing her or being picked up by the cops or me having to sweep in and smooth things over with her attorneys. This time, though . . ." He shook his head. "This time I'm afraid his obsession with her got the best of him."

"There were pictures of me all over his office," Kelsey said. "Has he ever mentioned me to you?"

"No. And I'm really sorry you've been sucked into this. Before yesterday, I had no idea who you even were. He doesn't talk to me about anything related to Vivienne because he knows how I feel about his obsession. The best I can figure is he saw your pictures in the news recently and convinced himself you're her daughter. You have to understand, my father wasn't just in love with Vivienne, he was convinced she was his soul mate. When she left him to make it big in Hollywood, it completely gutted him. Everything after that day was torture to him. Every movie she made, every other man she dated, every story about how her life went on without him. This missing daughter is pretty much the epitome of her life without him."

"The attorneys told us he's petitioned the state for half of Armstrong's estate," Hunt said.

"Yeah." Trey sighed. "I learned that yesterday as well. I had no idea he'd done that."

"That gives him a motive to try to go after Kelsey. Especially if he's convinced she's Armstrong's daughter."

"I agree. Which only worries me more." A buzz sounded, and Trey said, "Sorry. I have to check this." He pulled his cell phone out, read the text, then punched a few buttons and returned it to his pocket. "That was my attorney. I have to meet with him after this." Sighing, he looked at Kelsey. "I know people are going to tell you he's doing all this because of the money, but I'm not convinced that's what's really going on."

"What makes you say that?" Kelsey asked.

"Because my dad never really cared about the money. You saw where he lives. His place is a dump, yet he's not destitute. He's got cash in the bank, a nice retirement to live off; he's just not spending it the way most people do. The cops told me they've been going through all his records and that they've found numerous receipts for private investigators he's paid over the years to try to find Armstrong's daughter."

"So he was looking for her to get rid of her," Hunt said.

Trey frowned. "If you'd have asked me that six months ago, I'd have said no. I'd have guessed he was looking for her so he could present her identity like a gift to Vivienne. The one thing no one else has ever been able to get for her. But now . . ."

Kelsey tensed, and Hunt already knew what she was thinking. Now it looked like he just wanted to eliminate any evidence she'd ever existed.

"Do you have any idea where he might be?" Hunt asked.

"I don't, unfortunately. He hasn't contacted me. I gave the cops some locations he's escaped to before—a place up near Tahoe he likes to camp at, and a fishing village down in Mexico where he sometimes goes to get away. This is going to hit the news tonight or tomorrow morning, and when it does, his face is going to be plastered everywhere. If he's still in Oregon, he's not going to be able to hide out there much longer."

That was the only consolation in this whole gigantic mess that Hunt could see.

"Do you know Vivienne's friend Catarina Brunelli?" Hunt asked.

"Not personally. Why?"

"She mentioned your father when we spoke to her today. Sounds like she helped Vivienne deal with your father over the years."

"I'm glad for that. But I was never involved in any of that. I never had any contact with Vivienne or her friends. Anytime I had to intervene, I dealt with Vivienne's attorneys only."

"Are you married, Mr. Foster?" Kelsey asked.

Hunt glanced at her, wondering why she was asking.

"No." He smirked Kelsey's way. "Not unless you call being married to my job marriage."

When she didn't press for more, Hunt said, "And what do you do for a living?"

"I manage a small tech company. We create online security software."

"Growing field."

"Always. And the longer I'm away from it, the harder all of this is on my business."

"And your mother," Kelsey said. "Are you close?"

Trey Foster shook his head. "My mom passed when I was just a kid. Cancer."

"I'm so sorry."

He waved his hand, shifting in his seat as if the topic made him uncomfortable. "Thanks. It was a long time ago. I was bitter about it for a lot of years, especially after I had to go live with my dad and realized he didn't give a shit about her and never had, but I got over it."

"That must have been rough," Kelsey said.

"Yeah, well . . ." He exhaled a heavy breath.

When neither of them knew what to say in response, he pressed his hand against the table and sat up straighter, glancing from Kelsey to Hunt and back again. "So you two . . . are you sticking around here in California or heading back to Portland?"

Hunt looked Kelsey's way and lifted his brows, and in her eyes she wasn't sure if he saw regret or relief at the prospect of leaving.

Kelsey held his gaze. "Um . . ."

"We're heading home," Hunt said, knowing it was past time. He still had no idea what he was going to tell her family about them, but he had one more night to figure that out. "Not much reason to stay now. I think we learned everything we came here to find."

"Yeah, I guess you have. Well." Foster pushed back from the table and rose. "If either of you need to contact me, you have my number." He shook Hunt's hand as he stood, then Kelsey's as she rose. "It was nice to meet you, and I wish you both the best."

They watched as he headed for the front of the coffee shop, slipped on his sunglasses, and moved out the door.

When he was gone, Hunt looked down at Kelsey. "What do you think?"

She tipped her head, watching him go. "I think I wouldn't want to be him right now. As soon as the media gets ahold of this story, his life is going to be a nightmare."

"Yours, too, if he brings up your name."

"I'm not sure he will."

"Why not?"

"Vivienne was careful never to mention his father's name. She didn't use it in her book. Very few people knew about their past or that he was harassing her. That kept Trey's name out of the press as well. Why would he want to mention me now? Seems like it would just draw more attention he doesn't need."

His heart turned over. "Not everyone's like you, you know."

She looked up at him. "What do you mean?"

"Selfless."

"I'm not selfless."

"Yeah, you are. And you have a very forgiving heart, Kelsey McClane." Stepping toward her, he framed her face and tipped her mouth up so he could press a soft, tantalizing kiss against her lips. "There aren't many people who could sit here and listen to that whole story without getting upset."

"Getting upset won't change anything. I tried that last night, and it didn't get me anywhere."

"It got you here. With me."

Her eyes heated. "True. But I like being here with you."

"I like being here with you too." Wrapping an arm around her shoulder, he turned her toward the door. "And since this is our last night here alone together, I think we should make the most of it before your family starts asking questions about us."

Her smile widened. "What do you have in mind?"

He pushed the coffee shop's door open. "I was kind of hoping for a bottle of wine, a little room service, and you naked and at my mercy the entire night."

"I think you might be able to talk me into that."

"Good." He pressed a kiss to her temple. "Because tonight you're all I want."

And everything he wasn't about to lose.

CHAPTER SIXTEEN

Kelsey was glad to be home. As she followed Hunt out of the airport in Portland and crossed the sky bridge to the parking structure where he'd left his car several days ago, she drew in a breath of damp Pacific Northwest air, anxious to see her parents.

Hunt shifted the bag over his shoulder and glanced down at the phone in his free hand with a frown. "Your brother's texted me about ten times, wondering when we're coming down."

Holding his other hand as they moved into the parking structure, she said, "Which one?"

"Alec."

She grinned and stepped out of the way for a woman pushing a stroller. "Figures. He's impatient."

Hunt huffed. "Tell me something I don't already know." Pulling her to a stop several feet from his SUV, he dropped his bag on the ground at her feet and said, "Wait here while I check to make sure the car's clear."

Kelsey rolled her eyes but did as he said, knowing he was just being cautious. He'd already warned her not to get too far away from him when they landed, just to be safe. She wasn't particularly worried someone was waiting for them here in Portland, but she did hold her breath as she watched Hunt glance under the vehicle and inside the windows for any signs the car had been tampered with, then sighed in relief when he motioned for her to join him.

She grabbed his bag from the ground and met him steps from the vehicle. Frown lines marred his handsome face as he popped the back of the vehicle and tossed in their bags.

Amusement toyed with the corners of her lips. "You're nervous."

"About the vehicle?" He flashed her a *yeah, right* look as he slammed the tailgate. "It's fine."

Her grin widened as he moved to the passenger side and reached for the door handle. "No. About my brothers."

He scoffed as he held the door open for her. "Not a chance."

She slid into the seat. "You *are* nervous." She was extremely touched by that knowledge, but wanted only to put him at ease. "Which one's making you nervous? Rusty? I'll talk to him first before we say anything to the rest of the family."

He rolled his eyes as if she were being silly, but his expression softened as he leaned down to kiss her cheek, and he completely shocked her when he said, "I'd say it's a toss-up between Rusty and your father."

He closed her door and moved around the car, and even though she knew she shouldn't be happy by that admission, she was. Maybe it was childish, but she liked that he was nervous. It meant this was real.

Truth be told, though, she was a little nervous too. She wasn't sure what they were going to say to her parents and brothers, especially Rusty. He was immediately going to assume Hunt had done something to take advantage of her in her vulnerable state. For some reason, *"Hey, everyone, I know I just got divorced, and I know Hunt was technically my bodyguard, but we're sleeping together now,"* didn't seem like the smartest option.

Her phone buzzed as Hunt slid into the vehicle next to her and started the ignition. "Wonderful. Alec's texting me now."

"This shit's got to stop."

She reached into her jacket pocket for her phone. "You're going to tell him to stop?"

"Hell yeah." Hunt frowned again as he glanced over his shoulder to back out of the parking space. "After we figure out what we're going to tell all of them, of course."

She chuckled and looked down at her screen. Then froze.

Talking about me? I bet you are. You've been busy talking to lots of people about me. Pretty soon, though, you won't be talking at all. Enjoy that new boyfriend while you can, starlet, because I'm coming for you real soon.

A picture popped up on the screen just after the message. A picture of her and Hunt and Trey Foster, sitting together at that table. A picture that had been taken through the windows of the small coffee shop.

Kelsey gasped and covered her mouth with her hand. Beside her, Hunt glanced at her and went on instant alert. "What?"

She held up the phone with a shaky hand. He slammed on the brakes, stopping in the middle of the lane, and took it from her.

"Motherfucking son of a bitch. He was outside the damn coffee shop? The whole fucking time?"

Not just outside the coffee shop, she realized. He'd known they were in Palm Desert pretty much from the moment they'd arrived. A sick feeling passed through her when she thought of him looking in their hotel-room windows. Had she left the curtains open at all? When she and Hunt had been intimate, had he been watching? Bile rose up in her throat.

Every muscle in Hunt's body was tense and rigid as he dug out his own cell phone and dialed. Pressing it to his ear, he said, "Davies? Yeah, it's me. I need another trace on a text on Kelsey's phone. I'll forward it to you. And then I want to know how the fuck he got her number. This is a secure phone that *we* set up. No one has the number but us and her family. The fucker is messing with us, and I want his ass triangulated *now*."

Kelsey couldn't hear what Davies said in response, but the venom in Hunt's voice was unlike anything she'd heard from him, aside from that morning Julian had attacked her and he'd beat the shit out of her ex.

"Get me whatever the fuck you can and get it to me fast. If he's tracking her with her own goddamn phone, I want to know."

He hit "End" on his phone and tucked it into his pocket. Hers he powered down and tossed onto the console. Kelsey glanced down at the dark screen as he shoved the car into "Drive" and tore out of the parking garage with a squeal of his tires.

He was pissed. He had every right to be pissed. But she breathed easier, knowing they were back in Oregon, hundreds of miles from Foster now.

"Are you okay?" she asked as they headed out of the airport.

"Fine." He gripped the steering wheel and focused on the wet pavement. A rainstorm had come through within the last hour, and the traffic was thicker than normal because of the slick conditions.

"Fine," she repeated quietly. He didn't look fine, but she wasn't about to say that. If he was beating himself up that he hadn't noticed Foster watching them, she wasn't about to point out that wasn't his fault. He'd just disagree with her.

She looked out the window as they pulled onto I-205 and headed south. His phone buzzed, and he picked it up and glanced at it, then handed it to her. "Here. It's your brother again. Tell him you'll be there in thirty minutes."

She typed a quick response and hit "Send." Setting his phone on the console next to hers, she said, "I'm sure he'll settle down once he sees I'm fine."

"He'll settle down once he knows you're safe at your folks' place. You need to stay there for the next week or so. The guys aren't done installing the new security system at your warehouse yet, so you can't go back there. Your folks' place is wired tight. I did that system myself."

Confusion drew her brows together. "You want me to stay with my parents? Last night when we discussed what I should do after we got home, you said you wanted me to stay with you."

His jaw clenched tight. He glanced in the rearview mirror, then back at the freeway, not coming close to meeting her gaze. "You're safer at your parents' place. I'm clearly distracted by you." His shoulders tightened even more. "I'll be better able to figure out what the fuck Foster is doing by myself. I'll send one of my other guys down to stay with you and your parents until Foster's caught."

Oh no. He was not brushing her aside like that. She shifted in her seat, gearing up for a fight. "Hunt, I know you're upset right now about that text, but—"

"But nothing, Kelsey. I was hired to protect you. That's what I'm doing. That's what I should have been doing all along. Not fucking around and putting your life in danger."

"I really don't think—"

"That's the end of the discussion."

Her mouth snapped closed at the finality in his voice. She'd heard that tone before. Not from Hunt but from Julian. Spine stiffening, she angled her gaze out the side window, seething because she'd backed down from Julian more times than she could count, and she wasn't about to start doing that with Hunt.

He didn't want her to stay with him anymore? All because of one stupid text? Fine. She absolutely didn't want to stay with him. She was so *not* begging for a man's attention ever again.

They drove the rest of the way to her parents' house in Lake Oswego in silence. The second Hunt pulled to a stop in front of her parents' gate, rolled down the window to type in the gate code, then looked toward the house, though, she was more than ready to get out of this car and away from him.

The gate slowly swung back, and Hunt pulled onto the property. The driveway angled down and around. As they made the turn, Kelsey spotted her mom's Audi, her dad's Range Rover, her younger brother Thomas's Jeep, and all three of her older brothers' vehicles parked in front of the garage.

Well, the only good thing was now neither of them had to figure out what they were going to tell her family about them.

He pulled to a stop and killed the ignition. Kelsey immediately popped her door and climbed out. "Kels, wait a second."

She slammed the door and moved around the vehicle. Before Hunt could even climb out, the wide double front doors to the house opened, and Alec, Rusty, Ethan, and Thomas rushed out, sweeping her up in their arms with ear-splitting laughter.

Tears sprang to her eyes. Tears, and a relief she was home that she hadn't even thought she'd feel. She let them each hug her, one by one, and assured them she was really in one piece. Then finally said, "Enough smothering me already. I can't breathe."

Her brothers each laughed but listened and put her on her feet. And then she heard her mom's voice and felt her arms go around her, followed by a kiss on the top of her head from her dad and his happy voice that she was home.

"Yes," she said, reassuring them too. "I'm really fine. No lasting damage. Nothing a week of sleep won't heal."

"Oh, honey, we're so happy." Hannah McClane hugged her tight again. "No more morning-show interviews, though, okay?"

A reluctant smile tugged at Kelsey's lips. "Okay."

An excited little voice sounded behind her mom, and Kelsey glanced to the side then dropped to the ground just in time to catch Alec's five-year-old daughter, Emma, in her arms. "Aunt Kessey! You missed *all* the fun at Disney World. I went on Space Mountain, and Pirates of the Cawibbean, and Daddy wouldn't let me go on Peter Pan because he wanted to get his picture taken with Rapunzel."

Behind Kelsey, Alec gasped. "Emma! That was our secret. You weren't supposed to tell her that."

"What? It's true, Daddy." She looked at Kelsey again and rolled her big blue eyes. "He made me stand in line to meet *all* the princesses. It was ex-hausting."

Alec huffed. At his side, his wife, Raegan, grinned. "Oh, stop complaining. You know that was your favorite part of the trip."

"The only good part of the damn trip," Alec muttered.

"It really was," Thomas agreed quietly. "Rapunzel was seriously hot."

Kelsey pushed to her feet and gave Raegan and then Sam, Ethan's wife, a quick hug. From the corner of her eye, she spotted Hunt standing next to Alec with his keys in his hand, but she didn't fully look at him.

"Okay, come on," Hannah said, stepping back. "Everyone inside. It looks like it's going to rain again."

Kelsey hoisted Emma onto her hip and turned for the house, not bothering to glance back to see if Hunt was staying or leaving. She didn't expect him to leave right away, but she was not begging him to stay either.

Kelsey instantly relaxed as soon as she stepped inside. Her parents' home sat on two pristine waterfront acres. They'd bought the Craftsman-style home years before they'd adopted any of their kids and had remodeled and added on over the years as their family had grown. Today, it was all natural woods, beamed ceilings, slate floors, and walls of glass that looked out over a spectacular view of Lake Oswego. Kelsey loved this house. Had loved growing up here. And she told herself she would be just fine here for the next week, even if it wasn't at all what she'd planned last night.

Sam and Raegan followed Kelsey into the living room with Emma. "We're so glad you're home," Raegan said as Kelsey put Emma on her feet and the girl dropped to the carpet to play with her toys. "We were so worried. Alec was a compete basket case as soon as he heard the news from Portland."

"Ethan wasn't much better," Sam said. "He was desperate to get back here."

That didn't surprise Kelsey at all. Her brothers were all protective of her.

"It must have been terrifying for you." Sam pressed a hand against her throat. "Being in the dark like that for so long. How on earth did you get through that? I think I would have hyperventilated."

"Oh, you know. I just kept telling myself help was coming." But even as the words were out, she knew they were a lie. Her chest tightened with the truth. She'd gotten through it because Hunt had been there with her. Because he'd kept her calm and hadn't given up on her. Her gaze strayed to the kitchen where he stood talking quietly with her brothers and father. Only he didn't look like he was paying much attention to their conversation. He kept glancing toward her with a worried expression.

Well, good. Let him stew a little. She tore her gaze from his and smiled at her sisters-in-law. She wasn't going to put up with being told what to do. He'd tried that yesterday in California by scheduling that meeting with Catarina Brunelli. Yeah, it had turned out to be an okay meeting, but that wasn't the point. He should have asked her first before he set the damn thing up. And he absolutely should not be making decisions for her now without discussing them with her first.

"Sorry. What?" Hunt said in the kitchen.

"I asked how your head is," Alec said. "You've got a big-ass yellow bruise on the side of your forehead there. But I guess I already figured out the answer myself." He glanced toward their father. "Brain damage. Told you it wasn't smart to leave this guy in charge of your only daughter."

"Don't listen to him," Kelsey's dad said to Hunt. "He's still grouchy the airline lost his bag."

"Damn right I'm grouchy about that. It still hasn't shown up yet."

"How is your head, really?" Kelsey's mom asked. "That is a nasty bruise."

"It's fine."

"And your leg? Kelsey said you needed stitches."

This time Kelsey couldn't keep from glancing back toward the kitchen. Hunt was still watching her, barely even paying attention to the questions from her parents and brother. "My leg's fine. It was nothing."

Thomas slipped behind Hunt and tugged the fridge open. "When are we eating? I'm starving already."

"You're always starving." Hannah stepped around her husband and reached for the fridge door while her youngest son dug through the contents. "Thomas, don't eat that. It'll ruin your appetite. Rusty, I need you to go start the grill before Thomas devours everything that's not nailed down."

"Olives!" Emma jumped to her feet when she spotted the jar in Thomas's hand and sprinted into the kitchen.

"Emma," Raegan called, "Only three. Thomas don't let her eat too many of those. She'll get sick."

Chaos was already reigning supreme, just like at every other McClane family get-together, but it didn't stir Kelsey up, if anything it relaxed her a little more.

Alec moved into the living room and slung his arm over Kelsey's shoulder. Ethan moved up by his wife's side and slipped an arm around her waist.

"So tell the truth." Alec pointed over his shoulder to where Kelsey knew Hunt was still standing in the kitchen. "How relieved are you to get away from that smelly guy? He didn't try anything on you, did he? Cause if he did, we can kick his ass."

Kelsey tensed. From the corner of her eye, she didn't miss the way Rusty's gaze narrowed across the room and zeroed in on her as he lowered his book.

"Yeah, we're good at that." Thomas stopped on her other side, popping an olive in his mouth. He puffed out his chest and pounded his fist against his sternum with a grunt. "Just like cavemen."

A nervous laugh slipped past Kelsey's lips, and she quickly shrugged out from under Alec's arm, not wanting to give anything away. Alec might be teasing, but she could see Rusty was suddenly paying very close attention, and she didn't want to do or say anything that would set him off. "Why on earth would you think that?"

"Why are you acting so weird?" Alec asked, looking after her. "It was just a question."

Thankfully, her father pulled her to safety and steered her to the kitchen so she didn't have to answer. "Back off and give the girl some room so she can breathe. She's been through a traumatic experience."

Hell yeah, she had.

Her situation didn't improve though, because her father brought her to a stop only feet from Hunt. Who was still watching her like a hawk. Only in his familiar brown eyes she didn't see that same flash of anger she'd seen in the car, she saw a whole lot of guilt.

"Now, you two," her father said. "Tell us what's really going on. We saw the news about this man named Foster. How is he linked to what happened in Portland? And what, exactly, happened when you were in California?"

Kelsey's entire body grew hot, not just from the question but from the look she saw in Hunt's eyes. A look that told her he knew he'd seriously fucked up.

She just wasn't sure if that look was because of what had happened in the car, or with Foster, or with their entire relationship.

———

If Hunt was planning to leave, Kelsey wasn't sure why he was prolonging the inevitable.

They'd had dinner. Sitting around the table, they'd both rationally told her parents everything that had happened in Portland regarding the bombing and with Julian. They'd also relayed everything they'd learned in California about Foster and Vivienne Armstrong. Avoiding, of course, any discussion about what had happened between them personally.

Kelsey wasn't exactly sure if she was relieved or pissed off about that fact. She'd let Hunt take the lead talking about California, curious what he would say. Since they really weren't speaking to each other right now, it was probably a good thing he hadn't admitted anything. But at the same time, it only made her more anxious for him to leave.

Her brothers and father had immediately launched into a discussion with Hunt about what was best for her after that, and unable to listen to a minute more of the men in her life trying to decide her future, she pushed back from the dining table and looked toward her niece Emma, playing on the floor in the living area with two trucks and a Ken doll she'd dismembered. "Hey, Em. Wanna go downstairs with me and play cards?"

Emma jumped to her feet in her cute little pink dress and yelled, "Yes!" Rushing over to where the adults were sitting, she wrapped her little hand around Kelsey's and dragged her toward the staircase that led down to the daylight basement. "I know where Thomas keeps his special cards too. I'll show you. They're in his room. Some of them have naked boobies on them."

Alec, Rusty, and Ethan all busted out laughing. From the end of the table, Ethan said to Thomas, "As your former counselor, I can officially diagnose you as seriously screwed."

"Ethan McClane," Hannah admonished.

"Sorry, Mom, but it's true."

Thomas's face turned beet red, and he lurched out of his chair, chasing after Kelsey and Emma. "I told you to stay out of my stuff, Em. You're in big trouble now."

Kelsey let Emma drag her downstairs while the rest of her family returned to the topic of her psychotic stalker. Since Thomas had taken over the lowest level of her parents' house, it was a total man cave. There was a small bar area to the left that was never stocked with alcohol since Thomas was only eighteen. A pool table sat in the center of the room, and a couch and chairs on the far side faced a flat-screen TV surrounded by bookshelves filled with Xbox games. Another wall of windows looked out over a covered patio and view of the lake. And what used to be her dad's exercise room but was now Thomas's bedroom opened through a doorway to the right.

Emma let go of Kelsey's hand as soon as they stepped off the bottom stair and raced toward Thomas's bedroom door with a squeal. "I'll show you where his cards are."

Shoving past Kelsey, Thomas rushed after her. "Don't you dare touch my stuff, Em."

Kelsey looked after them, crossing her arms over her chest as she shook her head. She'd thought getting away from all the chitchat upstairs would make her feel better, but it hadn't. All she could think about was the fact Hunt had been in this house for several hours but still hadn't said a single goddamn thing to her. Was everything in California just a complete lie?

"Kelsey."

Her heart picked up speed at the sound of Hunt's voice behind her, and a little thrill shot through her, one that only angered her more because she knew if he touched her she'd probably completely back down like the weak woman she didn't want to be.

She dropped her arms and faced him. "Just go back up—"

Emma's high-pitched scream drew both of their heads around.

"I swear to God, Em," Thomas yelled, "if you don't get out of my room, I'm not gonna let you play on my Xbox ever again!"

From the staircase above, Alec yelled, "What the hell is going on down there?"

Kelsey took one breath and glanced up, ready to holler back that he should get down here and intervene, but before she could get the words out of her mouth, Hunt lowered his body, wrapped his arms around her legs, and hefted her over his shoulder.

She grunted as the air left her lungs and the room tipped. "What the hell, Hunt?" Pressing her hands against his back, she wiggled against his grip. "Put me down."

Seconds later she was in the wine cellar—or what used to be the wine cellar before Thomas commandeered the basement and her parents turned it into a downstairs pantry for his snacks—and was dropped to her feet. Hunt shoved the door closed after them, locking them both in darkness.

"What do you think you're do—"

His mouth closed over hers, cutting off her words. She didn't see him move. Couldn't see a damn thing in the dark. But she felt him. She felt him everywhere as he closed in at her front, wrapped his arms around her waist, pinned her against the shelves, then devoured her until her brain was complete mush.

She was seconds away from kissing him back, from caving and giving him what he wanted. Then she remembered all the times she'd caved with Julian, and it was enough to shore up her strength so she could shove her hands against his chest and push him back.

"You can't just kiss me and expect that to make everything okay."

"You're right. I'm sorry." His breath was hot against her lips. Hot and close and so damn tempting it was all she could do not to grab him and pull him back. "I'm not kissing you to make everything okay. I'm kissing you because I'm an idiot. The biggest idiot on the planet. You have every right to be mad at me for what I said to you in the car. I have no excuse except that it scared me. It scared the shit out of me to know he was that close to you and I didn't even know. The whole drive down here, all I could think about was what would have happened if he'd had another bomb or if, God forbid, he'd had a gun. I wouldn't have been able to stop him because through that whole damn conversation with Trey Foster, all I'd been thinking about was getting you back up in my bed."

Kelsey's heart raced in the darkness. She wasn't sure what to say to that. Hadn't expected him to be so honest with her. Or so open. And the tremble she felt against her confirmed just how scared he still was.

She swallowed hard, knowing he hadn't meant to upset her, but at the same time knowing she could not let that happen again. "You can't make my decisions for me."

"I know that."

"And I'm not going to let you tell me what to do. My brothers have been doing it for years. They're upstairs trying to do it now. And Julian used to do that to me all the time. I'm not going back to that kind of relationship."

"I don't want you to. And I don't want to tell you what to do. I promise."

Her anger ebbed, and she slowly curled her fingers in the fabric of his gray button-down. "It scared me too, you know. We were both in that coffee shop, and you were in just as much danger as I was. If Foster had done something and you were hurt, how do you think that would've made me feel? He's not trying to target you. He wants me. You don't get to corner the market on fear and guilt."

"I know." He pressed his forehead against hers. "Forgive me," he whispered. "Please forgive me for being a jackass."

The desperation in his voice pushed aside the last of her anger. Lifting her mouth to his, she kissed him. Maybe it made her weak, but she didn't care. She didn't want to fight with him anymore.

He groaned, opened to her kiss, and slid his tongue into her mouth. And as he pressed her harder against the shelf, she wrapped her arm around his neck to pull him closer, lifted to her toes so she could kiss him deeper. But something sharp on the shelf scraped against her back, jerking her back from his lips. "Ouch. Wait." She tried to twist around to see what had scratched her. "Let go for a second. There's something—"

The door swung open, and light spilled into the small room, blinding them both. Kelsey immediately slammed her eyes shut and lifted her hand to block the glare. "What the he—"

"You son of a bitch." Rusty's voice filled the small room. "I knew you couldn't be trusted."

Things happened so fast, Kelsey barely had time to react. One second Rusty was pushing Hunt against the shelves on the opposite side of the pantry, the next his arm was swinging back and his fist was plowing into Hunt's jaw, cracking Hunt's skull back against the shelf behind him.

Kelsey screamed and scrambled between her brother and Hunt, eyes wide and completely shocked. "Rusty!" She shoved hard against his chest. "Stop!"

Footsteps sounded on the stairs outside. Voices echoed. Thomas was frantically asking what was going on. Ethan and Alec were hollering at Rusty to calm the hell down and struggling to pull him out of the small closet. But the only thing Kelsey could focus on was Hunt standing in a pile of cracker and candy boxes, swiping at a bloody lip.

"Oh my God, you're bleeding." She ripped a paper towel off a roll to her left and held it up to his mouth. "Are you okay?"

"I'm fine." She searched his eyes for any sign he wasn't. Yes, he was bleeding, but it wasn't bad. He'd had worse from wrestling with Alec, she was sure. But he didn't look angry. He didn't look ready to swing back like Julian would have done in the same situation.

Her temper shot right back up, only this time it was directed at her brother. She whipped around and faced Rusty, standing in the doorway of the pantry, trying to shake off Ethan and Alec's holds. "What the hell was that?"

Rusty stiffened, his black hair mussed, his obsidian eyes a little less violent, but still entirely too on edge for Kelsey's liking. "You know exactly what that was. I heard you."

Alec's blue eyes narrowed. "Heard what?"

Rusty's jaw clenched down hard. "I heard her tell this asshole to stop and let her go, then when I opened the door, I saw him pinning her up against the wall as he shoved his tongue down her throat."

Alec and Ethan both tensed and seemed to grow two inches as they puffed out their chests. Even Thomas, behind them, got all brotherly bent out of shape, which was absolutely not going to help the current situation.

"Holy fuck, O'Donnell." Alec's eyes flew wide. "What the hell did you do?"

"Oh for shit's sake." What was left of Kelsey's patience bubbled right up and over. "For your information, I'm a grown woman who can make her own damn choices. I don't need any of your approval."

"So what was going on in here?" Ethan asked calmly, ever trying to be the peacemaker.

Kelsey glanced over her shoulder at Hunt. But he didn't meet her eye. He didn't look at her brothers either. He just stared down at the floor with a guilty expression. One that told Kelsey loud and clear he did not want to be having this conversation.

She narrowed her eyes, unable to believe he wasn't going to say anything. Especially after that amazing little speech he'd given her. Was he really just going to keep quiet about them now that they'd been found out?

Hunt finally sighed and scrubbed a hand through the back of his hair. "Kels. Gimme a minute with your brothers, why don't you?"

Gimme a minute. Which meant, let me take care of this on my own. Without your input.

Her jaw clenched down hard because they'd just had this damn conversation.

Shaking her head, she turned away from him and pushed past her brothers. "Fine, whatever. Kill each other for all I care."

Her father was standing at the bottom of the stairs with a concerned expression. "What's going on?"

"Men being idiots."

Emma rushed up and grabbed Kelsey's hand. "Way to tell 'em, Aunt Kessey. Wanna go run over Ken with my trucks?"

"Why yes, Em. I think that sounds like more fun than I've had all day."

CHAPTER SEVENTEEN

Hunt did not look good when he finally came upstairs almost thirty minutes later.

From Kelsey's spot on the rug in front of the fireplace where she was sitting with Emma, she glanced toward the stairs. Her brothers each emerged with a frown. Her father had an unreadable expression on his face. And Hunt, climbing the steps at the back of the group, looked pale and completely uncomfortable.

Emma made crashing noises as she rammed her Tonka truck over the top of Ken, but Kelsey barely noticed. Hunt's lip was no longer bleeding, and there were no other visible marks on him from whatever had happened after she'd left, but his uneasy expression told her loud and clear that whatever he'd said had not gone over well.

She took little joy in the fact he'd been grilled to within an inch of his life. She looked back at Emma on the floor in front of her. If he hadn't been so bullheaded and sent her upstairs, she could have helped him with that.

"Oh good." Kelsey's mother glanced up from the dishwasher where she was loading plates. "No one needs medical attention. I was starting to worry."

"I would have called you if it got bloody." Alec moved into the kitchen and kissed his mother on the cheek. "Hunt knew better than to fight back."

Ethan chuckled and dropped onto the chaise beside Sam where she was sitting near the windows with a magazine and slid an arm around her shoulder. Thomas moved straight to the fridge and pulled it open as if he hadn't just eaten an hour before. Rusty, looking a little more chill than he'd been earlier, but not by much, crossed to her father's favorite leather chair on the far side of the room away from the group and picked up the book he'd been reading earlier in the day.

Kelsey's father wrapped his arm around his wife and rubbed her arm reassuringly. "It's all good. Just normal male bonding."

"Uh-huh," she answered with a grin. "Why do I not believe you, Michael McClane?"

Hunt cautiously stepped onto the carpet where Kelsey sat, his hands tucked into the pockets of his worn jeans, his shoulders tight. Kelsey continued to play with Emma, not about to ask what had happened down there. He wanted to handle it on his own? Fine, he could handle it all on his own.

Across from Kelsey, Raegan, who'd also been sitting on the carpet, glanced up at Hunt, then pushed to her feet. "I think that's my cue to go hit my husband over the head with a two-by-four." She squeezed Hunt's arm as she stepped past him. "Don't worry. I'll talk to him."

"I already did. Though I'm not opposed to accepting help wherever I can get it."

Kelsey wasn't really sure what that meant, but she wasn't in the mood to ask. And she wasn't in the mood to argue anymore either.

Voices echoed lowly in the room as she shoved Ken's arms and legs back onto his torso again and set the doll up on the carpet once more so Emma could crash into it with her trucks and dismember the thing. Long seconds later, Hunt slid to the floor beside Kelsey and leaned back against the couch. But he was careful not to touch her, and she didn't know how to read that or even if she should.

"You should know," he said in a low voice as Emma made crashing sound effects and backed over Ken, "that your father is the only reason I'm still breathing."

Kelsey huffed and grabbed Ken's head before it rolled under the couch. "He's a total pacifist. He could have thrown Julian out of this house years ago and saved me a messy divorce, but he didn't because he doesn't believe in violence. Don't feel special."

Hunt sighed and glanced sideways at her. "You're really funny, you know that? I told him, Kelsey."

Her hand stilled against Ken's mangled arm, and something in her chest cinched down tight. "Told him what?"

He reached for Ken's arm and head from Kelsey's hands and handed them back to Emma. "I told him and your brothers that I'm crazy about you, that I have been for a long time, and that I'm a complete idiot for nearly messing this up."

"Thank you," Emma said, then hummed "Ring Around the Rosie" while she shoved Ken's parts back together.

"Why would you do that?" Kelsey asked, staring up at him with wide eyes.

"Because it's true." He slid one hand around her nape, pulled her toward him, and kissed her—right there in front of everyone as if it was a normal, everyday occurrence—then released her. "And because I am." Looking away from her toward Emma, he said, "So who taught you to run over guys like this, Em? Was it your dad? Is he teaching you to be a man-hater already?"

Emma threw her head back and laughed, showing off her little white teeth. "Daddy didn't teach me. I taught me." Jumping up from her spot, she picked up Ken's torso and one of her trucks, then plopped down on Hunt's lap. "Look. Ken can't fit in the seat with his legs. He's too big. I have ta cut them off so he fits."

Still too stunned to speak, Kelsey watched as Emma launched into a conversation with Hunt about the uselessness of legs, and Hunt let her boss him around like she did all the men in the McClane family. Kelsey glanced up and around and realized everyone was watching them—Ethan and Sam from across the room with amused expressions, Alec and Raegan near the dining room table, his arm over her shoulder, a reluctantly accepting look in his eyes, her with a knowing smile as she wrapped her arms around his waist. Rusty was still in his chair brooding, but he no longer seemed ready to pound his fist into Hunt's face, just resigned to the current situation. And in the kitchen, her parents didn't seem the least bit surprised. Her mom was grinning, and her dad stood behind her mom rubbing her shoulders and whispering something in her ear Kelsey couldn't hear. Even Thomas, eating straight out of a carton of ice cream, didn't seem fazed by what Hunt had just done. Which, after the scene only minutes before in the basement, didn't just strike Kelsey as bizarre, it told her loud and clear that whatever he'd shared with the men in her family had convinced them he was telling the truth.

"What?" Hunt looked sideways and smirked. "You look confused, Kels."

"I . . ." She was. Way the hell confused. Because something told her she never could have smoothed things over with her family the way he just had.

Hunt's phone in his back pocket buzzed. He shifted to the side and pulled it out. But when he stiffened, Kelsey knew something was wrong.

Her adrenaline spiked, and her pulse whirred in her ears. "What is it?"

Hunt sat forward, gently shifting Emma from his leg to the floor, then carefully held the phone out so only she could see the screen.

An image flashed. And Kelsey's heart shot straight into her throat when she saw the picture of the two of them, sitting side-by-side on the floor with Emma on Hunt's lap.

The picture that had been clearly taken through the windows of her parents' home only seconds before.

––––––

Hunt hadn't told Kelsey what to do.

He'd been careful about that. Wasn't about to make the same mistake again. But he'd been strung tight as a drum the whole time her family had been discussing what was best for Kelsey now that they knew Foster was still following her. And more relieved than he could show when she agreed that leaving with him and going back to his beach house was the best option at this point.

He'd taken every roundabout way between Lake O and the coast that he could, doing his best to throw anyone off their track. While Hunt had contacted PPD and the Feds about Kelsey's most recent text before leaving her parents' place, her brothers had hoofed it across the lake to where the picture appeared to have been taken. They hadn't found Foster—not that Hunt had expected him to be standing there waiting—but they had found a camera set up in the trees across the water that was most likely controlled by a remote cell phone app and a nearby nonsecure wireless signal.

The police were currently checking all security footage from PDX, searching for any sign Foster had come through the local airport either brazenly or in disguise. If he'd been in California just the day before, taking photos of them at that coffee shop, he had to have flown in. He couldn't have made the drive and set everything up in Oregon in time. Not unless he had an accomplice.

The thought that he might have someone working with him formed a knot in Hunt's stomach as he wound through the last part of the drive toward his beach house. Since they'd left her parents' place after dinner, it was already dark, and the storm moving in, slashing rain across the windshield, wasn't helping his mood. He was confident once he got Kelsey into the house, though, that everything would be okay. The beach house was wired tighter than Fort Knox. Since it was owned by his company and really only used when clients needed a safe getaway or he needed a place to think, it wasn't known to many. And just in case anyone got past the high-tech security—which they wouldn't—he always had the safe room that was completely impenetrable.

He rolled down his window to type in the access code at the main gate, then pulled onto the property and watched the gate close behind him. A winding, paved drive took them another half mile to the house. He used his secure cell phone app to open the garage, then pulled into the middle stall and closed the doors after them.

Kelsey hadn't spoken much on the drive. He knew she was likely freaked, still processing everything that had happened at her parents' place and trying not to let her emotions show. But he really wanted her to lean on him. Needed her to, especially because he knew she was still a little irked at him about earlier.

He met her at the back of the vehicle. She'd already popped the hatch, but he grabbed her bags before she could and tossed the straps over his shoulders.

She frowned up at him. "I can carry my own bags, you know."

"I know you can. And I'm a big feminist supporter whose mother taught him to be a gentleman." Shutting the hatch, he nodded toward the steps that led into the house. "Come on. Let's get inside. You can scowl at me in there just as easily as out here, only in there it's warmer."

He stepped past her and opened the door to the house. Since the house was built into a hill and the garage opened to the main level, he took her bags in and dropped them in the guest room she'd stayed in before. More than anything he wanted her stuff in his room, but he wasn't about to push things with her and risk another major fuckup.

He set her bags on the bench at the end of the bed, then glanced toward the door where she stood just inside the room with her arms crossed over her chest and an unreadable expression on her tired face. "It's late.

You're probably exhausted. I'll let you change and get some sleep. I need to go check the security system and make sure everything's running right."

She didn't say anything as he stepped past her. Didn't try to stop him or make any move to join him, and he tried not to be disappointed by that fact. She'd agreed coming here with him was the best place she could be at the moment. He hadn't coerced her into being alone with him. When her brother Rusty had asked her if she was sure she felt safe with Hunt, she hadn't hesitated to say yes—in front of her whole family. But he couldn't shake the reality that she hadn't kissed him back in the living room. She hadn't reached for him or held his hand in the car on the drive out here. And she hadn't once given any indication she was glad he'd laid his feelings bare before her and everyone else.

His chest was tight as a drum as he made a full sweep of the house, checking the entire system and all the monitors. He tugged on a coat and walked the perimeter of the property in the rain, trying not to think about Kelsey and what the hell was happening between them, failing miserably because thoughts of her just wouldn't leave his brain. Stepping back inside, he shook the rain from his jacket and headed down to his office to call Davies, hoping an update would get his head back on straight. But when he learned there was still no concrete news and that no one had a fucking clue where Foster had gone, his adrenaline spiked all over again.

He drew a deep breath. Told himself they were safe in this house. And headed into the kitchen to grab two cold waters from the fridge.

His feet slowed outside Kelsey's bedroom door, and he glanced into the room. She hadn't unpacked a single thing. Hadn't taken off her shoes, hadn't changed into pajamas. While she was no longer standing in the doorway, she hadn't moved far. She stood still at the end of the bed, staring down at her unopened suitcase as if it held the mysteries of the world.

Nerves churned in his belly. Cautiously, so he didn't spook her, he stepped into the room and set a water bottle on the nightstand. "Everything okay, Kels?"

"No." She shook her head quickly. "I'm not okay."

He tensed. *Shit.* She hadn't lost it when that building collapsed, or when Julian had attacked her, or when she'd seen Foster's pictures of her in California. But she was about to lose it now because the fear had finally gotten to her. He took a step toward her, desperate to console her. "Kels, you're safe here. Everything's going to be oka—"

She turned his way. "What did you tell my brothers and my dad?"

He stilled. Blinked once because that wasn't what he expected her to say. Then blinked again because the look in her light brown eyes wasn't one of fear or emotional instability, it was one of confusion. "I-I already told you."

"Did you tell them we slept together in California?"

Heat immediately rushed to his cheeks. "No. I didn't get into detail like that. I didn't need to."

"What does that mean?"

Cracking his water bottle with suddenly shaking fingers he hoped she couldn't see, he took a deep drink. "It means it wasn't necessary."

"Why not?"

Double shit. She wasn't just confused, she was angry. "Because your dad and your brothers aren't stupid."

"So you told them what? That you're crazy about me, then hinted we fucked, and they just were okay with it?"

He cringed. "Don't say it like that."

"Why not? That's what we did, isn't it?"

"Is that all it was to you?"

She stared at him long seconds in silence, and his chest tightened all over again because he couldn't read a single thing in her eyes. Had no idea if she was remembering their nights in California together or if this was her finally regretting what had happened between them.

Please don't be regretting what happened between us . . .

She broke eye contact before he could come up with an answer, shoved the suitcase off the bench, and sat. Dropping her face into her hands, she muttered, "This is a mess."

He wasn't sure what she was referring to—the situation with Foster, what had happened at her parents' house, or them—and instinct urged him to turn out of the room before she clarified and he got his heart broken for good. But he couldn't make his feet move. Didn't want to let this fester between them. Because even if she was having second thoughts, he needed her to know he wasn't.

Setting his water bottle quietly on the nightstand, he moved around the bed, knelt on the floor in front of her so they were at eye level, and gently pulled her hands from her face. She blinked several times and met his gaze, but he didn't see anger in her eyes anymore. He saw fear. A fear that gave him strength because it was the same damn fear he felt.

"Kels." He lowered her hands to her lap and brushed his thumb across her silky-smooth cheek. "I told them I'm in love with you."

"Why would you do that?" she whispered.

"Because it's true." He skimmed his thumb along her jaw. "And because I know you're in love with me."

Her eyes fell closed, and she drew in a shaky breath. But she didn't deny it. And that was all the encouragement he needed.

"Look, I know you're scared. And I know I didn't help matters much when I freaked out about that text. I told you in California that I suck at relationships. I will make mistakes, like I did today. I guarantee you'll want to slap me on numerous occasions for being such an idiot. But I'll never hurt you. Not intentionally. And if you give me a chance, I can prove that to you. I know what I want and that's you."

She opened her eyes and looked at him—really looked at him—and the emotion in her eyes was so raw, he felt as if he were seeing into her soul.

"It's hard for me to believe you. Not because I don't trust you but because I stopped trusting people who weren't my immediate family a long time ago. I could never believe anything Julian said to me, especially when it came to his emotions. Affection was something I got when he was in a good mood, or when I'd done something that pleased him, or when he wanted to prove to other people we were the perfect, happy couple. In public, he was the doting husband, but in private he was quiet, cold, and controlling, and I never knew what was going to set him off and send him into a rage."

"I'm not like that. You know I'm not like that."

"I know." She glanced down at his hands holding hers in her lap. "But I need you to understand why sometimes it seems like I'm freaking out about nothing." She met his gaze again with those open, honest, vulnerable eyes. "Because to me, it's not nothing. Julian didn't love me. He said he did, but he didn't. Not really. You don't treat someone you love the way he treated me."

The image of Benedict holding her to the floor in her warehouse slammed into him, tensing every muscle in his body.

She tightened her hands around his. "I know what you're thinking, and I need you to know what you saw the other day was the worst he ever did to me, physically at least. Most of the time it was mild. He'd grab me by the arm or push me up against the wall to get my attention. A couple of times I ended up with bruises, but not usually. And most of the time when he lost his temper, it happened when we were arguing, and I was yelling at him."

Hunt's jaw clenched down hard. "That's no excuse. No guy— husband, boyfriend, or whatever—should ever grab you or push you or hurt you no matter what you say or do. It's unacceptable, so stop making excuses for it."

"I know." She looked back down at their hands. "That's one of the big reasons I finally had the courage to leave. But the worst . . ." She bit her lip. "The worst things he did weren't physical. They were verbal, and they were emotional, and they damaged me. I know it's easy to say everything he said was a lie, but he knew how to tap into my fears and neuroses, and he used them against me. He was good at that. He knew how to make me feel like I was never enough, and those feelings have lingered, long after I got away from him. Even when I don't want them to."

She sniffled as she continued to focus on their hands, and a dozen different emotions swirled inside him, the strongest of which were the need to console her, and the urge to pound his fist through Benedict's face all over again.

"My parents raised me to be a strong, independent woman," she went on, "and ninety percent of the time, that's exactly what I am. I have a college degree, for crying out loud. I'm not stupid. But with Julian I felt stupid. And I was never strong or independent with him. I let him have control over my emotional well-being. If he was happy, I was happy. If he wasn't, it meant I'd done something wrong and needed to fix it. My whole life with him was trying to act like everything was perfect in public while walking on eggshells in private. I never stood up for myself. I let him call all the shots. I wasn't a partner. I was property."

A sick feeling rolled through his gut when he realized what she was trying to say. "That's not me. I wouldn't treat you like that. When I stupidly told you to stay at your parents' house, it was only because I was scared what Foster had plan—"

"I know." She squeezed his hands again and met his gaze, looking fierce and gorgeous and strong—way stronger than she even knew she was. "I know you're not like him, and I'm not upset anymore about what you said in the car. I'm telling you all this because I need you to understand. I stayed with him for a long time—way longer than I should have—because I thought if I could just make him love me, then it would prove I wasn't as worthless as he'd said so many times. And in some sick sort of way, I guess I thought it would prove my birth mother abandoning me wasn't really about me either. It took me a long time to trust Hannah and Michael. An even longer time to trust my brothers. And as much as I trust you and believe in you, and know you're not like Julian, I'm still . . . scared. Because what if you change your mind? Or get tired of my irrational reactions? Or just plain decide I'm not worth the effort anymore? I don't know what that would do to me."

Tears filled her eyes. She blinked rapidly to force them back. But just the fact she was confiding in him and not pulling away made him fall deeper in love with her.

He lifted his hands to her face. "I don't have any guarantees for you. I don't know what's going to happen tomorrow or next year or ten years from now. The only thing I know for sure is that I love you. I love all of you. The strong you, the feisty you, the nervous you, even the scared you. And the way I feel about you has nothing to do with what happened in the last week. I've been half in love with you for at least ten years. I love you because of everything you've been through and survived. I love you because even though you think you're weak, you're not. You're the strongest woman I've ever known. And I love you because you haven't let any of your past—the hurt, the anger, all the disappointments—harden you as so many other people would. You let it shape you into the amazing, talented, incredible woman you are."

Tears slid over her lashes and down her cheeks. Tears that caused his heart to swell inside his chest.

Sliding one hand to her nape, he gently tugged her toward him and pressed his forehead to hers. "I know you're scared," he whispered. "I'm scared too, but not of loving you. I could never be scared of that because it's the only thing I know is right. I'm terrified I'm gonna screw this up like I almost did today and lose you forever. Because that would gut me. Way worse than losing my mom ever did. Especially now, when I've finally realized you're the only thing in this whole wide world that matters."

She sniffled, lifted her hands to his elbows, and drew back from his forehead. "You're not going to lose me," she whispered. "As long as you keep loving me, you'll never lose me." She pressed her mouth against his and slid her arms around his neck. "I love you too. I've always loved you."

He couldn't breathe. Was almost sure he'd heard her wrong. But when he opened to her kiss, and she slipped her tongue into his mouth and groaned as she tasted him, he knew she was his. For as long as he wanted her. Forever.

All he had to do was keep her safe from a madman.

CHAPTER EIGHTEEN

Kelsey couldn't get close enough to Hunt. Couldn't touch him fast enough. Couldn't show him quickly enough just what his words meant to her.

Gripping him tighter at the shoulders, she spread her legs to make room for him where he knelt between her thighs. Her breasts pressed against his hard chest as he tugged her closer. Aching to feel him—all of him—she rocked her pelvis against his hips, torturing them both.

He groaned. Nipped at her bottom lip, then sucked the spot until she moaned. "I need you, Kelsey. I need to be inside you."

"Yes." *Oh fuck, yes.* Fingers trembling, she grappled with the buttons on his shirt and slipped the first one free. "I need you too." Desperate, she kissed him hard and whispered, "Now. Right now."

His answer was a low growl as he wrapped his arms around her waist and lifted her from the bench. She held on to his shoulder, kissing him again and again as he carried her to the bed and laid her out on the mattress.

She dragged him down on top of her, kissing him deeply while her fingers went right back to freeing his buttons. She needed skin, wanted him naked. He drew back so she had to arch up to keep reaching his lips, then slid his hand down her leg and flipped her right shoe free from her foot, followed by her left. They clattered against the carpet. Hooking his thumb into the top of her sock, he yanked off the first and then the second.

She braced her bare feet on the bed as he climbed back over her. Reaching up, she shoved the two halves of his shirt aside, then sucked in a breath at the sight of his chiseled abs and chest. He drew back from her mouth long enough to wiggle out of the sleeves, and she skimmed her fingertips over his chest, loving the way it made him shiver. Tossing his shirt behind him with frantic moves, he leaned down and closed his mouth over hers with a hot, wet kiss again, then wrapped an arm around her waist and tugged her higher on the bed.

She moaned as he kissed the corner of her mouth, her cheek, her jaw as he worked his way down her neck and pushed her soft sweater up her torso. Cool air tightened her already straining nipples to stiff peaks beneath the thin lace bra. He drew back and looked down with rapt attention. Licked his lips as if he couldn't wait to taste her. And knowing he wanted her that much, knowing he was hers, created a tidal wave of want inside her that condensed between her legs.

Her stomach caved in under his heated gaze. Grasping the hem of her sweater, she swept it over her head and tossed it on the bed. And wasting no time, he flipped the front clasp free on her bra, slid his palm around the outside of her breast, then lowered his mouth and traced her nipple with the tip of his tongue until she groaned.

"Hunter . . ." She arched her back and sifted her fingers into his hair, desperate for more, desperate to feel him everywhere. "That feels good."

"No, baby, you feel good." He moved to her other breast, licking and laving and tormenting until she was writhing beneath him. She flexed her hips against his chest, pressed her knees into his ribs, dug her fingernails into his shoulders, wanting only more. He took the cue and dragged a line of molten kisses down her belly. With one hand, he rolled her left nipple between his thumb and forefinger. With the other, he toyed with the right nipple until she arched her back and cried out. And then he licked a line of heat across her lower belly and popped the snap on her jeans open with his teeth. "And in a second I'm going to make you feel amazing."

He released her nipples, drew back on his knees, grasped her jeans at the waistband, and stripped them and her underwear straight down her legs.

She gasped and quickly tugged the straps of her bra off her arms and tossed the garment over her shoulder. And then, bracing herself on her elbows, she watched as he lowered his knees to the floor, hooked his arms under her thighs, and yanked her to the edge of the mattress with the hottest, sexiest, most gorgeous eyes she'd ever seen locked on her.

He pushed her thighs wide. Smiled that wicked, for-her-eyes-only grin she loved so much. And then he glanced down and breathed hot over her swollen flesh as he whispered, "This is what I've been craving."

She held her breath and bit her lip, anticipating that first touch. And when she felt it, when she watched him lick up her center with the flat of his tongue, she cried out and arched up to meet his mouth, wanting only this, wanting only more, wanting only the pleasure and emotions and perfection he could make her feel.

"Oh, yes, Hunter. Just like that." Her fingers gripped the comforter as he circled her clit and pleasured her with his mouth. She rocked against his touch, moaning and begging for more. He feasted on her, drawing her closer to the edge with every frantic flick of his tongue. And when he slid two fingers inside her slick channel and stroked in time with his licks, she lost track of time and space and everything that had happened the last few days and flashed like lightning into an orgasm that consumed every inch of her body.

She collapsed on the bed in a sweaty mess, still shaking from her release. But he only gave her a moment to breathe. Trailing his lips back up her body, he found her mouth and devoured her like a man starved, like he couldn't get enough, like she was his everything.

Desire resurged inside her. Lust morphed to an all-consuming need to feel him everywhere. Lifting one hand to his face, she pressed her tongue against his and reached down to help him push his jeans off. He was already ahead of her, though. Naked and already tearing a condom open. She reached for it, wanting to help him, but he pulled away from her mouth, grasped her at her hips, and flipped her to her stomach.

She hit the mattress with a gasp and tried to push up on her hands. Foil crinkled at her back, and then he was there, the rough scratch of his leg hair brushing her inner thighs, his hands tugging her hips up so she was braced on her knees, his fingers sliding through her wetness until she was so hot and eager for more, she pressed back against him and quivered.

"I like the way you tremble when I touch you." He nudged her knees farther apart with his thighs, then slid the thick head of his erection through her wetness. She held her breath as he leaned over her back and pressed a kiss to the corner of her mouth. And then he flexed and slowly pushed inside her, stretching her around his girth until she moaned. "But I *love* the sounds you make when I'm inside you."

He pressed all the way inside her, slow and deep, and held still as her channel relaxed around him. Just as slowly, he drew back, causing her to tighten every muscle to keep him from sliding free. His fingers gripped her at the hips. He sighed, then pressed in deep all over again, this time a little harder, groaning at the way she clenched to hold him tight.

"Kelsey . . ." His thrusts picked up speed. He drove inside her again and again, making her wetter with each plunge as her desire grew. Sliding one hand around her waist, he slipped his fingers between her legs and found her clit, stroking in time with his thrusts until she was rocking back against him, their pace growing more frantic and more desperate with every second.

"Oh, yes." Pleasure streaked through her body, tightening her nipples, making her skin hot and tight, centering every thought only on that place between her legs he was stroking and filling the way only he could.

He grunted in her ear. Thrust harder. Wrapping his free arm around her waist, he drew her up from the mattress and back against his chest. She gasped and spread her legs wider so he could continue to flick her clit, so he could press farther inside her with every sinful plunge. Gripping her face, he turned her mouth toward his. His hot breath tickled her lips as he whispered, "God, I love being inside you."

He captured her bottom lip and sucked until she groaned, then he pushed his tongue between her lips and consumed her like a man possessed. His thrusts grew frenzied. He drove deep again and again, rubbing hard against that spot that made her wild.

"Kelsey." He kissed her lips and smoothed the damp hair back from her face as she gripped his arm. "This is real. We're meant to be together. You know this is as right as I do."

Tears burned her eyes. Tears not just because he loved her, but because he loved her in spite of all her many flaws.

Her heart squeezed so hard it stole her breath. Tipping her head back against his shoulder, she pressed her mouth to his and kissed him deeply, tightening on every thrust so he could feel what was in her heart and she could take him over the edge with her.

"I do know." She grasped his arm at her waist for stability. "Just don't let go of me."

"Never. I am never letting you go. I promise." He swelled inside her and groaned against her lips. "Come with me, baby. Come all around me."

His entire body jerked with the force of his orgasm, and knowing it was consuming him triggered hers. Heat exploded inside her in a wave of bliss that was sweeter than anything had ever been. And as it washed over her, she cried out at the sheer force, savored it, and told herself she could make this last. That *they* could make this last. All she had to do was believe. Even if believing was the hardest thing for someone like her to ever do.

She didn't remember sliding to the mattress, but when she blinked, she felt Hunt's weight at her back and his body still twitching with the aftershocks of his release.

She smiled, loving his heat against her, and reached for his hand on the mattress near her head.

He groaned and rolled off her. But he didn't go far, and as soon as he was on his side, he tugged her up against his sweaty, sweet, tantalizing body.

She sighed as he trailed his fingertips down her spine. Against her forehead, he pressed a soft kiss and whispered, "I told you that you were crazy about me."

She grinned as she rested her cheek against his chest, loving that he knew the perfect thing to say, even now. "Proud of yourself, huh?"

"For that? No. For the way I made you scream my name a few minutes ago? Hell yeah."

She couldn't stop herself. She laughed. And, oh, how good it felt to laugh. She hadn't done much laughing the last few months. The last few years, really. "I did not scream."

"Okay, screeched."

She swatted his arm playfully. "I didn't screech either."

"All right, maybe it was a shout." He tipped his chin down and grinned at her. "Bet I can make you scream my name before this night is over, though."

The wicked heat re-forming in his eyes made her suck in a sharp breath. And this time she didn't even try to fight what she knew she wanted. "I would love to see you try."

Smiling, he rolled her onto her back and kissed her once more. "That is one challenge I will never decline."

Kelsey sighed in the dark and snuggled closer to Hunt under the covers. The storm whipped around outside, rustling trees and grasses, but in Hunt's big bed, she was warm and content and quiet. Well, her lips were quiet. Her brain was another matter entirely.

After he'd pleasured her thoroughly in her room, he'd taken her into the big shower in the master bedroom and soaped up every inch of her skin. He'd tried to drive her mad with his fingers under the spray, but she'd told him she needed food before he wore her out again, so he'd dragged her into the kitchen, pushed her into a chair at the table, and cooked her an omelet. And when hunger was sated, he'd proceeded to have his way with her right there on the table before dragging her back to his room and completely destroying her in this bed.

She couldn't remember the last time a guy had cooked for her. Couldn't recall the last time she'd been so relaxed. Wasn't sure she'd ever been so happy. But she was absolutely positive she'd never had so many orgasms in one night. And just thinking about all the delicious ways he could make her moan made her want another one, right this very second.

Biting her lip, she slid her hand across his chiseled abs. Above her, where his head rested in the pillows, he let out a low groan. "How the hell are you not exhausted? Every muscle in my body feels broken."

She smiled, remembering his acrobatics during that last round. "That's because you got too creative. All I had to do was lie there."

He brushed his hand down her arm. "Yeah, next time you get to do all the work."

Heat gathered between her legs.

He sighed and pressed a kiss to her forehead. "Let me sleep a little, baby. Then I promise to rock your world again. We both need the rest."

He was right. She knew he was right. She was probably too tired for another round, anyway. Sighing, she closed her eyes and let her mind drift, let her muscles relax, let all her worries slip away.

She wasn't sure how much time passed or how long she slept, but when Hunt jerked beneath her, it startled her awake. Blinking several times, she pushed up on her hands as he climbed off the bed. "What's wrong?"

"The fan's not running." He crossed to the closet and tugged on a pair of jeans.

Blinking because she was still half-asleep, confused because she had no idea what time it was or how long she'd actually slept, Kelsey glanced up at the ceiling fan blades unmoving above her. "Didn't you turn it off before we went to bed?"

"I didn't turn it off. I never turn it off. I need the white noise to sleep." He opened the bottom nightstand drawer, typed in a code on the small safe inside, and pulled out a 10mm. "Stay here." He checked the magazine. "Get dressed just in case. I'm gonna check the security system."

Her brain jolted wide awake at those words, and she sat straight up in bed. "Hunt. Oh my God."

He moved back to the bed and grasped her at the nape as he kissed her. "It's probably just the storm. Odds are good the power just went out. I'm a light sleeper. I'm sure the generator's going to pop on any second, but stay here and wait for me just to be safe. And lock the door as soon as I'm gone."

Her heart raced like wildfire as he moved into the hall and closed the door at his back. Scrambling out of the bed, she found her suitcase in the corner of the room where Hunt had dropped it after they'd decided she was staying in his room, tugged on her tank and a pair of pajama bottoms, then crossed to the bedroom door and flipped the lock like he'd said.

Seconds morphed to minutes, which lengthened and frayed her already tattered nerves. In the darkness, she paced and told herself he hadn't been gone that long, that everything was okay, that he'd be back any second. But every moment he didn't return shot her heart rate up and made her palms sweat even more.

"Come on, come on, come on," she muttered.

A buzzing sound startled her. With a quiet yelp, she jerked toward the bed. Hunt's cell phone illuminated the room in an eerie white light.

Heart in her throat, she lurched for it, sure it was Hunt calling from the landline downstairs to tell her everything was fine. But the second her fingers closed around the device and she read the words on the screen, her blood ran ice cold.

Do I look like a small dog kind of guy?
Even sporting dogs like Princess live ten to thirteen years.
That's not exactly short.
Not exactly long either. What's the point in getting attached to something that's going to be gone in ten years?

They were her own words texted back to her. Hunt's too. Spoken only days ago in this house. When they'd first arrived and she'd seen him playing with Princess on the beach after his run.

She swallowed hard. Somehow she knew the text was from Foster, coming through on Hunt's phone, not hers. But she didn't understand how. Or how he knew what they'd said to each other in this house.

The phone buzzed again, and another text appeared on the screen. Only this one wasn't a repeat of any conversation.

Poor Princess didn't make it to ten. Guess your boyfriend's going to be disappointed. He should learn to get used to disappointment, though, seeing as how he'll be next.

Fear clamped an icy hand around Kelsey's throat and squeezed so tight she couldn't breathe. She rushed for the door, flipped the lock, and raced into the darkened living room.

"Hunt!" Unable to find him, she tore into the kitchen, searched the entire upper level, then ran for the stairs, hoping he hadn't gone outside to check the generator. Hoping and praying that she could stop him before he did. "Hunter!"

Panic surged up her throat when she hit the basement level and he didn't respond. "Hunter O'Donnell, answer me!"

Only there was nothing. Nothing but the sound of her racing pulse echoing in her ears and her frantic breaths.

A new sense of terror consumed her. Shaking, she backed into a dark corner in the basement and tried to breathe, tried to think, tried not to completely break down.

And as she did, she felt it again. That sense of dread that told her something horrible was about to happen. Only this feeling was so strong, she knew it wasn't a false alarm.

———

Hunt flipped the switch on the generator, confused as to why the thing hadn't automatically popped on.

As he'd thought, the storm had cut out power all over this portion of the coast, and no lights could be seen for miles on the hillside around him. Shining his flashlight over the machine, he checked for any evidence it had been tampered with but couldn't find anything. There were no cut wires or broken pieces. In fact, the entire property checked out. Everything was normal. Which meant he'd scared the crap out of Kelsey for no reason.

He waited while the generator fired up. When it was running with a steady hum, he headed inside the garage, turned the light on, and looked up as the room was illuminated. The generator seemed to be running fine now, which he was thankful for.

He moved to the breaker box and checked the switches just to be safe. Just as he was closing the panel, a muffled scream echoed from inside the house. Kelsey's muffled scream. Coming from beneath him.

His heart lurched into his throat. Reaching for the gun tucked against his lower back, he tore into the house and raced down the stairs to the basement. The room was completely dark except for a sliver of light. He stilled as soon as he hit the carpet and squinted to see through the weight-lifting equipment set up to his left. Heavy breaths met his ears, putting him on high alert.

His stomach tightened as he gripped the gun. Someone was standing in the shadows in the corner. Someone he couldn't see. His adrenaline surged. A muffled sob met his ears.

"Kelsey?"

"Hunt?"

The air whooshed out of his lungs. Hitting the safety, he quickly tucked his gun into his back waistband and crossed to her. "What are you doing out here? I told you to stay in the bedroom. Are you okay?"

"Oh my God, I thought . . ." She moved into him in one swift move, wrapping her arms around his waist and pressing her cheek to his chest in a way that ramped up his pulse even more. "I was so scared."

"It's okay." He rubbed a hand up and down her spine. "It was just the storm. The generator already kicked on. We can turn the lights back o—"

"No." She shook her head and pushed back, fear making her voice lift an entire octave. "You don't understand. Your phone. It just buzzed. It just came through." She pushed his phone into his hand and tapped the button to illuminate the screen. The room glowed blue-white. "Look."

Hunt scanned the message, his blood turning to ice as the conversation replayed through his memory.

"How does he know what we said?" Kelsey whispered. "Was he here the other day? And Princess . . ." She covered her mouth with her hand. "What if . . . ?"

"Motherfucker." There was no way the fucker had been here the other day. There was no way he'd gotten into this house without Hunt's security being tipped off. Which meant only one thing. One thing he hadn't considered until right now. "He hacked your phone." He powered the phone down and shoved it in his back pocket. "The son of a bitch was using it like a microphone to listen to our conversations."

"But this is your phone."

"If he hacked yours, he could have easily gotten my number and hacked mine. Son of a bitch." He needed to get a screwdriver and pop the battery out of her phone so the asshole couldn't use it against them anymore. But first he had to get Kelsey somewhere safe, just in case.

"Can someone do that?" she asked in a small voice.

"Yeah, hackers can do all kinds of shit these days."

"But how? I don't understand. You gave me my phone after the bombing. You said it was secure."

He raked a hand through his hair, working for calm when he felt anything but. He didn't want to scare her more, but he knew Kelsey well enough to know she wasn't going to listen to what he needed her to do if he didn't explain this.

"Remember the cameras at your warehouse? You had the new phone with you when you went back there the morning after the bombing. My guess is he got access to your phone there, through your already compromised network. Remember the hacker who stepped forward and told the FBI how to hack the iPhone after the San Bernardino terrorist attack? Apple didn't even know how to do that. A good hacker can find a way into anything, even one of my secure devices."

He raked a hand through his hair, still not sure how Graham Foster had done it. Nothing they'd learned about the guy painted him as an elaborate hacker.

He froze, understanding widening his eyes as he remembered that photo that Kelsey had received when they'd stepped off the plane in Oregon. "Oh shit."

"What? What now?"

Hunt turned toward her. "Trey Foster designs online security software. He would absolutely know how to hack into your phone."

A memory flashed from their meeting with Trey Foster in that coffee shop. The man had paused to type something on his phone. He'd probably been signaling a camera to take their damn picture right there in front of them.

"Trey? The son? But—"

"Listen to me." Urgency pounded through him as he gripped Kelsey's shoulders. "I need you to go in the safe room and stay there until I come get you."

"What? No. You should come with me."

"I can't. I need to check the perimeter and call my team to get over here."

"Hunt . . ." Her voice trembled with fear.

It took every bit of strength he had to keep his voice even when he said, "I don't think he's here. I think he's just toying with us like before. But I need to be sure. And I won't be able to think straight and do what I need to do if I'm worried about you."

"But—"

He slid one hand under her hair and around her nape and cupped her cheek with his other hand, forcing her to look up at him. "I'll join you if there's any sign the system was bypassed, and we'll wait for the cops together. But I need you to do this for me. Please go in the safe room."

Her eyes searched his in the dim light, then she finally whispered, "Okay."

More relieved than he wanted her to know, he pulled her against him and held her, soaking in the rapid beat of her heart against his as she wrapped her arms around his waist. "It's going to be okay. I don't think he's here. And Princess is probably fine. He's just trying to scare us. Okay?"

But in the back of his mind, he couldn't be sure. The fucker had already set one bomb off and tried to kill him and her and dozens of other people. Hunt had no idea what he'd resort to next.

She clung to him and nodded. And though all he wanted to do was go on holding her, he wanted this over with more. He drew back and reached for her hand. "Come on."

The access to the safe room was off a closet in the back of the lowest level. It looked like nothing more than a shelving unit, but when Hunt tapped a special button on the side of one shelf, the entire piece swung back and revealed a steel, blast-proof door. After typing in the access code on the panel, he placed his hand on the screen for the fingerprint analysis. A click sounded, and he turned the lever and opened the heavy steel door with a hiss.

Since the house was built into a hill, the safe room was made of concrete, steel sheathing, and bullet-resistant fiberglass. It could withstand high winds, heavy rains, a tornado, a shitstorm of bullets, even a bomb blast. The lights immediately flipped on as the door opened, and he moved back to let Kelsey step past him into the room first, scanning the downstairs behind him as he went to make sure no one was lurking in the dark.

The interior of the safe room wasn't anything special. To their left was a leather couch, a coffee table, a couple of side chairs, and a flat-screen TV on the wall. Pointing to the doorway just past the TV, Hunt said, "There's a bathroom through there with a full shower." Adjacent to the doorway, he nodded to a counter that ran halfway down the twenty-foot wall. "There's water and nonperishable foods in the cabinets there, and a fridge." Moving to a metal cabinet just past the counter, he pulled the door open and showed her supplies he hoped she wouldn't need—blankets, extra clothes, flashlights and batteries, along with a first aid kit. "Anything else you need will be in here."

Wide-eyed, Kelsey nodded to her right, where floor-to-ceiling steel cabinetry bookended another counter, this one topped with a bank of monitors. "And that?"

"This is the command center." He moved to the counter, tapped a button on the keyboard, and typed in a code. All twelve monitors flipped on, illuminating different rooms in the house and locations outside on the property. "This room runs off its own generator, so regardless of what's happening outside, everything in here will still work." As she drew close he showed her how to toggle between screens to access different cameras. "From here you can see everything going on in and around the house. Cameras monitor every room. If you want to change the temperature in here or outside in the house you can do it from this panel. There's even an intercom system accessible here that lets you talk to anyone who might be out there, but don't use it. If there is someone lurking around, I don't want them to know you're in here."

She nodded, but her cheeks were completely pale, telling him she was probably only catching half of what he said.

Moving to the cabinets to his left, he typed in a code and flipped the door open, exposing the rack of guns and weaponry. Choosing a small 9mm that would fit her hand, he popped the empty magazine free on the Ruger LC9 and replaced it with a fresh one. "Do you know how to use one of these?"

Kelsey paled even more and stepped back, lifting her hands. "I-I don't want that."

"You're not going to have to use it. It's just a precaution." He closed the cabinet door, a click sounding as it locked. Moving toward her, he lifted the small gun so she could see it and said, "This is your safety here. It can't hurt you with the safety on. Once you flip that off, all you have to do is point and shoot. It's easy, and the kick isn't too bad on this one. Just don't point it at yourself, and don't shoot me when I come back."

He held it out for her, but she didn't take it, just stared at it in his hand with a nervous expression. Not wanting to push her, he set the gun on the command counter near the keyboard, then grabbed one of the two-way radios and clipped it to his belt. "If I need to talk to you, I'll do it with this. Yours is over there. I'll come back and get you when I know the place is clear."

He moved past her for the door, but she reached for his hand as he drew close, stopping him. "Wait. Just . . ." She curled into him and wrapped her arms around his waist. "Be careful, okay?"

He held her tightly, knowing she was scared. He was too, but he already felt better knowing she was safe in here.

"I will be. And I'll be right back." With one finger under her chin, he lifted so her eyes met his and added, "Hang out here and wait for me. And don't go outside no matter what you hear. Can you do that for me?"

She nodded.

"Good. Everything's going to be fine." Pressing a swift kiss to her lips, he pulled away from her and moved for the door. But one look back at her worried expression told him she wasn't convinced. "I do this for a living, Kels. And regardless of what you think right now, I'm actually pretty good at what I do."

"I know you are."

He flashed a smile for her sake and reached for the door handle to pull it closed behind him. "Relax, okay? Bolt the deadlock after me and find something to watch on the TV. I'll be back in a few minutes."

The door hissed closed at his back, and silence met his ears, followed by the shelving unit automatically sliding back into place to conceal the safe room door. Because the safe room was sound proof, he couldn't even hear her flipping the deadlocks, but he knew she'd listened and would do what he said. Knew because she was motivated by fear right now, which regardless of how much he hated that at the moment, just might be what could save her life.

Breathing easier, he decided to start with the basement. He checked every room and nook and cranny for signs of anything out of the ordinary.

Confident the bottom level was secure, Hunt moved into his office, shrugged into a light jacket, and powered up a new burner phone. Then he dialed Davies.

"It's me," he said when Davies answered. "I'm on a different number. My cell was compromised. I need a team out here ASAP."

"You got trouble?"

"I don't know. I'm going out to search the perimeter. Power went out and the generator didn't come on. System hasn't gone red, but I'd rather be safe than sorry."

Keys clicked in the background. "I'll get a couple guys out to you right away. Helicopter will be fastest."

"That's fine. Have you found anything yet?"

"About Foster? No. But just out of curiosity, I ran some searches on Vivienne Armstrong and Catarina Brunelli."

Hunt glanced toward the door, anxious to get outside and search the perimeter. "Give it to me fast. I've got stuff to do."

"This is probably unrelated to Foster, but Armstrong and Brunelli had a huge falling out a few years ago. I did a little digging, and it looks like the blow up was about a guy—Royce Sloane."

"I know that name."

"You should. He's a huge movie producer in Hollywood. He gave Armstrong her first big break on a really bad B horror flick, which was filming just about the time Kelsey McClane was conceived."

"Shit. You think the guy is her father?"

"That'd be my guess."

"Her autobiography mentioned a relationship with a guy not in the film industry."

"She was probably protecting him, don't you think? On her own or because he threatened her never to ever use his name. You know how some of those bigwig Hollywood producers are. Think they're gods."

"Her attorneys said the guy was married."

"Makes sense then."

"Maybe. But we met with Brunelli two days ago. She's the executor of Armstrong's will. If Brunelli was fucking her ex and the two had a huge falling out because of it, why would she trust Brunelli with her estate?"

"I don't know. Maybe they patched things up. Women do strange things. But this part is even more interesting. Brunelli is not only the executor of Armstrong's will, she's also the beneficiary."

"You're kidding."

"Wish I was. And she's in debt to her ears right now. Has been for a while, but it's been getting worse. Spends way more than she earns. She's a heartbeat away from filing bankruptcy."

"Shit. That gives her motive to want Armstrong dead."

"Yeah. Or Armstrong's long-lost daughter who stands to inherit the whole thing."

Hunt's mind tumbled, rushing back over the conversation with the actress in Beverly Hills. His pulse picked up speed. "She couldn't do it all on her own."

"No. She couldn't. Which was the first thing I thought. I mean, she's an actress, right? She's not a rocket scientist—especially if she's nearly bankrupt. So I looked at her past movies, and wouldn't you know, she starred in a thriller a few years ago called *Revenge* about a sociopath with a handful of names he's ticking off a list. And to disguise the fact he's actually committing targeted murders—"

"He plants homemade bombs." Hunt's stomach dropped. "Shit. I remember that movie."

"Thought you would. After I found that, I thought I'd see if Ms. Brunelli's been up to anything lately. I mean, if she devised this entire plot, she'd have to recruit people to do the dirty work for her, right? So I dug a little more, called some people, found out where her favorite hangouts are, where she likes to be seen—or not seen, and if she's been dating anybody recently. And I got a hit at a little bar in Malibu. Not unusual to see the Hollywood types there, right? She probably thought it was safe. Turns out, she's met with a guy in his late twenties or early thirties out there a few times over the last few months. I got a copy of his picture from the security system. It isn't super clear, and you can't see the guy's face, but his size and shape are pretty damn similar to Graham Foster's son Trey."

Hunt squeezed the phone tighter. "Take everything you found to Brett Callahan at PPD tonight. It might not be enough to arrest Brunelli, but it'll be enough for bring her in for questioning."

"So you don't think this is a stretch?"

"Hell no. I'm pretty sure Trey Foster is the one who hacked our phones. Kelsey just got another text, this time on mine. He was playing us the entire time. And it makes a hell of a lot more sense that Brunelli is the one who recognized Kelsey's face in those fashion photos. The woman was wearing ten different designer labels when we met her. She even brought up Kelsey's design company before we mentioned what Kelsey did for a living."

"Okay. I'm on it. What about the older Foster? Graham?"

"Do you really think he's still alive? He hasn't been seen since before the Portland bomb blew. Would you leave him alive if you were planning to set him up for a federal crime like domestic terrorism?"

"Poor fucker."

"Worry about the ones we can. Get over to Callahan. Then call me when you have news."

"Will do."

Thirty minutes later, Hunt stood on the covered side porch outside the kitchen, convinced Trey Foster was messing with them. A thorough check of every inch of the property had produced no security breach. Nothing indicated his system had been tampered with, and there was no sign of the neighbor's dog—dead or alive.

A shiver rushed down his spine beneath his jacket. As the wind whipped his hair back from his face, he typed in his closest neighbor's number and lifted the new phone to his ear. A buzzing sounded, indicating the phone lines were down. Since he knew his neighbors ran their phone through their Internet, that wasn't a surprise, especially since he'd already checked with the power company and gotten confirmation the grid in this area was down from the storm.

He stuffed the phone into his back pocket, pulled the door open, and moved into the dark kitchen. With a few key clicks, he rearmed the security system, breathing easier with every passing second. In the morning, when the storm had passed, he'd check in on Princess and his neighbors and make sure they were okay. They would be, though. He had no doubt Trey Foster just wanted to scare them. And hopefully by now Brunelli was already being questioned abou—

His phone buzzed. He reached back and pulled it out as he headed for the stairs that led down to where Kelsey was waiting. "Hey, Brett. Did Davies get to you with everything he found?"

"Yeah. I've relayed everything to the Feds, and Beverly Hills cops should be on their way to see her."

"Good."

"Thought you'd want to know I just got off with the Palm Desert Police Department. Hikers stumbled across Graham Foster's body in a ravine about five miles from his house. Looks like he's been dead at least a week."

Just as he thought. "They ID'd him already?"

"His vehicle was found a few miles away. Official ID will take a few days, but it looks like a match."

"Shit. They set him up to look like the bomber. He already had an unstable background."

"That's the way it's looking. Nice kid, huh?"

Yeah, really nice kid. Who'd told Hunt and Kelsey to their faces that he didn't like his father.

"We've been checking PDX cameras for any sign Trey Foster came through the airport in the last day or two. So far nothing, but we'll keep on it."

"Thanks. He's here somewhere. If he isn't here already, he's on his way. I know it." Hunt's phone buzzed. "Hold on, I'm getting a text." Callahan muttered something about needing to get back to work, but Hunt ignored him and pulled the phone away from his ear, then froze when he read the words on his screen.

Thanks for bringing her right to me. This was way easier than I ever planned. Don't you know how easy it is to fool a fingerprint analysis with some glue, a digital camera, and a glass? Thankfully I had plenty of time while I was hanging out here waiting for you to do just that. Ready or not, here I come.

His heart stuttered, then felt as if it completely stopped. And in a rush of understanding, he realized his security system had never tripped because he'd told Kelsey how to arm and disarm it when she'd been here just a few days before. Each time he'd given her instructions, she'd had her phone on her. Her phone that had already been hacked by Trey Foster and had been relaying their conversations like a microphone. And the fucker was right. The fingerprint analysis on his safe room was a minor security measure any person could bypass by creating a fake fingerprint with dried glue, a digital camera, and his own fucking fingerprints he'd left on a coffee mug in the kitchen before they'd left for California. All someone had to do was have access to those things and already be in the house.

He sprinted for the stairs, only one thought in his mind. "Brent? Get a unit to my beach house as fast as you can."

"Why? What's happened?"

"He's here." Fear wrapped like a boa constrictor around his chest and squeezed until all he knew was pain. "He's here, and he's got Kelsey."

CHAPTER NINETEEN

Kelsey flipped the controls on another camera, this one outside the kitchen door overlooking the porch, as she sat in front of the bank of screens in the safe room.

The porch was dark and empty. Since Hunt had just been there, and she'd looked away when he moved, she had no idea if he'd gone into the house or was at another location somewhere outside.

Sighing, she flipped to the kitchen camera, only it was dark too.

Impatience warred inside her. This was taking entirely too long. She'd tracked him through the house as best she could with the cameras, but he moved too quickly for her to completely follow him, and she didn't know the system well enough to know which camera to access next. He hadn't found anything out of the ordinary, though, which was a good sign. Hopefully, he'd be back in a matter of minutes and they could climb back in that big bed of his and forget that text had ever happened.

She moved to the living room camera and spotted him. "There you are."

He was standing in the middle of the room staring down at his new cell phone. Because he'd kept the lights off—she was sure just to be safe—the room was dark, and his face was illuminated by the eerie blue-white light from his screen. She couldn't see what was so engrossing on his phone, but her irritation kicked up even more because he was wasting time when she was stuck in this claustrophobic room.

She sighed as he lifted his head and pressed his phone to his ear. And something in his expression caused her stomach to tighten.

She sat up straighter. Narrowed her eyes. But he rushed toward the stairs and disappeared out of the camera's line of sight before she could figure out what had happened.

Her pulse turned to a whir in her ears. Swallowing hard, she pushed to her feet, told herself everything was fine, she'd probably misinterpreted that look, and frantically hit buttons with shaky fingers as she pulled up cameras in the upstairs hall and lower levels, searching for him.

He wasn't on the stairs. He wasn't in the weight room. She flipped again and again and finally spotted him when the camera right outside the safe room door came into focus.

The shelving unit was pulled back, but the steel door wasn't opening on her side. Squinting to see better, she realized he was banging on the door from the outside, but she couldn't hear a single thing where she stood. She looked toward the door just as the two-way radio on the counter squawked, jerking her back toward the screens.

"Kelsey," Hunt said in a frantic voice. "Kelsey, answer me."

She fumbled for the second radio and pulled it close. "I'm here. What's wrong?"

"Kelsey, dammit, answer me!"

Panic tightened her throat. She looked down at the radio, wondering why it wasn't working, then realized she needed to push the button for him to hear her. "I'm here," she said again, this time with the button depressed. She rushed toward the door to let him in. "What's going on?"

"He's in the house." His frantic voice crackled from the radio. "Let me in. We have to get the hell out of here."

Her heart seized. "Oh my God, what do you mean, he's in the hou—"

"Busted," a voice said at her back. A familiar voice. A voice that should not be in the room with her. "Guess the gig is finally up, and my hiding spot's been found."

Terror streaked down Kelsey's spine, chilling every inch of her skin. Slowly, she turned in a circle and stared in horror at Trey Foster standing in the middle of the safe room, watching her with icy-blue eyes that weren't the least bit friendly. Not at all as they'd been in that coffee shop in California.

"Kelsey!" Hunt screamed across the radio.

Her heartbeat pounded in her ears. Her breaths grew fast and shallow. Before she could even lift the radio to respond to Hunt, Foster swiped the unit from her hand and hurled it across the room. It smacked the wall and clattered to the ground. "I don't think we need that anymore."

Kelsey jerked to the side, her adrenaline soaring. "Y-you. B-but why?"

He didn't make any move toward her, just tracked her like a lion tracks it prey, putting himself between her and the door. "Why? Simple. Money. Money I deserve after all the shit years I spent with that man."

Kelsey didn't know what he meant, but she knew she had to keep him talking and distracted so she could figure out a way to open the door and let Hunt in.

Her mind raced. She fought the panic threatening to consume her. Hunt had said everything was controlled by the keyboard. Inching back toward the counter, she tried to remember what he'd showed her before he'd left the room. All she remembered was an intercom, but she couldn't remember what button triggered it. Reaching behind her, she searched for a button—any button.

"What do you think you're doing?" Foster tipped his head and glared at her.

"N-nothing." She tapped as many keys blindly as she could, hoping one would do something.

"Get away from that." He jerked toward her. His hand landed hard against her shoulder and flung her to the side.

Kelsey stumbled and hit the wall hard, lifting her hands at the last second so she didn't smack into it face-first.

Palms stinging, she gasped and braced herself, then shifted around to face him. Her legs shook. Her breath caught. Too late she spotted the gun sitting on the counter right where Hunt had left it. The gun she hadn't even thought to grab for.

She had to get that gun. It was her only chance.

She swallowed hard. *Keep it together. Stay strong. You can get through this.* Her old mantra raced through her mind, and she seized on it even as her arms and legs trembled with blinding fear.

"W-why are you doing this, Trey? What do you want? Whatever it is, you can have it."

He let out a malicious grunt. "What I want is my life back. Can you give me that?"

His eyes were no longer icy but filled with a fury that told her he wasn't just a murderer but a sociopath.

"I-I don't know what you mean," she whispered, sliding down the wall away from him.

"No, you wouldn't, would you? Because you're just like her. Selfish and spoiled rotten." He raked a hand through his hair and laughed, but the sound held no humor. "I read up on you, you know. After you were adopted, you had it easy. I saw that fancy house your adoptive family lives in on that lake. Pretty snazzy. Know where I grew up? That dump of a shack you and your boyfriend broke into. Wanna know what my childhood was like?" He swiped at a lamp on the table beside the couch, sending it shattering it against the floor. "It was fucking torture. My old man spent every miserable second whining about how she left him. And when he wasn't whining, he was bitching about the government for taking his money, bitching about her for being a whore, or shit-faced drunk and pounding on me for being the reason she left."

Kelsey was having trouble following him but one thing got through. One sickening comment that she didn't want to believe. "She . . . Vivienne was your mother?"

Disgust filled his features. "Now you've figured it out. Why the hell did you think they had to get married? Because of me. Only she quickly realized a husband and a baby and a shit life in a trailer wasn't going to win her any Academy Awards. So she ditched us and ran off to the glitz and glam of Hollywood. Oh, but when you came along . . . oh, she changed her tune about wanting to be a mother then, didn't she? The whole world knows how she changed her tune. Until that asshole producer who knocked her up wouldn't leave his wife and marry her."

"I-I didn't know her." Kelsey knew she should feel something, anything for what Trey had been through, but all she could think was that this man could not be related to her. "I never met her. I don't even know if I'm related to her."

"You are. Cat figured it out. She saw your picture in the media. Ironic that your fame is what tipped us off to you, huh?"

Cat? He wasn't talking about Catarina Brunelli, was he? Kelsey's eyes flew wide with shock and disbelief.

He exhaled a pathetic laugh. "If anyone should know who you're related to, I guess it'd be her. Seeing as how she was fucking your father too. Worked out good for us, though. Set up the perfect plan. You all were running around like crazies, looking for my dad. That was entertaining, I have to admit."

Kelsey didn't completely understand what he was saying, but she did understand that he and Catarina Brunelli had been behind the bombing and everything that had happened to her, and they'd done it all to get Vivienne Armstrong's money.

"I-I don't want her money." She frantically scanned the room for anything she could use as a weapon. Dammit, why hadn't she tucked that gun in her waistband? Why was this room so clean? "I never did."

"Good, because you're not getting it. With you dead, it'll either go to me or Cat. Just depends on how the court rules on her estate."

Her eyes snapped his way. "What about your father?"

"Oh, did I forget that part? He's already dead." He moved closer toward her, boxing her in between him and the small kitchen counter. He tugged a rope and a hypodermic needle from the pocket of his jacket. "Now, we can do this the easy way, or we can do this the hard way. One is going to hurt. I don't care which you choose, but you need to know right now that the outcome will still be the same. Overdose is easier." His lips twisted in a malicious smile. "The rope's a whole lot more fun."

Kelsey focused on the objects in his hands, and her whole body shook. In that moment, she knew Vivienne Armstrong's death had not been an accidental overdose.

From the corner of her vision, Kelsey spotted Hunt frantically pounding on the door, trying to find a way in. But this time, on the far right screen, she also spotted police in tactical gear slinking along the side of the house with weapons already drawn.

Her heart raced. Her palms were slick from fear. She was out of time. If she didn't try now, she'd never have another chance.

"I love you because even though you think you're weak, you're not. You're the strongest woman I've ever known."

Hunt's words gave her strength. Filled her with courage. With hope.

She lurched toward the keyboard. Her body smacked hard into the counter. She hit multiple buttons to open the door, praying one would be the right one before he killed her.

"You bitch!" Foster slammed into her back. The counter dug deep into her belly. She gasped as the air rushed out of her lungs. He shoved her sideways along the counter, and she grunted and threw out her hands, trying to stop her momentum. Her shoulder rammed into the cabinet on the far side of the counter. Pain spiraled through her arm and down into her chest. She cried out, ground her teeth, and tried to shove Foster's weight off her so she could breathe, but he was too heavy. Her muscles too weak. A click echoed through the room. Something sharp stabbed into her neck.

She screamed again and struggled against his hold. Something hard slammed into the back of her skull. Her forehead smashed against a computer screen. "You fucking bitch! It's definitely going to hurt now."

Blinding pain ricocheted through her head, slowing her fight. She groaned but barely had time to push away from the screen. She cried out as Foster grasped her by the back of the hair and threw her to the ground.

She hit the cement floor on her back. Pain spiraled through her head and shoulder and stomach and back, so much she could barely move. She groaned. Blinked through wavering vision. And looked up to see Trey Foster breathing heavily as he held the gun Hunt had given her in one hand and stared down at her with a malevolent rage.

Her adrenaline wavered. He was going to shoot her. She tried to roll to her side. Tried to get up. Couldn't seem to make her muscles work. He lifted the gun. She tensed, bracing herself for the bullet. But behind him, something moved. It was the door. No, it wasn't the door. The door was already open. It was . . . Hunt.

She wasn't sure what happened next. She jerked at the gunshot. Jerked again when Foster whipped around, lifted his gun toward the door, and another shot rang out. Jerked a third time when the final shot echoed through the room.

Gasping, hands shaking in front of her, she stared wide-eyed at the place where Foster had been standing only seconds before, ready to shoot her. The place that was now empty because he was lying motionless on the floor.

"Kels? Oh shit." Hands grasped her face, turning her from looking at Foster. "Look at me, Baby. Stay with me."

She blinked up at Hunt, kneeling over her, trying to see him better, but her vision was water. Turning black at the edges. He brushed a hand against her cheek, and she felt something warm and wet and sticky on her skin where he touched her. "I'm right here, Kels. Stay with me. You're okay."

She didn't feel okay. Had she been shot? She tried to figure out what was going on. Couldn't. She didn't feel any pain. Didn't remember being struck by a bullet. Even the pain in her head from hitting that computer screen was gone.

"We're down here!" Hunt screamed, looking away from her.

She didn't know who he was yelling at, but she suddenly remembered someone else was in the house.

Foster.

Panic seized her chest all over again. She opened her mouth. Tried to scream. Only managed to croak, "Fos-*ter*."

"He's dead." Hunt's sticky finger stroked her cheek again. "He can't hurt you anymore. Don't try to talk. Just keep your eyes on me. I've got you. Everything's going to be okay. Just keep breathing, baby."

She was trying to. But the panic in his voice wasn't making her feel like everything was going to be okay. And her vision was growing darker by the second.

She fought it. Tried to stay awake. Muffled voices echoed somewhere close. Someone was talking to Hunt, but she didn't know who.

"No, I'm fine," he said. "It's not bad. Take care of her first."

She reached for his hand, not understanding what was happening. His sticky fingers closed around hers. She squeezed tight, holding on to him. Not wanting to let go like he'd said he wouldn't ever let go of her.

"Dammit. Stay with me, Kels."

She tried to. She wanted to. But the darkness circled in before she could stop it. And the last thought she had was that she'd been right. Something terrible had been looming all along.

And neither of them had been able to stop it.

CHAPTER TWENTY

Kelsey woke to a bright light and the sound of voices.

Rolling to her back, she blinked several times and squinted to see who was mumbling. Her mother's familiar face registered, followed by her brother Rusty just past her. "Mom?"

"Oh, my baby." Hannah pushed to her feet and moved to Kelsey's side. She slid one hand over Kelsey's on the bed, and the other along her hair as she'd done when Kelsey was a kid. "You're awake. How do you feel?"

Kelsey blinked again as Rusty moved to the foot of her bed, confused as to why they were asking. "Fine, I guess. What's going on?"

"You've been out of it for two days." Rusty shoved his hands into the pockets of his worn jeans. "Mom's been freaking out even though she told all of us there was no reason to be worried."

"I was not freaking out." Hannah sat on the edge of Kelsey's bed and glared at her son, then looked back at Kelsey with a playful frown. "He exaggerates. I knew you'd be fine. Your body just needed time to get rid of all those drugs."

"Drugs?" Glancing past them, she took in her surroundings. An older, square TV was perched on a shelf high across the room. Below the

TV, a whiteboard with words scribbled in green was affixed to the wall. A small window sat to her left. Behind her were machines she could only barely see, and to her right, a closed drape, which she instinctively recognized from all the times she'd joined her mom on rounds at the hospital when she was a little girl. "Wh-what happened?"

"Foster injected a drug cocktail into your system just after you hit the button to open the safe room." Her mom ran a gentle hand down her hair again, using the calming doctor voice Kelsey knew meant things had been worse than she was letting on. "We were lucky the needle was found at the scene so the doctors knew exactly what you were given."

A wave of memories rushed into Kelsey's brain, and with it a blinding fear that shot her heart rate straight up. "Foster?"

"Dead." There was no mistaking the pleasure in Rusty's voice. "Hunt hit him square in the chest as soon as the door opened. Fucker's lucky he was already dead before I got ahold of him."

Hannah glared up at her son. "Rusty McClane. Language? And that kind of talk is not helping right now."

"Whatever. It's true, though. And the language is warranted on a piece of shit like that. She knows what I'm talking about."

Kelsey's stomach rolled because her brother was right. She'd seen into Trey Foster's mind when she'd been trapped with him. She'd seen how unbalanced he was, how vengeful, and she knew he was never going to stop blaming her for something she had no control over. But she didn't like thinking that he was dead because of her. "He . . ." She swallowed back the bile. "I think he was my brother. Half brother."

"No, I'm your brother," Rusty said with conviction. "Me and Alec and Ethan and Thomas. We're the only brothers you need."

She looked up at him. Saw the absolute conviction in his dark eyes. And slowly felt her heart rate come down. "You're right."

He didn't respond. But his clenched jaw and focused gaze made her remember how he'd been the one to go after Hunt at her parents' house when he thought Hunt had taken advantage of her. Remembered, also, all the times he'd looked like he'd wanted to go after Julian. Of all her brothers, Rusty was her fiercest champion. Not because she was closer to him than the others, she knew, but because of what had happened to his biological sister when he'd been just a kid.

"You're right," she repeated, reaching for his hand. He moved to the other side of her bed and closed his fingers around hers. And as she felt the strength and warmth in his grip, she smiled, wanting to tell him how much he meant to her, knowing at the same time if she tried, he'd just back away. That was the way with Rusty. He was fiercely protective but a total loner. He always had been.

She blinked back the wave of emotions. "And what about my other brothers? Is Hunt with them?"

"Um . . ." Rusty glanced toward their mom.

Confused, Kelsey looked at her mom too. Hannah smiled and patted her hand on the bed. "Oh, your brothers. Thomas was starving again so they took him to the cafeteria. I swear that boy never stops eating." She laughed, but something about it sounded off to Kelsey. Nervous. Her mom glanced toward Rusty. "He's worse than all three of you put together. I think he's hit another growth spurt. In a couple weeks he'll probably be taller than all of you too."

"In his dreams," Rusty muttered.

"You'd best be careful. Your father was showing him some of his old wrestling moves. Thomas is strong."

"I can still take him."

Kelsey wasn't sure what was going on, but the conversation felt forced, and she had the distinct impression something was going on. "Where is Hunt? And where's Dad? I want to talk to—"

"I'm right here." The curtain pulled back, and Kelsey's dad stepped into the room with a bright smile and two steamy cups of what smelled like coffee. "And there's my beautiful girl."

He handed the coffee to Hannah, then moved to the side of Kelsey's bed and leaned down to hug her.

A ridiculous wave of tears filled her eyes as Kelsey sat up and wrapped her arms around her father, trying not to get the stupid IV tube caught in the process. She was a full-grown woman who'd never needed a father's approval, but with him she'd always wanted it.

"It's good to see you awake," he said into her hair. "You had us all worried, pumpkin."

She held on tighter, fighting back the tears. He'd called her pumpkin from the moment she'd come to live with them, and though she'd loved it, she'd never felt as if she deserved it. One of her biggest regrets about her marriage to Julian was that she'd known that relationship had disappointed him. "I'm fine." She sniffled. "I didn't mean to worry you. I'm sorry."

He drew back and swiped at her cheeks. "You didn't do anything wrong so don't apologize. We were worried because we love you."

"I know."

He pressed a kiss to her forehead. "Everything's going to be okay now."

While her mother and brother spoke quietly about something Kelsey barely paid attention to, she released her dad and let him fix the pillows at her back so she could sit up higher. "So where are we?" she asked, interrupting them. "The hospital in Seaside?"

"No." Her mother sipped her coffee while Rusty set his on the table behind him. "Portland. You were flown here."

That made sense since her mom was a doctor and could arrange it all.

She glanced toward the door, wondering when Hunt and her brothers were coming back. She was anxious to see him. He'd obviously called the police and paramedics and gotten her help right away. Had he already talked to the cops? She needed to tell him everything Foster had admitted to her.

"There is something we need to talk about," Michael said, moving to stand next to his wife and placing a hand on her shoulder. "An Officer Callahan's been by a few times to talk to you, but you were still out."

"He's Hunt's friend. He knows all about the Fosters. Does he need to question me?"

"No," her father said hesitantly. "Not about Foster. The cops have everything they need about that case, though I'm sure they will want to talk to you at some point when you're feeling better."

Kelsey's brow lowered. Hunt must have heard everything then and already told them. She hadn't been sure she'd hit the right button on the control panel to turn on the intercom. "What did he want then?"

"To tell you he has the DNA results from the test you submitted in California. He's been in contact with the attorneys you met with there."

Kelsey's mouth grew dry, and her heart sped up all over again, this time with a different kind of fear.

"Do you want to know?" her mother asked.

"Do you know?"

Her parents looked at each other, then back at her. "Yes," her father said. "Since it's part of the criminal investigation, we were told."

Guilt hit her hard. Guilt that she hadn't told them she was submitting a DNA test to find out if Vivienne Armstrong was her biological mother or not.

Her mom rubbed a hand over her leg under the covers. "It doesn't change anything for us, Kelsey. You're still our daughter just as Alec's still our son. We want you to know who your birth parents are if you want to know."

She was right. Alec had found his birth parents, and they were now part of his life. And it hadn't changed Hannah and Michael's relationship with him at all. If anything, it had strengthened their bond and made him appreciate them even more. But this was different. They'd helped him find his birth parents.

"I'm sorry you found out this way. I should have told you about the test, I just—"

"We don't care about that." Michael cut her off with a sharp look. "We care about you. That's it. No more apologies."

Tears filled her eyes again. Tears she hated because she was not usually this emotional. She nodded. Took a deep breath. Then said, "Okay, tell me. What did the test say?"

Her mother squeezed her knee. "It confirmed that Vivienne Armstrong was your birth mother. That's it. Nothing more."

Kelsey blinked, feeling . . . nothing. Absolutely nothing. Which felt like an even bigger weight brushed off her shoulder than her divorce from Julian.

"It also gives Trey Foster and Catarina Brunelli motives for trying to kill you," her father added. "Sadly."

"Catarina Brunelli? She was really involved?"

Her mom nodded. "Apparently the mastermind behind the whole thing. Hunt found out while you were in the safe room. He had everything relayed to Callahan. Brunelli was arrested before you were even taken to the hospital."

Kelsey pressed her fingers against her suddenly throbbing temple, still confused about Brunelli's piece in all this but knowing she had plenty of time to find out. When her head didn't hurt quite so much.

"You're about to inherit a shit-ton of money, little sis."

Hannah glared at Rusty.

"What?" Rusty shrugged. "It's true."

It was true. *Holy hell.* "I don't care about the money."

"We know you don't." Hannah patted her leg. "Which means you'll do something good with it. Everything will get worked out. All you need to do is focus on feeling better."

"That and getting back to normal," her father added. "God knows we could use some normal in this family."

"Absolutely," her mother agreed.

"There is no normal now with Thomas around," Rusty mumbled. "Do you know he swiped my socks when I stayed at the house last night?"

Elisabeth Naughton

"He swipes mine all the time," their father said with a sigh. "And puts holes in the toes. I think his feet are growing again."

While her family launched into a discussion about Thomas's feet, Kelsey glanced toward the door again. The door Hunt still hadn't come through. Where the heck was he? Why wasn't he here? She knew he'd been frantic to get to her when she'd been locked in that safe room with Foster. Why hadn't he been sitting at her side, waiting for her to wake up?

"Relationships never work out."

Hunt's words from the rubble slammed into her, and in a rush of fear she remembered his story about his dad, how losing his mom had destroyed him and how Hunt had avoided relationships because he didn't want to end up that way. Followed by Hunt's admission to her the other night when he'd told her he loved her and how losing her would gut him.

She swallowed hard, for the first time she wondering if he wasn't here because it had all become way too real for him when she'd been hurt.

Her heart twisted hard. So hard it felt as if it might rip right in two. Followed by a wave of anger if he really had backed away from her because he was scared. She was scared too, dammit. He'd told her he wouldn't leave her.

"Where is he?" When her parents stopped talking to Rusty and looked her way, she said, "Why isn't he here? He said he wouldn't leave."

The room went eerily quiet. Her parents looked at each other. Rusty glanced down at his feet.

She sat forward in the bed, fighting back another rush of tears, these hotter than before. "Someone say something right now. Where is Hunter? Did he go back to his house?"

Her mother reached for her hand. "Relax, honey." She smoothed her fingers over the back of Kelsey's hand and used that aggravating calm doctor voice again, the one that made Kelsey want to scream.

"No, he's not at his house. He's . . ." Her mom glanced up her dad with a helpless look.

Kelsey looked to her dad, her frustration growing by the second. "Tell me what's going on. If he's not at his house, and he's not here, then where is he?"

Her father moved close and patted her knee, a sad look on his weathered face. "Hunter is here, he just . . . can't be here in this room."

That made absolutely no sense. She looked to Rusty, knowing he of all people would tell her the truth. "What's going on?"

Rusty sighed. "Hunt was shot."

Oh God . . . Her lungs seized. *"What?"*

"Foster got a round off before Hunt took him down."

Hannah McClane glared at her son.

"What?" Rusty said. "She has a right to know. You can't protect her from this."

"Where?" Kelsey demanded, already knowing it had to be bad for this kind of reaction. "How bad?"

"In the abdomen," her mother answered. "On the left side. It ruptured his spleen. Luckily, Hunter had already called the police, and they were already on scene, so paramedics were able to stabilize him so he could be airlifted to Portland."

What her mother was describing sounded like the best possible scenario. And yet she couldn't stop thinking about the fact he'd been shot. Because of her.

When she tried to pull her hand back, her mother only held her tighter. "He's going to be okay, Kelsey. It was touch and go for a little while, but he's doing better. He's in ICU now and will probably be moved to intermediate care soon. It's not as bad as it sounds."

Not as bad as it sounds . . .

It was worse. He'd almost died because of her. Was enduring horrible pain because of her. She knew how bad abdominal wounds could be. Her mother was a trauma surgeon. She'd heard too many of her mom's ER stories about abdominal gunshot wounds not to know what he was suffering. Because of her.

"If you want to go see him right now," her mom said, "I can make that happen."

She did want to see him. She desperately wanted to see him. But she was suddenly terrified. What would he say? Would he blame her? Julian would blame her. All those old neuroses she'd been fighting for so long came raging back to pummel her self-confidence from every direction.

Pulling her hand back, she rolled to her side and tugged the blankets up to her chin.

"I-I'm feeling really tired right now. I need to sleep. Maybe I can see him in a little while. When I'm not so tired?"

Silence met her ears. A deafening silence she hated because she knew they were all thinking the same thing she was. That she was a complete disappointment. Again.

A hand brushed her back, then her mom said, "Okay, honey. If that's what you want. We'll be back in a little while."

Kelsey didn't answer. Just listened to the sound of their steps leaving. And when the door finally closed behind them, she let the tears fall.

———

Hunt wasn't sure how long he'd been asleep this time, but when he woke, he was in a different room than he'd been in last time. And the person sitting at the side of his bed still wasn't Kelsey.

"Hey, Dad." Telling himself she was still probably groggy from the drugs Foster had given her, he shifted as best he could in the bed to get comfortable. Unfortunately, there was no comfort to be found in a hospital bed. The thin mattress felt like it was made of cardboard.

"Here, son." His dad pushed to his feet and fixed Hunt's pillow. "Better?"

"Yeah."

His dad sat back in his seat, his white hair catching the light coming in through the windows. "This is a nice room."

It was. A corner room with a great view down the hill toward the city and the river. And thank God it had its own bathroom. Not having one in ICU had sucked. "Did you get something to eat when I was asleep?"

"Yeah. I had a sandwich. The hospital cafeteria here isn't too bad. You worry about me too much, though. Need to be worrying about yourself right now."

He'd always worried about his dad. That was nothing new. "I'll be okay. Just a flesh wound."

His father frowned, which for some insane reason made Hunt chuckle. Then regret it when pain stabbed into his side.

His dad tensed and leaned forward. "You okay? Do you need the nurse?"

"No." He waved his hand, shifting the IV tubing stuck into his vein. "I'll be . . . fine. Just hurts a little. Thank God for pain . . . meds."

"Yes, they definitely help. Sometimes."

Silence settled over the room as his father leaned back in his seat. As the pain dissipated, Hunt looked over his father, noticing he looked tired and old. Older than the last time Hunt had seen him, which had only been a few weeks ago. Hunt knew what happened to him hadn't been easy on his dad, but nothing was easy on his dad. Nothing had been easy for the man since before his mom had died.

Memories of Kelsey locked in that room with a madman rushed through his mind, followed by the helplessness he'd felt at not being able to get to her. It was the same helplessness his dad had endured when his mom had been standing next to that car as it had blown. Except in Hunt's case, Kelsey was still alive—thankfully alive—whereas things had ended tragically for his mom . . . and his dad.

"I shouldn't have been so hard on you over the years," Hunt said, his throat thick with an emotion he didn't expect. "I know how hard it was for you to lose Mom. I'm sorry I wasn't easier to deal with when I was a teenager. Even when I was older."

His dad's brow wrinkled. "What made you say that?"

"Life. What happened." He shrugged, then ground his teeth because even that small movement made his side hurt. "I just keep thinking about Kelsey and what I'd be like right now if things had gone the other way. This gunshot wound is nothing compared to the pain I'd be in if I knew she was gone for good."

His dad was silent for several seconds, then said, "You love her, don't you?"

His chest warmed. "Yeah. A lot. Which scares the shit out of me because after we lost Mom, I vowed never to let myself feel anything for any woman."

His father crossed his arms over his chest and stared at him for several moments with a sorrowful expression. "I shouldn't have let you think that way. That's my failure as your father. I loved your mother very much. Maybe too much. And when she died, all I could do was focus on my grief. I should have focused more on you. I'm sorry for that."

A familiar pain burned through his chest. One he hadn't let himself feel in years. "It's okay, Dad."

"No, it's not. Not if you haven't let yourself fall in love because of that." Scooting forward in his seat, his dad rested his forearms on his knees. "Love isn't something you should be afraid of. When it comes along, you should grasp it and hold on as tightly as you can, because it's the only thing that truly lasts. I don't regret a single day I loved your mother. Not one. And I'd go through all the pain all over again, just to have those few precious years with her. Because not knowing her, never loving her, that would have been the real tragedy."

Tears burned Hunt's eyes, and he blinked rapidly to hold them back. He still missed his mom every single day. Nothing and no one could ever replace her, but his dad was right. Not knowing her love, never having had her in his life would have been the greatest tragedy.

His mind drifted to thoughts of Kelsey. To what his life would be like if he'd never met her. How empty everything would seem now. And that burn intensified right beneath his breastbone.

"She's gun-shy," he said quietly, his throat tight. "Kelsey. She went through a really bad relationship, and it's made her hesitant."

"Does she love you?" his father asked.

He thought of the way she'd opened up to him at the beach house. The way she'd kissed him and told him she wanted him. The way she'd looked at him. As if he was her everything. And, man, he wanted to be. He drew a deep breath that did nothing to ease the burn. "Yeah. I mean, I think she does. But she's scared."

"Then don't give up on her. If she's the one, be what she needs. Be patient and understanding and wait for her. Then don't let her go. You'll never regret loving her. I can promise you that. No matter what happens. You will regret never taking the chance, though."

His dad was right—again. And it only made him want to get out of this damn bed right this second and go find Kelsey to tell her that. But he couldn't. For the moment, he had to be patient.

"I love you, Dad."

His father smiled. "I love you too, son. I—"

A knock sounded at the door, then the door pushed open a crack. "Hey, loser," Alec said, sticking his head into the room. "Are you up for visitors?"

Hunt's dad stood and looked toward the door where Alec, Rusty, and Ethan were already filing in. "Come on in, boys."

"Hey, Mr. O'Donnell." Alec shook his hand. "We can come back later."

"No, no." Hunt's dad shook Rusty's and Ethan's hands as well. "I was just leaving."

He stepped around them and glanced at Hunt. "I'll be back tomorrow to check on you. Think about what we discussed."

"I will. Thanks, Dad."

His father smiled and disappeared out the door.

"What was that about?" Alec asked, moving around the bed.

"What a failure you are for not smuggling me whiskey." Hunt relaxed into his pillows, already feeling better.

"Hey, I'm a recovering alcoholic," Alec said. "You expect an alcoholic to get you his drug of choice?"

Hunt grinned, knowing Alec was only teasing. He thought of Kelsey. "If you were a real friend, yes. Especially when I have a hole in my belly because of your family."

Paper wrinkled; then, from the foot of the bed, Ethan held up a bottle of Jameson. "Good thing I'm your real friend."

Hunt nearly drooled. "You are a saint, Dr. McClane."

Alec rolled his eyes.

Rusty tugged three paper cups from the bag. "No, I'm the saint. It was my idea."

Ethan poured three shots, and Rusty handed them out. With his hands shoved into the pockets of his jeans, looking frustrated as hell, Alec said, "I hate you all. Just for the record."

Hunt tossed back the shot and relaxed even farther into the pillows. "No, you don't. You love us." Warmth spread down his chest. "Damn, that's good."

"Sadly, that's all you get." Rusty took the cup while Ethan hid the evidence so the nurse wouldn't see. "When you get sprung from this place and get home, you can have more."

Home made Hunt think of Kelsey. Made him want her at his home even more. Opening his eyes, he bit the bullet and asked the same question he'd asked every time the McClane brothers had come to see him. "How is she?"

"Better." Ethan sank into the chair Hunt's dad had left. "Looks like she'll be discharged tomorrow. They're just waiting for a few more tests to come back."

And she still hadn't come by to see him. A sick feeling rolled through Hunt's gut and pushed up his chest. That was not a good sign. "She's dealing with a lot of shit," Alec said. "Foster. Armstrong. You."

"Right." Hunt hoped like hell he hid the disappointment in his voice but knew he probably hadn't. "Who's she staying with when she leaves? Your folks aren't letting her go back to her warehouse alone, are they?"

"She's gonna stay with Mom and Dad for now." Rusty crossed his arms over his chest. "At least until things get back to normal."

For now. Shit. He needed to call his team. "The security system at her place should be up and running in a week or so. She can probably go back then." He tried to sit up and reach for his phone from the table to his right. Pain shot through his gut, but he ground his teeth and kept reaching. "Would somebody hand me that damn thing?"

No one moved a muscle.

"You were right, Ethan." Alec tipped his head. "He is completely and totally fucked."

"Told ya."

Giving up because he couldn't even reach the stupid rolling table, Hunt collapsed back into the pillows, sweating and breathing heavily from the pain. He glared at his friend. "What the hell does that mean?"

Alec smirked. "It means you're upside down in love with our sister, you loser. Which we should each deck you for. But we won't."

Hunt glanced warily at Rusty, standing still and silent with his arms crossed and a not entirely amused expression on his face. "I already told you guys I was in love with her."

"Yeah, but it's different now," Ethan said, pushing to his feet.

"Why?"

"Because she's in love with you too," Rusty answered.

"She is? How do you know? And if so, why the hell hasn't she been here to see me?"

Ethan chuckled.

Rusty sighed and reached for the whiskey again. "I need another shot for this."

"So fucked it's pathetic," Alec said with a shake of his head.

Ethan stepped forward, drawing Hunt's attention. "She has been here. Every night since she woke up and found out you were injured."

"What? When? I haven't seen her."

"That's because she didn't want you to know she was here," Alec said. "She's come by when you're asleep. She was terrified you were gonna up and die on her. I don't think she could stay away."

Emotions rolled through Hunt's chest, so many he could barely think. She'd been here. And he hadn't known. "Why?" He looked from one brother to the next. "Why hasn't she come by when I'm awake?"

"Because she blames herself for what happened to you," Ethan said. "She's been having panic attacks, isn't sleeping, has completely shut down from all of us. She's acting the way she did right after she got away from Benedict."

"No, she's acting the way she did when she first came to live with us," Alec said to his brother.

Ethan nodded.

Hunt's heart squeezed tight, and his chest filled with warmth and an urgency to climb out of this bed, to go find her right this second, to comfort her, to reassure her none of what had happened was her fault. He had to figure out a way to get down to her room. The nurses were never going to let him go down there, though. They were tightly monitoring his activity level. He'd have to sneak out, to find a way to—

"Which is why we're here." Rusty tossed back his second shot and dropped the paper cup in the garbage. "We don't want you to fuck this up any worse than you already have, so we're here to set you straight on a few things."

Hunt looked among the three, anxious only to get to Kelsey before she was discharged. "What things?"

Ethan rested his hands on the railing of Hunt's bed. "What to expect from Kelsey and her issues."

Hunt stilled, almost too afraid to hear what they were going to say.

"It's not that bad," Ethan assured him. "Kelsey's issues run way back to her childhood. Those feelings of abandonment, of not being able to trust, those are ingrained in her. And Benedict fed on those, which only set her back in her recovery. You need to be patient with her. What she's doing now—blaming herself for what happened to you—is classic for kids and women who've been through what she has. It's a defense mechanism."

Everything Kelsey had told him about her childhood slammed into him, followed by the way Benedict had preyed on her insecurities. More than anything he wanted to find the son of a bitch and break his nose all over again, but he fought the urge, sitting up a little straighter instead, gritting his teeth through the pain so he could focus on what her brothers were telling him.

"There are lots of different kinds of abuse," Ethan said, sounding like the psychiatrist he was. "Not all of it is physical. Most of the worst stuff isn't. It's emotional and mental, and it destroys a woman's self-confidence. It's very common for domestic-violence survivors to overthink everything, to blame themselves when things go wrong. To apologize for stuff they don't need to apologize for. To expect the worst at all times. And to push people away when things get to be too much."

"That's always been Kelsey," Alec cut in. "She's never felt like she deserved anything good, and she pushed all the nice guys she dated away until she wound up with Benedict. He was the only one who stuck around, and he was a total shit. And she convinced herself she deserved that too."

Everything they were saying made sense. Yes, Kelsey was strong and resourceful, and she found a way to pick herself up and go on whenever tragedy struck, but inside she was vulnerable and fragile in a dozen different ways, and she struggled daily not to listen to the negative voices in her head. They were just winning right now. And Hunt had never been more desperate to get through to her and prove they were wrong.

"So what are you saying?"

Ethan slid his hands into the pockets of his jeans and narrowed his eyes. "What we're saying is this. She's back in counseling, which is a good start, but you need to know right now that Kelsey's issues aren't going to be fixed in a week or a month or even a year. It's going to be a long recovery for her, and even five years from now she might react irrationally to a situation simply because something triggered an emotional response inside her. Abuse survivors often suffer from PTSD, from anxiety attacks, even depression. The good news is, the safer she feels, the more she trusts the people around her, the easier it's going to be for her to heal."

"Which means," Alec said, "if you really love her—"

"I do."

"—then don't let her push you away," Rusty finished. "Be patient and prove you're not going anywhere."

Hunt wasn't going anywhere. He knew what he wanted. He knew what mattered, and both were her. And since his words hadn't been enough to prove that to her, he could think of only one way to make her believe it once and for all. "Done."

"Done?" Alec's brow lifted in surprise.

"Yeah. You said she's come by my room every night?"

Ethan glanced over the bed at his brothers. "Yeah."

"So since this is her last night in the hospital, odds are good she'll stop by sometime again tonight?"

"Probably." Alec narrowed his gaze. "What are you thinking?"

"I'm thinking I need a favor."

"Another one?" Rusty frowned. "Dude. We already brought you whiskey."

Hunt smiled because he was confident this was a favor they wouldn't refuse. "It's going to involve someone driving out to my place on the coast. But you have to be back before she shows up here tonight."

———

The halls were quiet when Kelsey ventured out of her hospital room sometime around two in the morning.

Tightening the belt of her robe around her waist, she ran her hand along the railing in the hall and moved down the corridor. An orderly passed her with barely a glance. It was the nurses she had to watch out for, but she'd figured out when their shift change was and had timed her nightly excursions when they were distracted so she wouldn't be noticed.

She managed to slip out of her wing of the hospital without being caught and darted into the elevator. Nerves twisted through her belly as she rode up to the sixth floor where Hunt was currently in intermediate care, hoping and praying that tonight he looked better than he had last night.

The doors opened with a whoosh. She hesitated, glanced in both directions to make sure no one from her wing was here who might recognize her, and then moved onto the floor when it looked clear. The young blonde who'd been on night shift the last few days glanced up from her paperwork and smiled. "You're back."

Kelsey stuffed a hand into the pocket of her robe, her smile wobbling. "I won't stay long. Is he asleep?"

"Yes. I just checked on him. You know, I don't think he'd mind if you wake him. He's had other visitors."

"Oh no. I don't want to do that. He needs his rest." She stepped toward the hall. "I'll be quick."

The nurse didn't answer, and Kelsey was glad as she moved quickly around the corner and spotted Hunt's room two doors down. She wasn't sure what the nurse thought of the crazy lady in a robe who only visited at night when he was unconscious, but she didn't care. She needed to see him. Needed to know he was actually getting better. And didn't know what she was going to do tomorrow when she had to leave the hospital and couldn't check on him nightly.

Her fingers closed over the handle, and she turned it as quietly as she could. Pushing the door open several inches, she hesitated and listened. When the only sound she heard was Hunt's steady, even breaths, she slipped inside and gently closed the door at her back.

The room was dark, the curtain drawn, blocking her view. Quietly, she stepped around the curtain and stopped at the end of Hunt's bed, watching him sleep in the dim light.

He looked huge in that bed. It was the same thought she had every night when she came in here. Someone needed to get him a bigger bed so he could be comfortable. Holding her breath, she moved to the side so she could see his face. He was lying half on his side, his cheek pressed against a pillow, his skin a little pale, but not as bad as it had looked yesterday. There were still wires and tubes attached to his arms, but he seemed to be sleeping peacefully, not showing any signs of pain, and she took that as a good sign, especially after the other nights she'd been in here when he'd been restless and uncomfortable and still obviously on heavy painkillers.

Her gaze drifted back to his face. To his thick hair mussed against the pillow, his long eyelashes curled against his cheeks, and the steadily darkening stubble on his jaw she suddenly ached to skim her cheek against.

Her heart beat faster, and her hands flexed at her sides. She desperately wanted to climb into that bed with him, to wrap her arms around him, to kiss those tempting lips, to hear him say her name as he had that last night they'd spent together at his beach house. But she couldn't because she was scared. Scared of what he'd say when he opened his eyes and saw her. Scared that almost dying had made him realize her baggage was way too much. Scared that he'd blame her for what had happened to him. How could he not? It was her fault. Her past catching up to her was the reason he was lying in this bed now.

"I know you're scared." Out of nowhere, Hunt's words echoed in her head. The same words she'd heard him say that last night. *"I'm scared too, but not of loving you. I could never be scared of that because it's the only thing I know is right."*

Her pulse inched up, growing louder until it was a whir in her ears. Her palms grew damp. Her breaths, fast and shallow. He hadn't been lying to her that last night. He wouldn't lie to her. He was the one person she could always trust to be honest with her, even when she didn't particularly like his honesty.

"I'm terrified I'm gonna screw this up like I almost did today and lose you forever. Because that would gut me. Way worse than losing my mom ever did. Especially now, when I've finally realized you're the only thing in this whole wide world that matters."

Emotions overwhelmed her, stole her breath, made her lungs feel two sizes too small. He loved her. *Really* loved her. Not superficially, but with every part of his heart. And that meant there was no way he would ever blame her for what had happened. The only person who'd been casting blame these last few days was her. Which made her a complete fool for ever having questioned what he felt for her.

"Hunt?" Urgency pushed her forward to grip the railing of his bed. She had to tell him she was sorry. She needed to wake him. She needed him to know she was here and that she was the idiot, not him, for having stayed away. "Hunt?" she whispered. "I'm here. I—"

A high-pitched whimper echoed from the direction of the bathroom, followed by a scratching sound so startling it cut off Kelsey's words midsentence.

She whipped around and looked in that direction. The whimper echoed again, but Hunt didn't wake. Didn't stir. Didn't make any indication he'd heard it.

Confused, she quietly crossed the floor and reached for the bathroom door. The second it pushed open a crack, a golden fuzzball tore into the room and raced around her feet.

Kelsey jerked back and swallowed a gasp, then realized . . . it was a puppy. "What the heck?"

She hesitantly moved back into Hunt's room. The puppy whimpered and darted back to circle her feet. Afraid it was going to start barking and wake Hunt, she reached down and picked it up, cradling it against her chest.

It was adorable. Golden fuzz, blue eyes, and a—she swallowed a laugh as it licked her nose—sandpaper tongue.

"She likes you."

She sucked in a surprised breath at the sound of Hunt's voice and glanced to the bed where he was still lying on his side. Except his eyes were open now, locked on her in the dim light, and a ghost of a smile toyed with his tempting lips.

Her mouth went dry, and her heartbeat rushed right back to racing. "I . . ."

Words wouldn't form. She had no idea what to say.

"She's a golden. The last of Princess's pups."

She blinked, completely confused. "What?"

"My neighbor? On the coast? Remember I told you Princess was their dog and she'd just had puppies? This is one of them. The last from the litter, actually. They called her Three. They named all of the pups in the litter by numbers so they wouldn't get too attached. She's only six weeks. Not old enough to leave Princess for good yet, but she will be soon."

"She . . . Princess . . . she's okay?" Kelsey stroked the puppy's soft fur, confused why the dog was here.

"Totally fine. She was sound asleep at the neighbor's house with the pups when everything went down at my place. Foster was taunting you when he sent that text about her."

Relief—a relief she hadn't even known she'd needed—filled her chest. "I'm so happy to hear that. No one told me."

Silence echoed in the room. A heavy silence she was suddenly afraid to try to break. Why wasn't he asking her what she was doing here? The puppy wiggled in her arms. And what was he doing with a dog in a hospital room? No way the nurses had allowed this. She had a million questions. She had a million things she needed to say, but she was suddenly deathly afraid to start any topic when she had no idea where it would end up.

"She needs a home, Kels."

Kelsey blinked again, looking at him still lying on his side in the bed and watching her. He was talking about the pup. "She does? Oh." She looked down at the puppy, already settling down to sleep against her. "I could take her."

"Actually, you can't."

"Why not?" Now he was completely confusing her. "You just said—"

"Because I already bought her. Only I didn't buy her for me, I bought her for us."

Us . . .

That word echoed in her ears, and reflexively, her heart bumped.

"I'm not going anywhere," he said softly. "And the way I see it, if we have a dog we have to share, that'll prove it to you."

Oh . . .

"But . . ." Tears blurred her vision. Tears of hope she was almost too afraid to reach out and grasp. "But you told me you didn't want a dog. That you didn't want to get attached to one because it wouldn't live long enough."

"I was wrong."

He shifted in the bed, gritting his teeth so he could sit upright, and it was all she could do not to rush right over and help him. "I was wrong to think a dog wasn't worth the emotional investment. Just as I was wrong to think the same about relationships. I realized that after the week we spent together. I don't want to go back to being alone. I want you, and this dog, and a million more weeks with you waking up by my side. Nothing that happened with Foster changes that. Your pulling away from me now doesn't change that. I'm not your ex. What happened to me was not your fault. And I'm never going to let you blame yourself for any of it. So you can take as much time as you want, but just know I'm not going anywhere. I'll wait as long as it takes for you to realize you can't live without me either. Because I know you can't. I know you're head over heels in love with me the same way I'm crazy in love with y—"

All the worry and fear and stress and guilt bubbled right up and over, pushing tears from her eyes and her feet across the floor. She reached the side of his bed and leaned down to kiss him, desperate to touch him and hold him and show him he was right. And he was right there to grab her and pull her close and not let go.

"I'm sorry," she whispered against his lips, sinking to one knee so she could sit beside him. "I'm so sorry for everything. I was so scared you'd hate me for what happened that I didn't know how to tell you I was sorry and . . ."

He brushed the hair back from her eyes and looked up at her. "Don't you dare apologize. You're done apologizing. None of what happened was your fault. Do you hear me?"

Her heart swelled. He'd told her he loved her. He'd promised he wouldn't leave her. She'd been afraid to believe him before, but she wasn't now. And it wasn't because of the puppy, though she absolutely loved that he'd given her this gift. It was because in her heart, she'd always known she could believe in him. She'd just been too afraid to trust herself.

"Are you okay?" she whispered. "I've been so scared. I thought—"

"I'm fine." He scooted to the side to make room for her on the mattress. "Better since I found out you'd been coming into my room every night."

Her cheeks heated. "Who told you that?"

He smirked. "Couple guys I know."

Her brothers. She shook her head. "They're playing matchmaker now? They're such girls."

He grinned. "They totally are. And you love them for it."

She did. They had her back. Always would. And she had theirs just as fiercely.

When the puppy grunted, Hunt glanced down at the sleeping bundle of fur in Kelsey's arms. "So what do you think?"

She didn't bother to look at the pup. Instead, she focused on the man who hadn't just protected her, he'd saved her life in more ways than one. "I think . . . no, I *know* that you are the best thing that ever happened to me." Holding the puppy tighter, she leaned down toward his lips. "I can't promise I won't freak out again. That kind of seems to be my pattern. But I can promise I will never stop loving you, just so long as you never stop loving me back."

He slid his fingers through her hair and pulled her down for a kiss. "That's an easy promise to keep. And one you can count on."

No, she could count on him. He would forever be the one person she could always trust to support her through anything life threw her way. And that made him the most precious gift she'd ever received.

ABOUT THE AUTHOR

Before topping multiple bestseller lists—including those of the *New York Times, USA Today,* and the *Wall Street Journal*—Elisabeth Naughton taught middle school science. A voracious reader, she soon discovered she had a knack for creating stories with a chemistry of their own. The spark turned into a flame, and Naughton now writes full-time. Her books have been nominated for some of the industry's most prestigious awards, such as the RITA and Golden Heart Awards from Romance Writers of America, the Australian Romance Readers Award, and the Golden Leaf Award. When not dreaming up new stories, Naughton can be found spending time with her husband and three children in their western Oregon home. *Protected* is the third book in her Deadly Secrets series, following *Gone* and *Repressed*, which was a 2017 RITA winner in romantic suspense.

Learn more about Elisabeth at www.ElisabethNaughton.com.